The Midgard Serpent

A Novel of Viking Age England

Book Ten of The Norsemen Saga

James L. Nelson

Fore Topsail Press
64 Ash Point Road
Harpswell, Maine, 04079

Maps by Chris Boyle

ISBN-13: 978-0-578-69642-3

To Lisa, my shipmate, my partner, my wife of all these years,
with all my love: then, now and forever.

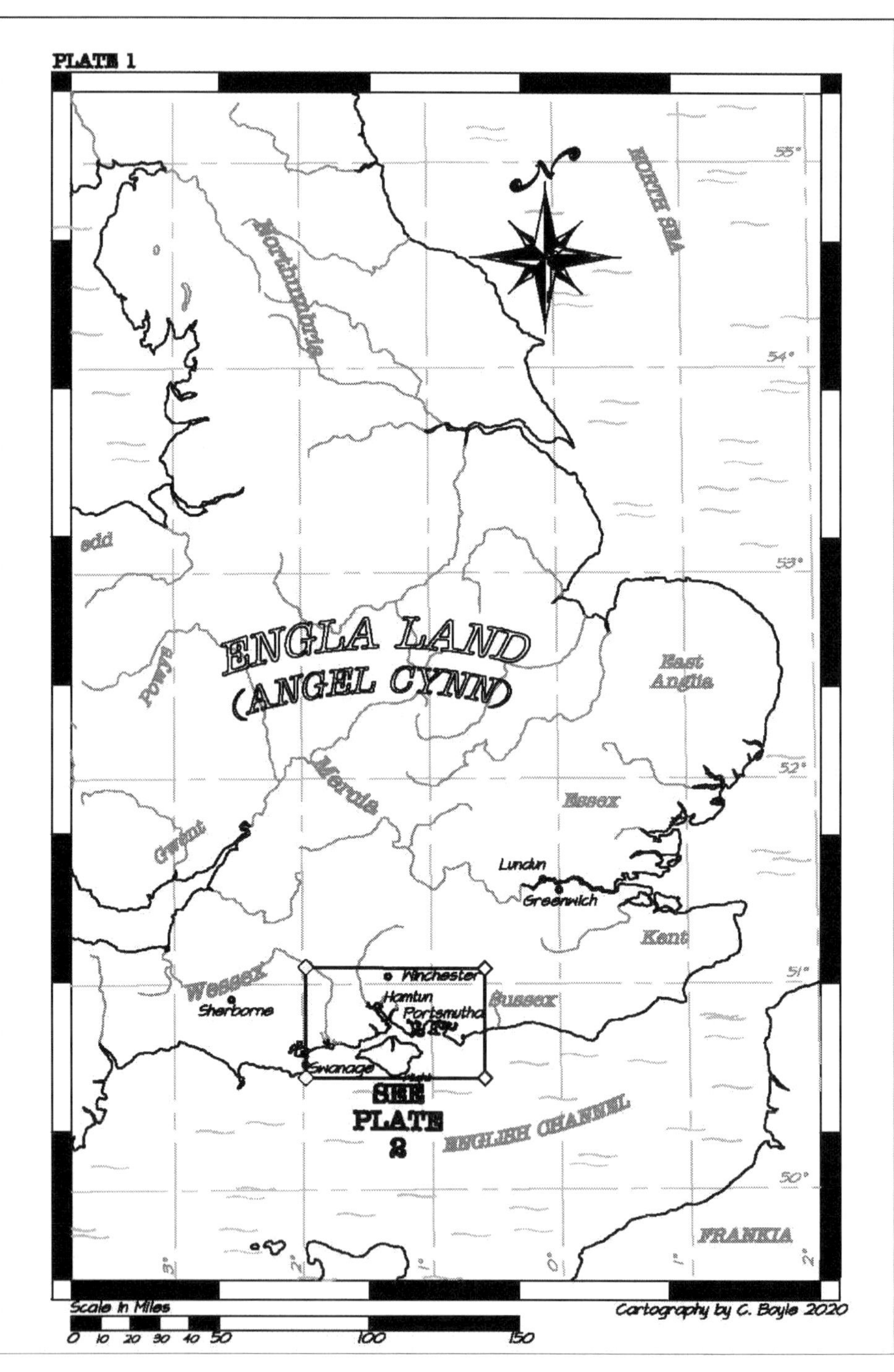
PLATE 1
55°
NORTH SEA
Northumbria
54°
edd
53°
ENGLA LAND
(ANGEL CYNN)
East
Anglia
Powys
52°
Mercia
Essex
Gwent
Lundun
Greenwich
Kent
51°
Winchester
Wessex
Hamtun
Sherborne
Portsmutha
Sussex
Swanage
SEE
PLATE
2
ENGLISH CHANNEL
50°
FRANKIA
3°
2°
1°
0°
1°
2°
Scale in Miles
0 10 20 30 40 50 100 150
Cartography by C. Boyle 2020

PLATE 2

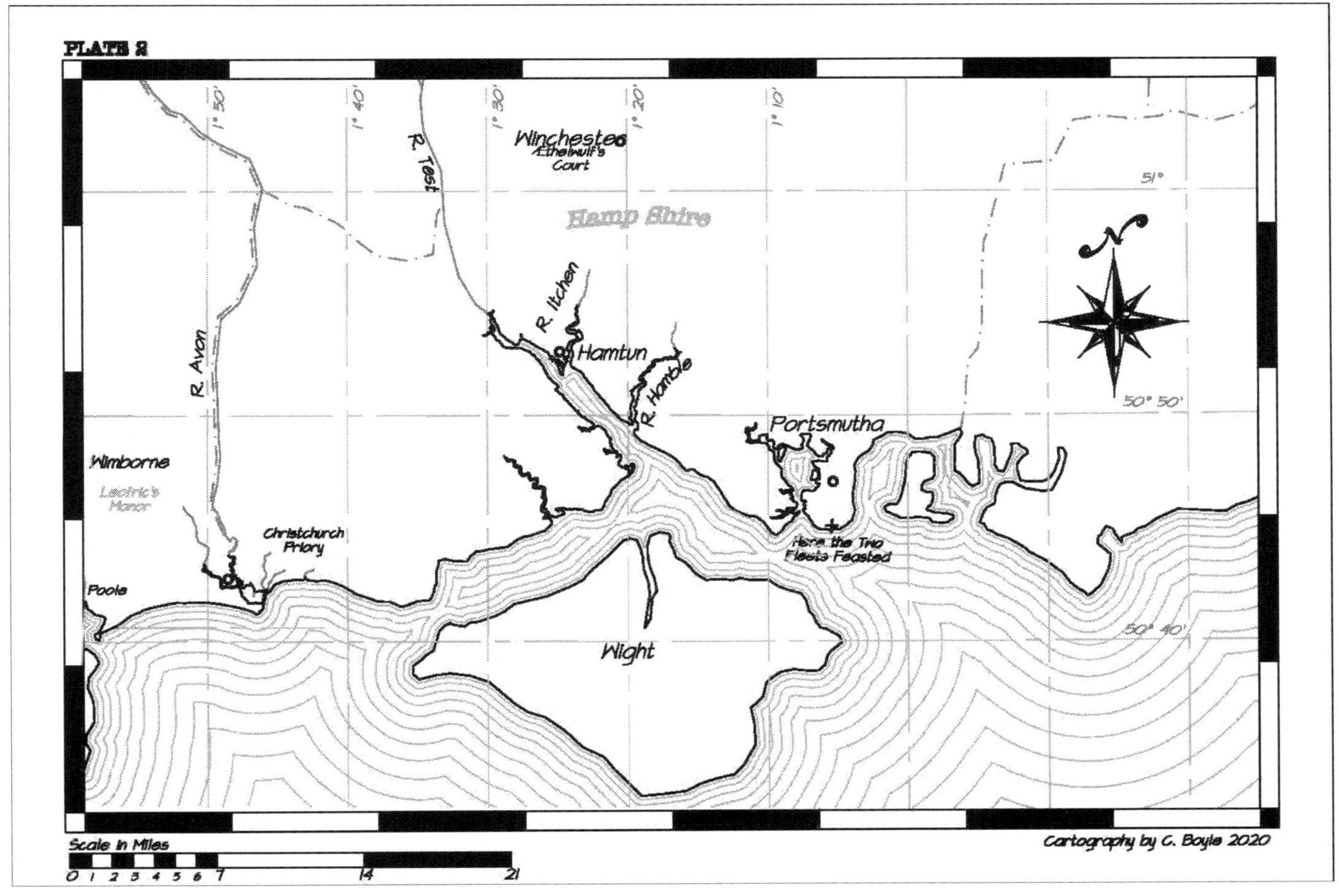

1° 50'
1° 40'
1° 30'
1° 20'
1° 10'
R. Test
Winchestea
Æthelwulf's Court
Hamp Shire
51°
N
R. Itchen
Hamtun
R. Hamble
R. Avon
50° 50'
Portsmutha
Wimborne
Laefric's Manor
Christchurch Priory
Here the Two Fleets Feasted
Poole
50° 40'
Wight
Scale in Miles
0 1 2 3 4 5 6 7 14 21
Cartography by C. Boyle 2020

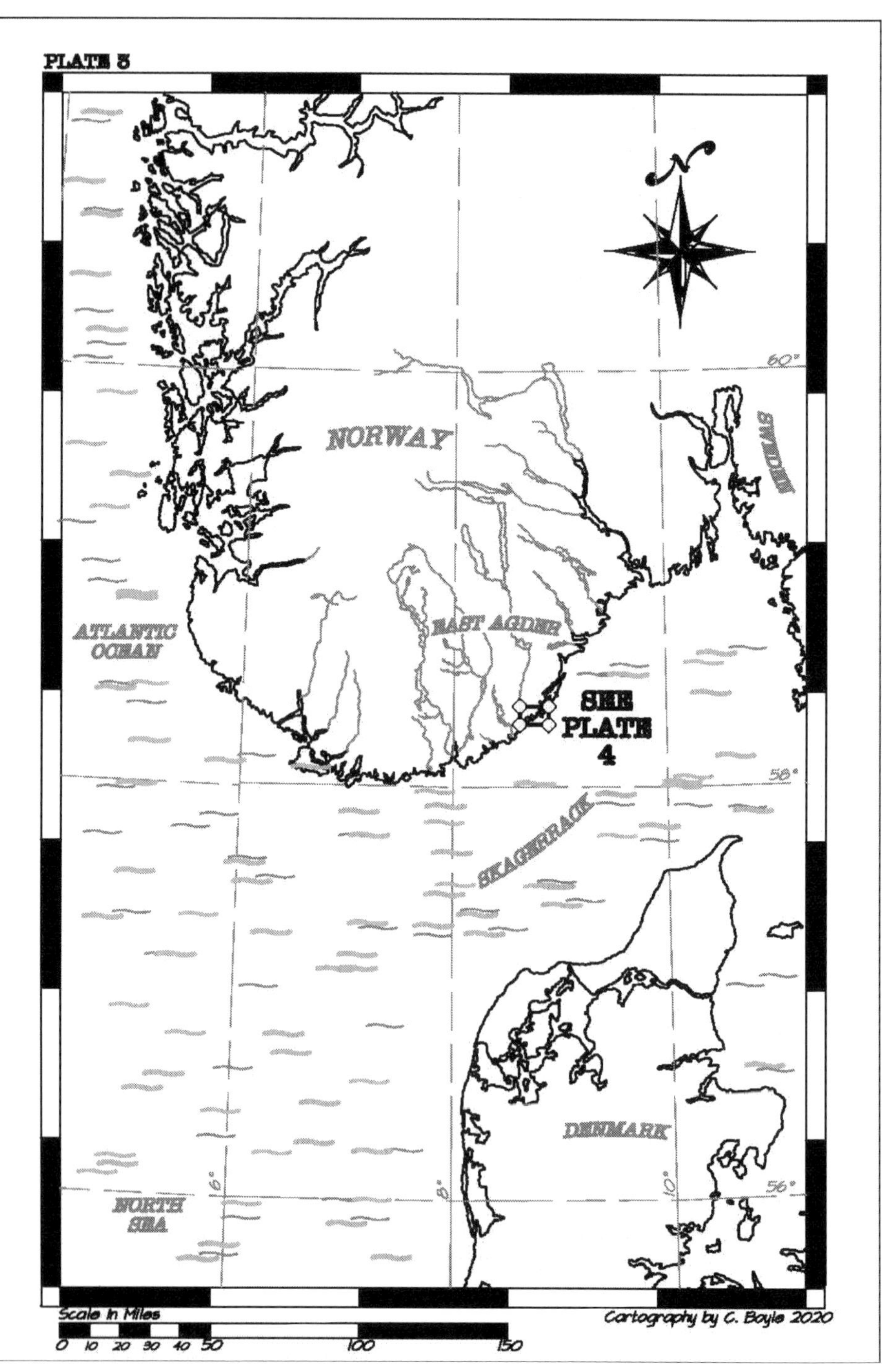
PLATE 3
N
NORWAY
SWEDEN
EAST AGDER
ATLANTIC OCEAN
SEE PLATE 4
SKAGERRACK
DENMARK
NORTH SEA
60°
58°
56°
6°
8°
10°
Scale in Miles
0 10 20 30 40 50 100 150
Cartography by C. Boyle 2020

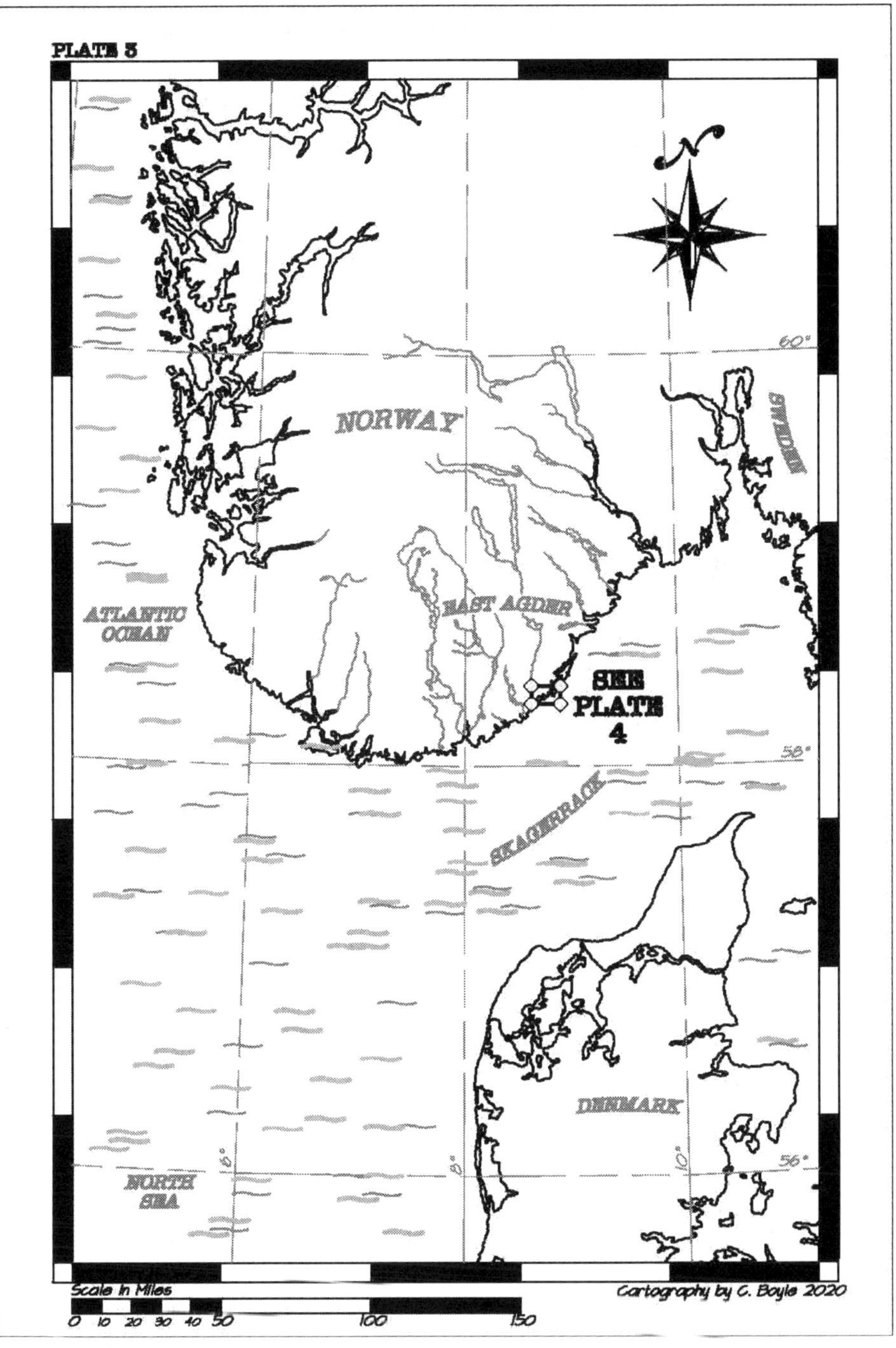
PLATE 3
NORWAY
SWEDEN
EAST AGDER
ATLANTIC
OCEAN
SEE
PLATE
4
60°
58°
56°
SKAGERRACK
DENMARK
NORTH
SEA
6°
8°
10°
Scale in Miles
0 10 20 30 40 50 100 150
Cartography by C. Boyle 2020

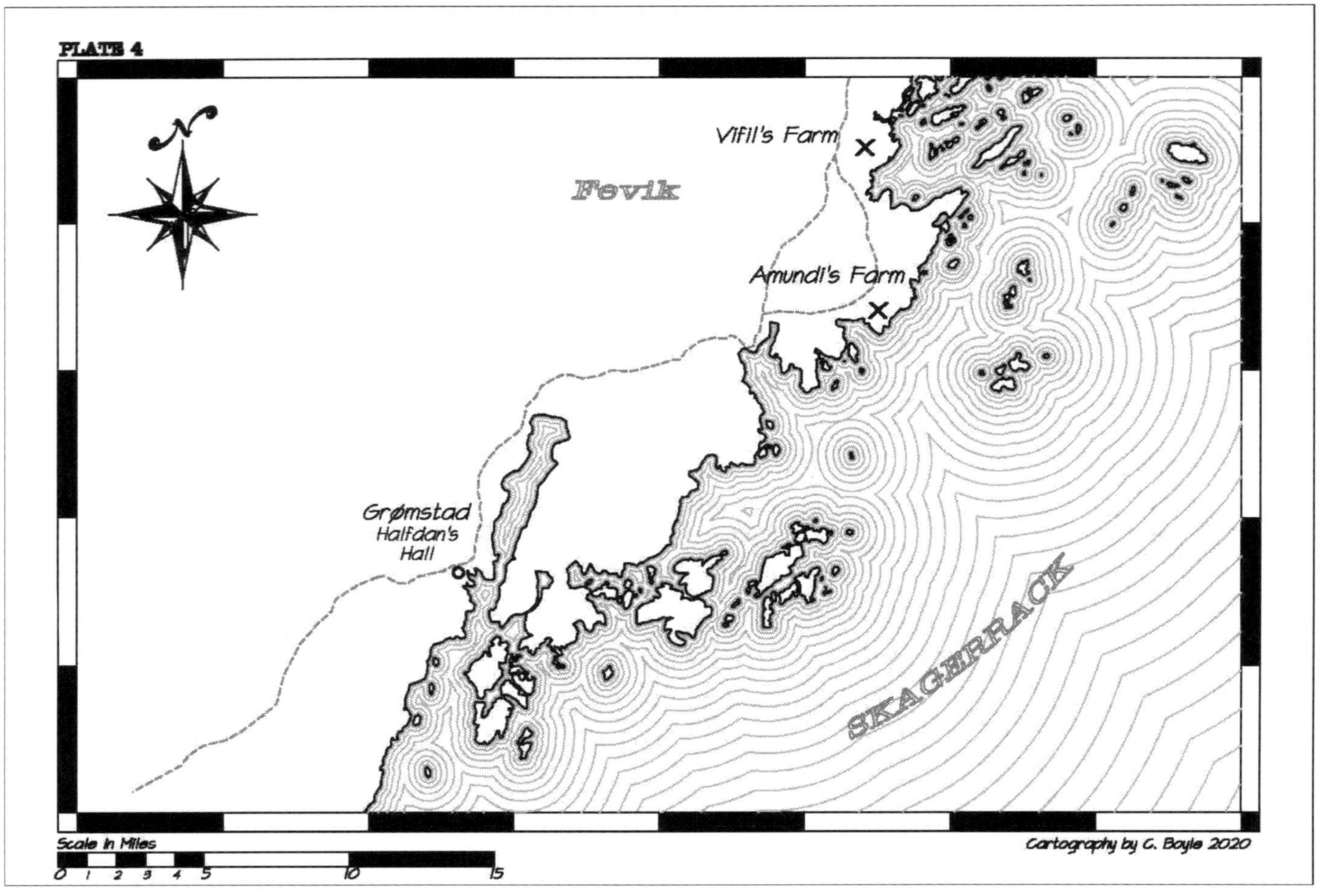
PLATE 4
N
Vifil's Farm
Fevik
Amundi's Farm
Grømstad
Halfdan's
Hall
SKAGERRACK
Scale in Miles
0 1 2 3 4 5 10 15
Cartography by C. Boyle 2020

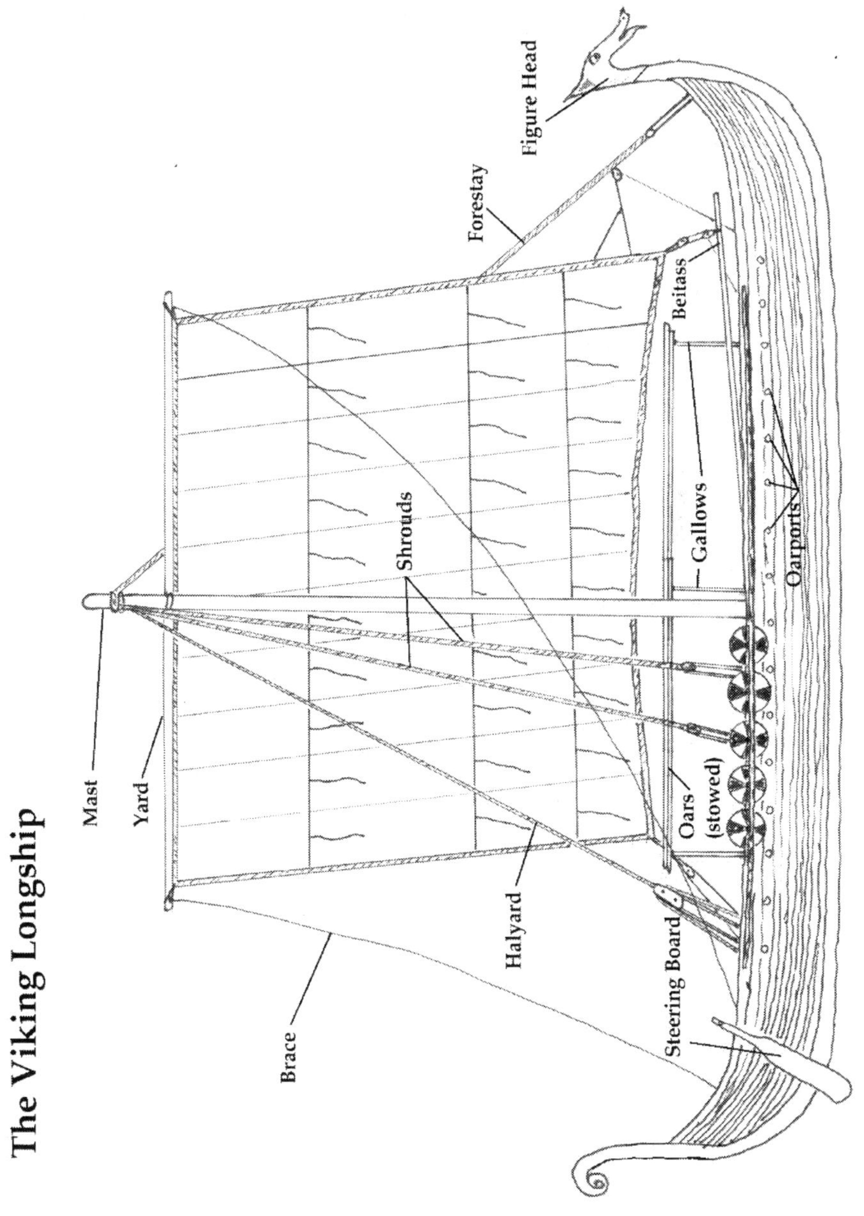

For terminology, see Glossary, page 451

Prologue

The Saga of Thorgrim Night Wolf

There was a man named Thorgrim and he was called Night Wolf because it was believed by some that his spirit from time to time would take on the form of a wolf. Thorgrim was known as a man who was generally fair and honest, and, as he grew older, one who was not quick to anger or violence. But sometimes as the day drew to a close he would become very irritable, so much so that none dared approach him, and he would go off on his own and it was at those times that some thought he roamed the night in the form of a wolf.

Thorgrim himself did not know the truth of his wolf dreams, as he called them, but he would often see things that proved to be true. At those times he would suffer no one to be near him, save for one man who was named Starri Deathless. Starri was of those men called berserkers, a warrior to whom the gods gave great power in battle and other mystical powers as well. When the wolf dreams came on Thorgrim, Starri would remain near him through the night, but if Starri ever witnessed Thorgrim's spirit shifting into the form of a wolf he would not say.

After earning great wealth and reputation going a'viking as a young man, where he raided along the coast of Engla-land and Frankia, Thorgrim bought a farm in a country called Vik and there he and his wife Hallbera, known as Hallbera the Fair, started their family. They had two sons, the oldest named Odd and the younger named Harald, and a daughter named Hild. From his days of raiding Thorgrim Night Wolf had gained a reputation as a warrior of great skill and a gifted leader of men, and that reputation only grew stronger over the years as Thorgrim led his neighbors in defending their lands against bandits and sundry raiders, and joined in fighting for the king when called upon. It was for that reason that few men been gifted by the gods with an innate sense for weather which was honed by a lifetime at sea, sailing the coast of Norway and raiding in foreign lands. If his gut told him the weather would not change soon, he believed it, and he knew the others would as well.

It was a crucial point, because the next decision depended on the weather. The direction they wished to go was already set: east, always east. But Thorgrim had no way of knowing how far these cliffs extended, or how long they would have to sail before they found another place to come ashore. He did not care to sail that coast after dark, and he certainly did not want to be caught by a wind that was trying to drive them onto land. Or, worst of all, a wind trying to drive them ashore at night. He might not care about himself so much, but he had six ships and nearly four hundred men under his command. And one woman.

Failend. His lover. His former lover? Thorgrim was still not sure of his standing with her, and had found neither the time nor the inclination to inquire after her feelings on the matter.

He looked inland again. His instinct told him they were on an island, not the mainland. When they had come that way days before he had seen a stretch of water off to the north. It might have been the mouth of a very wide river or bay, or it might have been the open water that separated a great island from the shore. If he suspected the weather was going to turn on them he would lead his fleet back that way, to see if they could sail east between the island and the shore. But now it seemed that would not be necessary.

"What do you say, Louis?" Thorgrim asked. Louis the Frank had also come with the small band to the top of the cliff, more out of curiosity, Thorgrim guessed, than anything else. He certainly had nothing to offer in the matter of seamanship or navigation.

In reply to Thorgrim's question Louis shrugged, as Thorgrim knew he would. "As long as we can sail to the east, that's all that matters," he said.

Why do I ask him? Thorgrim wondered. *I didn't even ask Harald, or Godi.*

It was a curious thing, his relationship with Louis. Thorgrim was not much given to introspection, but he did wonder at this. Louis had been his prisoner at first. He had escaped, and nearly gotten Thorgrim and his men killed in the process. He had fallen into

Thorgrim's hands again. Thorgrim had nearly killed him half a dozen times.

And through all that, Louis had remained unflappable, unmoved, as if it made no difference to him. He certainly had never shown fear. Thorgrim would expect that of a Northman, but somehow he was impressed when he saw it in a Frank. Louis claimed to be a nobleman, he claimed to be a trained warrior, and his manner and his skill in battle suggested he was not lying about that. Thorgrim believed him, though he would never give Louis the satisfaction of admitting it.

"You wish to sail east because your home is to the east?" Thorgrim asked. Louis had only one immediate concern in life, and that was to return to Frankia and run a sword through the brother who had betrayed him.

"And your home as well," Louis said. Because Louis knew that Thorgrim's only concern was to get back to his native land and never leave again.

"The east?" Thorgrim asked. "Frankia's to the east?" They had been blown across the sea from Ireland to the shores of Engla-land, but where in that country they had made landfall Thorgrim had no idea. And so far they had not met anyone who was much able to enlighten them.

Louis turned and looked north. He turned and looked south. He turned and looked at Thorgrim. "That's Engla-land to the north," he said, "and the ocean to the south, and so we must be on the south coast of Engla-land."

Thorgrim nodded. He did not really seek Louis's opinion, he was just needling the man for amusement. If Louis knew more about the twisting, irregular nature of shorelines he would know that his reasoning did not necessarily follow. But it was as good a guess as they could hope for, and it was in fact Thorgrim's guess as well.

"This is a rich land," Starri Deathless said. He and Hardbein, captain of *Fox*, and Halldor who commanded *Black Wing* were the rest of the party who had climbed to the cliff top.

"A very rich land," Starri said again. "Lots of silver, gold. Churches plump with it. Ireland looks like a poor man's hovel compared."

This was met with grunts of agreement from the others, though Thorgrim remained quiet. He knew Starri was right, but the talk made particularly benevolent king, and he was not accustomed to resistance of any kind.

He had tried to make Odd and his family prisoners and take Odd's farm, along with Thorgrim's, for himself. He led an attack on the long hall, set it on fire, prepared to capture or kill the people as they came racing out. But it had not worked that way. Odd was not alone: all of his neighbors were there, some rich and powerful men, and they had their warriors with them. Worse, Odd had some means of getting out of the hall undetected. Halfdan still did not know how. But they had launched an attack against Halfdan and his men which seemed to come out of nowhere, and the surprise alone was enough for them to carry the day.

So, after an ignominious retreat back to Grømstad, Halfdan found himself in a state of wild rage, but along with the rage were feelings of uncertainty, confusion, strange and unaccustomed emotions. He had to react, and quickly, that much he knew. Such an act of treachery could not go unanswered. Ignoring it would be a greater threat to his rule than all the swords and spears in Norway.

He assembled his men, his elite warriors, his hird, and his foot soldiers as well, and they marched. Halfdan meant to punish those who had dared defy him, but his thinking had not really moved much beyond that. He had no plan for just who he would punish, or what he would do to them, or to what end. He was just letting the rage drive him now.

They had come first to the farm of Amundi Thorsteinsson, probably the wealthiest man in the region after Thorgrim Night Wolf. Odd Thorgrimson might be the leader of the rebellion, but Amundi was certainly a big part of it. Amundi could have stopped the people from joining in with Odd if he had wished to do so. But he did not, and in fact it was Amundi who had first refused to join Halfdan in his raid on Odd's farm. Amundi needed punishment, and Halfdan was ready to dole it out.

But Amundi's farm had been abandoned, stripped of people, livestock and stores. Halfdan considered burning the long hall and the outbuildings to the ground, and the thought pleased him, but before he gave the order he forced himself to think it through.

If Amundi was a traitor, then he would forfeit all this property. If it came into Halfdan's possession it would be far more valuable as it was, rather than as a heap of charred wreckage. So he and his men spent the night, and left the farm undisturbed as they headed out the next day.

They had continued their sweep through the country north of Grømstad, the bulk of the army moving from farm to farm while riders were sent to the more far-flung places. But they did not find any of those whom they sought to punish, nor anything else such as food or drink that might be of help to the army. Each farm they marched on was deserted.

Of course, Halfdan realized, the freemen who had stood up to his rule would have anticipated their king's vengeance. Of course they would have had people watching for the army on the march. Of course they would have retreated in the face of such a threat. They were not going to wait in their homes to be slaughtered.

At the same time he realized that he, the king of Vestfold, had better start thinking things through rather than raging like a chained bear set upon by dogs.

The anger was subsiding, and in its place he found only his own confusion, his own uncertainty.

"Just a few miles to Odd's farm, lord," Onund ventured. Unlike Skorri, Onund knew this part of the country well, having been born and raised in Fevik. It was exactly the reason Halfdan did not make Onund sœslumadr after Einar Sigurdsson's disappearance. Onund was too close to the people there. Halfdan could not be certain to whom Onund, in the deepest recesses of his heart, was most loyal.

"Right," Halfdan said. He thought Odd's farm was nearby but he was not certain, and he was not going to let that uncertainty show. "Let's ride."

He climbed back up into his saddle and the others did the same, and the air was filled with the noise of hundreds of armed men regaining their feet. It was a sound of weary protest that emanated from the group, a collective sound, such as no single individual would have dared utter. Halfdan ignored it.

They rode on and soon they crested a hill, and spread out below him was Odd's farm. Halfdan reined his horse to a halt and moved his eyes over the place, and behind him the rest stopped as well. Halfdan had led his earlier attack at night, so he had seen none of this, but he had visited Odd several times before that, during annual tours of his kingdom, and he recognized the land and the buildings. Mostly. It was changed in many ways. There were more outbuildings

Halfdan squatted down and picked up one of the chips and examined it. Pine. He sniffed it. He could still smell the sap and the odor of green wood. He stood. Onund and Skorri were standing near, close enough to be on hand, not so close as to be obtrusive.

"Fresh chips," Halfdan said. "Was Odd building a ship?"

The two men looked uncomfortable. They obviously did not know, but did not care to admit ignorance, either.

"I think he was," Onund said at last, an easy statement to make given the evidence at their feet. "He had a shipwright. Fellow named Ari. Good shipwright."

Halfdan nodded. This at least was new information. Clearly Odd had a ship, built and launched recently. Some or all of his people and his goods must have gone off that way. But where? Had he left the country? What about the other freemen, Odd's compatriots? Were they also waterborne now?

Halfdan began to get an uncomfortable feeling in his gut. An army on land could not move very fast and could not remain unseen, but an army carried aboard a fleet of ships could move very quickly indeed, and appear suddenly over the horizon. It was a lesson the Northmen had been teaching all of the western world for the past sixty years.

Ships…

"So, he had a ship, a new-built ship," Halfdan said at last. "And now he and everyone else are gone. Did they all go by ship? Where did they go?"

That was met with more uncomfortable silence. Then, once again, Onund, who knew Odd and knew the people of Fevik, was the one to speak up.

"Odd might have gone to where his sister lives, lord. To hide out. Or maybe as a gathering place, to figure what he would do next."

Halfdan frowned. "His sister?" Thorgrim Night Wolf and Ornolf the Restless were prominent enough in that region that Halfdan knew of their family, of their comings and goings. "I thought his sister married and moved off to the north country."

"The older sister, lord. Hild. She married a few years back. I mean his younger sister. Hallbera. The one named after Odd's mother, Thorgrim's wife, who died in childbirth."

Halfdan said nothing as he thought about that. Of course there was a younger sister. She must be three or four years old, Halfdan figured. As he understood it, it was Thorgrim's grief at the death of his wife that had led him to agree to go a'viking again with Ornolf. He was about to ask more when some bustling behind him, some disturbance, broke into his train of thought. He and Onund turned to the sound.

A cluster of warriors stood in something like a circle, spears lowered. There must have been someone in the center of the circle, someone who presented some threat, but Halfdan could not see him through the press of men. But he heard him, heard him say in a loud voice, touched with panic, "I came to speak with King Halfdan!"

A few of the warriors turned to look toward Halfdan. Halfdan gave a nod of his head and the man was led over to him.

"My lord," the man began, "My name is Vandrad…I'm…I was a sheepherd on the farm of Odd Thorgrimson. This farm, lord…"

"Yes?" Halfdan prompted.

"I was sent by Odd, lord. Not to speak with you, but to watch you. But I would not betray my king, lord, and if you'll give promise that I won't suffer the fate of the others then I'll tell you of his plans, lord."

You'll tell me whether I pardon you or not, you silly worm, Halfdan thought. He knew these sorts of men and despised them, though he knew that this one might be of use. But first he wished to hear more about the business that had so intrigued him, before this Vandrad's arrival.

"Hold a moment," Halfdan said. He turned back to Onund. "You were telling me of a younger sister? Where is she now? The girl Hallbera?"

"She lives part of the year with Odd and his wife, Signy, lord," Onund said, "and part of the year with Signy's mother and father to the west of here."

Halfdan looked at Onund as he spoke. *You know a great deal about these people, don't you?* he thought. *That's a helpful thing…*

Then Halfdan's thoughts were racing off in another direction.

A sister…Odd's only sibling still in Fevik…still just a child. The daughter born to his mother who died giving birth to her.

How much would such a girl be worth to Odd?

Chapter Three

How do men call thee?
Thy king confides in thee,
since in the ship's fair prow
he grants thee place.

The Poetic Edda

Harald Thorgrimson crouched low, his legs adjusting unconsciously to the slow roll of the ship as he examined Fostolf's red, sweat-sheened face. *Dragon* was a little to windward of the rest of the fleet and near the back of the pack. Only *Fox* trailed behind. It had nothing to do with *Dragon*'s sailing qualities or Harald's ability to coax speed from her; she was simply a smaller ship than the others were, and hence a slower ship.

The fleet had been under sail for hours, hoisting their long yards and hauling sheets aft as soon as the rowers had backed the vessels off the beach. The wind was from the west, twelve knots and coming just over the ships' larboard quarters. The sea was moving in long, easy rollers with a slight ruffle on the surface kicked up by the breeze. The sun was warm and the sky dotted here and there by high white clouds. It was perfect, absolutely perfect.

It was, however, a perfection that Fostolf, burning with fever and nearly delirious, could not appreciate. He had begun to feel sick the night before, his stomach inexplicably twisting up with nausea. The Northmen had just sacked a bountiful monastery and were well supplied with an abundance of fresh meat and ale. They were not eating the half-rotten stores that would tend to make a man sick, yet here was Fostolf, half-bent with discomfort. And along with the nausea he felt sharp pain in his gut that came and went like a knife stabbing him from the inside.

He kept the pain to himself as best he could, with only the occasional audible groan escaping. In the dark hours he had started vomiting, staggering off as far from the fire as he could get before heaving up on the sand. By dawn he was sweating with fever, his head lolling side to side, the soft groans coming at regular intervals.

Thorgrim and the others had gathered around the man, prodding him and discussing the case. The Northmen were skilled in treating such things as broken bones or the gaping wounds left by edged weapons or the damage caused by any of the many accidents that happened on shipboard. But this was different. This was the sort of internal malady brought on by evil spirits. It could not be fixed with splints or stitches or bandages. There were probably plants or herbs of some description that could have helped, but none of the men knew what those might be, or if they even grew in Engla-land, so they made no mention of them.

Instead, Thorgrim found some dried bones and carved on them the runes that would drive the spirits away, if the gods chose to help. He laid them on Fostolf's chest and pressed a damp cloth to his forehead. And that was about all that he could do.

The gods might help Fostolf or they might not. That remained to be seen. But there was no question that the gods were giving the rest of them the gift of fine weather, with the wind just right for driving them east, ever east. Harald knew that his father hoped it was a sign that the gods would allow him to go home. He also knew that Thorgrim would never say such a thing out loud or even dare think about it too much. Nothing would ruin a man's luck quicker than that.

Instead, Thorgrim ordered the ships underway as if there was nothing at all to be hoped for. They strapped Fostolf to a plank and carried him aboard his ship, *Dragon*, with as much care as possible. They laid down on a bed of fur and blankets, but his pain seemed only to grow worse, his grasp on the world around him more tenuous.

Now, with the coast of Engla-land passing down the larboard side and several miles off, Harald squatted next to Fostolf and frowned as he looked at his flushed face. He reached out and pressed his fingertips to the man's forehead and was startled by the heat that came off his skin.

He felt pity for the man. This was not how a warrior such as Fostolf should leave Midgard, the world of men. Harald was sincerely unhappy to see Fostolf die this way. His pity was genuine. And that was good.

He feared that he might actually delight in Fostolf's death, and that was not a proper thing to feel, not when the man was a fellow warrior, a man with whom you had stood in the shieldwall and in whose company you had braved the worst that the sea could dole out. A man should never long for his fellow warrior's death, even if his death could mean finally achieving the thing he longed for most: command of a ship.

As they lifted Fostolf over *Dragon*'s side, Thorgrim had called Harald over to him. They stood apart from the others. "The gods may yet heal Fostolf," Thorgrim said, "but I doubt they will."

Harald nodded.

"Even if they do, it'll be some time before he can be master of *Dragon* again. Herjolf is second to Fostolf, a good warrior, a good sailor, but he's too foolish by far to be master of the ship."

Harald nodded again. Herjolf was a few years older than himself, a strong, burly young man with a wide smile and an easy laugh. He was a joker and the other men found him very amusing. But Thorgrim had little patience for men who were amusing and Harald knew he would show Herjolf no preference. He felt a spark of hope and possibility spring to life in his breast, but he kept his face stoic.

"I know you've wished for a command of your own," Thorgrim said, "and you've been good about not asking for it. You did good work when you took command of the ships back at Loch Garman. I know you're an excellent mariner."

"I learned from the very best of mariners," Harald said with a smile, but Thorgrim only grunted and did not smile in return.

"I want you to take command of *Dragon*," Thorgrim continued. "I'll make it clear to the others, to *Dragon*'s company, that that's my wish. Even if they're unhappy about it they'll keep their mouths shut."

"Yes, father," Harald said. He paused for a moment, unsure if he should say what he wished to say, then decided he would. "Thank you."

Thorgrim nodded. "It's not a gift, you've earned it," he said. "Earned the chance. But understand this: even though I can make you the master of the ship with one word, it'll be up to you to show the others that you deserve it. That you're the right man to have his hand on the tiller. And it may not be permanent. If Fostolf recovers I'll give the ship back to him."

"Of course," Harald said, but he did not think that was likely, and he knew that his father did not think so either.

Harald was not sure how he should feel about all of it. From the moment Thorgrim announced that he would be the temporary master of the ship, Harald felt a roiling sensation of delight and trepidation, confidence and uncertainty, concern for Fostolf's life and fear that that his concern was in no way genuine. It was an odd mix of feelings, like the wind blowing against the direction of the waves.

The men of *Dragon* took the news well enough. They liked Fostolf but they could see that he was in no condition to command, and likely never would be again. And they liked Herjolf, as most did, but Harald had the sense they would not have been pleased to have him as master of the ship. They could see his shortcomings in that regard.

As for Herjolf, he did not seem in the least unhappy about the change. He had never struck Harald as one who was eager for command. In truth, he seemed relieved to not have to take on such a responsibility. His wide smile never faltered as Thorgrim announced the new arrangement.

So Harald took his place on the small afterdeck, hands on the tiller, the wood warm and smooth under his rough palms. He ordered rowers to the benches and others over the side to give the ship a shove out into the water. He waited as the other ships got underway: *Sea Hammer* and *Oak Heart*, *Blood Hawk*, *Black Wing* and then his own ship, *Dragon*.

He heard echoes of his father's voice as he called for the rowers to back water, for the men under the bow to heave, for the larboard side to pull, the starboard to back water so the ship turned in place like a dancer. He reveled in shouting, "Cast off the gaskets on the sail! Hands to the braces and halyard!"

All through the morning the fleet held its steady course south-east, following the fairly straight coastline. High, white cliffs flanked the beach where they had spent the past few days, but soon those yielded to a jagged, broken shore, as if the gods had picked up the land and snapped it in two and set the northern half back down again. But along the edge of the low, sandy cliffs were miles of flat beach, and their larboard sides. Whatever was beyond that point had been hidden until then, but as they came around they could see that the land tended away toward the north-east where it ended in another headland which once again hid the rest of the coast from view. But not entirely. There was open water straight ahead of them, but at the far edge of the horizon a dark line suggested that there was more land there, which Harald guessed was either Frankia or more of England's southern coast. The latter he thought most likely.

Not that such things were his concern. He might be master of *Dragon* now, but his father still commanded the fleet. Harald's job was to run his ship as well as he could, and to follow his father's orders.

He had a pretty good idea of what thoughts were turning over in Thorgrim's mind at that moment. There were really two choices that Harald could see. They could continue to follow the coastline and discover if and where it joined up with the lands on the horizon, or they could strike out across open water and hope to reach the far shore before night was on them. He looked up at the sun. He looked out over the water. He made a guess as to which Thorgrim would choose.

And he guessed right. Half a mile ahead he saw *Sea Hammer* turn to larboard, her sail bracing around to set on the new course. His father was following the coast because he gauged it was too late in the day to make the crossing to the far side. Harald felt a sense of relief. He did not care to be caught in the dark on an unfamiliar shore, or any shore for that matter. He certainly did not care to spend a night aboard the ship in the company of her former master's corpse.

Herjolf had been sitting on the sheer strake just forward of the afterdeck, and as Harald turned he stood and stepped closer. "I'm sure you didn't know this," he said, his voice low and conspiratorial, "but Fostolf has…had…a small horde of silver. There, under the deck, with his other things. I think it would much improve the men's mood if we were to divide it up among them."

"No doubt," Harald said. He felt the prickly sensation of wariness and uncertainty. It made sense that the late captain's wealth should be shared by his men. It would certainly help to lift the gloom. But it did not feel quite right.

"I think we should wait until we get to shore, see what Thorgrim says about that," Harald said, hating the words as they left his mouth. He was master now. He should make decisions on his own. Not ask for his father's help.

"As you wish," Herjolf said, a hint of his irrepressible smile on his face. "Your father's a fair man, that's certain. He'll want to share it out with all the men of the fleet, would be my guess." There was a note of disappointment in the words, Harald felt certain.

They continued on for some time more, with the sun sinking down astern of them. Finally *Sea Hammer* turned again, turned further to larboard, and the ships astern of her dutifully did the same, with Harald turning *Dragon* in the wake of *Oak Heart*, the ship immediately ahead of her. He could see what they were making for: a strip of sandy beach, an inviting place for the ships to run ashore for the night.

One by one the narrow vessels ground up on the sand and the men tumbled over the side and landed knee-deep in the surf. They waded ashore, bringing anchors and lines with them, and once the ship was secure Harald followed behind. As he made his way up the beach he saw Thorgrim standing just above the wrack line, waiting with arms folded. His father spoke just one word. "Fostolf?"

Harald shook his head. Thorgrim nodded.

News of Fostolf's death spread quickly along the beach, and the mood turned somber among all the men, just as it had for the crew of *Dragon*. "Fostolf's men…your men…should see to his pyre," Thorgrim said to Harald.

Harald, aware that his father was watching, turned and ordered the men of *Dragon*'s company to arrange a funeral pyre. Soon a great stack of driftwood had been built some distance from the ships, the beach being well endowed with that material. Fostolf's body was dressed in his mail shirt and helmet and laid on top of a bearskin at the peak of the wood pile. His sword and spear were laid at his side, and his shield set over his chest.

Thorgrim carved runes into a plank from *Dragon*'s deck and placed it beside Fostolf's body. There were a few live animals aboard the ships, part of the plunder from the monastery, and Thorgrim selected the most robust of the goats. This was slaughtered and the blood collected in a bowl. Then Thorgrim stood beside the pyre and called on the gods to welcome Fostolf and guide him on his journey as he used a small tree branch to scatter the blood over Fostolf and the pile of bleached and twisted wood.

It was fully dark by the time they kindled flames and lit the ends of torches and used the torches to set fire to the driftwood that supported Fostolf's body. It caught quickly and spread upward and the men backed away, step by step, as the flames grew higher and hotter. Soon the entire thing was a great blazing mass of heat and light and Harald guessed it would be visible many miles out to sea, if anyone was so unlucky as to be caught at sea at night. Inside the flames, Fostolf's body made a dark outline, human-shaped, visible for some time, and then it, too, became part of the fire, indistinguishable from the rest.

The men watched in silence as one of their own, a man loved and admired, set off on the journey they all would take. Harald could see Failend standing near Thorgrim, though not by his side. He saw her make the Christian sign, the one in which they touch their forehead, chest and shoulders, an odd gesture but one he had seen many times since arriving in Ireland. He was not certain how he felt about her doing that. The sign would have meant nothing to Fostolf, and might even offend the gods. On the other hand, if Failend was asking her Christ God to come to Fostolf's aid in the other world, he supposed that was all right. It was possible that the Christ God was a real god, such as Odin or Thor. He did not see how it could hurt.

Harald considered making the sign himself, but it did not feel right for him to do so. Instead he asked the gods to look with favor on Fostolf and welcome him into the Corpse Hall, despite the manner of his death. He imagined he was not the only one thinking those thoughts.

The men formed a circle around the pyre and watched as the flames grew smaller and smaller until there was little more than a dark circle on the sand, illuminated by those bits of wood still burning, and pressed in by the dark on all sides. Then one by one, somber and silent, they moved off to find their places to sleep.

The sun rose the next morning, another fine day in an improbable stretch of fine weather. There was nothing left of Fostolf and the funeral pyre beyond a black oval shape in the sand, littered with bits of charred wood and a few tendrils of smoke rising up. But as the men went about getting their morning meal it was clear their mood was much improved. They had done right by Fostolf, sent him off in a fitting manner. Time for the living to get on with life.

Thorgrim's voice came rolling down the beach. "Get these stores and gear stowed away! We'll get to sea directly! No time to lose."

Up and down the beach the men moved visibly faster in reaction to Thorgrim's words, and Harald wondered if the day would ever come that he, too, could make more than two hundred warriors move faster with the application of just a few sentences. He hoped so. He intended for it to be so.

And then they were underway again, the ships once more pushed free of the sand, their sails spread to the wind, their bows turned toward the open water. East, always east.

Chapter Four

Now something comes
to the king's house,
but no consolation
to thralls given,
filth eats the chair;
a cold wind blows.

The Poetic Edda

A scattering of low islands lay half a mile east of Grømstad's shore. The islands formed a loose, broken peninsula, three miles north to south. They looked as if they had once been a continuous point of land before some god had crushed it underfoot and left the shattered bits where they lay. To the east of those islands was the open ocean, eighty miles of open ocean, that separated that kingdom from the land of the Danes.

The islands were granite ledge, inhospitable, no place to pull a ship up on shore. But there was water enough between them for a ship to tuck in, sheltered from the waves rolling in from the east. Room, indeed, for a fleet of ships. And it was just that thing, a fleet of ships, that Odd Thorgrimson found himself looking at.

The fleet was not insubstantial: twelve ships of various sizes, from the thirty-five foot, twelve-oared ship belonging to Ragi Oleifsson, a fishing vessel, really, though still sleek in the way of the Northmen's ships, to Amundi Thorsteinsson's stately thirty-oared longship. That ship had been built sometime after Amundi had given up raiding on foreign shores, but he had sent others a'viking in her, and she was well built to that purpose. Now she lay near the center of the rafted vessels with bright-painted shields lining her sides, and she looked every inch the warriors' craft.

Sea Hawk, Odd's own ship, seemed somewhere between Ragi's and Amundi's in design and construction. She was recently launched and had been waterborne for only a few weeks. Ari, the shipwright who built her, was an old and skilled craftsman, a man who had built ships for Odd's father and his grandfather, Ornolf the Restless, as well.

Odd was not entirely certain why he had Ari build her. Fishing. Hauling the produce of his farm up and down the coast. Travel. He built her because a man should have a ship. And because the gods told him to build her. He knew he could find other, stronger, perhaps darker reasons if he really plumbed the depths of his motives, so he did not think too deeply about it.

Ari had built *Sea Hawk* but Odd had been with him throughout, sometimes discussing the properties she should have, sometimes hefting an ax or an adze or a draw knife himself. The ship combined the qualities of a merchant vessel, a knarr, with those of a raider. She was strong-built and wider than most raiding vessels, but she was sharper than most knarrs, her stem and sternpost rising up in stately arcs, ready to take their carved figureheads when and if the ship was needed for more war-like work.

Which she was now. At her bow, the oak stem arced around and seemed to meld into the shape of a screaming bird of prey, an almost magical transformation, the product of Ari's skilled hand and chisel. Aft, the tall sternpost looped forward in an elegant curl, crisscrossed with intertwined beasts. Like the other ships, *Sea Hawk*'s sides were lined with the shields of the warriors she carried aboard. There was nothing of the tubby merchantman about her now.

All dozen ships of the fleet were tied side by side and floating between two of the larger islands, making an island of their own. They were in two rafts of six ships each, and each six-ship raft was tied stern to bow. A steady stream of people — men, women, even children — moved from one to the other, climbing over the rails where they were not blocked by the shields mounted in their racks.

"She looks a proper raider's vessel now, doesn't she?" Signy asked. Signy, Odd's wife, stood by his side, their daughter of four months, Hallbera, propped on her hip.

"She does," Odd agreed. *Sea Hawk* was still a bit beamy for a raider's ship, but with the shields and the figurehead no one could argue with her war-like appearance.

"Just as you imagined her," Signy said. She had always been suspicious of *Sea Hawk*, dubious about Odd's reason for building her, and had not been shy about saying so. She suspected his real aim was to go a'viking like his grandfather, his father and brother. She feared that the dull routine of life as a farmer and husband made him feel restless and impotent. Whether she was right or not, Odd did not know, because he made an effort to not look too closely at that part of his life either.

So he shrugged at Signy's words and said, "Raiding, fishing, cargo. Escape. I built her for all those reasons. And a good thing I did."

Escape it had been. Not just himself and his family but all the people on whom Halfdan the Black was likely to pour out his rage. Which was all the prosperous men of Fevik. Odd looked out over the low granite island just to the east of where the rafted ships floated. There were boats pulled up on the ledge and women and children there, a fire burning near the water's edge, a great iron pot hanging from a tripod. A gang of men had a sail spread out on the warm stone and were mending a seam that had come apart. One of Amundi's men had set up a small portable forge and was making spear points.

In the end, Halfdan and his army had come for them all, though it started in a far less dramatic way.

Halfdan had tried to take the farm that belong to Odd's father, Thorgrim Night Wolf, claiming that Thorgrim was dead and he had died owing taxes to the king. Odd did not actually know if his father was dead or not, and neither did Halfdan. But Odd was quite certain that no taxes were owed, so he resisted Halfdan's incursions. Diplomatically at first, and then with sword and shield.

And his neighbors had joined him, because they understood that if Thorgrim's farm was not safe then neither were theirs. They were freemen, after all. They owed allegiance to their king, they owned him tribute, but they did not owe him whatever he wished to take.

The last fight had been at Odd's farm, when he and the other freemen had gathered to decide on what they would do next. Halfdan and his men had come for them, set fire to the hall in which they were feasting, intent on forcing them out and slaughtering them as they came. But Odd had been ready for that, and he had another way out, and they had instead sprung a surprise on Halfdan and driven him off. They had won the day, but it was not a victory that would last and they all knew it.

Halfdan would have his revenge. He had to. He could not let such defiance stand, it would strike at the foundation of his rule. He would come for them all, and he would come with more force than they could counter with. So they took to the sea.

They all had ships, all the wealthy freemen of Fevik, for the same reasons that Odd had built *Sea Hawk*. Travel was hard enough over land; moving any sort of cargo was impossible at certain times of the year. The sea offered mobility that roads could not. So when word came that Halfdan's army was on the move, they loaded their families and their warriors, their weapons and what food and drink and goods they could manage into those ships, and they hid the rest out in the countryside, and they put to sea.

"Here comes Amundi, and the others," Signy said, nodding toward the big ship in the middle. Amundi, conspicuous in a red tunic, was climbing over the stern of his ship and onto the bow of *Sea Hawk*. Odd could see the other freemen also coming that way.

"I had better go," Signy said. "It's time for the wise men to decide the fate of us all." Signy had always had a sharp wit. It was one of the things Odd so loved in her. But it could become uncomfortably sharp when she was worried, which now she was.

Amundi stepped down the centerline of the ship, his pace brisk but unhurried. Dignified. It was the way he did everything, the air he projected, and it came as naturally to him as breathing.

"Odd," he said and nodded his head in greeting.

"Amundi, welcome," Odd said. There was a gravity in Amundi's demeanor that was not always there, and Odd knew he would find it in the others as well. It was born of uncertainty. Fear. There was not a man among them who would ever show fear for his own life, but their families were there now. Wives, children, grandchildren, even. That made things very different indeed.

The rest gathered around: Vifil, whose farm lay to the south of Odd's, Thorgeir Herjolfsson, the second most prosperous farmer there after Amundi, Ragi Oleifsson, Hakon Styrsson who was just a few years older than Odd and had a reputation as a hard man in a fight, and the half dozen other farmers who had thrown in with Odd. If they regretted that decision or not, Odd could not tell. But either way it was too late. Halfdan was not a man known for forgiveness.

Once they were all assembled Odd said, "There's been no word from Vandrad, as you know. If Halfdan turned back or marched off in some other direction, Vandrad was supposed to bring word back. He knows where to find us. So it seems Halfdan's either still in the field, still to the north, or Vandrad is dead."

"Or he's betrayed us," Ragi offered, which brought a murmur from the men and an uncomfortable feeling in Odd's gut. Signy had earlier expressed her suspicion of Vandrad but Odd had dismissed her. He felt certain that Vandrad could be trusted. But he had been wrong before. Often enough.

"Well, we can't spend the rest of our lives sitting here and wondering," Odd said. "It's time to move. Are you ready? Your men ready?" He felt his concern ease a bit, with the decision made.

All around heads nodded. "We're ready," a few said out loud.

"Ready as we're like to be," Hakon said.

"Good," Odd said. "*Sea Hawk* will lead the way. We'll see what we find when we get ashore, base our actions on that. Thorgeir, your men will see to the ships with the women and children?"

Thorgeir nodded. "They're aboard already, with the men we could spare."

"Good," Odd said again. He looked around. There was nothing else that he could think of. "Then let us be underway, and we'll hope the gods give us good luck in this."

The men dispersed back to their ships, and Odd called his own men to the oars. A few weeks before they had been the men who worked his farm: Vermund Jurundsson, the overseer, Gnup and Valgerd, the men who did the butchering and the men who did the smithing and the planting and the herding. Even old Ari, the shipwright, was there.

They had been farmers or craftsmen then, but they were warriors now, and in the way of the Northmen they were trained and experienced in both fields. They all had weapons and shields and armor of some sort, leather mostly, with a few iron helmets among them and a couple who even had mail. There was not a man among them who had not been in one bloody fight or another.

Odd had donned his own fighting garb earlier. He wore a mail shirt, the links finely wrought and polished until they shone. His helmet sat on the deck at his feet. His sword, Blood-letter, hung from his belt. It had been given to him by his father, Thorgrim, who had received it from his father, Ulf of the Battle Song. Ulf was a legend, as was the sword, and Odd was both honored and hesitant to carry it. It was an honor he was not certain he had earned.

Not all of the men aboard were farmers, however. Many were the freemen's sons and men-at-arms, many of whom had gone a'viking and were well used to a good fight. They wore mail and carried swords, as fitted their station. They had come with Odd and the rest when they had first called on Halfdan the Black, when they were still looking for a peaceful resolution to all this.

And some of the warriors were Halfdan's men, or had been, warriors who had been taken prisoner after the battle at Odd's farm and who had elected to join with Odd and the other freemen. Their loyalty was still in question, but if they proved themselves then they would be good men to have when things got ugly. Which they were likely to do, and soon.

Ari was standing nearby with a gang of men ready to haul the anchor up over the stern. Odd nodded toward them and the men began to pull the dripping rope in, fathom by fathom, and coil it down on the deck.

"Cast off, there!" Odd called next and the lines that lashed *Sea Hawk* to the other ships by her bow and either side were untied and pulled aboard and *Sea Hawk* floated free. Hemmed in by ships on either side there was no room to run the oars out, so the men of *Sea Hawk* and the ships alongside heaved and pushed and eased her along until she drifted clear of the others.

"Ship your oars!" Odd called next, and he felt his stomach twist a bit as he did. He was not very experienced at this sort of thing, commanding a ship and so many oarsmen in such a confined space, and that left considerable opportunity to humiliate himself. He thought of his father, as he so often did in such circumstances, and the ease and skill with which he could drive a ship. Odd did not think he would ever achieve that level of competence. It was yet another thing in which he would never be Thorgrim's equal.

"Starboard, back, larboard, pull!" he called, and awkwardly the men followed his command. If Odd was not much accustomed to commanding rowers, these men, these farmers, were not much accustomed to rowing. Like fighting, ship work was part of who they were. But they did not do it often, not enough to gain any great skill.

It had been worse a few weeks earlier, when they had first taken to the sea. Then they had rowed like drunken men, each intent on pulling an oar in his own fashion. Between their inexperience and Odd's they had nearly wrecked the ship a few times. But they were doing better now, and Odd thought they had a good chance of making it unscathed through the tricky set of islands.

As *Sea Hawk* straightened on her course and gathered way the other ships cast off from one another, the artificial island broke apart, and the vessels fell into *Sea Hawk*'s wake, oars moving more or less together, bright painted shields lining the sides, a long line of swift, silent menace. And making up the tail end of the line, the two least nimble ships of the fleet carrying the women and children, who had no business in this sort of work but who could not be left behind, unprotected.

They moved south, with the largest of the islands, large enough to sport trees, off their starboard side. They rowed through deep water channels which Odd had already explored by boat, sounding as he went. At last they emerged from among the islands and turned north into the wide channel that ran up to Grømstad.

Near the shores fishermen pulled nets up over the sides of their boats and watched warily as they passed by. Odd could well imagine what they were thinking. They would be hoping that whatever upheaval was going on, whatever struggle for power or wealth, would not touch them or interfere with their precarious existence.

There was less than two miles of water to cover, and the ships covered it fast, the rowers picking up the rhythm of the stroke until they pulled like men who had been doing that work for years. Odd gave the tiller to Ari and headed forward, climbing up onto the sheer strake at the bow, one hand on the thick, tarred forestay. He could see a headland off the larboard bow, and another beyond it, and he knew that between them was the small harbor to which they were bound.

He climbed down and went aft again and instructed Ari to turn a bit to the west. He looked astern. The other ships were following behind, figureheads mounted on the stems of those that had them. They wanted to make a frightening, intimidating display, and they pretty much succeeded.

They rounded the headland and the harbor opened up before them. Not much of a harbor, really, more a deep cut in the shoreline, a half-moon shaped indent a couple hundred yards across the mouth. Various wooden docks jutted out from the shore with some larger fishing boats tied alongside, and a few knarrs and three longships floating at moorings. And set back from the water, a quarter mile away, the high dirt and turf walls, crested by a palisade fence, that surrounded the great hall of Halfdan the Black.

There was no one moving that Odd could see, but that was not a surprise. The fleet's approach had been no secret, and no one there would be foolish enough to wait around to see what the strangers wanted. The shields on the racks, the figureheads mounted on the bows, would tell anyone all they needed to know — that it was time to fight or to flee.

Odd took the tiller from Ari and steered *Sea Hawk* toward an empty stretch of dock. He called for the oars to be run in and the ship's way fell off as she came alongside, the more nimble of her crew leaping off with dock lines in hand.

One by one the rest of the fleet came up, finding docks of their own or rafting up alongside the ships that preceded them. And then they were all there, all the raiders, with the ships bearing the women and children dropping anchor a hundred feet off shore.

"Let's get ashore and make ready," Odd called. He picked up his helmet and set it on his head and slung his shield over his back. He headed forward and when he reached the place where the ship's side bumped against the dock he climbed over and stepped ashore, his men making room for him. He strode down the length of the dock toward the beaten ground ashore, and behind him he heard the bustle of the other warriors following. There was nothing else to hear.

He continued on, thirty paces from the dock, leaving room enough for the men to form up. His eyes were on the walls beyond and the roof of the long hall that rose up behind them, the center and the heart of Halfdan's massive compound. It was nearly twice as big as it had been when Odd had first seen it as a child, riding with his father and Harald for a visit to Halfdan's court.

Smoke from a fire burning in the hearth was lifting up from the peak ends of the long hall, escaping from the holes left there for that purpose. There was another column of smoke to the right, a smith's shop, perhaps, or a smokehouse for meat. There was nothing to suggest alarm, but then, Odd was pretty sure there were not many men present to raise an alarm.

Amundi stepped up beside him on one side, Thorgeir on the other, and Ragi, Hakon and the rest gathering around. They had helmets on, but their shields were still slung over their backs, swords still in sheaths. Odd turned around. The rest of the men were in a ragged line. Those who had helmets were wearing them, and most had their shields on their arms and spears and battle axes held loosely in their hands.

"Let's go," Odd said and stepped off again and this time he heard the semi-coordinated sound of the two hundred or more men marching behind him. His eyes remained on the high walls as they approached, his ears open for any hint of danger.

Should we form a shieldwall? A swine array? Are we fools to approach in so haphazard a way? Odd wondered as he walked. He wished he knew these things. He felt his inexperience, his ignorance, profoundly, and it unsettled him.

The big oak doors were shut and no doubt barred from inside, but as they approached Odd could see activity on the walls, men watching them, others running here and there, more heads appearing. Forty feet from the base of the wall Odd stopped and held up his hand and he heard the men behind him stop as well: an army of warriors with only the wooden gates and twenty feet of earthen wall, and another five feet of palisade on top of that, between them and nearly all the people and worldly goods that Halfdan held dear.

"Stop there! Who are you?" a voice called out, and it took Odd a moment to see which of the dozen men on top of the wall had spoken.

"I'm Odd Thorgrimson," Odd replied. "And the other freemen of Fevik are with me. We've come to speak with King Halfdan."

"King Halfdan is not here," the voice called back. "But I think you know that."

"Oh?" Odd said. "Where is he?" But Odd already knew that as well. The man on the wall did not reply.

"If you'll open the gate we'll come in peaceably and await the king's return," Odd said.

There was a pause, and then the man on the wall said, "I think not."

This came as no surprise. They would have to fight. Better for the men on the wall to die in battle against Odd and his men than to admit to Halfdan the Black that they had surrendered his hall without even trying to defend it. Death in battle was bound to be quicker, easier, and nobler than anything Halfdan would dole out.

And the fellow above was in a good position to be obstinate. Not a great position, but a good one. The walls were substantial, and anyone attempting to scale them could be killed with little trouble. If Odd and his men had, say, a half dozen ladders, they might attack the wall in more places than the handful of warriors left inside could defend. But they did not have a half dozen ladders.

They did, however, have something Odd hoped would be just as effective. He turned to the men behind him. "Bring it up, these fellows want to be stubborn."

The crowd of warriors parted and a dozen men came hustling through. They carried a thick section of log, twenty feet long, with handles lashed underneath that would allow six men per side to bear its weight. As they pushed through, Odd stepped in front of the first of them and two dozen more men swarmed up on either side. They unslung their shields from their arms and held them up overhead, forming a roof over the men with the ram.

They covered the distance to the doors quickly, paused for a heartbeat, then swung the ram back and then forward again. The blunt end hit the oak door with a shuddering impact and the men on the wall above began to yell as they saw what was unfolding.

The men on the ram swung again and again and Odd could see the oak doors give, just a bit, before the first of the arrows came. He felt the jarring blow of the iron point hitting the wooden face of his shield and imbedding there, and he saw an inch of the arrowhead where it had gone clean through.

The ram was swinging slower now, and the arrows coming faster. Odd could see point after point sticking through the wood of his shield, and he could see gaps in the boards as the shield began to shatter, and he guessed the other men's shields were in no better shape. They did not have much longer before the thin wooden slats that stood between them and deadly missiles raining down were torn apart and useless.

"Come on, come on, swing it, you bastards!" Odd shouted. The faces of the men heaving the battering ram were red and dripping with sweat, their mouths set with the exertion or open and gasping. They swung the ram and the gate jerked under the impact. Toward the back an arrow struck a man's shield and the shield fell apart over his head and the arrow continued on down, driving through one of the rammers' chests at a near vertical angle. The man screamed, fell, and the one whose shield had been destroyed threw the useless thing away as someone took his place.

Another blow from the ram, and then another, and then the bar holding the oak doors gave way. They swung open, just a little, the narrow gap between them revealing the open ground outside the hall beyond. Odd lowered his shield, which was bristling with arrows like some giant sea urchin. He raced toward the doors, kicking them further open as he did and drawing Blood-letter.

He was the first through and he could feel his blood rising, and he felt the onset of the madness he had only recently discovered was in him. He charged through the doors and into the yard beyond, the others just behind him.

In front of them stood Halfdan's warriors. There were about thirty of them, all the men Halfdan had left to protect the hall and the people and the rest of the compound while he went off to run Odd and the others to ground. Thirty men against the two hundred who charged through the gate.

Odd slowed, then stopped, and he felt the fight drain away. Halfdan's men were arranged in a shieldwall. It was a brave attempt, and an utterly futile one as well. It would not be a fight or anything like a fight. It would be no more of a fight than when they butchered lambs in the late summer.

The rest of his men came up on either side, forming a long line facing Halfdan's men and they, too, stopped. Odd lowered Blood-letter until the tip was just inches off the ground.

"Bravely done," Odd called across the thirty feet between the lines of men. "Halfdan could find no fault in how you've behaved. But now, I beg you, throw your weapons down. We don't want to do this. We really don't."

It was quiet for a moment. Somewhere far off a child was wailing in fear. Odd pressed his lips together. He had not lied. He genuinely did not want to kill these men.

And then the man in the center of the defenders' line cursed and threw his sword on the ground between them.

Chapter Five

Has the sea him deluded,
or the sword wounded?
On that man
I will harm inflict.

The Poetic Edda

The wind had come more southerly, which was not ideal, but it was not so bad, either. *Sea Hammer* had her yard braced hard around, almost fore and aft, with the starboard clew hauled down hard to the end of the beitass and the larboard hauled well aft. If the wind had been stronger the ship would have been dipping her larboard sheer strake under, scooping up great quantities of seawater which the unhappy men aboard would have to fling back where it belonged.

But the wind was not strong. Six knots or so, enough to push the ship over at an easy angle and drive her along, not terribly fast, but faster than she could have been driven under oar, and with a lot less effort. It was a gift from the gods for which the men were properly thankful.

They had set off that morning at first light with just enough breeze to make tolerable headway. Thorgrim watched with some amusement as the men glanced impulsively to windward, looking for the tell-tale dark patches on the water that would herald stronger winds. He could practically hear their thoughts as they implored the gods, *Please send wind, so that bastard Thorgrim doesn't make us break out the oars.*

And the gods listened, and let the wind build with the rising sun. The fleet pushed east, across the open water that separated the shore astern, where they had spent the night, from the shore that lay on the horizon. To the north the land tended away in what might have been an enormous bay, but more and more Thorgrim felt that they had actually been on an island for the past week, and what they were seeing now was the water that separated that island from the mainland.

Interesting, but not of any real concern to him. He felt no need to learn the contours of that coastline. He meant to leave it all in his wake and had no intention of returning.

The fleet spread out as they sailed, the faster ships — *Sea Hammer*, *Blood Hawk* and *Oak Heart* — opening up some distance from the smaller ships behind. But that did not concern Thorgrim much either. As long as the fleet stayed reasonably close, well within sight of one another, he did not think there would be any problems. No reason to bunch up and risk a collision, which was more likely to happen when conditions were good and vigilance relaxed.

Thorgrim turned the helm over to Armod, who was a good helmsman, and took his place on the other side of the afterdeck, looking out over his command. There was little to do and little to see, just the open ocean to the south and the unremarkable shoreline to the north and east. There was some activity on the water a mile and a half or so to the north, a cluster of boats doing something or other, though what it was they could not tell. Fishing, most likely. They were not boats of any substantial size, not enough to be of interest to Thorgrim, either as a potential threat or a potential source of plunder. So he ignored them.

Just a little way forward of where he stood, Failend was sitting on the deck, her back against the side of the ship. *Sea Hammer*'s motion was easy in the low swell and light breeze, so Failend's vomiting had been minimal. She did not look good, Thorgrim had to admit, but again, he had seen her look much worse.

He stepped down to the lower deck and walked over to her, crouching down at her side. Her eyes were closed, her head tilted back, and she seemed to not be aware that he was there.

"Failend," he said softly. With some effort she turned her head his way, opened her eyes and looked up at him. She had big eyes, deep brown, like well-oiled wood.

"Is there anything I can get you? Anything I can do for you?" he asked.

A hint of a smile seemed to play on her lips, not what Thorgrim would have expected. She shook her head slowly, more as if it was lolling with the motion of the ship rather than moving of her accord.

"You're sure?" Thorgrim said, keeping his tone as considerate as he could. "Very well, then. Just call out if you need anything…or wave or some such." He stood and returned to the afterdeck, somewhat puzzled by that whole exchange.

And then he remembered something that he had been meaning to give her, something that kept slipping his mind, and he thought this might be a good moment. It might help take her mind off her misery. He dug into the leather bag hanging from his belt until he found it: a small, silver amulet, intricately decorated. Mjölnir, the hammer of Thor. He stepped off the afterdeck and knelt down beside her again.

"Look, I have something for you," he said. "I've had it some time and I've been meaning to give it to you." He opened his hand. The amulet looked tiny lying on his calloused palm.

Failend looked down at it and smiled faintly. She looked up at him. "Thor's hammer?" she asked.

"Yes. A nice one. Well-wrought," Thorgrim said.

"You think I should wear your heathen symbol?" she asked and Thorgrim could not tell if she was teasing or not.

"Certainly. I wear your Christ symbol," he said. He pulled the leather thong that he wore around his neck out of his tunic. Hanging from the cord was an image of Mjölnir as well as a small silver cross. The cross had been given to him by another Irishwoman, years before. It seemed like several lifetimes before.

Failend nodded. She knew perfectly well that Thorgrim wore the two symbols. "You have many gods," she said. "My God tells us we must have only one God. Just him."

Thorgrim frowned. He thought the Christians had three gods but he knew it was not that simple. It had been explained to him several times by several people but he could never remember, so he let it go. "Maybe your God will think of it just as jewelry, and he will not be bothered by you wearing it," he said.

Failend smiled a little wider and nodded her head. "Maybe so," she said. "Thank you."

Thorgrim smiled as well. He took the delicate cord that Failend wore around her neck, untied it and lifted it carefully off. He slid the image of Mjölnir on to it and tied it back again. "There, now we match," he said. He laid his hand on her leg, a gesture of reassurance, then stood and returned to the afterdeck.

Once there he looked aloft, up at the rigging and sail, then looked astern at the fleet strung out behind them. He ran his eyes quickly over the ships and let them rest on the last in line, *Dragon*, now a good two miles astern. He considered the set of her sail, her angle of heel. It was Harald's ship now, his son's ship. He was proud of the boy, and he was concerned and he was curious as to how he would do with his first real command.

There had been no grumbling when he had named Harald master, at least none that Thorgrim was aware of, and he did not think there would be. Harald was well-liked, he was competent and he had proved himself many times over.

Still, if he did poorly, if he bungled his command, made stupid mistakes, it would be a bad thing all around. Bad for Harald and his place among the men, bad for Thorgrim if it seemed he had favored his own son, giving him a command for which he was not ready.

But so far, all seemed fine. The sail was set well, the ship making as much speed as she could hope to under those conditions. This of course was no real test of Harald's seamanship, but it was something.

Thorgrim's thoughts were interrupted by Starri Deathless's sharp, barking laugh. "You can stop your constant looking back toward Harald's ship, Night Wolf!" he said. "It hasn't sunk yet and it's not likely to."

Thorgrim turned back to look at Starri. "Well, you should know, excellent mariner that you are," he said. Starri had little understanding of, or interest in, ships and sailing. He considered ships as little more than a means to get him from one fight to another, and he let others worry about the actual sailing of them.

"I'm mariner enough to know what should concern you and what shouldn't," Starri said. "You worry about young Harald who's already a better sailor than you, and you don't even notice the ships ahead."

It took Thorgrim a moment to register Starri's words. "What ships?" he said at last.

"There," Starri said, pointing to a spot just off the starboard bow. "Five ships by my count. Do you see them?"

Thorgrim squinted a bit, cocked his head to one side. He thought he might see the vaguely square patches of color on the horizon, but he was not certain.

"Yes, I see them now," he said, hesitantly.

"No, you don't," Starri said. "No one aboard could see them, save me. I've been watching them for some time now and not one other man has noticed." Starri had keen, sometimes even preternatural eyesight. Hearing as well.

"Good of you to mention them," Thorgrim said. "How about you scamper up to the masthead and see what else those sharp eyes of yours can pick out."

"Gladly, Night Wolf," Starri said, and Thorgrim knew he was sincere. Starri liked being at the masthead. It was not an easy climb, going hand over hand up the shrouds, or at least not easy for most men. To Starri it seemed no more burdensome that strolling down a path.

He jumped to his feet and jumped again and grabbed onto the shroud, then clamped the thick tarred rope between his feet and began to climb. Thorgrim looked off to leeward. The cluster of English boats was still there, which surprised him, since the sight of even one longship was generally enough to make any English race off as fast as they could. But something was occupying them and he wondered if maybe they had not even noticed the fleet sailing by.

Despite himself he turned again and looked back at the ships astern, at *Dragon*, but now his view of that ship was blocked by the others ahead of it. No matter. Starri was certainly right. She was not likely to sink anytime soon.

He looked toward the east, past *Sea Hammer*'s bow, and this time he was fairly certain he could make out the sails in the distance. A couple of whitish patches against the blue sky and dark shoreline beyond. Another of a reddish hue, a common enough color for a ship's sail. He thought he could make out a few other irregular patches of color as well.

Starri might have been the first one to spot the ships, but word of his discovery spread quickly, and the men crowded along the weather side and pointed and speculated. "Five of them, and the one in the lead's a big bastard," Thorgrim heard one man declare, and another say, "Third in line's got a checked sail. I'm pretty sure I saw her in Dubh-linn this year past."

Can these whore's sons really see that much? Thorgrim wondered. He could hardly see the sails at all. He had been assuring himself that his sight was not particularly worse than that of most men, but now he began to wonder.

"Ships, is that it?" Louis de Roumois asked. He had been on the leeward side, leaning on the sheer strake just forward of the small afterdeck. "Ships ahead?"

"Come see for yourself," Thorgrim said, nodding with his chin toward the ships off the starboard bow. Louis pushed himself off and stepped up the deck against the ship's slight heel. He leaned over the side and looked forward.

"Ah, yes!" he said in his odd-sounding way, speaking the Northman's language, which was still somewhat strange to him, with the accent of a Frank. "I see them, five of them. I see the one with the checked sail as well."

Thorgrim grunted. He doubted Louis had yet lived beyond twenty-five years. Of course his eyes were still sharp as daggers.

Louis turned back toward Thorgrim. "Who are they?" he asked.

Thorgrim smiled, despite himself. Louis knew even less than Starri did about ships and the sea, and it often led him to ask stupid questions. Had they been on shore, Louis would have understood right off that Thorgrim could not possibly know who someone so far off might be. But somehow at sea the same thought did not occur to him.

"I don't know," Thorgrim said. "Too far to tell. We'll see if Starri can make anything out."

They waited for a few moments as the two fleets continued to close the distance between them. Finally Starri called down a report.

"Five ships for certain, Night Wolf!" he shouted. "Don't think they're English, not fat and clumsy enough for that. Northmen, more like. I think I can see shields mounted on their sides!"

"Hmm," Thorgrim said. Northmen. "Are they changing course at all?" he called back aloft.

"Not that I've seen since I got up here," Starri called back. "They're sailing in a line, like we are, but they haven't changed course or the set of their sails. They're heading more northerly than we are, they'll pass us right by. It'll be close, but they'll pass us!"

Thorgrim considered that. Northmen, sailing with shields mounted. They had not reacted to the sight of Thorgrim's fleet, which likely meant they wanted nothing to do with it. Just as Thorgrim wanted nothing to do with them. Let them go about whatever business they had, let them visit their terror on whatever unfortunate place on the coast of Engla-land to which they were bound, it was none of his affair. He had only one goal. East, always east.

But that did not mean he would be caught with breeches around ankles.

"Forward there! Ease off that tack some!" he called. He turned toward the leeward rail. "Hall, Vestar, ease the sheet!"

Men fore and aft grabbed onto the lines that held down the corners of the sail and freed them from the cleats to which they were tied, then eased the ropes out, a foot, two feet, three feet.

"Good! Make that fast!" Thorgrim shouted. The wind spilled from the sail that was now more bellied out than flat, and *Sea Hammer* sat more upright, her speed slacking noticeably. Thorgrim's fleet was spread out over miles of ocean, and that was fine if they were just sailing. But if there was the possibility of trouble then he wanted them close together where they could support one another. And since the smaller ships could not sail any faster, *Sea Hammer* and the others would have to slow down.

He looked astern. *Blood Hawk*, under the command of Godi Unundarson, was surging up behind, a few hundred yards back. Godi would have seen *Sea Hammer*'s sail eased out, Thorgrim was certain, and he would slack his own sail to match. The same was true for Asmund on *Oak Heart* behind her.

Thorgrim looked forward once again. Even he could see the newcomers now, their sails standing out sharp against the horizon and the distant shore. They were no more than a mile and a half off, still holding a steady course, north-west, heading for the water between the big island and the shore.

What are you up to? Thorgrim wondered. *Where are you going?* There seemed to be some purpose, something deliberate, in the way they were sailing.

They must know this coast. They seem to know where they're going. In the same way that he had once known the coast of Ireland.

The two fleets stood on for some time more, *Sea Hammer* drawing to within a mile of the lead ship as it passed from starboard to larboard, and the rest following astern of her.

"I can see her well now, Night Wolf!" Starri called down from aloft. "Big bastard, like I said. Big as *Sea Hammer* at least. Next in line is near the same! Thirty, forty oars? I can see the men aboard, and there's plenty of them! No change in course! Bastards don't have the balls to come and fight!" Thorgrim could hear the genuine disappointment in that last bit.

Just as well, Thorgrim thought. He was perfectly happy to fight when fighting was called for, but unlike Starri he did not crave it. Or at least, not anymore. When he was a young man it had been different. But now he wanted only to return to his home. He had riches and reputation enough.

He looked astern. *Blood Hawk* was in his wake, no more than a hundred feet separating her bow from *Sea Hammer*'s stern. He could see Godi's massive form standing at the tiller. Behind *Blood Hawk*, *Oak Heart* had also drawn up close, and *Black Wing* behind her.

Thorgrim leaned farther outboard. He could just make out the edge of *Fox*'s sail around the other ships. He could see nothing of *Dragon*, but that was hardly a surprise. The line of ships' sails made an effective screen, hiding the smaller ship from sight. Thorgrim crossed to the leeward side and looked astern from that vantage. Still no *Dragon*.

He frowned and turned and there she was. No longer in the line of ships, she was running downwind, almost directly away from her consorts. There was already a half a mile at least between her and *Sea Hammer*.

"Harald!" Thorgrim said, speaking out loud out of sheer frustration. "What by all the gods do you think you're doing?"

Chapter Six

Hither to the shore
are come rapid keels,
towering masts,
and long yards,
shields many,
and smoothshaven oars

The Poetic Edda

It was not long after the fleet got underway that Harald Thorgrimson began to feel agitated.

They had set sail once they were clear of the beach, all six ships, and with *Sea Hammer* in the lead they turned their bows east, aiming to cross the open water to the far shore.

Dragon had been right among them at first, just to windward of *Fox* and a little astern of *Black Wing*, the ships so close the men barely had to shout to be heard from one to the other. Harald had no illusions about matching *Sea Hammer*'s speed, nor would it have been proper to get ahead of Thorgrim's ship even if he could. As long as he was keeping pace with the other ships he was happy.

But that did not last long. As the morning wore on the fleet began to spread out, each ship settling into its natural pace, which left *Dragon* last in line. Harald tried to imitate his father's natural stoicism, the aura of calm command that Thorgrim seemed to radiate. Whether he was succeeding or not, Harald could not tell. But he did not think he was, and that only added to his annoyance.

He looked forward, past the bow, and realized *Fox* had gained a ship-length on them.

"Shift the beitass a little aft!" he called, and a dozen men turned to the work of moving the thick spar. The beitass itself was heavy enough, but now it had the corner of the sail made fast to its end, and that too had to be shifted. However, if the change in sail shape gave them even half a knot more, it would, in Harald's view, be worth it.

But it didn't. In fact, as *Fox* continued to stretch out her lead, Harald realized that the change had only made things worse. Now he had another decision to make: have the beitass moved back where it had been and admit his mistake, or keep it as it was now and continue to fall behind.

I'm not fooling anyone, Harald thought. *They can all see we're going slower now. It will only make me look more like a fool if I don't admit it.*

"Very well, put it back the way it was. That was a mistake," Harald called forward, wondering as he did if it was a mistake to admit to his mistake. Again the men moved to obey. Harald looked closely at their faces, looking for some sign of disgust or amusement, but he could see nothing.

He studied Herjolf's face as Herjolf supervised the task of shifting the spar and sail. Herjolf was his biggest concern, the fear that Herjolf would think he was not up to the job. It was possible, maybe even likely, that Herjolf felt that he himself deserved to be master of *Dragon* and was just looking for Harald to make a mess of it. Herjolf had never seemed unhappy with Harald's taking command, though that was not proof of anything.

But there was nothing untoward in Herjolf's expression that Harald could see, no suppressed look of delight at the mistaken change in sail trim, no gloating or disgust. Just the same simple, slightly amused look that Herjolf always wore.

The fleet stood on that way as the morning passed, the ships spreading farther and farther apart until *Sea Hammer* was at least a mile and a half ahead, with the rest strung out behind her like beads on a string.

"Give a pull on that leeward sheet," Harald called. He felt as if he had to do something, and tightening down on that corner of the sail might give them the increase in speed that shifting the beitass did not.

Men pushed themselves to their feet and shambled over to where the leeward sheet was made fast, but there seemed to be less enthusiasm now than before. Harald opened his mouth to say something, then shut it again.

"She's not a fast ship," Herjolf said. He had made his way aft and was standing on the weather side, just forward of where Harald stood at the tiller. "That's just the way it is. Even Fostolf couldn't make her go faster than *Fox*."

Even Fostolf... Harald thought. *Even Fostolf...*

"Well, we'll play with the set of the sail, see what we can get out of her," Harald said, trying to sound as confident and knowledgeable as he could.

"Of course," Herjolf said.

They plowed on east in *Fox*'s wake, and Harald struggled to keep from calling for further adjustments to the sail. He thought of ordering all the men to sit up on the windward side, which would make the ship sail more upright and probably give her a little more speed, but he resisted that as well. In his heart he knew she was the slowest ship in the fleet and there was nothing he could do about that, and trying and failing would just make it worse.

Once he called for the yard to be braced around a bit sharper, and then left it at that.

The men forward were taking their ease, with little to do, but Harald's vigilance did not flag as he continually scanned the horizon. For that reason he was the first to see the boats.

"Herjolf," he said. "Look to the north there. Looks like some boats. Half a dozen or so."

Herjolf stood straight and looked in the direction Harald was pointing. For a moment he said nothing. "Strange," he said at last. "What do you think they're up to?"

"I don't know," Harald said. "Fishing, I guess."

"Maybe," Herjolf said. "But you'd expect them to be spread out if they were hauling nets, not all clustered around."

"Whatever it is, it must be pretty interesting," Harald said. "Most English race for shore when they see the likes of us."

Herjolf smiled and nodded. "Yes, they do. I wonder if these fellows are doing something that might be of interest to us."

Harald glanced ahead as if concerned his father could overhear this speculation, though of course *Sea Hammer* was a good two miles ahead by then.

"Like what?" Harald asked, his curiosity now trumping his attempt at stoic detachment.

"I don't know," Herjolf said.

Dragon continued on, the distance closing between her and the cluster of boats off the larboard side, the men aboard watching the activity, which was no more than half a mile away. There was nothing very remarkable about the boats, to be sure, but on a day of clear skies, steady wind and open water they were the most interesting thing around.

And the more they watched, the more inexplicable their business became. The boats seemed to be engaged in some sort of dance, some racing off in one direction, some in another, some stopping where they were and bobbing there as if waiting for something. The rest of the fleet of longships was well beyond them now; only *Dragon* was still to windward of them, and they seemed to show no interest at all in the powerful enemy so close by.

"I don't know, either," Harald said, and just as he said that the sea in the midst of the boats seemed to erupt, rising up and roiling white and black. All along *Dragon*'s side the men shouted in surprise and wonder. And then up out of the thrashing patch of water came a massive fluked tail, seemingly as high as a ship's mast. It hung there for a moment then came slamming down in a welter of salt water, slamming down on one of the boats, which seemed to simply vanish as if some conjurer had made it disappear.

"A whale!" Herjolf shouted, his tone a mix of surprise and delight.

"Big bastard," Harald said. He had seen many, many whales in the few years he had been to sea, and he had seen them lift and slam their tails as this one had done, but this beast seemed bigger than any he had seen before. It was hard to say — they were half a mile off — but it seemed that way to him.

"Yes it is! Yes it is!" Herjolf said. "Ha! Look at them run now!" The boats, which had been swirling and dancing, now all turned and headed off toward the shore and away from the beast they had apparently been hunting. From where he stood Harald could see no sign of the boat that had received the crushing blow of the tail.

Herjolf turned toward him, his eyes wide, a wild grin on his face. "Oh, we have to go after it! We have to kill that beast!"

Harald felt the conflict in his heart, and his stomach twisted up even before Herjolf finished talking. He glanced over at where the boats had been and saw the great, black back of the whale rise above the surface and slide down again.

"Too late," Harald said. "Thing will be gone by the time we get there."

"No, no, it won't!" Herjolf said, his enthusiasm not diminished at all. "Anyway, it'll probably swim this way, come right for us. It'll stay on the surface, that's what they do!"

Harald glanced forward at *Sea Hammer*, far ahead of them now. He looked back at the whale. He looked at Herjolf. He didn't know what to say.

"Think of it!" Herjolf said. "Whale meat! A feast for all of us, on all the ships! Won't they thank us for that!"

Harald looked back at the whale, at the slick patch of water where it had been. He knew why his stomach was twisting up. Because he, too, wanted to go after the beast. Because he loved the idea of killing it. He and the men of his ship. What a feat that would be! How better to prove themselves as a ship's company?

"No," Harald said. "We're supposed to be making this crossing, following the others." The words sounded weak even as they left his mouth.

"Following the…look, it will take no time at all to kill this thing!" Herjolf said. "Those English, they probably tired it out, wounded it. We'll have it before the others even see we've gone out of line!"

"Ahh…" Harald said because he couldn't think of anything else.

Herjolf took a step closer. "Here's why I think this is a good idea," he said, his voice low so that only Harald could hear. "The men, they're still sorry about Fostolf's death. They liked him. They like you too, don't get me wrong, but they're not a crew like they were. But something like this…" He nodded toward the north and as he did the whale arched out of the sea again. Closer this time.

Harald took a deep breath. Herjolf was right. Nothing brought a crew together more than battle, and if that battle was with a whale, that was just as good. Here the gods were giving him the chance to show he was a leader, he was decisive, that he knew no fear. Not even fear of his father.

"Yes, let's do it!" Harald said, and, decision made, he felt a great sense of relief. "Listen up, you men!" he shouted forward. "We're going to go and kill that bastard whale, show the rest of the fleet how it's done. We'll make a feast of it, and won't those others thank us!"

He saw looks of surprise, looks that quickly turned to enthusiasm as the men understood what Harald was saying. A cheer broke out and Harald smiled because he knew just then that he had made the right decision, that the echoes of that decision would sound far into the future.

"Hands to tacks, sheets and braces!" Harald shouted next and the men ran to the various lines; there was no hesitation now. Harald pushed the bar of the tiller away from him and *Dragon* turned to larboard while the men heaved away on the braces and the big yard swung around overhead. More eager hands grabbed onto the sheets and pulled them tight and the ship danced ahead.

It was harder to see forward with the sail square to the ship. Harald bent down and looked under the foot of the sail and was rewarded with a sight of the whale once more rolling out of the water. It was not coming directly toward them, but they were on converging courses and it would be no time at all before they were on top of the beast.

Then what? Harald wondered. In his burst of enthusiasm he forgot that he didn't know how to kill a whale.

Stab it, like you'd kill anything… he thought. He knew that a whale's blubber was many inches thick, that it would take some stabbing to reach anything vital.

"Grab up spears, as many spears as you can find!" Harald shouted. "I'll put the ship alongside, you finish it off!"

Again the men shouted with enthusiasm as they grabbed up their long-shafted spears. They were all, as far as Harald could see, just as game for this sport as he was. The whale would be a feast for them all, all the fleet, and the killing of it would make the men of *Dragon* a united crew, united under his command.

He pulled the tiller a bit toward him, turning *Dragon* to starboard, pointing her bow at the patch of water where the whale had last surfaced. He looked up at the sail. The yard needed bracing again for this new course, but there wasn't time or men to do it. All of *Dragon*'s crew, more than thirty men, was crowded near the bow, leaning over the sides, larboard and starboard, spears held upright as they waited for their target to appear out of the sea.

Harald looked to the east. The fleet was noticeably farther away now as *Dragon* sailed a course perpendicular to the one they sailed.

Not a problem, Harald thought. *Kill this thing in no time, haul it along behind us. Father and the rest will be grateful for it, once they see it.*

A burst of shouting rolled down the deck and Harald pulled his eyes and his thoughts away from the fleet and back to the whale. The creature was arching out of the sea, the black flesh gleaming wet, the water rushing down its sides. It was not more than a couple hundred feet away. It seemed to have changed direction, as if it was trying to reach *Dragon* rather than fleeing the oncoming ship.

"Stand ready!" Harald shouted, his eyes on the animal's back as it slipped under the water again. He had a feel now for where the whale was going and how fast. He would turned *Dragon* just to windward of the beast, bring her up into the wind alongside the whale, and as the whale surfaced again the spears would be there to greet it.

"Everyone to the larboard side! Larboard side!" Harald shouted. "I'll put the larboard side right against this bastard's flank!"

The men were grinning as they leaped and jostled their way to larboard, leaning out over the sheer strake, spears leveled now and ready to plunge down. Harald could see the roiling in the water, the mark of the whale just below the surface, right where he had figured it would be. He realized he was grinning, a great broad grin, and he shouted with exhilaration as he pulled the tiller toward him and swung *Dragon* up into the wind, and the men lined the larboard side, braced for the throw.

But there was nothing to throw at, no black hump breaking the surface, no rush of water running down the whale's side. Silence swept the ship fore and aft as the men stared into the water, then the sail flogged and came aback and *Dragon* slowed to a near stop.

Harald opened his mouth and the first guttural sounds of his next words were forming in his throat when the whale appeared. Not on the larboard side, as anticipated, but to starboard. And not the easy arch of its back but a great mass of head and back cresting up out of the sea then slipping down again.

In the brief time the whale was out of the water Harald had time enough to glimpse the odd square shape of the beast's head, the dark spot of its eye. He saw a row of teeth in the partially opened mouth which shocked him because he had thought whales had no teeth, and he wondered if this was a whale at all or some other creature of the sea. Or the gods.

The thought was barely formed in his head when the massive tail lifted clean out of the water, so close it doused the ship along its whole length, and Harald was put in mind of his father spraying blood with a branch over Fostolf's body. Then the tail came down hard, the end of one fluke catching *Dragon*'s side and tearing the shields from the rack and smashing the sheer strake and the strake below it as well. The ship lurched to starboard and half the men forward were sent tumbling to the deck, their shouts drowned out by the horrible sound of shattering wood and rushing water.

"Oh, you bastard!" Harald shouted as the great tail slid beneath the surface. *Dragon* had rolled hard to starboard with the impact and now she was rolling hard back the other way, and the men who were trying to regain their feet were flung to the deck again. The sail was fully aback now, the ship making no headway, the tiller useless, so Harald abandoned it and ran forward as the ship settled back on an even keel.

"Herjolf!" he shouted as he ran, and then suddenly he found himself staggering, the deck beneath his feet moving in an unnatural way, out of rhythm with the swells striking *Dragon* on the starboard bow.

"By all the gods..." he managed to say before he stumbled and fell forward. His hands hit the warm, smooth planks and broke his fall, or slowed it enough anyway that he did not hit the deck hard.

The ship was still rolling under him and the men forward shouting — surprise, shock, anger, he could hear it all in their voices. He pushed himself to his knees. The whale was on the larboard side now, its back cresting up out of the water as it passed under *Dragon*'s keel, pushing the ship from under in a way that ships were not often pushed. She rolled hard to starboard once more, dipping her shattered sheer strake into the sea and scooping up a rush of water before rolling back again.

The whale passed under, and Harald knew what would come next, and he was not wrong. Once again the massive tail lifted up out of the water, rising like the hand of some god come to crush the puny men below it. Harald had seen whale's flukes often enough, but never from just thirty feet away, and never as they were reaching up overhead, ready to come down on him, his ship and his crew.

His mouth hung open, his eyes went wide. He felt as if he was in a dream, the sort in which he was trying to act but could not will his body to move. Then the tail came flailing down, once again flinging water the length of the ship, and Harald clenched his fists. The ends of the flukes hit just aft of the stem, slamming down on the larboard rail and once again stripping the shields from the rack and tearing a length of strakes from the side.

Some of the men forward had recovered from the first blow and managed to keep their feet through the second, and they flung their spears at the great bulk of the whale. Harald saw the weapons strike, the points imbed themselves in the whale's side, the shafts sticking out at odd angles. He did not know if they had wounded the beast or not. He doubted it. He doubted that the whale could even feel them.

He pushed himself to his feet, mind and body moving fast but neither one with much control. He felt no sense of doubt or confusion or fear. He felt only rage, near blinding rage. He had risked quite a bit to come after this beast — his reputation, his ship, his father's approval — and now he risked losing it all. To a fish.

"You bastard!" he shouted as he ran forward. He snatched up a spear that was lying on the deck and the men along the larboard side stepped away as he raced up. He stopped at the broken section of rail and flung the spear at the whale, which was lying all but motionless twenty feet away. He threw with the considerable power in his arm and saw the spear sail straight over the water and drive itself into the whale's side. He saw the animal twist a little, which gave Harald a tiny bit of satisfaction, but he got no more reaction than that.

"Give me that!" Harald shouted, pointing to the iron grappling hook lying on top of a coil of rope near the bow. The hook and line were there mainly to lash the longship alongside an enemy in the middle of a fight at sea. Perfect.

A man named Brand, about Harald's age, a man who had already impressed Harald with his competence, grabbed up the hook and passed it back.

"What do you mean to do?" Brand asked, and Harald thought he heard a touch of concern in the man's voice.

"We came to kill that son of a whore and we're not going to let him escape now!" Harald said, taking the hook and letting it hang from the rope made fast to its eye.

Herjolf spoke up next. "I don't think it's trying to escape," he said, but Harald made no reply. He didn't much care what Herjolf thought or anyone thought at that moment. The anger was driving him now. He swung the hook around in a circle, building momentum, and then let it fly. The forged iron grapple sailed through the air in a smooth arc, the line trailing out clean behind it. It passed over the whale and fell into the water behind, the line draping over the whale's back, and it occurred to Harald that it might not be as easy as he had hoped to hook the smooth-skinned creature.

He closed his hand around the line and stopped it from paying out, then he grabbed it with the other hand as well and pulled back. He felt the hook come toward him with no resistance and he had an image of it just sliding easily over the creature's hide. He pulled again, and again the rope came easily. He pulled a third time and he felt the hook catch, felt the rope go taut in his hands. With that the whale thrashed more vigorously and Harald knew it had felt the thick hook dig in, in a way it had not felt the long, thin spear points.

"Come on! Grab on here!" he shouted and Brand and the other men close by took up the rope as well, as if they were ready to hoist the yard or sheet the sail home.

"Heave!" Harald shouted and the men leaned into the rope. The whale thrashed more violently as the hook dug deeper. The rope quivered under the strain and *Dragon* was hauled nearly sideways through the water, closer to her quarry.

"We'll get alongside, close enough for the spears!" Harald shouted as they pulled again. "Kill it that way, with the spears!" He hoped it would seem as if that had been his plan all along. In truth he had had no plan until that very moment, and even now he knew it wasn't much of a plan.

The men heaved again, *Dragon* slewing around as they pulled. The whale arched its back, rolled a bit to one side as if trying to rid itself of the iron hook. The prong of the hook was eight inches of curved iron bar, sharpened to a wicked point, but it seemed little more than an irritant to the whale. And that made Harald angrier still.

"Get that other hook back here!" he shouted. There were at least four of the grappling hooks aboard, Harald was sure. The men on the line heaved again and *Dragon* was pulled through the water in an awkward, part sideways direction. Then the bow hit the whale, sending a shudder through the fabric of the vessel. The whale shifted again, as if readying itself for a big move.

Harald was not worried about that. He was beyond worrying about much. The second hook was passed back to him and once again he took the line in hand, letting the hook swing as he ran his eyes over the whale's gleaming back.

Where do you want this, you bastard? Harald thought. Halfway down the beast's length he saw a fin of sorts, a meaty point standing proud with a series of humps behind it. Perfect, but there was no way he would ever get the hook to catch on the short, smooth protrusion.

Or perhaps there was.

"Clear away, clear away!" Harald shouted as he pushed his way forward and the men at the rails stepped back to let him pass. "Mind that rope, pay it out!" he shouted over his shoulder. He reached the place just near the bow where the first rope was running out over the side. He tossed the hook he was holding across the gap between ship and whale and saw it land on the whale's back, bounce once then come to rest. He swung one leg over the sheer strake and reached out for the taut line made fast to the first hook.

"Harald, by Thor's ass what do you think you're doing?" Herjolf called.

"Going to hook this son of a bitch fish right," Harald said. He swung his other leg over the sheer strake and slid down, his hands on the first grappling hook's rope. The rope sagged under his weight and he found himself pressed against the cool dark side of the whale, his body submerged from the waist down. He could see swirls of blood on the surface now and he knew his men or the English had managed to do the whale some hurt.

He clenched his teeth and took a renewed grip on the rope. Hand over hand he hoisted himself up, and as he did the hook dug farther into the whale and the whale in turn began to thrash and twist.

I wonder if it's tired, Harald thought. Maybe that was why it was not reacting more violently. Maybe the fight with the English boats had worn it out.

He pulled himself up over the whale's side and onto the relative flat of its back and was able to get his knees under him. He let go of the rope and picked up the second grappling hook where it lay. He looked over at *Dragon* and nearly laughed at the looks on the men's faces: leathered, bearded faces with mouths hanging open and eyes wide in surprise. They made no sound, as if fearful of waking a sleeping giant.

Harald stood awkwardly, realizing that this was going to be harder than he thought, not that he had thought much at all. The whale's back was just breaking the surface of the water, and was more round than he realized, with only a narrow crest running down the center of the arch. Walking on that slick, smooth surface would be no easy task, and if the whale moved too violently it would be impossible. He considered crawling but dismissed the idea. Too slow. Too undignified.

Grappling hook in hand he stood slowly, then took a tentative step, moving aft along the ridge of the whale's back. His leather shoes were soaked through and that gave them more grip, for which he was grateful. He took another step and the whale shifted and Harald felt himself thrown off balance. He stopped, held his arms out, spread his feet as wide as he dared and found his balance again. He could see the fin, no more than twenty feet away. Ten more careful steps.

He started moving again, getting the feel for the slickness of the surface, the curve of the back. He glanced over at *Dragon* and saw that the ship had drifted away, leaving a narrow but widening gap between it and the whale. And just as he noticed that he heard Herjolf call out in a loud whisper, "We're drifting away! Give a pull of that line!"

Harald's eyes went wide, the word "No!" forming on his lips, but he never got it out. The dozen men who were still loosely holding the rope now grabbed it tight and pulled, leaning back into it to haul the ship back alongside the whale.

And the whale felt it. It arched its back and rolled to the right and Harald felt his feet going out from under him. He abandoned his careful steps and turned and raced toward the fin on the animal's back. The whale rolled left and lifted its head and the part under Harald's feet seemed to drop away. He could see the water boiling along the whale's length as it began thrashing harder.

He was going over the side and he knew it. His feet slipped as they searched for traction on the whale's back. He planted his right foot and pushed off, flinging himself the last few feet toward the fin, one last desperate attempt to stay aboard.

Harald came down hard, on top of the fleshy hump. He threw his left arm around it as the thrashing grew more violent and knew right off that he would not be able to hold on. The skin was too smooth and slippery, the fin too short and wide to offer any real grip. With his right hand he whipped the hook around and dug one of the barbs into the fin, pulling it hard toward him to sink it deep. And he knew immediately that the whale felt that, too.

He took a tight grip on the rope just as the whale lifted its tail out of the water. Harald looked up in amazement as the massive flukes rose higher and higher until they were nearly overhead. He felt a twist in his gut, the familiar sensation of death coming close. And then he realized that he was the one person there whom the whale could not crush with its tail.

Then the tail came down again. It came down hard on *Dragon*'s stern. Harald saw the sternpost with its elegant carving snapped off and the entire aft end shoved down into the sea so that the water poured over the sides. The men forward shouted and the water rushed down the deck and Harald was certain that the ship was going down, that it would fill and sink right there.

But it didn't. As the flukes slid off and hit the water and threw up a terrific spray, *Dragon*'s stern lifted again, rails clear above the surface, her deck awash.

One more and they're dead… Harald thought. He was amazed that his ship had survived that blow, but he knew she would not survive another. It did not occur to him to wonder what might become of himself.

He felt the whale buck and twist under him, felt the entire body ripple down its whole length. He saw the head go under and he thought the beast must be diving, but instead it made the rippling motion again and Harald saw *Dragon* moving astern, which confused him.

And then he realized *Dragon* was not moving astern, the whale was moving ahead. It had started to swim, trying to get clear of the danger it found itself in. Its body undulated again, head to tail, the big fluke propelling the beast forward, its speed increasing with every stroke. Harald felt the rope in his hand grow taut and he shifted his grip before it could trap his hand against the fin. He looked behind. The rope he held and the one made fast to the first grappling hook were still tied off aboard *Dragon.* As the whale made headway it was dragging the ship along.

He heard Herjolf shout, "Cut the ropes! Cut the ropes!" and then Brand yell, "No! No! We'll lose Harald for sure!"

The whale twisted and Harald felt himself slip but he adjusted his stance to gain a more secure perch. He wondered for the first time just how he was going to get out of this situation. It seemed that there was nothing he could do but hang on and see what happened next. He wondered if maybe this had not been such a good idea after all.

Chapter Seven

Along the edge
a bloodstained serpent lies,
and on the guard
the serpent casts its tail.

The Poetic Edda

The rope that Harald was gripping was bar taut, running straight back from the hook in the whale to the cleat on board *Dragon* to which it was tied off. And then it went slack again as the whale slowed for a beat and *Dragon* slid down the back of a swell.

Harald renewed his grip, wrapping fingers around the tough walrus-hide line, when the whale gave another stroke of its tail. He felt the line going tight again, threatening to trap his hand against the fin, and he jerked it free. As he did, the whale twisted under him and again Harald felt himself sliding down the animal's rounded back.

He grabbed desperately for the hook. He felt the cold iron under his hand and grabbed tight as his legs slipped down the side of the whale.

"Hold still, you bastard!" he shouted as he pulled himself back up. He spat out a mouthful of salt water, repositioned his hand, and once he felt as secure as he was going to feel he looked around. The whale was really swimming now, pumping its tail with a steady rhythm, driving its massive body forward, its back now just above the surface, now just below. The water rushed down its length and sometimes Harald was clear of it, and sometimes he was chest deep.

Dragon was twenty feet astern. They had not cut the ropes after all, but had slacked them away, opening up some space between the battered ship and the whale's deadly flukes.

Good, good… Harald thought. It was what he would have done, or what he hoped he would have done. *Dragon* was being pulled along like a toy boat on a string, like the plaything of a child in the surf.

The best way for the whale to escape this danger, Harald realized, was to dive, to plunge down as deep as it could go and stay there as long as it could. He wondered if the whale would realize that. He hoped that Herjolf had men standing by with axes ready to cut the ship free. If the whale dove there would be a heartbeat or two, no more, before it dragged the ship down with it.

The whale dipped its head and the water rushed down its back. It hit Harald like a wave and he guessed this was it, the whale was going under. But its head came up again as the tail pumped and drove the animal forward. In the strange equilibrium of the moment Harald looked around. He could see the fleet off to the south and east. There seemed to be more ships than was right, but he was in no position to count them, clinging to the whale, spitting salt water from his mouth and blinking it from his eyes as he was doused over and over.

The whale was charging away on a more northerly heading, opening up the distance between itself and *Dragon* and the rest of the ships, and Harald could see there would be no help coming from that direction. And as that thought occurred to him it brought a new sense of resolve. He didn't want help. He shunned the idea of help. He alone had made the decisions that put him in this danger — danger that was both mortal and ludicrous — and it would be by his own doing that he would get out of it.

He took his eyes from the ships and turned them back toward the whale. It was still driving along but Harald had the distinct impression that it was moving slower now and he wondered again if it was getting tired. Powerful as the beast was, it could not be easy to pull an entire ship behind it. Would it just stop? And if it did, what would he do about it?

How do you kill one of these things? Harald wondered. He had never seen it done, not close up. From the shores of East Agder he had watched men go out in boats, men equipped with long lances and spears, and he had seen them later towing dead whales back. But how they had actually dispatched the things, he did not know.

Lance in the heart, or the lungs… he thought. It seemed as if he had heard that before. There was a way to kill a whale by driving a lance into its heart or lungs. But you had to know where to drive the lance so it would hit one of those organs, and then you had to get into a position to do it.

Well, I have to do something, Harald thought. If he didn't want help then he would have to help himself. He looked toward the whale's head, and as he did a great cloud of mist burst from the animal's blowhole with a hissing sound, jetting up twenty feet in the air. The spray drifted back toward Harald, and with it a revolting fishy smell that nearly made him gag.

But he was certain now that the fish was swimming slower, its motion less violent. His first thought was to get back aboard *Dragon.* He could probably climb back along the rope that bound the ship to the whale. But that seemed like running away, backing down from a fight. He couldn't do that. Even if his entire crew had not been watching, he couldn't do such a thing. He would know that he had fled from danger. The gods would know.

But he also could not remain where he was since he could do no good there. He thought it might be possible to work his way forward, up to the animal's head. Surely there he could reach some part of the creature that was vulnerable, find some way to kill the thing.

He pressed his lips together, let go of the iron hook, and began to move, half crawling, his legs wide to give him as much grip as possible, his hands trying and failing to get a hold on the thick, slick flesh. He knew now that standing was not a good idea, and he no longer worried about looking foolish in front of the men.

The whale twisted under him, its back dipped below the water. Harald felt himself begin to slip, sliding down the larboard side. He reached around and snatched the dagger from his sheath and plunged it into the whale's body and steadied himself with that precarious handhold. He braced for the whale to begin thrashing with the pain, but it seemed not even to feel the point of the blade.

Harald let his breathing settle, then pulled the knife free and began moving toward the head once more, stabbing into the whale whenever he felt himself losing his perch. The water rushed down the sides of the beast, tugging at his leggings and his leather shoes. He had a fleeting glimpse of the shoreline, far away, and sails off to his right, but he could spare them no more than a glance.

He was fifteen feet from the whale's blowhole and still had no idea what he was going to do when he saw one of the spears thrown from *Dragon*'s deck jutting from the whale's side and flailing in the rushing water.

There, Harald thought. *There*. It wasn't much, but at least he had a more realistic chance of killing this thing with the spear than he did with his knife. He inched his way forward, working himself as close to the spear as he could. It was sticking out of the whale's right side, but too low for Harald to reach. And then the whale rolled to its left, and as it did Harald reached down and grabbed the shaft of the spear, rolling back as the whale came more upright.

"Ha!" Harald shouted in triumph as he held the spear up. He shuffled a bit further along. The whale dipped its head and the water rushed waist deep over him, but he had his knife plunged into the whale's hide and managed to hold on that way. He considered his situation. He did not know how to find the heart or lungs, but he guessed he was now over the beast's brain, which should also do, though it would take some effort to drive the spear down into it. For this he would need all the strength of arm he could muster, and all the leverage as well.

He held tight as the whale dipped again, held on as the water pulled at him and swirled around. And then the whale rose, its head and back lifting a foot or two above the surface and Harald leaped to his feet, balancing on the slick, rounded back. He lifted the spear up above his head and with both hands on the shaft he drove it down with all his considerable strength right into the head of the whale.

The spear was on its way down when Harald realized that the spear point was going to hit the whale's skull and it was unlikely to go further. But the point hit and drove on down and Harald kept driving it on. He could feel resistance, the point going through something firm and thick — muscle, perhaps, or a thicker layer of blubber — but he could not feel it hit anything as solid as bone. He kept driving it down until the shaft was half buried in the whale and he could push it no deeper.

Whatever he hit, it was not a vital organ, apparently. The whale did not die, as Harald had hoped, or show any sign of being mortally wounded. Quite the opposite. The anger and pain the animal had felt from the Northmen's spears was nothing to the reaction it had to Harald's attack. Its forward momentum stopped and it seemed to double over, its head plunging down into the sea, its back arching above. Then it straightened again, its head coming up and thrashing side to side. Harald could hear the massive tail beating the water but he did not dare turn and look.

"Cut the ropes! Cut the ropes!" he shouted back toward *Dragon*, though he doubted they could hear him over the terrific thrashing of the wounded whale. It twisted from side to side, bucking and plunging, but Harald had driven the spear so far in that it made for a solid handhold. He clung to it now with both hands as the whale pounded and flailed under him.

"Will you die, you son of a bitch?" Harald shouted. He remembered the teeth. Didn't know whales had teeth. He wondered again if this was a whale at all, or if he had involved himself and his crew with something that mortal men should not tamper with.

Jörmungandr, the Midgard Serpent?

The whale rolled to its left and Harald grabbed tighter onto the spear, bracing for the fish to roll back, but it didn't. Instead it kept rolling, turning clean over, and Harald found himself under water, under the whale, which was now twisting above him.

Harald was a good swimmer and not afraid of the water, but this was something different. He had managed to suck in a lungful of air before he was rolled under, but he knew he could not hold that for long. In another moment he would have to let go of the spear and kick for the surface, in which case he would be beside the whale, not on top of it, and very much in the path of its fury.

But the whale did not remain upside down for long. Instead it kept rolling, turning completely over, and Harald found himself rolled up above the surface again. He took a deep breath and coughed and took another, but his thoughts were entirely on *Dragon*. If they had remained tied to the whale then they were certainly sunk or stove in already.

He twisted around as best he could and at first he didn't see his ship and he felt a swell of panic in his gut. And then he saw her, a good two hundred feet away and floating on her waterline. They must have cut the ropes free, just as he hoped they would, just as he had called for them to do. At least his ship would be safe, regardless of what happened to him.

Wrong place, I speared it in the wrong place, Harald thought. Whatever he had driven the spear into had only infuriated the whale, not killed it. He had to try again, in a different spot, which would not be easy given the frenzied motion of the beast.

He grabbed tighter onto the spear and pulled up to free it, but the spear did not move, not even a tiny bit. Whatever he had plunged it into was dense and had a grip on the point that even Harald Broadarm could not break loose. He tried again and with no better results. And then the whale rolled again.

"Ahhhh!" Harald shouted in frustration as the whale turned over once more. He felt the cold water close over him, the force trying to tear his hands free of the spear, the only thing he had to hold on to. His feet lifted off the whale's back and he knew he was streaming behind the spear shaft like a flag in a high wind as the whale drove forward.

His lungs were aching as he made a conscious effort not to breathe. He knew his time was about up, and then it was kick for the surface or die. But before he released the spear he felt the whale rolling again and once again he came sputtering up out of the water, hands on the spear, legs splayed out behind. But this time things had changed, because this time there was a ship alongside the whale, driving hard under a bellying sail, her high, curved stem cleaving the water as she came on.

The ship was no more than fifty feet away and seemed to be driving at the whale as if it meant to ram the thing. Harald blinked the salt water from his eyes but his vision was too blurry to see much, to tell what ship it was. He was pretty sure it was not *Dragon*, but beyond that he did not know.

Nor did he much care. It was a ship, and that was all that mattered. His stubborn resolve that he kill the whale himself had been washed clean out of him. He was ready for a bit of assistance. He knew he was done for if the whale rolled him under one more time.

He opened his mouth to shout to the men in the ship and received a mouthful of seawater for his trouble. He spat it out, choking and coughing. The ship had not changed course — it was still charging down on the whale with its sail full and the water curling around its stem. And up in the bow Harald could see a man, a big man with a long beard and wild hair, and he was holding an oar up over his head as if it was a spear.

For an awful moment Harald thought he must be dead, or near dead, to be seeing such strange things. Then just as the ship's bow was about to ram into the whale's side the man with the oar yelled, "Now!"

Harald wasn't sure if that was directed at him, and if it was he did not know what to do, but in that instant the ship turned hard to starboard, running its larboard side against the whale.

Harald was no more than twenty feet from the man in the bow and he could see now there was a spear lashed to the oar, extending the reach of the weapon by twenty feet. The man plunged the spear down, right into the whale's side, just behind the fin. At that the whale convulsed in a way that Harald had not seen, slamming its tail, twisting and rolling. Harald grabbed tighter to the spear and felt something hit him on the shoulders.

He looked down, almost too numb to understand what was happening, and he saw a rope lying there, draped over his arms. He looked up and followed the rope back to its origins. It had come from the ship, fifteen feet away, and now a crowd of men were beckoning him and pointing to the rope and shouting.

Then he understood. He released the spear and grabbed the rope just as the whale rolled away from him. The men on the ship heaved and Harald was dragged down the side of the whale, which was twisting and thrashing under him. He hit the water and did not let go, but instead gripped harder on the rope and felt himself lifted up. He bounced against the side of the ship, the smell of oak and tar sharp in his nose, the wake from the dying whale slamming him against the planks.

And finally his hands reached the sheer strake and a dozen others grabbed onto his arms and grabbed handfuls of his soaked tunic and hauled him up and deposited him on the deck. He lay there for several moments, gasping for breath. He looked up at the mast which was sweeping wildly back and forth against the clouds as the ship rocked in the maelstrom kicked up by the whale alongside.

And then the motion of the ship slowed and an odd quiet came over the world. It lasted for a moment, no more, and then the men aboard burst out into wild cheers. The cheering was so infectious that Harald almost smiled, and he might have done so if he had any idea what the cheering was about.

A shadow fell across his face and he looked up there was the man he had seen standing in the bow, the big man with the big beard and the oar and spear. He no longer had the oar and spear, but he was smiling a great smile.

"Harald Thorgrimson!" he said in a loud voice. "Don't you know how to kill a whale?"

Harald did not reply. He had no idea who this man was.

Chapter Eight

This sumptuous house shall,
for ages hence,
be but from hearsay known.

The Poetic Edda

A blacksmith shop stood a couple hundred feet from Halfdan's great hall, a big shop, big enough to satisfy the considerable smithing that a king might require. Big enough to house all thirty or so of Halfdan's warriors who had surrendered to Odd's overwhelming force.

The captain had been the first to throw his sword aside and the rest had immediately followed suit. Odd's men gathered up the swords and relieved the warriors of their helmets and mail as well. These were the accoutrements of an elite band of fighting men, part of Halfdan's hird, Odd imagined, though they did not look so elite locked in the smithy with a guard posted around.

Odd had assured them that Halfdan could find no fault in their surrendering. It would have been pointless for them to fight. No reasonable man could think they had failed in their duty. But then, Halfdan was not always a reasonable man.

I'll give them the chance to join with us, Odd thought. It was quite possible those men, those warriors, would choose to throw in with Odd and the others rather than wait to hear Halfdan's opinion of their behavior in battle.

With the fighting men secured, Odd turned his attention to the rest of the people in Halfdan's compound, all of whom were keeping out of sight. He called to the men behind him, his warriors and the men brought by the other freemen. "Spread out, search the hall, the outbuildings. Anyone you find, bring them out here. If you find any wine, any mead or ale, you keep your hands off it. Any man here gets drunk, I'll see they regret it for a long time."

The men headed off, nearly all of them in the direction of the great hall because they knew that anything worth taking was likely to be in there. But Amundi, Vifil, Ragi Oleifsson and the rest of the freemen stopped them and split them up, sending bands of men in various directions, assuring them all that any plunder would be shared out equally.

"Well," Amundi said to Odd once the men were off, "this little scene, taking the fort, it played out just as you thought it would. I'll give you credit there."

Odd nodded his thanks. There had been some debate as to how easy the taking of Halfdan's compound would be. Odd knew it would depend on how many men Halfdan had left behind. But he also knew that Halfdan wished to crush the rebellion under the weight of greatly superior numbers, which meant he would take nearly all his men with him.

He knew also that if he was wrong, if the compound had been too heavily defended, they could simply abandon their attempt to capture the place. The biggest risk was a trap: a few defenders on the walls, three hundred warriors waiting inside when the gates were broken open and Odd and his men came swarming in.

But that had not happened.

The gods are with us, Odd thought. He almost said as much out loud, but he did not think that would be wise.

Soon the men began to return, and they did not come alone. They came driving servants and wives and children, slaves and craftsmen, all the people who occupied Halfdan's fortress, the folk who made it a home and made it productive. Well over a hundred of them, all the people who were not part of the army marching off over the countryside.

Many of the women and children were crying, and many had to be pushed or half dragged along. They all looked terrified. The men for the most part were moving only because they were driven at spear point. Most of these people had been hiding before Odd's men had flushed them out. And now they came to discover their fate, and none of them seemed to think it would be very pleasant.

There was one woman among them for whom Odd was looking. A tall woman with long dark hair, a dress made of silk held up with silver brooches, a strand of lovely, delicate beads strung between them. She was not crying, and she was not being pulled along. She walked defiantly, with long strides, her eyes on Odd as Odd's were on hers.

"Ragnhild, good day," Odd said. A young boy, three or four years old, was standing behind her, his hair a wild mop of blond curls. He seemed to be struggling to appear as bold as his mother, but he was not meeting with much success.

"Good day, Harald," Odd said to the boy, and the boy took another half step behind his mother's dress.

"You're a fool, Odd Thorgrimson, and now you're a dead fool," Ragnhild said, her voice calm, her tone matter of fact, as if commenting on the weather.

"Perhaps," Odd said. "I mean, the part about me being dead, perhaps. I'm certainly a fool, I won't argue that."

The reply seemed to throw Ragnhild off her stride just a bit. She frowned and her eyebrows bunched up. "And you, Amundi Thorsteinsson?" she said. "You've been loyal to my husband all these years, and now you piss that all away? Your farm, your wealth? Your life?"

"Those things are of no use to a man if he's nothing but a slave," Amundi said.

"Slave?" Ragnhild spat. "Halfdan has never treated you as a slave! He's treated you like the freeman you are. All of you!"

"If everything a man has can be taken at the whim of his king, at any time, then he's no better than a slave," Odd said. "If the king is a master with no regard for his people, then his people are slaves."

"That's not at all…" Ragnhild began but Odd cut her off.

"We're not here to debate," he said. "We're here to show Halfdan that we're not slaves. To show him that if he turns on us, there will be consequences."

"You won't be slaves, but you'll make us slaves, is that it? All of us?" Ragnhild asked, gesturing toward the crowd of people around her.

"No," Odd said. "No one will be harmed. Not if they do as they're told and no more. Nothing stupid. We've suffered by Halfdan's hand. Homes lost. Lives lost. We're here to get compensation for that. We'll take what's fair and be gone."

Ragnhild opened her mouth to speak again but Odd was done with her. He called out in a voice that all the people there could hear.

"We don't mean to harm you, any of you. Our fight is with King Halfdan, not you. We're here to take what's owed us. Payment for our losses. You men..." He pointed to a knot of laborers standing together. "You round up wagons and oxen. Bring them here. The rest of you, and the women, when the wagons are here you'll load everything in those storehouses into them. Now, go."

The men went off to follow Odd's directions, taking care to appear as unwilling as they could, so that Ragnhild would see they were not being any more helpful than they had to be. A dozen of Odd's armed men accompanied them.

Odd looked over the people who remained. They had naturally segregated by their relative status: the wives and children of the more important men standing near Ragnhild, the families of the lesser men further back, the servants and slaves off to one side.

"You, you, you and you," Odd said, pointing to four of the women there, women whose simple but clean dresses told him they were servants in the great hall. "Come with me."

He could see the hesitation in their faces and it did not surprise him. Ragnhild understood what was happening, knew why these invaders had come. Some of the other wives of the leading men might also understand, but these poor creatures did not. It would seem perfectly reasonable to them that they were being led away to be raped or killed.

"Come," Odd said, more emphatically. He pointed to a handful of men standing near. "You, too." He headed toward the hall and the women and men followed behind.

"That hall is my home," Ragnhild announced. "You won't enter there without me."

"Yes, we will," Odd said over his shoulder, in a tone that did not welcome argument. He reached the main door of the great hall with the women behind and Amundi by his side, and behind them all a dozen of his and Amundi's warriors. He pushed the door open and stepped into the cavernous space. It was dark compared to the light of day outside, the only illumination coming from the fire in the central hearth and the smoke holes in the roof. Odd turned to the women behind.

"You know where Halfdan keeps those things most valuable to him. Any treasure, his own weapons, that sort of thing. Show us where."

For a moment no one moved.

"Go on," Amundi said. "Do as you're told and you won't be hurt." He left it to them to imagine what would happen if they refused.

And apparently they did imagine it, and they realized that there was no benefit to them in standing up to this conquering army. They crossed the packed earth floor to the far side. Two of the women threw open a set of doors built into the wall to reveal a sleeping chamber of startling size. The walls were hung with elaborately embroidered cloth and the floor was covered with luxurious rugs that Odd guessed had come from lands far off. A wide bed occupied a good portion of the space, enough to accommodate Halfdan and Ragnhild and their children and anyone else they saw fit to invite.

There were large wooden chests along the walls and Odd lifted their lids and looked inside. Clothing, Halfdan's and Ragnhild's, blankets, furs. In one there was an array of weapons: swords, seaxes, daggers, as well as a few helmets, spurs and the like. They glinted in the muted light of the torches the women had brought. Silver, with inlays of gold and precious stones. Beautiful weapons, too good for actual combat. Odd could see why Halfdan had not brought them on his campaign.

He turned to the men, Halfdan's men, he had ordered to accompany them. They were lurking in the hall, just beyond the open doors, terrified at the thought of violating the king's bedchamber.

"Two of you, grab onto this chest and get it outside" Odd said. "If the carts are here set it in one of those."

They hesitated and exchanged uncertain glances, but no one moved.

"Come along," Amundi barked. "You can do as Odd says or you can die heroes protecting the king's riches. Your choice."

But not a hard choice, apparently. They swarmed into the bedchamber and two of them grabbed onto the handles of the chest and found they could barely lift it. So two more joined them, and with grunts and muttered curses they carried the heavy oak box out the door.

Odd and Amundi continued their search, but now the servants had a sense for what was happening, and what the invaders were looking for, and they became surprisingly helpful in the locating of it. They showed the men where hidden caskets of silver and gold could be found, stashes of arm rings and brooches, stores of wine too good for the guests' table. Odd suspected that the occasional ring or armband or coin was finding its way into the women's pockets or into the folds of their clothes but he did not mind that.

Once they had finished with the bedchamber the women led Odd and Amundi and the rest to the western end of the hall where yet another door stood. This was opened to reveal a throne room of sorts, smaller than the bedchamber, with benches set against the walls and a raised platform at the far end that held a massive, intricately carved oak chair. The posts that supported the roof, fifteen feet overhead, were artfully carved as well with twisting serpents and vines.

In the light streaming in from the smoke hole in the roof Odd looked around in wonder. In all the times he had been to Halfdan's hall he had never seen this room. He had not even known it existed.

Once again he and Amundi and the others spread out and began looking for whatever they might find. The women, however, remained in the long hall and showed no interest in joining them. Entering the throne room, apparently, was too audacious, even with their queen outside and under guard and their king many miles away.

There was less of interest in that room. A small casket of silver, a few things apparently plundered from some Christian temple overseas, a sword. Odd toyed with the idea of taking the throne itself. If he was trying to make a statement, that would certainly do it. But he set the notion aside. It was too much. Halfdan would be furious with what they had already done, but if Odd heaped such pointed humiliation on top of it there was no telling what the man would do. The idea was to convince Halfdan to bargain, to end the war, not escalate it.

Evening was coming on by the time the last of the wagons rolled down to the harbor, and the last of the plunder was loaded aboard one of the ships. The slaves and servants who worked in the hall were put back to their former tasks, cooking, serving, pouring ale and mead and wine. The great hall was big enough to easily fit the two hundred warriors who made up Odd's army, and now they lined the tables and feasted on the best that Halfdan's pantry had to offer, which was very good and very plentiful.

Odd and the other freemen sat at the head table and Ragnhild sat with them, though not through any choice of her own. She glared at the plate set down in front of her and glared at the servant who set it there, enough that the servant backed away in terror, then turned and fled.

"What we've taken will pay us back for the harm Halfdan has done," Odd said to her, speaking loud enough to be heard over the feasting men. "Anything beyond that we'll gladly return once peace has been made."

Ragnhild looked up at him with even more disdain than she had had for the plate or the servant.

"Really?" she said. "You self-righteous prick. You think Halfdan will listen to that foolishness? Just forget all this?"

"I don't know," Odd said truthfully. "But something has to be done. To end this. And now I'll tell you something so that you might relate it to Halfdan, when he returns."

"What makes you so sure he's gone far? That he won't be back this night?" Ragnhild asked.

"Because he's being watched," Odd said. "Because I don't like surprises, so I guard against them."

But even as he said it he felt a qualm of uncertainty. He had sent Vandred off to keep an eye on Halfdan because Vandred, being a sheepherd, knew the country well and would not stand out. And then he had sent another to find Vandred and see what news he had. But he had not heard from either man. There were a hundred reasons why that might be, and Odd was trying not to think of the worst of those possibilities.

"You're a clever one," Ragnhild said. "Or so you think. But you are not your father, Odd Thorgrimson. You remind me more of your grandfather, that old fool Ornolf."

That old fool was more loved than your bastard husband ever will be, Odd thought, but he kept that to himself.

"When Halfdan does return," he said, "when he finally tires of searching all over Agder for us, then you tell him what I said. Tell him we still do not want war, we do not want to be an enemy to him. We want to be his subjects, loyal to him, but we will not be his slaves. We'll pay the tribute that's fair, but we won't stand for him to take whatever he wants from us. Tell him we want to talk, and if we can talk like honest men then we can agree like honest men."

Ragnhild laughed, a short, sharp laugh. "I'm Halfdan's second wife, as you know, and I have not been his wife very many years. But I've been his wife long enough to know that he won't be much interested in talking to any of you, 'like honest men'."

Odd looked at her and she looked back at him, still as bold and defiant as she had been from the first. He had a feeling that if he burned her at the stake she would still wear that expression, and it would never change.

He, in turn, did not allow his own expression to change, though his thoughts were roiling. This plan had always been a gamble. While Halfdan was abroad hunting them, they would use their ships to come behind and capture his great hall. They could burn it all to the ground but they wouldn't. They would just plunder it, and be gone long before Halfdan returned with his army. They would show Halfdan that he would never be safe, that he would never be free of the threat, as long as he was at war with the freemen of Agder. Show him the wisdom of coming to an agreement.

Amundi and the others had harbored serious doubts about the whole thing. They were skeptical that Halfdan's compound could be taken that easily, and skeptical that Halfdan would learn any lesson from it, or at least the lesson they wanted him to learn. They had debated it, argued it back and forth, and in the end Odd had convinced them that it would work, and that they had no other choice.

And so far Odd had been proven right. The taking of the hall had been as easy as he hoped. Easier, really. They had gathered enough plunder that Halfdan would feel the loss, but not enough that he would be in any way impoverished. Now, on the morning tide, they would be gone, and they would wait for word from Halfdan, and from there decide their next move.

"Very well," Ragnhild said. "I'll tell Halfdan all you wish me to tell him. I'll tell him as soon as he returns. Which will not be long, I shouldn't think."

"Good," Odd said and gave a half smile and a nod of his head. But Ragnhild's words had struck just as she hoped they would. Time was short. There was no leaving now, not in the dark with the tide well out. Nor did Odd want his men, or Halfdan's men, to think they were scurrying away like thieves. First light, that was when they would go. Halfdan just had to stay gone until first light.

It was some time later that Odd finally went to bed, stretching out on blankets on top of the platform that ran most of the length of the hall. He sent Ragnhild and the boy Harald to sleep in the king's bedchamber and set two guards at the door, more of a formality than anything else. He did not think any of his men would be stupid enough to do anything untoward, though he thought it possible that one of Halfdan's servants or slaves, feeling liberated now with the hall in enemy hands, might decide retribution was in order.

Odd stretched out, worked the stiffness out of his legs and shoulders. He closed his eyes and kept them closed for a moment, then opened them again. He sighed. Sleep was not going to come, not for a long time, if at all.

First light… Their luck just had to hold out until first light. He felt an ugly sensation in his gut and he tried to dismiss it. *You're sleeping in the king's hall, which you've captured…of course your gut is fighting you…*

It did not help. He could not reason away this sensation. But sleep did come at last, an unrestful, tossing sleep filled with strange, swirling, unsettling images.

He woke suddenly, covered with a film of sweat. The sleep, such as it was, had done nothing to lesson his sense of foreboding. And then he realized that Amundi was crouching beside him, that it was Amundi who had woken him up. There was light enough in the hall to see the man's face. To see the awful expression on his face.

Odd closed his eyes. He knew what Amundi was going to say, knew with as much certainty as if he had already said it.

Halfdan had returned.

It was first light, but they would be going nowhere.

Chapter Nine

There was a dash of oars,
and clash of iron,
shield against shield resounded:
the vikings rowed;
roaring went,
under the chieftains
the royal fleet
far from the land.

The Poetic Edda

Situations changed, and they changed quickly. Thorgrim knew that.

A storm could blow up out of nowhere, and suddenly a calm day at sea became a struggle to survive. A battle that seemed headed for an easy victory could change course and a thousand lives would be sent off in another direction. A healthy man might ride away in the morning, fall from his horse in the afternoon, and by nightfall find himself a broken cripple.

But for all that, he was still surprised by how quickly the course that he and his men were on, both literal and otherwise, had changed that day.

Suppposed to be an uneventful sail, Thorgrim thought, and then smiled at his own foolishness. As if the gods would ever let such a thing happen. Sure, they had hinted that such might be the case. Beautiful morning, a moderate swell from the south, wind from a near perfect direction. Sun, warmth. Any man could be excused for thinking he was in for an easy run across open water to the far shore.

The first half of the day had been just that, with the fleet making good progress: east, always east. And then the strange ships had appeared, crossing their heading from south-east to north-west. They showed no interest in Thorgrim's fleet, but that did not mean Thorgrim would be unprepared if they did. He slowed *Sea Hammer*'s speed, let the other ships come up, told his men to be ready to fight if that was what these strangers had in mind.

And then Harald decided to add his own contribution to the madness, abandoning his position at the end of their neat line and racing off toward the cluster of fishing boats to the north.

"Harald! What by all the gods do you think you're doing?" Thorgrim shouted across the water, though he knew that the boy could not hear him over that distance. He shouted out of surprise, a surprise which changed quickly to anger. He turned and looked aloft. "Starri! What is Harald doing?"

"How should I know, Night Wolf?" Starri called back. "He's your son! But he looks to be going after those fishing boats we passed!"

Thorgrim took his eyes from Starri and scowled out over the water toward Harald's ship. He could feel his anger rising like a fast-moving flood tide. Harald was leaving the fleet to go after some ridiculous bunch of fishing boats? That foolishness alone would have made Thorgrim furious. Now, with a fleet of strangers bearing down on them, it was inconceivably stupid.

He stepped forward along the weather side until he came to the aftermost shroud. He grabbed onto the thick, taut line and using it to balance stepped up onto the sheer strake. He could feel the tar in the rope, soft and warm under his hand, as he leaned outboard as far as he could and looked east toward the fleet crossing their course.

Two, three, four…five… he counted. Five ships to his six. Maybe two hundred men to the more than three hundred he still had after all the blood-letting of the past months. If it came down to it he and his men would prevail, he was sure of it. But if Harald and his crew were off on some idiot venture, unable to help, or in need of help themselves, then that might change everything.

I hope the boy has a good reason for this, Thorgrim thought, though he could not imagine what that reason could be. Still, he knew he was holding onto that hope as firmly as he was holding the thick hemp shroud. If Harald was acting as stupidly as he seemed to be, it would reflect badly on the boy, stain his reputation throughout the fleet. And it would reflect badly on his father as well, the man who had given him that command.

And then he would have to decide if Harald should no longer be master of *Dragon*, a decision he did not care to make.

He looked back at the unknown fleet to the east. No change that he could see, no change of course, or position of the ships, or the set of the sails. He considered asking Starri if he had seen anything but he was too angry to tolerate the ribbing Starri would give him about his eyesight. Thorgrim found it ironic, and not in any amusing way, that the one man aboard with the keenest vision was also the only man in the fleet who would dare mock him for his own poor eyesight.

Then he heard Starri shouting from the mast-top, a wild, whooping shout of exhilaration.

"Whoa! Yes, yes! Ya-ha!" he called. Thorgrim looked up. Starri was looking north toward Harald's ship and waving his free arm in the air.

"What is it, Starri?" Thorgrim shouted.

"Did you not see that! It's a whale, Thorgrim, a whale! Harald's gone to kill himself a whale!"

Whale?

"Harald's killing a whale?" Thorgrim shouted back.

"Well, he's hunting one!" Starri called down again. "But right now the whale seems to be winning! Just smashed in half of Harald's ship with its flukes!"

The corner of *Sea Hammer*'s sail was blocking Thorgrim's view of *Dragon*, so he hopped back down to the deck and made his way aft in a few long, hurried strides. He leaned on the leeward rail and looked out over the water toward Harald's ship. It was nearly a mile away, and to his eyes looked more like a smudge of gray and black than a ship and its sail. If *Dragon* had suffered damage he had no hope of seeing it from that distance. But as far as he could tell she was still on her waterline, and showed no sign of going down.

"Harald, you blockhead, if you lose your ship because of this fool notion, and live to get home, I swear by the gods you'll never leave the farm again!" Thorgrim said out loud, too angry and frustrated now to keep the words inside. And just as he finished with that promise he saw the whale's tail rising up out of the water again, like a sea god rearing in anger. Thorgrim knew what it was despite the distance. In his years of seafaring he had seen flukes often enough to recognize them even from so far away.

He squeezed hard on the edge of the sheer plank as he watched the tail hang motionless, just for the briefest of instances. He had no doubt that the whale could crush *Dragon* under the power of the downward stroke. And even if it didn't sink the ship outright then it might shatter her badly enough that she would flood and go down before *Sea Hammer* or any of the others could reach her.

Down came the tail and *Dragon*'s mast rocked violently as if trying to wave the whale away. Overhead Starri whooped again and all along the leeward rail the men, who had abandoned watching the distant fleet in favor of this new amusement, all shouted or moaned in sympathy or called for Harald and the others to kill the great beast.

Thorgrim released the sheer strake. He stood upright, his lips pressed hard together. He looked out toward the fleet crossing their track and then back at *Dragon.* Reflexively he wanted to turn downwind, run to the northward, come to the aid of Harald and the men of *Dragon.* But if he did that then he would be further dividing his fleet, putting them in greater jeopardy. Perhaps these newcomers had no interest in attacking a superior enemy, but if they discovered they could pick off half the fleet then they might change their minds.

"This is your doing, Harald," Thorgrim said, as if his son was right in front of him. "You get yourself and your men out of it."

He left the rail and stepped back to the center of the small raised deck aft. Armod was still holding the tiller. As Thorgrim took his place Armod looked at him and said, "Lord Thorgrim?" as if wondering why Thorgrim had not yet given the order to turn and go after *Dragon.*

But that was something Thorgrim did not intend to do, and he did not care for Armod's prompting. He looked at Armod with an expression both angry and uncompromising and watched the man start to squirm under the gaze.

"Hold this course," Thorgrim said and Armod nodded and looked forward, suddenly very intent on maintaining a true heading, his eyes fixed on the water beyond the bow.

No change, Thorgrim thought, watching the fleet of strangers ahead. All but the last ship in the line had crossed *Sea Hammer*'s path, crossing from her starboard side to her larboard. If he had not slowed *Sea Hammer* down the two fleets might have become entangled, but as it was there was at least a mile between them.

He looked over his shoulder. *Blood Hawk* and *Oak Heart* were close up astern of his ship now, a hundred feet or so between them, and the smaller vessels right behind. If these strangers meant to fight then they would have to fight all of Thorgrim's ships at once.

Except *Dragon.*

Thorgrim frowned. He wanted to look off to larboard to see what Harald's ship was doing now, but he also knew that would just make him more angry still, and that would not help matters. He resolved to keep his eyes forward when Starri called out again, another wild, undulating shout of enthusiasm.

Harald, son of a bitch, Thorgrim thought. Whatever Starri was shouting about had to concern Harald, and despite his resolve Thorgrim turned and looked. He looked just in time to see the massive tail coming down once more, but this time it came down more directly on top of *Dragon*'s stern. The after end of the ship was driven down, lost from sight in a great burst of spray, and Thorgrim sucked in his breath.

And then the tail slid off and *Dragon* came bobbing up again and Thorgrim could not help but feel a flash of pride. He had built *Dragon*, he and his men at Vík-ló, and no miserable fish was going to sink her, no matter how big it was.

That feeling did not last long. Almost immediately it began to dissipate and the anger began to reassert itself. Then, before the anger worked itself up to gale force, it was swept away by surprise and confusion. *Dragon* had been rolling and pitching violently as she recovered from the blow of the whale's tail, but now she was making headway again, driving forward as if her sail was set to a stiffer breeze than *Sea Hammer* was finding.

Thorgrim was not at all sure what was happening because he couldn't see much detail from that distance. He could see *Dragon*'s hull and her sail, and he could see that the ship was moving, her speed building, but that did not seem possible. Already her speed seemed all out of proportion to the easy wind blowing from the south.

"Ha!" Starri shouted. "They've hooked the bastard, Night Wolf! I'll bet my life they have a hook in the beast and it's pulling them along! Oh, what a ride!"

This announcement brought a swell of shouting and laughing and pointing from the men lining the larboard side. Thorgrim could see them smiling as they looked over the water, and he thought he saw some of them placing bets, Harald against the whale, he imagined. He thought of telling them all to get up to the starboard side, maybe tell them, by way of excuse, that their weight was needed to counter the heel of the ship. But that would be petty and untrue and the men would know it. And Thorgrim knew it would not help his mood anyway, so he kept his mouth shut, his eyes forward.

He could see only water. Both *Dragon* and the strange fleet were now hidden behind the sail where Thorgrim could not see them. And that was fine.

"Night Wolf!" Starri called down from aloft. The wild enthusiasm was gone and there was a different note in his voice now. "The lead ship of this fleet, this strange fleet, they seem to be heading for Harald and his whale!"

That Thorgrim could not ignore. He crossed over to the larboard side and leaned outboard, looking past the tight leech of the sail. He could see *Dragon*, still moving at a surprising speed, bobbing and twisting, dragged along, apparently, by the enraged whale. But he could not see the lead ship of the other fleet. He hopped down from the after deck and leaned over the side, looking under the foot of the sail.

Starri was right. The ship had clearly altered course. The whale had pulled *Dragon* closer to it, but the ship was turning now, her yard bracing around as she turned, her bow pointing more directly at *Dragon* and the whale.

"Son of a bitch!" Thorgrim shouted in frustration. It was just as he feared. These strangers would not dare attack Thorgrim's fleet, but neither would they resist the chance to snatch up a single ship that was cut off from the rest. And now he had no choice but to go to Harald's rescue.

"All right, you whore's sons!" he shouted down the rail at his gawking crew. "Get on the sheets and braces! The rest of you get your weapons, armor, shields! It looks like we'll have to go save those blockheads aboard *Dragon*!"

The men moved fast. They, too, had heard Starri's call and they anticipated this order. They ran to the sheets and the braces and loosened off the bar-taut ropes. Thorgrim turned to Armod on the tiller.

"Fall off to leeward!" he ordered. "Right at them!"

Armod nodded and pushed the tiller away and *Sea Hammer* turned north, the distant shore sweeping past. One by one the ships of this strange fleet came into sight around the edge of the sail as *Sea Hammer* took up her new heading. Above them the yard swung round until it was perpendicular to the centerline of the ship and *Sea Hammer* was running downwind.

Starri came sliding down the after shroud, hit the rail and dropped to the deck, like a bird going from one branch to another. He was smiling. Thorgrim imagined he had been smiling for some time now, with all the amusements of the morning, but nothing would excite him quite like the prospect of a fight.

Down the length of the ship men were pulling on leather armor or mail shirts, for those fortunate ones who had such luxuries. Starri, however, pulled his tunic up over his head and flung it away, revealing his lank, sinewy body, which was all hard muscle and scars. It was how Starri in his berserker's madness chose to go into battle. Leggings, two battle axes, and around his neck the split arrowhead he wore on a cord for luck. That was it.

Thorgrim glanced at the wicked scar near Starri's shoulder, the result of a spear thrust while fighting in Ireland. That one, Thorgrim had thought, would be the end of him, the voyage to Valhalla that Starri so craved. But no. The gods would toy with Starri just as they toyed with him.

Louis de Roumois came aft at his usual, unhurried pace. He wore his sword but no helmet, no mail. He stopped at the break of the after deck and looked up at Thorgrim.

"We're going to rescue young Harald, is that what I understand?" he asked.

"If he needs rescuing, yes," Thorgrim said, wondering yet again why he bothered to answer this man's questions. Perhaps because Louis was the only one with the guts to ask. Except for Starri, but Starri was insane.

"You'll bring your ship next to the other?" Louis asked. "We'll go aboard them, fight them there?"

"Yes," Thorgrim said. "What else would we do?"

Louis shrugged. "I've never done anything like this before," he said. "Fighting on ships."

"It's much like fighting on land," Thorgrim said. "Kill the other fellows. Don't let them kill you."

Louis nodded. "Except when you fall down on land, you stay put. Here you might sink."

"If you're unlucky," Thorgrim said. "Is that why you aren't wearing mail?"

"Of course. I'll take a sword through my heart before I sink down to the bottom of this God-forsaken ocean."

Thorgrim nodded. "Probably a good choice. Not that the gods ever give us a choice as to how we die."

With that he was done with Louis de Roumois. He was about to fetch his sword, Iron-tooth, and his mail, when he saw Failend there, on the weather side. She was wearing the mail Thorgrim had given her, mail made for a boy, and the seax he had also given her, an edged weapon that seemed scaled for her. Small as she was, the big knife looked more like a sword in her hand. She was holding Thorgrim's mail shirt, and Iron-tooth and the belt on which it hung.

"I brought these for you," she said unnecessarily.

"Thank you," Thorgrim said. It had been this way for some time, since Failend had become his lover, and not his captive. Before a fight she would bring him his mail and his sword. At night she would share his bed. But she had stopped doing the latter, and he was somewhat surprised she was still doing the former. What thoughts were going through her mind, what feelings she had for him, Thorgrim did not understand.

And, as usual, he had neither the time nor the inclination to think about it.

He took the mail shirt and slipped it over his head, thinking as he did of Louis's choice to not wear mail in a sea fight. Once, during a battle not long after coming to Ireland, Thorgrim and an adversary had gone overboard. Thorgrim had not been wearing mail; his opponent had; and that had made a big difference in who lived and who died. But this time he would take his chances and make an effort to stay onboard.

He settled the mail, wound the belt around his waist and buckled it. He looked out past the bow. *Dragon* had stopped now and she was rolling in the ocean swell, no longer made fast to the whale, apparently. Thorgrim thought he could see the whale's back, a dark line against the dark ocean, water foaming white around it.

The ship, the lead ship from this strange fleet, was bearing down on *Dragon* and the whale, her sail full, her sharp bow cleaving the water. She was a couple hundred yards away from Harald's ship and closing quickly. *Sea Hammer* was more than twice that distance away. If these strangers were coming to fight, Harald and his crew would have to hold them off by themselves for some time before Thorgrim's men could come to their aid.

He looked up at *Sea Hammer*'s sail and he knew there was nothing that he could do to make his ship go faster. All he could do was wait, and the waiting filled him with impotent frustration. And the frustration turned quickly into fury as he remembered that it was his own son who had put him in this situation, created all this unnecessary bother, when all he, Thorgrim, wanted to do was to sail across a stretch of water to the far shore.

A collective shout went up from the men and Thorgrim looked forward. The strange ship had turned and seemed to come to a stop, like it had hit something, and that something had to be the whale, since *Dragon* was floating free several ship-lengths away.

Now what? Thorgrim thought. Was that an accident? Had they not seen the whale? Or did they mean to do this?

Sea Hammer rose and dipped as the swells passed under her and she raced toward the two ships ahead, now both nearly motionless in the water. Thorgrim's men were crowded together at the bow making it hard to see, but rather than order them away Thorgrim stepped down from the afterdeck and moved forward and the men parted and made room for him.

He stepped up onto the foredeck and looked around the tall stem, frowning as he tried to understand what he was seeing. The sea ahead was churning, breaking white, and two ships were rolling in the chaotic water.

"They've lanced it!" cried one of Thorgrim's men, a man named Thorkel. "We used to hunt these things back home, I've seen this often! They got a lance in it, and now it'll swim in circles before it's dead. They better stay clear!"

Thorgrim watched, fascinated, as *Sea Hammer* came swooping down on the odd scene, her bow rising and dipping as the following sea made it lift then fall away. He could see the whale clearly now, or as much of it as was visible above the water and the churning foam. It was indeed thrashing around in a great circle, rolling and twisting, slamming its tail up and down with quickly diminishing vigor. The white water around it was stained pink with the dying creature's blood.

The whale had, until that moment, been moving away from the two ships, but now in its death throes it turned and began moving back toward them, toward *Dragon* most directly.

"Get your oars out, get clear of there!" Thorkel shouted toward *Dragon*, though there was no possibility of his being heard. "I've seen them take ships near as big as *Dragon* down with them at the end," he added to the men looking on.

But the time to watch was over, Thorgrim knew, and now it was time to act. "The lot of you, get away from the bow so I can see!" he called out. "Stop staring with your mouths hanging open and get ready to fight!"

He turned and hurried back to the helm, unwilling to let Armod do the tricky job of bringing *Sea Hammer* alongside the other ship. He stepped up onto the afterdeck and Armod handed the tiller over and Thorgrim swung in behind it. It felt good in his hands, it felt familiar. The afterdeck, the view forward: it was all familiar, and that eased his mind in a world that seemed to make no sense.

He felt the stern lift, gentle and smooth, then dip under him as the bow came up. The strange ship was straight ahead and not more than a hundred yards away, the whale still kicking in the space between that ship and *Dragon*.

"Get ready to clew up the sail!" Thorgrim shouted, and a handful of men set down shields and spears and axes and ran to the lines they would need to loosen or haul. Thorgrim waited for one more swell to pass under, for the wind and water to give the ship that one last push.

"Clew up!" Thorgrim shouted and the sheets and tacks were let go, the clew garnets hauled and the big woolen sail was pulled up to the yard above, spilling her wind and flapping uselessly.

Good, good, Thorgrim thought. He had timed that right, he was sure. The ship's momentum would carry her right up to the stranger's side. *Sea Hammer* would come alongside and stop and his men would pour onto the enemy's deck.

He heard cheering, yelling and whooping, but it was not coming from his ship but from across the water. He looked forward. The whale had stopped its flailing and seemed to have rolled on its side, one massive flipper sticking straight up, bobbing motionless like the two ships nearby.

"Get ready!" Thorgrim shouted as he pulled the tiller near, swinging *Sea Hammer* to starboard as the last of her way carried her up to the strange ship's side. He could see a bustle of motion on the other ship. The crew preparing for a fight, he guessed, but he saw instead, to his surprise, they were heaving heavy rope fenders over the side of their ship. They were taking care, apparently, to see that neither ship was damaged when they came together.

Forty feet, thirty, and Thorgrim could see the men lining the side of the other ship, men much like his own in the manner of their clothing and beards and hair. But while his men stood grim and ready for battle, these men were smiling, arms up in greeting.

This is not what I was expecting… Ten feet separated *Sea Hammer* from the other ship and Thorgrim was about to call to his men to stay put, tell them not to fight until they knew a fight was to be had. Tell them to grab hold of Starri Deathless if he went on the attack.

Before he could speak, the men on the other ship parted to make way for another, a big man with a big beard, who was smiling even wider than the rest.

"Thorgrim Ulfsson!" he shouted. "Do you come with swords and shields to fight me like I'm some sorry Englishman?"

Bergthor Skeggjason.

He and Bergthor had gone raiding together, years before, though they had been on the crews of different ships. His farm was in Fevik, twenty miles north of Thorgrim's. Thorgrim had seen him on and off over the years, though not for some time before he had left for Ireland with Ornolf the Restless.

Now Bergthor was there. With Harald at his side.

Chapter Ten

Tell me, Fjolsvinn!
That which I will ask thee,
and I desire to know:
whether there is any treasure,
that mortals can obtain,
at which the pale maiden will rejoice?

The Poetic Edda

Thorgrim pulled the tiller back and *Sea Hammer* came gently against the side of Bergthor Skeggjason's ship, bumping noiselessly against the heavy fenders Bergthor's men had set in place. His own men had taken a step back from the side and lowered shields and weapons. Whereas a minute ago they had looked primed for battle, now they just looked confused. But at least they had sense enough not to attack men who were waving and smiling at them.

Starri, too, seemed to understand that there would be no fight that day. He was standing amidships, and Thorgrim expected to see four men trying to hold him back, but Starri was still unrestrained, watching the goings-on, his axes held loose at his sides.

You're getting old too, my friend, Thorgrim thought. Starri was forever suggesting that age was quenching the fire in Thorgrim's belly, but now Thorgrim wondered if he was not alone in that. A year or more past he would have expected Starri to be launching himself into the fight whether there was a fight or not. But now he seemed to be waiting for events to unfold in a way that was…calm. Reasonable. It was a strange thing to see.

"Thorgrim!" The sound of his name shouted out with loud exuberance pulled Thorgrim from his thoughts. He let go of the now useless tiller and turned. With the vessels side by side Bergthor, still aboard his own ship, was only twenty feet away and calling across the space between them.

He was just as Thorgrim remembered him: a big man with a thick, bushy beard, remarkably thick even for the Northmen. His long hair was pulled back and braided and the gap between beard and moustache revealed a broad smile. His big arms were spread as if he meant to hug Thorgrim despite the water that separated them.

Thorgrim looked at Harald, standing next to Bergthor. Harald was looking back at him, a happy but wary look, an uncertain smile on his face, as if he was not sure what sort of reaction to expect from his father.

You're in more trouble than you can imagine, boy, Thorgrim thought, and Harald's smile faded quickly, as quickly as if Thorgrim had shouted the words across the space between them. Harald was soaking wet, and Thorgrim wondered how that had happened, and how he had managed to get aboard Bergthor's ship.

"Thorgrim, by the gods it's good to see your ugly face!" Bergthor shouted. "Who'd have thought we'd meet here? I recognized young Harald right off, though he didn't know who I was! Just a boy when I saw him last, now he's a man!"

"Good to see you too, Bergthor," Thorgrim said. This was all so very strange, and only getting stranger. "How does…" he continued, but Bergthor cut him off with raucous enthusiasm.

"Oh, Thorgrim, you should have seen it! Your boy…only you could have such a son! I see these poor bastards trying some fool thing like hunting a whale, looks to me like they're in trouble, so we come over to help. And there's Harald! Get this, Thorgrim, he's on the whale's back and he's stabbing at the rutting thing with a spear! A spear! What balls the boy has! More balls than brains, I'll warrant!"

Thorgrim had no idea what to say to that, but Gudrid, ten feet away, called out, "Harald Whale-spear!" and that was met with laughter which turned quickly into cheering and yelling, the celebration spreading over the crews of both ships. The men all around Harald slapped him on the back and clapped hands on his shoulders as the rest shouted out their enthusiasm. The uncertain smile returned to Harald's face as he looked around, nodding his thanks, laughing at the adulation. He was careful not to meet Thorgrim's eyes.

Thorgrim looked astern. *Dragon*'s sail was clewed up and the men had broken out her oars, and she was drawing closer to *Sea Hammer* and Bergthor's ship. He turned and looked to the south. His fleet and Bergthor's were all converging on them, ten ships with sails set to a following wind making for the same patch of ocean.

"I'll be honest with you, Night Wolf," Bergthor continued, "Part of the reason I'm surprised to see you…back home, most thought you were dead. We had word of Ornolf's death…what? Two years ago? And never a word about you since, so we all figured the worst."

Thorgrim nodded. He still did not know what to say.

"How about this, Thorgrim," Bergthor said. "I reckon this is Harald's whale. I might have lanced it, but it's his whale, sure. But even he can't eat it all! Let's tow it to the beach north of here, get it ashore and we'll have us a grand feast! Your men and mine! By the gods, I want to hear everything you've been up to these years past!"

Thorgrim looked down the length of *Sea Hammer*, at the eager, expectant faces of his men. He looked at the rest of the fleet closing on them. He looked at the far shore, which he had hoped to reach by dark, but now was not so sure he could. They'd run pretty far downwind coming after Harald, and now they would have to work to windward to get back, and that was a much slower proposition.

"Very well," Thorgrim said. "Do you know there's a beach north of here?"

"I got a fellow aboard, knows this coast well," Bergthor said. "He says there is and he's usually right about such things."

"I've got to get back aboard my ship," Harald said, but he sounded as if he was choking on the words. Thorgrim could guess why Harald had faltered in his speech — he wasn't sure that *Dragon* still was his ship. Neither was Thorgrim.

But he was willing to let Harald have it for now. Herjolf, at *Dragon*'s helm, brought the ship in carefully until her bow touched the stern of Bergthor's ship and Harald was able to swing himself across. Herjolf ordered the rowers to pull astern and *Dragon* backed away as Harald made his way aft to assume command. Thorgrim's men cast off the lines that Bergthor's had tossed over to lash the two ships together.

"I'll pull around the larboard side of this dead beastie, hook on there!" Bergthor shouted.

"Good! I'll hook it on its starboard side!" Thorgrim replied. The two ship, unbound from one another, began to drift apart, and soon there was space enough to run the oars out. Bergthor backed his ship away, clear of *Sea Hammer*, then ducked in on the whale's other side, the maneuver neatly and skillfully done.

Forward, Hall and Bjorn stood ready with two of *Sea Hammer*'s grappling hooks. Thorgrim brought the ship closer alongside the whale and the two men leaned over the side and swung the hooks down onto the whale and watched them bounce off again, half a dozen times each, before they finally managed to sink them in deep enough to hold.

Thorgrim ordered the oars in and the sail set, to the great relief of the men pulling the looms. The wind had dropped a bit but it was still from the south and strong enough to drive the ships faster than the rowers could. One hundred feet away Bergthor's men did the same, and soon the two ships, nearly even in size and complement of men, were rolling north with the swell behind and a dead whale between them.

It was not long before the rest of the fleet caught up and word was passed from ship to ship that they were bound for the beach to the north. Thorgrim ordered Godi in *Blood Hawk* to go ahead of the fleet and scout out the landing and make certain it was safe, free of navigational hazards and English men-at-arms.

The land to the west tended away as they sailed north, revealing a stretch of water that seemed to reach far inland. Thorgrim was sure now that they had been on an island all that time, and not on the shore of Engla-land. But he still did not care very much.

It was late in the afternoon, the sun hanging lower on their larboard side, when they finally reached shore. Godi had built a fire on the beach and piled it with driftwood to create a thick column of smoke as a marker for the landing place: a long sandy beach running for several miles east to west. The western end of the beach, about half a mile from where Godi had landed, ended at the mouth of what Thorgrim was certain was a river or the entrance to a narrow harbor.

One by one the ships beached and the crews hopped out and pulled them far enough up onto the sand to keep them in place, but not enough to make it difficult to float them again. Last of all came *Sea Hammer* and Bergthor's ship, with the whale floating at the end of the towropes fifty feet astern.

Thorgrim hopped down into the surf and trudged ashore and Bergthor joined him on the warm sand. "So, how do we get this bastard up on the beach so we can eat him?" Bergthor asked.

"Not sure, exactly," Thorgrim admitted. "But I have a man knows about this sort of thing. Thorkel!" he shouted and Thorkel broke off from the knot of men with whom he was conversing and came jogging over.

"Yes, Lord Thorgrim?"

Thorgrim nodded toward the whale. "How do we get this thing up on the beach so we can eat it?"

Thorkel turned and looked at the whale for a moment. "Not sure we have to," he said. "We can just pull him in a little closer and me and a few others can go aboard it and cut in and fetch off all we can eat. You weren't planning on drying any of the meat, were you? Or making oil from the blubber?"

"I wasn't planning anything except sailing to the far shore," Thorgrim said.

"Good, then," Thorkel said. "I'll get some men and we'll be at it. Back aft on the whale, where it gets narrow by the tail, that's where the best meat's to be found."

Under Thorkel's direction, and with the considerable enthusiasm of hundreds of men ready for a feast, the whale was hauled in close to shore. They set at the massive fish with axes, knives, and seaxes, stripping away blubber and carving out great chunks of red meat which were passed lovingly to shore, while further up the beach other men built smaller fires for roasting. Soon there were fires enough, and meat enough, for the five hundred Northmen there to eat their fill. And while that was taking place, the rest of the men off-loaded the mead and ale and wine from the ships resting at the surf line.

The celebrations were full underway by the time the sun set behind the land to the west, the evening filled with the smell of roasting whale meat and the chaotic noise of drinking men. In such situations as this, two fleets of Northmen flung together, Thorgrim would have expected to see the men divide into camps, his men in one camp, Bergthor's in another, from which each would regard the other warily. But that was not happening now.

Maybe it was the shared effort in killing the whale, or in butchering the whale, or the need for both armies to share one whale, but Thorgrim's men and Bergthor's were mixing as if they had been sailing in company that year past. Nor were they entirely strangers. Just as Thorgrim and Bergthor knew one another from their homes across the water, so a few of the others also knew each other from before they went a'viking, or from encounters in Frankia or Ireland or Engla-land or any of the many places where the longships carried them.

"All right, Thorgrim, now, at last, tell me what trouble you've been up to these years past!" Bergthor said, taking a seat next to Thorgrim on the big driftwood log that had been hauled over by the fire. Bergthor had a cup of mead in one hand, a wooden plate with a massive slab of blackened whale in the other, but he managed to seat himself gracefully despite those burdens and his ponderous size.

"Well," Thorgrim said because he did not know where to begin. He did not particularly care to recount the death of his wife, the despair that came on the heels of that, the decision, perhaps the stupid decision, to sail with Ornolf the Restless.

A stupid decision?

No, he could not say that. Not entirely. For all the hardship of those past years, all the desperation he now felt to return to his farm in East Agder, he had to admit that the seafaring, the raiding, the adventuring had not been so bad. He was now wealthier by far, even after having made and lost several fortunes, and that wealth he would pass on to his four children.

These past years had seen Harald grow to manhood, or mostly. Thorgrim was still furious with the boy, still intent on teaching him a lesson about the stupidity of doing what he had done, but for the most part going a'viking had done for Harald what it had done for Thorgrim, when Thorgrim had been Harald's age.

Where to begin the story? But Bergthor saved him that decision.

"I heard…we all heard…of Hallbera's passing," he said. "I never had the chance to say how sorry I was about that. She was well loved. Everyone loved her. But I don't have to tell you that."

"Thank you," Thorgrim said. "Yes, you don't find women like her too often. So, after she was gone, I sailed with her father, Jarl Ornolf. But you know that, too."

Bergthor nodded.

"We reached Ireland and had some luck in raiding. Not much. Some. We took this Irish boat, and there wasn't a thing on it, save for a crown…"

Thorgrim told Bergthor, in broad strokes, the tale of the crown and the fighting at Tara, the taking of Vík-ló, the struggles at Loch Garman and more recently in Engla-land. And though he himself had lived it, from arriving on the shores of Ireland until this chance meeting with Bergthor that afternoon over the body of a dead whale, the events of the past years seemed extraordinary laid out like that, end to end.

"Ha!" Bergthor said when Thorgrim finished. "Incredible! A story worthy of Thorgrim Night Wolf!"

"And what of you, Bergthor?" Thorgrim asked. He was curious as to how Bergthor happened to be in that place, and even more curious for the news of what was happening back home. And Bergthor, Thorgrim knew from past experience, would be eager to tell him.

But he did not get the chance, at least not just then. A voice called for attention through the general roar, and when Thorgrim looked over he saw Herjolf standing on something so that he could be seen by all the men on the beach, and calling and waving his arms.

"Listen to me, you drunken fools!" Herjolf shouted and was greeted with hoots and sundry insults, but high-spirited, friendly. "Listen here! We've seen feats today such as no men have seen before! Feats performed by the great Harald Broadarm, beloved of the gods, and you should make him stand up and tell you of them!"

Thorgrim frowned. He meant to give Harald the dressing down that he deserved, meant to do it that night, make him tremble for the stupid things he had done. He did not want the boy to be celebrated for them.

But Thorgrim seemed to be alone in that thinking. The rest of the crowd were calling for Harald to speak, demanding he tell his story, encouraging him to take his place beside Herjolf. And when he finally did, standing up on whatever Herjolf was standing on, the men assembled around them cheered louder still.

"Well, it's not so much of a tale," Harald began, and Thorgrim knew his reluctance to talk was not feigned. The boy was no braggart, of that Thorgrim was sure. If he had been, Thorgrim would have put a stop to that a long time ago.

"Come on," Herjolf shouted. "It's a whale of a tail! A whale's tail!" That was met with a mix of laughs, hoots, boos, curses. Harald smiled and looked around and took it in.

"Very well," Harald said at last. "We were crossing the water, do you see, when we saw a bunch of these boats, these English boats, but what they were doing we could not tell…"

He went on from there, and just as Thorgrim had related to Bergthor the past years, so Harald related to the other men the events of that afternoon, from seeing the whale to going in pursuit of the thing, to finally leaping on its back so that he might set the hook in well. As he spoke Herjolf interjected comments, urged Harald to continue the story, added his own recollections to it. He confirmed Harald's story, bit by bit, as did others of the *Dragon*'s crew, standing around close by.

Thorgrim looked at Bergthor, a question on his face.

"Yes, it's true, Thorgrim!" Bergthor said. "At least what I saw. When we come up, Harald was on the fish's back! Right on its back and stabbing away! The boy's bold as a wolf and fearless as can be!"

And an idiot, Thorgrim thought. None of what he had heard changed his opinion in the least. Putting himself and his men and ship in danger, ignoring orders, leaving the line with a strange fleet in the offing? Thorgrim did not care how bold Harald's actions had been, there was no honor in boldly acting stupid.

And it was not just that. Bergthor had saved Harald's life. Neither he nor Harald had mentioned it, but it was true and every man there knew it. And because of that, Thorgrim felt that he was in Bergthor's debt. Bergthor was a friend, and not a man to take advantage, but still Thorgrim did not care to be in another man's debt. He did not care for it at all.

He considered pushing his way through the crowd and pulling Harald down off his perch and leading him away, but he knew he could not do that. The boy might have done some stupid things, but he did not need to suffer that degree of humiliation. At least not yet.

Harald continued, giving due credit to Bergthor and his crew for arriving just as he feared the whale would roll him under for good, and to Bergthor himself for knowing where on the whale to stab his spear so as to actually kill the thing.

"And that's why we feast on whale tonight!" Harald concluded with a shout and raised arms, and that in turn led to the others yelling louder still. A gang of men rushed forward and grabbed Harald, lifted him up and set him down on their shoulders. They then proceeded to parade him around the beach, his smiling face sometimes illuminated by the brilliant flames from the massive bonfire, and sometimes lost in shadow.

Thorgrim could not stand to witness any more of that, so he turned back to Bergthor. "And you, what brings you here?" he asked.

"It was time to go a'viking," Bergthor said. "A man can get rusty, just farming, year after year. Some of the men in the neighborhood, they wanted to go as well, so I built this ship, which I call *Wave Splitter*, and we made ready to sail. The owners of the other ships, they heard about me going, and they knew I had had some good fortune raiding in years past. Back in the younger days when you and me were raiding together, heh, Thorgrim? So they joined in with us.

"Sailed to Frankia and did some raiding there, and then crossed over to Engla-land. We've had some luck, but not what I'd hoped. Of course, we haven't been here long. We were at a place the English call Dover, or something like that. Met this Englishman, a fisherman with a greater love for silver than for his fellow English. He speaks our language and knows the coast well. He says just north of here is a place called Winchester which is the seat of their high king and the Christ church as well. It's thirty miles from here, but this fellow says we can get there by ship, or nearly there."

"And that's where you're heading now?" Thorgrim asked.

"We are," Bergthor said. "The raiding's getting harder, I tell you, not like before. You've see it, I'll warrant. There are so many of these young men who want to go a'viking, and the Danes too. So the English are moving anything worth taking inland. So it's inland we must go."

Thorgrim nodded. That made sense. If he had any intention of staying he might well take that advice himself.

"May the gods look with favor on you, Bergthor," Thorgrim said. Harald had been set back on the ground and the riotous voices had quieted considerably. "But tell me, how are things back in Agder? You've not been gone so long, have you? How were things when you left?"

"We sailed in Sumarmál, just as the weather was turning warmer. And I have to tell you, Thorgrim, things were not good. Not good and seemed ready to get worse."

"How so?" Thorgrim asked. This was not what he wanted to hear, not what he expected to hear.

"Halfdan," Bergthor said. "King Halfdan, he's most of the problem. He's always been ambitious, you know that."

Thorgrim nodded. "I know."

"Well, age has not made him less so. The opposite. He's grabbing up land as quick as he can. He's taken most of Agder and parts of Rogaland to the west and Geirstad to the east, and even looks to Vestfold and Vingulmarken."

"And will he take those places, make himself king over them?" Thorgrim asked.

"He might. He's spent a great fortune on these conquests, and now he must pay the warriors he needs to keep control of them. He must be stretched thin. I don't like to think what he'll do to fill his treasury again."

Thorgrim could feel an uncomfortable sensation in his gut, a sick and helpless feeling that such problems should be playing out at home while he was stuck on a beach in Engla-land with five hundred drunken men and a partially eaten whale.

"What of East Agder?' he asked. "Our people, our neighbors, any word of them?"

"Not that I've heard. I saw your son Odd…what? A year ago? A year and a half? He seemed well and prosperous, and he said your farm was doing well, too. Waiting your return. He may have been putting on a good show, but I don't believe he ever thought you were dead."

That was good news, anyway, but still Thorgrim felt the nagging in his head, the need to be back. Returning home had been foremost in his thoughts for some time now, but with Bergthor's words he could feel the need redouble.

Thorgrim had urged Odd not to go a'viking, not to leave his family, as much as it disappointed and angered the young man. To see his father, his grandfather, and his younger brother set off raiding while he remained behind…Thorgrim could well imagine how Odd felt. But he knew it had been the right decision.

Ornolf had died on the point of a sword. In more than two years of raiding Thorgrim and Harald might also have been killed a hundred times over. Why the gods preserved them Thorgrim could not imagine. His best guess: the gods found it more amusing to watch him struggle than to end his life.

But it was one thing for him or Harald to die. They did not have a wife and young children depending on them. Odd did, and he had no business seeking out trouble.

But if trouble had come to East Agder, then it was quite possible it had found Odd, and that Odd had embraced it. The boy was more like his grandfather, Ulf of the Battle Song, then even he himself realized. It was not something that Thorgrim had ever pointed out, not a similarity Thorgrim was eager to reveal. But neither did he think it would stay hidden forever.

All of those considerations, and Bergthor's words, made Thorgrim's desire to return home build like a rising wind, and it made his eagerness to move even more unbearable.

East, always east.

But Thorgrim knew what Bergthor was about to say next. He was going to offer a proposal, Thorgrim was sure of it. A reasonable proposal, a good one, in fact, and one that Thorgrim would feel he could not decline, as desperately as he wanted to.

"You know, Thorgrim," Bergthor said. "I've been thinking on something. Our men, mine and yours, seem to be getting on famously. All together we make a powerful army. What say we join up, you and me, and together we'll sack this Winchester right and proper?"

Chapter Eleven

Army comes
hasty running,
fire they set
in the king's castle.

The Poetic Edda

Odd Thorgrimson did not wish to confront Halfdan the Black, but that was not what troubled him most. Not at all.

More than that, far more, he did not wish to confront the men who had joined him in this raid on Halfdan's home: Amundi Thorsteinsson, Vifil, Ragi, Hakon Styrsson, all his neighbors and the men his neighbors had brought with them. All the men whom he, Odd, had led into this fight. All the men he had assured that his plan — taking Halfdan's compound, plundering it, sailing off long before Halfdan had returned from chasing ghosts around the countryside — was certain to work.

But he had been wrong. His arrogance had blinded him, their success in fighting Halfdan thus far had deluded him into thinking it would continue. He had led them into a trap, apparently, and his pride would be the death of them all.

At least the women and children can get clear, he thought. They had left the women and children aboard the ships, riding at anchor, with a handful of men to sail them. The women and children could get away, return to their homes.

And then what? Starve for want of men to work the farms? Be captured by Halfdan anyway, and sold as slaves? Or worse?

All this Odd considered as he leaped out of his bed, pulled his shoes on and lashed them tight with the leather thongs. Amundi, who had woken Odd with the news of Halfdan's return, headed off to wake the others as well. Odd settled his mail shirt on his shoulders and strapped on his sword, Blood-letter.

Halfdan will never get this sword, he thought. He would break it in two before he let Halfdan take the precious blade. But then he recalled that he meant to die with Blood-letter in his hand, to go down fighting, the blade covered in blood. After that, he would have little to say about what became of the sword.

At least I will see Ulf in Valhalla, and I'll be able to look him in the eye, he thought. At least he would die a death worthy of that blade.

With that he crossed the dim-lit hall and opened the big door that led to the grounds outside. He guessed that the sun had just come up. It was still hidden behind the high walls of the compound, leaving the compound itself still mostly in darkness, with the buildings barely visible like the spirits of giant beasts. Here and there the bright light of a fire stood out as servants stoked up coals in preparation for the day.

Odd walked quickly across the ground and climbed a ladder that led to the top of the wall. Sentries were posted at intervals all along the perimeter, men belonging to each of the freemen who had brought their own contingent of warriors. Those close to the gate, the first to see the enemy, were Amundi's men, which was why Amundi had been alerted first.

"What do you see?" Odd asked the man nearest the top of the ladder.

"Not much now, Master Odd," he said, nodding out toward the ground beyond. There was more to be seen outside the walls where the dawn light was not obstructed, but farther off all was hidden in shadows.

"It was still dark and we heard sounds," the sentry continued, "like men moving, horses, that sort of thing. A couple of riders come up to the gate. They stopped, just over there." He pointed to a place forty feet from the wall. "They just stopped and looked. Finally I ask who they are and they say 'Open the gate for King Halfdan,' and I say, 'King Halfdan don't rule here now,' and that's it. They rode off."

Odd said nothing but just stared out into the dark. No one had yet seen Halfdan or his army, but it would be foolish to think they were not there.

"Very well, keep your eyes and ears sharp. Let me know if you discover anything more." He climbed down from the wall and was heading back toward the hall when he saw the others, Amundi in the lead, coming toward him. They, too, were in mail with swords on their hips.

Well, there's no avoiding this in any case, Odd thought. He met them on the grounds outside the long hall and they gathered in a circle, the hauldar, the ten wealthiest and most influential men in Fevik, and a few of the more prosperous farmers of lesser rank, men rich enough or experienced enough that they were welcome to join with other freemen.

"The sentries didn't see Halfdan or his army," Odd started in, even before anyone asked. "And I couldn't see anything either. But the fellow there told me he heard movement out in the dark, and two riders came up and demanded the gate be opened for Halfdan. He refused them and they rode off."

He glanced around. There was light enough to see the looks on the others' faces. The looks of concern.

"What do you think?" Ragi asked.

"I think Halfdan is there. Halfdan and his men. I think the riders were sent to make certain we were actually in possession of the compound. Somehow Halfdan must have discovered what we were planning."

The others listened to that and some nodded their heads. Odd braced for the criticism, the reminders that he alone had thought this plan a good one, that he had convinced the others.

That he had led them, all of them, to their deaths.

He waited, but no one spoke, and he could see no indication that any of the men were blaming him. He may have been the one to think of this plan, and been the one to advocate for it, but the others had chosen for themselves to go along, and they were honest enough to not blame him now. Odd was not sure if that made him feel better or worse.

"What next?" Vifil asked. It was the question that Odd had been pondering, and he had some definite ideas, but he was not much in the mood for giving orders that morning.

"We don't really know what we're up against," Amundi said. "How many men Halfdan has, if indeed he's out there with his army. What he wants."

"Our balls, that's what he wants," Hakon said and that earned a few muted chuckles.

"I say we wait for now," Amundi continued. "Wait until it's full light and we can see what's out there. If Halfdan's there I don't think he'll keep us waiting long to find out his demands."

That was met with more nods, and, indeed, there was not much else that they could do.

"Good, that's good," Thorgeir Herjolfsson said. "But see here. We can pretty much guess what Halfdan'll say. He'll tell us to open the gates, and tell us if we do he might be willing to bargain, but if we don't he'll take the place by force and kill the lot of us."

"He might tell us he's willing to bargain if we open the gates, but can we believe him?" Ragi asked. "Can he just let us go, after us taking his great hall like this? I think he'll want us dead no matter what we do, or what he says. He'll feel that he has to kill us all. For honor's sake."

That, too, made sense, and no one argued otherwise.

"The only other choice is we fight," Amundi said. Odd said nothing, gave no reaction. *Fight.* That was exactly what he was thinking, but he did not want to suggest it. He no longer wanted to suggest anything.

"We have, what, two hundred, two hundred and fifty men?" Vifil said. "Against Halfdan's…?"

"Three or four hundred, I would guess," Thorgeir said. "After what happened at Odd's hall I don't think he'd march out with less." No one disagreed.

"Let's remember one thing," Amundi said. "We're in a fortification. Halfdan is not. If he attacks he'll lose a lot of men. A lot. Even if he manages to beat us. He can only attack the walls in a few places at once, if that. And being on the inside we can move men to defend the walls a lot quicker than he can move to attack them."

"And we're in possession of his home," Ragi said. "His treasure. His wife and children, and the wives and children of all his chief men. We have a lot to bargain with here." The others nodded at the truth of that.

We have a lot to bargain with… Odd thought. That was true. But at some point, after a deal was made, they would have to open the gates, and then everything would depend on Halfdan's keeping his part of the bargain. And Odd was not terribly optimistic about that happening.

But for the time being, until some word arrived from Halfdan, there was nothing more to do, so Odd ordered the servants to bring them breakfast. Soon after they were seated at the table in the long hall with oat porridge and white bread and butter and honey and fresh berries and ale spread out before them. And they ate with more enthusiasm than one might expect from men who had every reason to believe they would not live to see the end of that day.

"A fine way to live, being king and all," Hakon Styrsson noted.

"Halfdan seems to think so," Ragi said.

"I can bloody well see why," Thorgeir said.

Hakon was still polishing off what Odd thought was his third bowl of porridge, which actually was equal parts honey and porridge, when Amundi's man from the wall arrived. Odd could see he had no glad tidings to relay. He spoke loudly enough for all to hear.

"Riders at the gate, masters," he said. "A dozen, and King Halfdan in the lead. The king says he would speak to one of you. Or all of you."

The men at the table exchanged glances. "The time has come," Odd said, and he stood and the others stood as well. Amundi's man led the way across the open ground and up the ladder to the top of the wall. The sun was high enough now that it reached over the palisades, sending long, sharp shadows over the trampled earth in the wake of the buildings and wagons and such.

Odd stepped off the ladder and made his way along the top of the wall, making room for the others following behind, his eyes on the ground beyond the gate. A dozen riders, just as Amundi's man had said. They were in two columns, sitting on tall horses, and their mail shirts and helmets seemed to glow like embers in the early morning sun. The rider at the front of the left column carried a pole from which flew a banner, long and pointed like a serpent's tongue. It was white with a broad red border and at the widest part was the outline of a bird in flight. A bird of prey. This was Halfdan's hird, his most elite warriors, fitted out in the finest armor and weapons to serve as a reflection of their king's wealth and power.

A dozen feet in front of them, alone, Halfdan himself sat his own horse, palms resting on the saddle, the picture of patience and forbearing. He was looking up with his head slightly cocked, a silver helmet framing his face so that his neat beard, more gray than its original brown, seemed to be an extension of the polished iron.

Odd glanced to his right. Amundi was next to him and the rest spread out beyond him. Vifil, who was last in line, was just climbing up onto the wall. Odd looked back at Halfdan and waited for Halfdan to speak. But he did not.

For a moment or two they remained motionless, regarding one another across the hundred feet that separated them. Even the horses seemed to recognize the gravity of the moment and remained silent and still.

Halfdan still did not speak.

Oh, is this the silly game we're to play? Odd thought. For a moment he considered playing as well, refusing to speak first. But one of them had to stop being childish, so he figured it might as well be him.

"King Halfdan, good morning," Odd said. Halfdan gave a courteous nod of the head, acknowledging the greeting, but not returning it. Odd remained quiet. He felt that he had done more than his share of the talking.

"Odd Thorgrimson," Halfdan said at last. "Amundi. All of you. This is a strange situation. It seems you are in my home, and I am out here."

"It seems so," Odd said.

"Yes," said Halfdan. "So, might I ask that you leave my home, and allow me and my men to come in? We've had a long march." Odd could hear the unspoken parts of that as clearly as the words Halfdan had said. *You didn't expect to see me, did you? And now you don't know what to do.*

"I don't think so, King Halfdan," Odd said. "I think we have a lot to discuss — you, me, the hauldar and the others. Much to discuss, agreements to reach. I wish we might have done so under better circumstances."

"I imagine you do," Halfdan said.

"We stand ready," Odd said. "Ready to talk, or whatever you wish. But until then we'll remain here. Your wives, your children, they're safe enough, I give my word. But they'll remain here as well."

The words were meant as a threat, or a warning, neither very subtle, and Halfdan took them as such, though he seemed neither threatened nor warned. Instead he smirked, just a bit, just enough to ensure that the expression was clearly seen by the men on the wall.

"Very well," Halfdan said. "I'm sure the servants have already shown you where the good wine and the silver are hidden, so you don't need my help there. Good day." With that he pulled the reins of his horse to one side and the animal turned and began walking away, presenting its wide posterior to the men watching. The hird parted neatly and let Halfdan ride down the center of their two columns and then fell in behind him, riding away. In the distance Odd could see the tents set up on the open ground half a mile from the wall. The smoke from cook fires was rising up into the pale blue sky.

"Well, that wasn't exactly what I was expecting," Hakon said, breaking the silence.

"No," Amundi said. "Halfdan's too smart to do what we expect. There's no guessing what he'll do. So we have to be ready for…whatever it is."

How they might make ready they did not know. They had never discussed what they would do in a situation such as this because they had never envisioned being in this situation. But here it was, and now they needed to scramble for a response.

The top of the wall was not the place to do that. Not in the presence of the men standing sentry. They did not need to learn that their leaders had been taken by surprise and did not know what to do next. So Odd and the rest climbed back down to the ground where they could speak with some degree of privacy, and deal with this crisis in the most logical way.

There was a small fire ring nearby with benches arranged in a circle around it, and it seemed as good a place as any for a council of war. Better than a table, certainly, because there was no head at which to sit, and Odd wanted any further decisions to be arrived at mutually. He led the way over to the ring and seated himself and the other men sat as well.

"Very well," Odd said, by way of starting. "Halfdan is out there. We're in here. What next?"

"For us, we just keep doing what we're doing now, mostly," Amundi said. "We'll keep vigilant watch, get the blacksmiths here to start making more spears. Search for more weapons…there must be some stored around here…maybe start making up more arrows. Get stones up on the walls that we can throw down. Get as prepared as we can to defend this place. I don't see what more we can do. It seems to me that anything beyond that will be Halfdan's move."

Heads nodded. Thorgeir Herjolfsson spoke next.

"We have to find out what Halfdan wants. Or, I should say, what he's willing to accept. We know what he wants. He wants his hall back and he wants us put down. But is he willing to talk? Make some sort of deal? Or will he only be satisfied if we're all dead?"

"That's the question," Odd said. "If he'll only be satisfied with our deaths, then, speaking for myself, I don't mean to make it easy for him."

At that the others nodded again. Odd had meant to add that if any man there wished to make some separate agreement with Halfdan, to find some way for him and his men to be set free from this trap, then he, Odd, would not hold it against him, or think less of him in any way. But he could see that such an offer would be an insult. None of these men would march off and leave their fellows to fight to the death. He just hoped that the warriors under their command, the men on the walls, felt the same way.

"I must say, Halfdan did not seem too interested in talking," Amundi pointed out.

"Trying to rattle us," Ragi said. "Unnerve us. He hopes to get us fighting amongst ourselves."

"He can play that game of waiting and we can too," Vifil said. "We have plenty of food here. Three wells that I counted, so we won't run out of water. We have hostages. We can wait a long time for Halfdan to decide what he'll do next."

And so it was agreed. They would wait. Let Halfdan decide when he had enough of living in his tent and was willing to talk.

With that decision made they set about preparing for the fight they knew would come. The warriors remained on the walls, watch upon watch, and the people in the compound went about their new, siege-induced routine. The sound of hammers banging iron rang through the air as the blacksmiths turned out more spear points. Weapons were cleaned and sharpened, inventories of food and drink made, defenses organized. But Halfdan did not come.

He did not come the next day, or the day after that, either. Odd could feel the uncertainty grow, and with it tension and fear. Waiting. Not knowing. Nothing was more corrosive to morale than that.

And then something changed. Odd was inspecting the blacksmiths' work when he heard voices on the wall, the sentries calling out with an urgency they had not shown before, and he set down the spear point and started moving for the ladder with no conscious thought. He took the rungs fast and stepped onto the wall.

"Riders coming, Master Odd," the nearest sentry said, pointing. Odd followed his finger. A group of horsemen were approaching. He could see their mail shining and, bobbing up and down, a bright spot of color that he took to be Halfdan's banner at the end of a pole. As far as he could tell from that distance it was the same group of riders that had come that first morning.

As he watched he became aware of a great swell of noise behind him. He looked down at the grounds below and saw all the men who were not on the wall scrambling to get armed and up to the places they had been ordered to go. It was not orderly, to be sure, but it was not utter chaos either, and that was good.

Amundi, Ragi and Thorgeir came clambering up the ladder and stepped out onto the wall, their eyes fixed on the riders who were clearly visible now.

"Halfdan, looks like," Thorgeir said.

"Come to surrender, no doubt," Amundi said.

The horsemen came to within fifty feet of the gate, the same well-equipped warriors of the hird, with Halfdan in the lead. The guards reined to a stop, their horses in two neat lines, as Halfdan approached.

"Odd Thorgrimson, I'm glad to see you," Halfdan said. "Amundi, Ragi. Thorgeir." He nodded his greeting to each man.

"Good morning, King Halfdan," Odd said, the only one of them to reply. "Why are we honored with your visiting us?"

"Actually," Halfdan said, "it was not so much me who wanted to visit. There's someone else wishing to greet you. Someone you know. Know well, I think."

He turned in the saddle and nodded toward the guards. One man near the center of the line nudged his horse to a walk and rode up to Halfdan's side, and as he drew closer Odd recognized him as Onund Jonsson, captain of Halfdan's hird, a man Odd had known for many years. Onund had someone on the saddle in front of him, a child, clearly. Odd squinted and looked closely at the child's familiar features, the round face, the long tousled blond hair. He felt his stomach twist and thought he might vomit. He could hear his breath, loud, as he sucked in air. He felt his fists curl tight enough to be painful.

"Ah, you recognize her!" Halfdan said. "I myself haven't seen her since she was a baby. I would have never known her. But you? Of course you would recognize her. Hallbera. Your very own sister."

Chapter Twelve

In the same year the aforementioned worshipful
King Æthelwulf freed the tenth part of his kingdom
from every royal service and tribute, and offered it up
as an everlasting grant to God the One and Three…

Asser's Life of King Alfred

King Æthelwulf was the pole star, and all the others were minor points of light whirling around him. That was how it had seemed to Felix when he first arrived at the Royal Court at Winchester, and it seemed that way to him still. Æthelwulf was the North Star — not just there, but in all of Wessex — and the rest were little gleams in the blackness, growing less and less significant the further from the pole star they were found.

Mon Dieu, he thought, and shook his head at the madness.

It was not new to him, this position of the king in the royal firmament. Felix had been sent from the court of Charles the Bald of West Frankia, and in that kingdom it was Charles who occupied the place of the pole star. But the Frankish court had never seemed quite so mad as that of Wessex.

There were always many of these points of light in the royal household — ealdormen, thegns, various court functionaries and hangers-on, stately and serious men, comely, richly dressed women — but now, with Æthelwulf's departure imminent, there were more, far more, lighting up the court until it blazed. Men from all over Wessex and beyond, drawn in by the irresistible pull of power, as if dragged there by chains. All spinning around the king. But he, Felix, spun closer than any of them.

That was the image that Felix saw in his mind. The stars in a circle spinning around the North Star, and he himself so close to that pole star that they seemed to almost touch, his circle was much smaller than the others, his orbit much faster. And he was not turned inward, not looking to the North Star. He was turned outward, out toward the others, standing like a sentry between them and the king.

The image was metaphorical, of course, but on some days, such as that one, it seemed very literal indeed. The crowd of nobles in their bright, fine linen and furs and decked out in jewels, swirling through the hall and the grounds, circling in for a word with Æthelwulf, a final grant of a favor or the hope of being bequeathed this or that. Thegns arriving with their retinues, their house guards, all needing food and drink and stables and whatever else to which they thought themselves entitled.

"Ah, Felix, there you are!"

Felix looked up, unsure if he had heard the words or if they were just an echo in his head. He had been hearing them all day.

"Lord Baldred, *bon jour*, I'm honored to see you," Felix said with a shallow bow. Baldred was one of the wealthiest of the thegns in Hampshire, near the border of Sussex, and an overbearing, pompous fool.

"Felix, I need to see the king before he's off, and it must be soon, do you hear?"

"Of course, Lord, though King Æthelwulf is quite pressed, as you might imagine. At the moment he is attending a private mass."

That was actually true: Æthelwulf attended mass daily, often with the bishop as celebrant. The king was, among other things, a pious man.

"Pressed? I'm sure," Baldred said. "And I'm sure in your Frankish courts you might put off a man of influence such as myself, but that won't answer in Wessex, not at all, do you see? I must have my audience. Pray see to it." With that Baldred turned and walked off, his fine cloak like a flag fluttering behind him.

Felix watched him walk away. *You may have an audience with my posterior, but you'll get no higher than that, monsieur*, he thought, and that was all the time he had for Lord Baldred. By the time he looked back down at the parchment in his hand he had already forgotten the man.

Six years earlier Felix had arrived at Æthelwulf's court, sent there by his former master, the king of West Frankia, Charles the Bald. Felix had long before proven his intelligence, loyalty and organizational skill in Charles's court, and so Charles had dispatched him to bring order and competence to the court of his friend King Æthelwulf. Felix had begun his tenure as Æthelwulf's notary, taking charge of his correspondence, but his realm had expanded until he seemed to be responsible for all aspects of keeping the royal court functioning properly.

Which was really why Charles had sent Felix in the first place. He had sent him as a favor, thinking that Æthelwulf could use a man of his experience, a man who had no stake in the political machinations of Wessex. And he had also sent him because Charles was not averse to the idea of having eyes and even a voice inside the court of the most powerful kingdom in England.

Felix looked up from the list in his hands and scanned the bustle in the great hall, the line of servants like ants carrying food and rolling barrels of wine out to the courtyard. He looked down at the list once more, a list of all the things that Æthelwulf would need for the arduous trip to Frankia, which was bound to take a week or two.

The sailors, Felix knew, survived on dried fish or salted beef and coarse, unleavened bread. But that would not do for the king and his entourage. In truth, Felix admitted, it would not do for him, either.

He ran his eyes down the list, item after item: fresh beef, rabbits living and otherwise, ducks likewise, venison, fresh carrots and greens, bags and bags of bread which would be as unlike the sailors' bread as the king's silk tunic was to the sailors' oiled shirts. A third of the items on the list had a small *X* beside them to confirm they had been loaded aboard one wagon or another.

"See here," Felix said, looking up at the man who, during his brief discussion with Baldred, had stood fidgeting beside him. Felix's English had been good when he left Frankia; now it was better than most native speakers', save for a few Frankish words he still used reflexively, and a trace of an accent which he knew the servants mocked behind his back. "It says here there were six barrels of wine, but I saw only five go past."

"You sure?" the steward said, looking down at the list as if it might do some magical thing. "I thought I counted six."

"Pray, count again," Felix said, and to himself added, *You thieving bastard…*

The steward nodded and hurried off and Felix had no doubt he would discover his "mistake" and see that there was a sixth barrel on the wagon. There was some pilfering he could tolerate, and some he could not catch, but he would not risk having Æthelwulf and his party come up short on wine.

He rolled up the list and headed for the big doors through which the line of servants was snaking, the steward's men checking off lists of their own as they passed. The courtyard, incredibly, was even more chaotic than the great hall. A line of wagons ran from the doorway through which Felix stepped all the way up to the gates in the massive stone wall that surrounded the royal manor, a small, self-contained town within the larger town of Winchester.

More wagons stood off to the side, but those were not rough carts built to haul barrels or heavy sacks. They were high-wheeled and lightly constructed, made to carry the nobility over the countryside in as much comfort as was attainable, which admittedly was not much.

They would be making the trek to Hamtun, about twenty miles distant, down a road built centuries ago by the Romans. The road had clearly been a magnificent thing in its day: wide and paved over with carefully fitted stones and slightly arched to shed rain. There were such roads in Frankia too, and throughout most of Europe. Felix knew a little about the Romans, mostly from the remnants of their civilization that still stood and the ancient stories he had heard, many of which he thought were no more than children's tales, but he imagined that the roads had been kept in good order while Rome still ruled the world.

But, alas, road repair had gone the way of Pax Romana. Now great gaps existed in the paving where folk had plucked stones out to use for one purpose or another. In other places time and weather had eaten away at the surface, revealing the layers of pebbles and sand which the Romans had meticulously laid down to support the stones.

Magnificent. Far better than anything anyone would be willing to do in present times, even if they knew how. And damaged as the old road was, it had been maintained after a fashion and so was still better than any that were English-built. Given the fine weather and the tolerable road Felix did not think it would take more than two days for the train of wagons to cover that distance. Three if they were unlucky.

But first he had to see it loaded, organized and well manned. He looked around the grounds. Dozens of men-at-arms were standing in clusters or sitting on benches, most with cups in their hands. These were the house guards who had come with their masters, the ealdormen and thegns who came to pay respect to the king and ask those last favors.

There was a keen sense of urgency among them. Æthelwulf, king of Wessex, was bound for Rome, off on a magnificent pilgrimage to meet with Pope Benedict III. It was unprecedented, as far as Felix knew. And, he was sure, it was a very bad idea.

The pilgrimage itself was not unprecedented. English kings had made the journey to Rome before. But they had been kings who were in exile, driven from their thrones by more powerful rivals, or kings who, worn down by consideration or fearful of assassination, had handed power over to their successors and then made the long journey to live out their final days in the footsteps of the Apostles.

But no king that Felix knew of had ever gone to Rome while he still ruled his kingdom, with the expectation that he would return to resume his reign. Æthelwulf was leaving his eldest son, Æthelbald, to be king of Wessex in his stead, and his next oldest boy, Æthelberht, to be king of Kent. When he returned, Æthelwulf expected his sons to hand the kingdoms back to him.

That was where Felix thought there might be some difficulty.

He had hinted at his concerns as forcefully as he dared, but Æthelwulf had dismissed him, and Felix had only so much influence. All he could do now was to see things as organized as possible, ensure that Æthelwulf's people did not steal too much from him, and fend off the nobles looking for favors from their king while he could still grant them, since they did not think he would be king for very much longer.

All this Felix would report to his real master, King Charles of West Frankia, when Charles was playing host to Æthelwulf and his party in a month's time.

A little ways beyond where the men-at-arms were gathered, another group of men stood in close conversation, their colorful tunics and capes and bright points of silver giving them a festive look, though Felix doubted there was anything festive about their discussions. Among them was Nothwulf, ealdorman of Dorsetshire, who had achieved some notoriety recently by defeating a band of Northmen who taken the monastery at Christchurch.

Felix shifted his eyes a bit. Thirty feet from where Nothwulf stood in conference there was a fellow named Leofric, engaged in his own discussion with fellow thegns. They were all wealthy men, but Leofric was wealthiest of all. He and Nothwulf had been close, but something had happened, some falling out. Felix did not know what it was, and seemed unable to discover the truth, but whatever it was it was causing considerable friction in the neighboring shire.

Yet another gaggle of men stood beyond Leofric's group, these men of Kent, thegns and nobility. Sitting on a bench nearby was a young boy, seven years old. His clothes were as fine as any of the nobles, his expression was one of complete boredom as he made slow work of eating an apple. He looked up and met Felix's eyes and for a moment they looked at one another. Then Felix gave the tiniest flick of his head to beckon the boy over. Slowly, with apparent reluctance, the boy stood and shuffled over in Felix's direction.

Alfred, youngest son of Æthelwulf's surviving four, small and not terribly robust, with big, brown eyes that hinted at the boy's depth. He would be accompanying his father to Rome, but it would not be Alfred's first time there. He had been sent the year before as part of a retinue intended to pave the way for Æthelwulf's pilgrimage.

Felix was actually surprised the boy had survived the rigors of the journey, but was pleased that he had. Felix liked Alfred very much. He hoped he would survive the second trip. Alfred was certainly the brightest of Æthelwulf's sons, and even if there was almost no chance of him ever assuming the throne, Felix felt certain that the kingdom of Wessex was better off having him there.

"Alfred, how do you fare?" Felix asked.

"Well enough, sir," Alfred said. His voice was soft, his tone always polite.

"And what do you hear?"

"Lord Forthhere wants my father to grant him the hundred that abuts his land in Cisseceaster, but Godhold wishes it as well. The thegns are divided on this, but it seems to me that Godhold has the majority of support."

Felix nodded. These men of Kent could be a supreme annoyance. But they would soon be the problem of Æthelberht, Æthelwulf's second son, who had been set as king of Kent until Æthelwulf's return. Æthelberht favored Forthhere, Felix knew, so it was no wonder that Godhold was trying to secure the grant before Æthelwulf departed.

"What do you think?" Felix asked.

"I think my father favors Godhold, which is why Godhold hopes to get the grant now. Before we leave."

Smart boy… Felix thought. Alfred was a good ally. No one concerned themselves with what they said in his presence: in their eyes he was only a shy, possibly stupid boy. The fourth son, one of no consequence. So he heard a great deal, and most of what he heard he understood. And passed along to Felix.

"I think this will be your brother's problem," Felix said, "because I do not think your father will care to involve himself in this just now."

"Particularly if you don't tell him about it," Alfred said with a shy smile.

"Indeed," Felix said. He was about to ask the boy what else he had heard when the thought was interrupted by someone heading his way, a messenger by the look of his mud-splattered leggings and rumpled tunic. A messenger who had ridden hard, as gauged by his red and sweating face, his wet hair, his open-mouthed look of exhaustion. Felix felt an ugly foreboding. Messengers did not generally ride hard when they brought good news.

"Sir," he said, bowing as he came to a stop just a few feet away. Anyone who had business with the court, whether it was delivering messages or begging an audience with the king, knew that Felix was the man to approach first.

"Yes?" Felix asked.

"I come from Portesmutha," the messenger said. "Hunwald, the shire reeve, sends me. He bids me tell you that the Northmen have arrived there."

"Arrived?" Felix asked. "Have they plundered the place? The abbey?"

"No," the messenger said. "They're…they've killed a whale, lord, and they're eating it. On the beach."

Felix felt his brows come together. "A whale…" He thought about that oddity for a moment, then asked, "How many?"

"Just the one whale, lord," the messenger said.

"No, how many Northmen?" Felix snapped.

"Oh…shire reeve says eleven ships, lord."

Eleven ships… That could be as many as five or six hundred men. Not a number that could be ignored.

Felix looked down at young Alfred. "What think you, Prince Alfred?" he asked.

"I think my father's plans are suddenly much altered," Alfred said.

Felix nodded. "Indeed they are."

Chapter Thirteen

Daughter of my father,
there you grinded hard,
but you saw crowds
of giants fall.

The Poetic Edda

Odd heard Amundi, to his immediate right, make a low, grunting sound as the implications of Halfdan's words came to him.

He heard Thorgeir ask in a soft voice, "That's…Odd's sister?"

"Yes. Hallbera," Amundi said.

There was quiet for a moment, then Thorgeir said, "I thought Hallbera was his daughter."

"Hallbera Oddsdottir. This is Hallbera Thorgrimsdottir. Odd's sister. They were both named after Odd's mother, who was much loved. She died giving birth to this one."

Odd heard the words but they passed through him like water through a net. His whole attention was focused on his sister, his beloved sister, sitting awkwardly on Onund Jonsson's saddle. She had been off with Signy's parents, far from Odd's farm, and he had thought her safe. In truth, he had not really thought about her at all, with all the other concerns he had.

But Halfdan, apparently, had thought about her. And found her. And now she sat fifty feet away with Onund's arm around her waist, looking up at him, eyes wide, face smudged with dirt. Fear radiated off her like heat. Her mouth was slightly open, as if she were silently imploring him to save her.

Odd wondered how Halfdan had found her. Anyone who was likely to have known where she was had left the farm and sailed off with Odd and the others.

"Now, Odd Thorgrimson," Halfdan said. "Now I think it's time for us to talk. And you, Amundi, you should be part of this as well."

Odd's mind was tumbling and spinning like a drunkard trying to keep his feet. He wanted to speak but no words would come. Amundi, however, did not feel so tongue-tied.

"Very well, Halfdan," Amundi said. "Speak. We're listening."

"I hope you are. I hope Odd is," Halfdan said. "He seems a little confused right now. So here we are. I am in possession of young Hallbera. Odd's sister. I hope you won't force me to actually threaten the child. I don't think I need to do that. You can imagine what might happen to her. Selling her into slavery would be the least of it."

Once again Odd tried to talk and once again it fell to Amundi.

"That's your idea of not threatening the child?"

Halfdan shrugged. "There's been a lot of talking at cross purposes as of late. I just want to make sure we all understand each other."

"I'm sure we do," Amundi said. "I'm sure you understand that we have your wife and your child in here. And the wives and children of many of your men as well."

"Now it seems that you're the one threatening children," Halfdan said.

"I just want to make sure we understand each other," Amundi said.

"We do," Halfdan said. "You see, even if you butcher all the women and children in there, you'll still have to fight us at some point. You can stay behind those walls for a long time, but not forever. And the longer you wait the more of my warriors will arrive from the garrisons abroad."

Odd waited for Amundi to speak, but apparently the man had no reply to that. Instead, Halfdan continued.

"I think we also know that you won't slaughter the women and children," he said. "I don't think your honor would allow for that."

"And your honor?" Amundi asked. "Your honor would allow you to kill that child?"

"My honor lies in being king of Agder and the lands beyond," Halfdan said. "My honor lies in sitting unchallenged on my throne. And I'll do whatever I need to do to preserve that honor."

A bargain… Odd thought. *A deal, make a deal.*

"I have no argument for any of that," Odd said. Halfdan looked from Amundi to him and smiled.

"Ah, you can speak!" he said.

"I know you for a liar and a coward, but what you've said here is all true enough," Odd continued. "Every man in here is willing to fight to the last, and that would mean a lot of your warriors dead as well. It will cost you dear to take your great hall back. But I'll offer you a bargain. Swap me for Hallbera, and let the others here go free. You get what you really want and you get it cheap." The offer was sincere, the best that Odd could make, though he doubted that Halfdan would ever agree to such a thing.

But Halfdan surprised him

"You and I think alike," Halfdan said. "I wouldn't have guessed it, but it seems we do. I can accept your offer. You for the child. You open the gates and I let the rest march free."

Odd was making the first syllables of agreement when Amundi cut him off.

"Very generous, just as we would expect from so kind a king," he said. "But we must discuss this. The decision is not Odd's alone."

"No?" Halfdan said. "I should think it is. His and mine. But whatever you say. I'll be back at midday, and I'll expect your answer then." He turned his horse and Onund Jonsson who held Hallbera turned as well and they rode back toward the camp, the rest of the hird once more following behind.

Amundi turned to Odd. "The fire circle," he said. "Let's gather at the fire circle and we'll talk about this with the rest."

They climbed down the ladder and walked over the ground to the ring of benches. Odd felt as if he was floating, as if his mind and body were not connected. Once again Halfdan had done something that he had not foreseen, not even a hint of it. Here Odd had concocted this idea of plundering Halfdan's long hall, taking him by surprise, and instead Halfdan had pummeled him with one shock after another, until he was backed into a corner from which he would not cscape with his life.

Odd sat and waited as the others came over and sat as well. He looked over the set, angry, concerned faces of the freemen, the men he had led to this place, and he found his senses returning, mind and body joined as one once again.

"Most of you heard what Halfdan had to say," Odd said. "He has my sister, my little sister Hallbera, as hostage. How he laid hands on her I don't know, but he has."

"Onund Jonsson," Amundi said.

"Onund…?" Odd asked.

"Who else? Onund's from Fevik. Knows everyone. I always counted him as a friend. Of course he would know where you sister was to be found. And he also commands Halfdan's hird."

Onund Jonsson…of course… Odd thought. He might have felt a stabbing hatred for the man if he had any feeling left in him. But he didn't, so he continued.

"However he got her, he got her," Odd said. "And now he's offered a deal. A fair one. Hallbera for me. Straight trade. And the rest of you and your men, you're free to go."

Ragi spat on the ground. "As if we could trust the word of that bastard!" he said. "We open the gates and we're dead men, all of us. Sure, we can take plenty of Halfdan's men with us, but in the end he'll kill us all."

"One thing Halfdan said is true," Thorgeir said. "We can garrison in here for a long time, but we can't stay forever. Halfdan has hundreds more men far afield, but he can call them back. Outnumber us even more. The longer we wait the worse our chances get."

"If that's true," Odd said, "then why does he go to the trouble of taking Hallbera hostage? To save time?"

"There's one person here who probably knows Halfdan's mind better than any," Amundi said. "I think we should fetch her."

Word was passed, and soon after Ragnhild came striding defiantly up to the fire ring, two spearmen behind her. Her face was set in a scowl and there was not a trace of fear in it.

"What do you want of me?" she demanded to the gathering in general.

"I beg you, sit," Odd said, gesturing to an empty spot on one of the benches, and Ragnhild just glared at him and did not reply and did not move. "Suit yourself," Odd said.

"This is what we want of you," Amundi said. "We want you to tell us what Halfdan has in mind."

"And how could I know that?"

"Your best guess," Thorgeir said. "Halfdan has offered…"

"I know what's he's offered," Ragnhild cut him off. Her scowl turned into something more like a smirk as she looked at Odd. "You're a special man, Odd Thorgrimson. Halfdan's gone to a lot of trouble to get his hands on you. You should be honored."

"I am," Odd said. "But what I don't understand is, why would Halfdan be willing to let the rest of these men go? Why does he only want me? Sure, this all started with me, and my father's farm, but the rest here have stood up to him as well. Why does he not want them? Or will he betray us, kill us all if we open the gate?"

Ragnhild looked over the assembled men, as if gauging how much, if anything, to tell them.

"You're not escaping, none of you," she said at last. "Oh, maybe with your lives, but Halfdan will see that you pay, and pay well. Taxes, tribute. Warriors, slaves. He'll take all that, and you'll have the example of what becomes of Odd to remind you of why you would rather pay than suffer at my husband's hands. Of course he could kill you all now, but you're worth much more to him, for much longer, if you're allowed to live. Dead men don't pay tribute."

"Halfdan takes a big risk, making us choose," Vifil said. "We have you, and Halfdan's son, as hostage. And the other women and children."

Ragnhild looked at him, a scornful look. "Halfdan is not risking anything that is of any real worth to him," she said. "He cares only about his throne. If that's threatened then nothing else matters."

"You believe that Halfdan will be true to his word?" Odd said. "Let these others go if I give myself up?"

"I don't know what Halfdan will do, any more than you do," Ragnhild said. "I just know he has good reason to want you and just you, Odd Thorgrimson. To make an example of you. And to let the others live. You know what your choice is. Take your chance and open the gate, or stay in here until we all starve."

With that she turned and pushed through the two spearmen and headed back toward the hall, and no one tried to stop her.

"Halfdan must know how long we can stay here," Vifil said. "Even if he doesn't know how much food is in here, one of his men must."

"How much food is in here?" Amundi asked.

"Two, three weeks' worth, if we're careful," Vifil said. Silence followed that assessment as Odd and the rest considered what would might happen over that short span of time. The brutal hunger. The fighting for scraps. Death from wounds and from starvation. And finally, the desperate attempt to battle their way free of the compound, the crazed, half-starved men against Halfdan's large and well-fed army.

"This is a simple thing," Odd said at last. "Hardly worth discussion. There's a chance, a good chance, I think, that all of you can get free of here if I give myself up to Halfdan. Weigh that against the certainty that we will all be butchered if we remain. And Halfdan will do what he will to my sister."

There was silence in the wake of that pronouncement, then Amundi said, "We came into this together and we'll stand together. We're not going to feed you to Halfdan like scrap meat to the wolves."

Odd looked around. Heads were nodding.

"There's no choice," Odd said. "I will not ask you to stand and fight in hope of saving my life. Not when it means that many of you will die, and my sister as well. That I cannot do."

"We all die eventually," Amundi said. "You, me. Your sister. All we can hope for is to die like men, weapons in hand. If we can take Halfdan with us, then no harm comes to your sister."

"We must act fast. Now," Ragi said. "Any time wasted is a gift to Halfdan. At midday he'll be just outside the gate with only his hird to guard him. He'll come to talk, and when he does, we throw open the gates and come out under arms."

"Go right at 'em, take them by surprise," Thorgeir said. "Snatch Halfdan and Odd's sister, and then we're the ones who have hostages worth bargaining for."

Odd looked around once more. Heads were nodding again but faces were grim. It was a plan, the only one they could think of, perhaps the only one available. Odd doubted that any man there thought it would work, that they could grab Halfdan in time, or that Halfdan's army would not be ready for them. It was just about the worst of plans, but the alternative was waiting around to see what fate would bring to them, and that would be worse still. Better to force fate's hand. Better to act than to be acted upon.

So they made ready. They moved quietly, explaining to the men how this would go — once Odd was talking with Halfdan then the gates would fly open and the men inside would come screaming out, weapons in hand, shields on arms. If they hit hard and hit fast then there was a good chance they could roll right over Halfdan's unprepared men.

The sentries were left to walk the tops of the walls, the smoke from the cooking fires inside the compound still rising up into the blue sky. The smiths still hammered away at their forges. Halfdan and his men would see no change from that morning; they would not see the two hundred men standing silent and grim behind the heavy oak door.

The sun was nearing its high point when all was ready, the men in place, each of the freemen at the head of those warriors he had brought with him. They stood in two columns behind the doors, shuffling in the dirt and seeking firm footing to launch themselves off. They cleared their throats and yawned in nervous anticipation. The worst part, the waiting.

"Riders coming!" the sentry called out from the top of the wall and Odd saw some men jump in surprise. Odd turned and looked from Amundi to Ragi and Vifil and the others. He nodded to each in turn and each nodded back. Then he walked quickly over to the wall and scaled the ladder that led to the top. He stood on that section above the gate where there was no palisade so he could see the country out beyond the walls.

He could see Halfdan's camp, the various tendrils of smoke from a dozen small fires, the white dots of the tents. He thought he saw men standing in a line as if ready for battle, but he could not be certain. It was what he would expect to see. Halfdan was no dim-wit. He would guess what the men in the compound were planning and prepare for it.

Odd turned and looked down at the armed men on the ground behind him. "Something's going on, I don't know what," he said as loudly as he dared. "Stand ready, but don't move until you have my signal." The men nodded their understanding and Odd turned back toward the enemy outside.

The riders were still far off, half a mile at least, but Odd was certain it was Halfdan and his guard. A small cloud of dust trailed after them as they approached over the dry, trampled earth. Whether or not they had little Hallbera with them he could not tell from that distance. It did not matter.

Without a word, without looking back, Odd stepped around the edge of the palisade and stood on top of the earthen wall that sloped at a near vertical pitch down to the ground. He unbuckled his sword belt and set Blood-letter and his seax down on the wall's flat top, then half climbed, half slid down the slope. He heard the sentry on the wall above say, "Master Odd?" but he did not reply.

His feet hit the ground and he pushed off the wall and began walking quickly toward the riders who were closing the distance. He heard the sentry call, "Master Odd?" once more, a bit louder, a bit more emphatic, but the man had no way of knowing whether or not this was part of the plan. Odd picked up the pace. He and Halfdan were quickly converging.

Behind him he heard more sounds of confusion, words passed back and forth, but he could not hear what was said. He was a few hundred feet from the gate already, and by the time Amundi and the others figured out what was happening he would have already given himself up to Halfdan.

And that was how it had to be. There would be no surprise attack, no desperate battle. Odd would not allow anyone, save for himself, to die because of his mistake.

Chapter Fourteen

Night was in place,
the Norns there came,
to the highborn they
destiny pronounced.

The Poetic Edda

Thorgrim Night Wolf kicked his son Harald awake. It was something he had done countless times before, but this time he kicked him harder than was necessary. Quite a bit harder.

Even as his foot was in motion he knew he was going to kick the boy harder than need be. On one level he felt bad about it, though he seemed unable to stop himself. On another level he wished he had kicked him harder still.

Harald was sleeping half curled on his side, mouth open, long blond hair in the sand. It was a warm night and Harald had no fur or blanket over him and Thorgrim suspected he had not so much gone to sleep as passed out. The top of Thorgrim's soft shoe connected with Harald's gut and Harald's eyes shot open and his mouth opened wider and he doubled up more around Thorgrim's foot. Thorgrim watched the rapid change of expressions on Harald's face: surprise to confusion, to understanding that someone had kicked him, then anger and then, looking up and seeing who it was, a sheepish confusion once again.

"Daylight," Thorgrim said. "Get up."

Harald nodded and pushed himself to a sitting position and then up to his feet, a move that was made harder by the soft sand and Harald's general unsteadiness just then. It was daylight only in a manner of speaking; the sun was just approaching the distant horizon, the sky illuminated with soft, pre-dawn light. Light enough to see anything that was not too far away. Light enough for a man lying nearby to see Harald stand and shout in a weak voice, "Harald Whale-rider!" and Harald to give a weak smile in return.

It was perhaps the worst exchange that might take place in Thorgrim's presence at that particular moment. He felt his anger flare red hot once again, and he grabbed Harald by the shoulder of his tunic and half dragged him down the beach, toward the water where they would be out of earshot. He could feel Harald stumbling as he tried to keep up but he did not look at the boy. He could hear Harald's weak, mumbled protests and the confused sounds he made.

They arrived near the water's edge and Thorgrim let go of Harald and turned and faced him. In all that had happened, the arrival at the beach, the butchering of the whale, the feast that followed, the celebration of Harald Whale-rider's feat, Thorgrim had had no chance to speak to the boy, to express his considerable displeasure. But now he intended to do just that.

Harald in turn straightened and smoothed out his tunic and tried to look as if he had some understanding of what was going on, some sense of how to react. He opened his mouth to speak but Thorgrim did not give him the chance.

"You're a great hero now, it seems," Thorgrim said.

Harald stood for a moment, mouth open, clearly unsure how to react, what answer he should give. "It seems that way," he said at last. "At least…the others seem to think it."

"Do you think you're a hero?" Thorgrim asked.

Harald's brows went together. "I…I don't know…" he stammered and then his confidence seemed to fill in like a sea breeze. "No one had ever heard of anyone doing such a thing as I did with the whale," he said. "Maybe not heroic, but it was something."

"Something…" Thorgrim said, his voice trailing off. "Did I not tell you when we sailed to keep your place with the fleet?"

"Well…yes…" Harald admitted. "But that was before we saw the whale."

"And before we saw Bergthor Skeggjason's ships. Which we were not ready to meet, thanks to you and your foolishness."

"Bergthor's no threat to us. He meant us no harm," Harald protested and Thorgrim wanted to smack him, one of the few times in his life he had felt that way. He had actually done so on a few occasions, when Harald was younger. A good swat on the backside.

It had been good for the boy. He wondered if it would do any good now.

"We didn't know that," Thorgrim said, trying to remain calm. "We didn't know it was Bergthor Skeggjason at all. It might have been someone wanting a fight, and here you were off playing with some fish, and not there to help if we needed you."

Harald stood a little straighter still. "Are you calling me a coward, father?" he asked.

By the gods, does this boy understand nothing? Thorgrim thought.

"No, I'm not saying you're a coward. I'm saying you're foolish. That you acted foolishly. By leaving the rest of us and going off to play your little game you made the whole fleet weaker. And you divided us, so we would have been in a bad place if it had come to a fight. You couldn't have helped us. We couldn't have helped you."

Harald might have acted like a fool, but Thorgrim knew the boy was not stupid. He expected Harald to understand what he was saying, to feel chastened as he realized his mistake. But looking into Harald's face he did not see a humbled, chastened young man. He saw defiance. And arrogance.

"The others don't agree," Harald said. "The others don't think it was foolish, they think it was a fine thing I did."

"The others are not responsible for all these ships and men. I am," Thorgrim explained. "And don't be so sure you're a great hero. The men who pull the oars might think you're some sea god, but the men who hold the tillers don't. I don't think you'll find that Godi or Halldor or Asmund or any of the other ship masters think you did such a great thing."

"Then maybe they should eat dried fish, and not join in with us, feasting on the whale meat I provided," Harald said. Thorgrim frowned, squinted at the boy, hardly believing he had just heard what he had heard. He wondered when and how the boy had come to be so arrogant.

"I can see that you're not understanding why…" Thorgrim began but Harald cut him off.

"Or maybe it's just you who aren't happy about this," he said. "Maybe you can't stand anyone else being the hero. None but Thorgrim Night Wolf gets to show his cleverness or his courage."

Thorgrim shook his head. That was it. Harald had gone over the cliff with that accusation. "You're done as master of *Dragon*," he said. "Herjolf will have command. You're done."

For an instant the arrogance was gone from Harald's face and Thorgrim saw the little boy that Harald had once been. But it was only a flash, and then there was anger and defiance in its place.

"I'm…you're taking my ship from me? Because I killed a whale?"

"Bergthor killed the whale, not you," Thorgrim said. "And that's not why I'm taking the ship, not because you acted like a fool. I'm taking it because you don't seem to have learned from the stupid thing you did. And until you can admit mistakes and learn from them then you have no place as master of a ship. Or a leader of men."

Harald glared at him. "The others…" he began, then stopped.

""The others' what?" Thorgrim asked. He knew what Harald intended to say, and he wanted to see if the boy was so far gone in his arrogance that he would dare to say it. But Harald held his tongue, so Thorgrim said it for him.

"The others won't stand for you being treated this way? For me taking your ship? What will they do? Who among them will dare question me?"

The sun lifted above the horizon and the early morning light fell on Thorgrim and Harald and it did not soften the look of fury on Harald's face, not in the least. For a long moment he continued to glare at Thorgrim and Thorgrim held his glare and waited for Harald to speak. He could see the conflicting desires tugging and pulling at Harald's mind: the desire to lash out at his father wrestling with the desire to not further anger the man who controlled so much of his fate. The conflict of being a man, his own man, while also and inextricably being the son of Thorgrim Night Wolf.

Finally, without a word, Harald turned and marched off up the beach, his heavy footsteps silent in the sand, and Thorgrim let him go.

That was the right thing, Thorgrim thought. *It was the right thing, what I did.* He had no real doubt about it. But it was not easy, and he knew there would be more trouble to come.

He turned away from Harald's retreating figure. He turned to the east, to stare off down the beach, into the distance, because staring off into the distance helped him think. But now he found himself staring at the carcass of a whale, fifty feet away. The tail end of its long, black body was still in the water, its square head resting on the beach. A swarm of gulls circled and screeched and pulled at the tendrils of meat. They seemed to be fighting over the remains despite the fact that there was more there than a thousand gulls could eat.

Just aft of the head, great swaths of the whale's flesh had been cut away, revealing a thick layer of greyish white blubber, and under that the pink and red meat. From the look of it, the men had taken quite a bit from the beast, and there was still quite a lot left. Thorgrim could detect only a faint odor from the massive fish, but he knew it would not be long before the stench would be unbearable.

His mind moved on from the whale. He thought of Harald and the exchange they had just had. And that brought him around to those thoughts that were most central to him these days. He was closer now, closer to Agder, to his farm, than he had been in nearly three years, and he was moving even closer all the time.

The gods had let him leave Ireland, at least. They had allowed him to make some progress along the south coast of Engla-land. How far he was from that stretch of water that separated Engla-land from Frankia and Frisia he did not know. Not too far, he imagined, not more than a few days' sail with a fair wind behind him. He did not believe that the southern coast of Engla-land was any longer than the distance from, say, East Agder to Hedeby, a voyage he knew well.

Agder. Vik. His farm. To return to that place and remain until death finally came for him. He had longed for his home since that first winter in Dubh-linn. But now the longing was more acute, far more. His conflict with Harald, his aching body, the turmoil in his mind, it seemed to him it would all be cured by returning to his home.

He smiled to himself. *Your home is a fantasy to you*, he thought. *In your mind it's become like some magic place dreamed up by a child.*

Agder was not free of troubles, he knew that. And just yesterday Bergthor had reminded him of that fact.

The gods had dropped Bergthor right in front of him to goad him with news of his home. Thorgrim had probed the man for any word he could get, any half-remembered news of Agder. And Bergthor had obliged him, telling him what he knew of the neighbors, the freemen and their success or failures, births, deaths, marriages.

He told Thorgrim of how Halfdan had expanded his great hall and the walls of his compound, made them higher and greater in circumference. He told of Halfdan's ever increasing greed for land and for expanding his kingdom, for putting more and more people who could pay taxes and tribute under his rule. Halfdan was ambitious, and growing more so, and Thorgrim and Bergthor both agreed that no good would come of that.

And from where he stood, on some empty beach on Engla-land's south coast, Thorgrim could only hope that Odd had the good sense to stay clear of those troubles. Odd was a smart one. Smarter than Harald, Thorgrim guessed. Smarter than himself, probably: the boy's intelligence came down from his mother. But being smart did not always mean making the right choices. Sometimes a man was driven by something more primitive than his brain.

He sighed a loud sigh because there was no one there to hear him. He headed back up the beach toward where the others lay spread out over the sand like wrack tossed there by a storm. The men were just starting to move, to roll out of whatever covers they had, or to push themselves up off the sand where they had fallen. The more ambitious among them were stoking up the fires to cook the morning whale.

He reached the place where he and Failend had made their bed the night before. Failend was sitting cross legged on top of the bear skin that had served as a blanket. She was wearing leggings and a tunic and was running a comb through her long, dark hair.

Thorgrim stopped a few feet away and let his eyes rest on her. He and his men had become so accustomed to her that she attracted no more notice than any of the others, but being in the company of Bergthor's men had reminded Thorgrim of how unusual she was. To see a woman dressed in men's clothes was odd enough; to see one carrying weapons was odder still.

And for all her manly attire, Failend was a great beauty: petite and shapely, with fine features and a gorgeous fall of black hair. Thorgrim had seen the appreciative looks on the men's faces as she walked by. He imagined there had been considerable discussion of her status and circumstance. He wondered if any of Bergthor's men would be bold enough or eager enough to try and win her favors.

She looked up at him and smiled and he smiled back. "Good morning," he said.

"Good morning," Failend answered. Her speech, like everything else about her, was quite unique. She and Louis de Roumois had picked up the Norse tongue quickly, she quicker than Louis because she wanted to learn it, whereas Louis simply felt he had no choice. And just as Louis spoke the language with a Frankish accent, which was ugly to Thorgrim's ear, Failend spoke with the accent of her native Ireland which, to Thorgrim, was not ugly at all. It might have been more the soft, melodic quality of Failend's voice, rather than the accent, but he did not find her speech unpleasing in the least.

"Did you sleep well?" Thorgrim asked. In the past, when they made love, which was often, they had both slept soundly, but that had not been the case for some time.

"I did sleep well," she said. "Whale meat agrees with me."

"We were at sea nearly the whole day yesterday," Thorgrim said, "and I never saw you throw up once. You're becoming quite the seafarer."

Failend smiled, her lovely, full-tooth smile. "Hardly," she said. "If the seas had been an inch bigger I would have been face down over the side." She seemed in a good humor that morning, and that made Thorgrim happy and eased the trouble in his mind a bit.

She looked off to the west, still running the comb slowly through her hair, then looked up at Thorgrim again. "I saw Harald go by. For a great hero he didn't seem too happy."

"He wasn't very happy," Thorgrim said. "I didn't treat him like the hero he thinks he is."

"Why not?"

"If folk think a man's a hero, then the worst thing he can do is start believing it himself," Thorgrim said.

"And you told Harald he was no hero?"

"I did."

"And did he believe you?"

"No," Thorgrim said. "And that worries me."

A familiar smell came playing around Thorgrim's nose, the smell of roasting whale, and he realized that he was hungry. He looked down at Failend. "Looks like it's whale again. Can I fetch you some?"

"Thank you," Failend said as she stood easily from her cross-legged position. "But I will get some for you, and some ale as well." She tucked her comb into a small leather bag that hung from her belt, snatched up two wooden plates and two cups and headed off toward where the cooking fires were burning. Thorgrim watched her walk away.

She's in good humor, he thought. He had seen her moods change from cheerful to melancholy to angry and back again. He knew there must be a great tangle of thoughts and feelings churning around in her head, but he could not fathom what they might be.

Soon she was back with food and drink. They sat side by side on a driftwood log and ate, while the men of the two fleets, a formidable army of more than five hundred warriors, woke, stretched, urinated, scratched, ate and drank as they started their day.

They were nearly finished when Bergthor approached, smiling as he seemed always to be. "Thorgrim, good morning! Good morning, Failend!" Thorgrim looked up, but Bergthor's eyes were lingering on Failend, not him.

"Good morning, Bergthor," Thorgrim said and Bergthor turned his gaze quickly, with something of a guilty look on his face.

Been some time since you've been with a woman, is it? Thorgrim thought.

"Thorgrim, much as I'd like to spend my life on this beach drinking mead and eating whale, I guess we'd better do something more worthwhile. I was hoping we could have a gathering of all the ship masters this morning, figure what comes next."

Thorgrim nodded. Bergthor seemed to believe that they had joined up now, their two fleets, but he was getting a little ahead of himself.

"That would be fine," Thorgrim said.

Bergthor had his men arrange driftwood logs in a circle big enough for them all to sit, and when they were done all the ships' masters were asked to come together. Thorgrim did not invite Harald because Harald was not the master of a ship anymore. And he did not invite Herjolf because, despite what he said, he was not sure that Herjolf had it in him to command a ship, nor did he care what Herjolf had to say. But that could all be straightened out later.

Starri Deathless was there, of course, but Bergthor did not question that. Bergthor, too, had one man extra — a fellow who did not look like the master of a ship, or even a Northman, but Thorgrim did not ask.

"Very well," Bergthor began in a faltering way. "We should…that is, I think…perhaps we should talk about what's next."

Thorgrim smiled, just a bit. Back in Agder, Thorgrim, son of Ulf of the Battle Song, son-in-law of Ornolf the Restless, was a well-known, prosperous and important man. Far more so than Bergthor

Skeggjason, who was liked and respected, but held no position of importance. Even without considering his bloodline, Thorgrim had a reputation as a warrior that was second to none, and great wealth besides. The relative status that the two men enjoyed back home had been transferred to this beach in the south of Engla-land, it seemed, and Bergthor was loath to take command with Thorgrim there.

"I think we better do that, Bergthor," Thorgrim said. "I can tell you, for us, what our plans were when we met up with you. We were sailing home. We were making for Norway, nothing more. Done with raiding." Thorgrim had explained all this to Bergthor earlier, but he repeated it now for the other ships' masters. And for his own men, in case they had lost sight of his intentions.

"I've been years away from home," Thorgrim continued, "as have many of those with me. Time to return."

"Well, it's the opposite with us!" Bergthor said with enthusiasm. "We're not done plundering these English bastards! We've hardly started. This fellow here," he continued, pointing to the odd man in his party, "this fellow is named Geldwine, he's the one I told you about. A Briton, speaks our language, has no love of the Saxons. He's a fisherman hereabouts. Knows these waters, and the towns, too. Geldwine, tell Thorgrim and the rest where we're going."

Geldwine nodded, though he did not seem like a very talkative sort. "Just to the west of here," he said, "there's a great bay. Looks more like a river but it's not, though several rivers run into it. At the head of the bay is a village called Hamtun. A church and an abbey there. Big ones, rich ones. But the real wealth's to the north, a place called Winchester. It's there the king lives."

Heads nodded, Bergthor's men and Thorgrim's. "This Winchester," Godi said. "We can get there in our ships?"

Geldwine shook his head. "Winchester's about thirty miles from Hamtun, but there's a good road, a road built by the ancient people. A day or two's march, if you march hard. Might even find some horses about."

"A king's court, it could be well defended," Bergthor said. He glanced around at the men who sailed under him. "But we're willing to give it a try. Hit them fast and hard, be gone before any of the other men-at-arms are summoned from the country around. It could be risky, of course. But now…" He let the words hang in the air.

Now you've doubled your number of fighting men, Thorgrim thought. And if this Winchester was as rich as Geldwine suggested there would still be plunder enough to satisfy them all.

He looked around at his own men. They were paying attention, sitting upright, eyes on Bergthor, listening. Some were still nodding. Starri was trying to contain his excitement.

Thorgrim had assumed that, like himself, they all wanted to get back to Norway, back to their homes, though he had never actually spoken to any of them about it. Louis certainly made no secret that his only desire was to get back to Frankia, not that Thorgrim cared what Louis wanted. As to the others, Thorgrim realized he had no idea how they felt.

How many here have been with me since we sailed from Agder? he wondered. Not many. Vali and Armod. Harald, of course. A handful of others. Even Godi and Starri Deathless had only joined with him after he had been some time in Ireland.

It did not matter. He was going home. He was done with raiding. He would take *Sea Hammer* and *Blood Hawk* and sail for home with any who wished to join him. Any who did not could have the other four ships and do with them what they wished. But he was done.

Starri spoke next. "The gods must wish it, that we come with you," he said, looking at Bergthor. "They put you right in our path, and sent Harald after the whale so we would meet up."

Bergthor nodded, though it was clear he did not know what to make of Starri.

Thorgrim felt a wave of misery wash over him. Bergthor had saved Harald's life. Certainly any man there would have done the same, but that did not change the fact that Bergthor had indeed saved the life of Thorgrim's son. What did he owe a man who did such a thing?

His thoughts moved on to Harald, sulking somewhere down the beach. What had he just said to the boy? *You made the whole fleet weaker by leaving. You divided us, and we would have been in a bad place if it had come to a fight.*

And now he, Thorgrim, was planning on doing the exact same thing.

"I won't decide for everyone," Thorgrim said at last. "We'll meet on it. Me and the masters of my ships. Together we'll decide whether or not to join you in your raiding."

Chapter Fifteen

In the same year [Æthelwulf] went to Rome with much honor and taking with him his son, the aforesaid King Alfred, a second time on the same journey...

Asser's Life of King Alfred

Felix listened to the messenger's report, the Northmen landing on the beach at Portsmouth with a dead whale. He took a moment or two to ponder the situation. It was a complication he did not want or need just then.

Like a street performer on a tight rope, Felix was trying to maintain his careful balance between Æthelwulf and his real master, King Charles the Bald. This had all been set up so carefully: the pilgrimage, the royal visit to West Frankia, the audience with the pope. And now the damned heathens had come blundering right into the middle of it.

For that reason, Felix's first impulse was to just let the heathens be, ignore them while they rampaged around the country, knowing that God in his own time would take them all to Hell. He considered keeping word of their arrival to himself. But of course Alfred had heard it too, and if Felix was going to tell Alfred to keep quiet he would have to give him a very good reason why he should.

"The heathens..." Alfred said. "The messenger says they're at Portesmutha. If we leave from Hamtun as we've planned we'll have to sail right past them."

"You're right," Felix said, impressed, if not surprised, by Alfred's grasp of the geography of the area. He had thought of that himself — they could not leave from Hamtun now without sailing right into the heathens' murderous arms.

"In truth I think we'll meet them before that," Felix continued. "Northmen come for plunder, and there's nothing worth stealing at Portesmutha. Some fishermen's huts, that's it. No, they'll come to Hamtun if they know what they're about. Plunder Netley Abbey and the church there."

And that settled it. There would be no hiding the presence of the Northmen.

When at last Æthelwulf was finished with his private mass, Felix informed him of this new threat that had come to the shores of Wessex. And Æthelwulf reacted exactly as Felix knew he would.

"Heathens? Damned heathens? Vermin! We must stamp them out like vermin!" Æthelwulf all but shouted. He was not a young man, but he was not feeling the ravages of age as some did. He could be forgetful, and sometimes not entirely clear on the circumstances, but the prospect of the pilgrimage, the royal visit with Charles the Bald, the papal audience, all seemed to have had a wonderful effect on him, mind and body. His energy was that of a man twenty years younger, which was a welcome thing. Or mostly a welcome thing, though not always.

"Felix, see the men-at-arms are turned out, and let word be sent to raise the fyrd. No delay, we must crush these whore's sons before they do too much damage."

"Sire, we should tell the nobles and the ealdormen. Of course you are eager to be at the heathens, but it would be best if the other men of import were at least made aware of your plans." Æthelwulf, in his enthusiasm, was ready to plunge into battle alone, without even knowing how many of the heathens there were, or where exactly they had come ashore.

Word had already spread throughout the court by the time the nobles and ealdormen were summoned to the great hall, a magnificent building of stone walls and a high, vaulted ceiling supported by intricately carved beams. Benches and tables filled much of the space, and at the far end, the dais on which Æthelwulf's massive marble throne was perched. Those in attendance filled the benches, each jostling as forcefully as he dared to be as close to the dais as he could, though they mostly sorted themselves out by wealth and stature. Sunlight streamed in through the high, narrow windows and fell at regular intervals in great squares across the hall, illuminating the rich cloth and silver jewelry of the eager seated men.

So much arrogance, Felix thought, looking out over the important men of Wessex from where he stood at Æthelwulf's right hand. *How does it all fit into this building?*

But, he had to admit, if the Northmen were going to land in Wessex, they had picked an advantageous time and place, at least as far as Wessex was concerned. All of these men crowding the hall had come to see Æthelwulf off on his pilgrimage, or to accompany him, and they had brought their house guards with them, their elite warriors, so that they could each make a great show of their power and wealth. As a result there was quite a number of skilled and experienced men-at-arms at Winchester just then, and even better, they were not in Æthelwulf's pay.

"You've all heard by now," Æthelwulf said from the dais, then paused and waited as the men in the hall reluctantly stopped talking. "Heathens have landed in Portesmutha, and they'll be intent on sacking Hamtun I'll warrant. The abbey there and the church and whatever else they can get their damned hands on. Felix, how many are there?"

"It was not clear, sire," he said. "But there were eleven or twelve ships. Five hundred men, perhaps?"

Æthelwulf waved his hand dismissively. "I fought those bastards three years ago, and there was three times that number!" he said. It was a battle that every man in that room had heard of, in some detail, and in which many had fought. The kingdoms of Wessex or Kent or Mercia were not always successful in keeping the heathen host at bay, let alone defeating them. But Æthelwulf had done so, and quite decisively, an impressive victory against a large heathen army.

"A lot of you here, you fought with me then. Egbert, you were there. And Leofric. Do you recall?"

"Yes, sire," Egbert called, pleased to have been singled out.

"I recall, sire," Leofric called. "Many of us were there. Alhmund was there, as were Byrnhorn and Ingwald. And Lord Nothwulf, ealdorman at Dorsetshire."

"Of course, of course," Æthelwulf said, nodding and smiling at the memory. "Wait," he said, "Nothwulf? Nothwulf, were you there?"

"No, sire," Nothwulf called, trying not to sound as pathetic as Felix knew he must feel.

"Right," Æthelwulf said. "It was your brother, Merewald, wasn't it?"

"Yes, sire," Nothwulf called and Felix, despite have no particular love of Nothwulf, almost winced with sympathy. That was no mistake on Leofric's part, he was sure, and he wondered what had happened between the two men that Leofric should want to humiliate his ealdorman so. But Leofric was a wealthy man, and a powerful man who had fought beside the king, and that gave him considerable influence in court.

"Sire, we had best get back to our discussion of the Northmen in Portesmutha," Felix prompted.

"Of course," Æthelwulf said. "Leofric, you just fought a fleet of these bastards, down at Christchurch, did you not?"

"Yes, sire," Leofric said. Felix knew for a fact that Nothwulf had also been part of that fight, and he wondered if Leofric would be so egregious as to leave him out, but he added, "And Nothwulf was there as well."

"Do you think these are the same heathens?"

"I don't know, sire. There were seven ships that we fought. We burned one of them. There's eleven or twelve ships now. Perhaps they've joined up with some others."

"Perhaps," Æthelwulf said. "Anyway, it doesn't matter. I've sent orders for the fyrd to be raised, and I would think any man within five miles at least should be here in time to join us. Twenty if he has a horse. When will you and your men be ready to march?"

"An hour, sire!" a man called from the back of the hall and the rest called out their concurrence. Just as they had fought to be nearest to the dais, they would fight to be first in readying themselves for battle.

Because this was an opportunity not to be wasted. The heathens, whom Æthelwulf hated more than sin itself, had landed and were now stopping him from proceeding on a holy pilgrimage. Here was an opportunity for each man to ride into battle at his king's side, where the chances for glory were great, as was the chance that one of his neighbors would be killed, thus making his lands available to be given by the king as a gift of appreciation.

"An hour, then," Æthelwulf said. "Then we'll form our men in the courtyard and march off to battle! Felix, see that the arrangements are made!"

Felix, see that the arrangements are made, Felix thought. Six or seven hundred men marching off to battle, a battle they could not reach in one day, or maybe even two. They would need food and drink, tents, spare horses, wagons.... Even with all the servants swarming over the royal court it would be nearly impossible to get that arranged in an hour's time.

Or would have been, had God not given his servant Felix a blessing for once and arranged to have a train of wagons already waiting and loaded with everything they would need for the march. Rough, simple food and drink for the fyrd were even now stacked on the carts, along with something better for the men-at-arms, and the finest for the king and his court. Tents for the warriors, pavilions for the nobility, equipped with furniture for campaigning in the field that was finer than anything that most anyone in Wessex would ever own.

Yes, he was ready.

It took two hours, not one, for the men-at-arms and those who commanded them to assemble in the courtyard, but that was still less time than Felix had thought they would take, and they all still had to wait for Æthelwulf and his closest advisors, the bishop among them, to emerge.

They made an impressive column as they rode out of Winchester, all the men in their best armor and helmets. Anyone of any importance was on horseback, the rest on foot. Poles with bright banners streaming from their peaks rose up above the line of men to signify whose warriors were whose.

Æthelwulf, of course, was at the head of the column, his horse a lovely black stallion, its armor, like the king's, polished to a brilliant shine. Both horse and king wore elaborate helmets. Æthelwulf's was adorned with gold filigree and a bright burst of plume on the crest. A smile cracked his gray beard. Æthelwulf was clearly enjoying this. It was, Felix imagined, was as close to reclaiming his youth as the old man was likely to get.

They rode south through what was left of the day, which was not much, until they came to some fields where the grass had been grazed short, and made camp there. They had been careful to not outmarch the train of wagons, which meant that they did not have to wait on their tents and food and drink to catch up, but it also meant that they did not cover much distance at all.

The evening turned into yet another banquet, another in the long series of feasts they had been enjoying at Winchester since gathering to see the king off. But this time the celebrations were sharpened by the esprit de corps that comes from being fellow soldiers in the field, free of the censure and moderating influence of their wives.

And as the men-at-arms and the nobles and the court enjoyed their bacchanal, more and more of the fyrd, those citizens called up for duty as soldiers, arrived in camp, swelling the ranks of the Wessex men.

The next day nearly all the daylight hours were taken up with the march. The army, crawling at the pace of the heavy-laden carts, managed to covered a full fifteen miles toward Hamtun. Once again camp was made and food and drink served out, but this time the men, tired and saddle-sore from the march, feasted with considerably less enthusiasm. It was not long after the sun had set that every man was asleep, save for the sentries, the servants, and those of the fyrd who continued to find their way into camp.

Felix woke before dawn on the third day. His eyes opened and he stared out into the blackness of his tent, fully awake and cognizant of where he was, what he had to do. He tossed his blankets aside, swung his feet off his traveling bed, stood and stepped outside. A small table was set up there with a bowl for washing, and Felix's servant was busying himself getting his sword and mail ready.

The morning was cool and still, with the undercurrent of noise that comes from so many men sleeping or moving softly about in so small a space. Felix washed his face and ran water through his hair. He allowed his servant to ease his padded tunic over his head, and his mail shirt on top of that, and finally to belt his sword around his waist.

Felix was no warrior and he knew it. Certainly he had fought in enough battles, had killed, wounded and been wounded often enough that no one could ever accuse him of shunning the more brutal aspects of power. He did not lack in physical courage, but swords and spears and mail were not the sort of weapons that most appealed to him.

Politics, intrigue, statecraft, those were the fields of battle where he felt most comfortable, most in command. But sometimes the field of combat could not be avoided. No amount of diplomacy was likely to make the heathens go away. And, that being the case, there was nothing much that Felix could do but shuffle into his mail and ride off with the rest.

Once he was properly dressed and fitted out he walked the fifty feet to where Æthelwulf's pavilion stood, ringed by the smaller tents of the nobles, which themselves were ringed with guards standing semi-erect, spears in their hands. The sun was still below the horizon but the light had spread enough that the guards could see Felix clearly. They stepped aside without a word as he made his way toward the royal tent.

He paused just outside. He could hear movement within, men shuffling around and occasionally a gruff but indecipherable word from Æthelwulf himself. Felix knew the king's habits well, and he knew it was still a few minutes too early for him to disturb Æthelwulf's morning.

He waited patiently, silently, and listened to Æthelwulf's servants get their lord prepared for the day, and when one of them stepped through the flap that served as a door to the pavilion Felix said, "Is the king ready to receive?"

The servant nodded, though he looked unsure. "Reckon so, lord," he offered. Felix nodded and ducked through the door and into the king's tent.

It was well lit, with candles standing in tall iron candleholders placed liberally around the space. Æthelwulf was in the center of a cluster of servants fussing over him. They looked to Felix like a pack of hounds that had run a bear to ground and now were doing their best to bring it down. Finally Æthelwulf had enough, and with a wave of his hand sent the men scurrying away.

"Ah, Felix, there you are!" Æthelwulf said. "We must get the men fed, quick as can be, then we march."

"Yes, sire," Felix said. "And you'll be pleased to know that another sixty-three men of the fyrd arrived in the night. Our army is more than seven hundred strong now, by my figuring."

"Excellent, excellent," Æthelwulf said.

"And sire?" Felix continued, getting to the real purpose of this visit. "We have but a dozen miles or so to Hamtun, but that could take us the bulk of the day with the wagons. Might I suggest we leave the wagons behind to catch up to us as they will, and make for

Hamtun as quick as we can? Before the heathens arrive and do whatever wicked thing they might do?"

Felix was not one to be taken by surprise, so he had been making arrangements with the captain of Æthelwulf's house guard. They had sent regular patrols south to the coast to keep an eye on what the heathens were up to. He knew for certain that as of yesterday they had not arrived in Hamtun, in fact had not yet left the beach on which they had first landed. The whale, however, was starting to get a bit ripe, and the patrols suggested that the beach would not be habitable for much longer.

There were any number of directions in which the heathens might go when they did finally leave the beach, but Hamtun, the closest place where they might find churches and monasteries filled with plunder, was a good bet. Heathens seemed to have a nose for those things.

It was possible, too, that they would not be satisfied with Hamtun alone. The largest concentration of wealth in the kingdom of Wessex, one of the largest such concentrations in all of England, would be at the royal court at Winchester. If the heathens knew that, they might find an attack on Winchester irresistible.

Felix did not think Æthelwulf would argue with his suggestion of a quick march, and he was right. The king sent his servants to summon the nobles, the ealdormen and the thegns. Once they were assembled outside his pavilion he gave orders for the men to make ready to move, the men-at-arms and the fyrd alone. They would leave it to the servants to break camp and follow. They would get to Hamtun as soon as they could and turn their attention to killing their enemies.

This announcement had a wonderful rejuvenating effect on men who were heartily sick of traveling at the speed of oxen. They scattered and summoned their men and called for their horses and soon the column was riding south out of the camp, leaving tents, servants and wagons behind. Some of the men-at-arms, and some of the fyrd, were still eating their breakfast as they marched.

They made their way south over the old Roman road and they made good time of it. Felix rode near the head of the column, just a little behind King Æthelwulf and his retinue. They rode in silence. There was nothing for them to discuss, not yet.

The tall spire of the church at Hamtun came into view first, and Felix knew they had only a few more miles to ride, which was good since his legs and posterior were no longer accustomed to long hours in the saddle.

Felix knew Hamtun well. He traveled there often, it being the closest port to Winchester. The church he was looking at now was a wooden affair, impressive in its massive timber frame and commanding spire. But it was not as impressive as the cathedral at Winchester, which, along with Æthelwulf's hall, was a rare, stone-built structure.

No smoke, Felix thought as he rode. There were no great columns of black smoke roiling up from the unseen town, and that was good, because it probably meant that the Northmen had not yet arrived. And there were no thin columns of smoke, either, at least not many, which meant that most of the folk there had probably run off for what they hoped would be safety. And that was good, too. It was one less thing to worry about, and meant there would be more food to feed Æthelwulf's army.

The first of the houses soon came into sight, the thatched, board-sided cottages that were scattered around the edges of the town and grew more numerous as they rode toward the water. Felix looked off to his left, across the river that formed Hamtun's eastern boundary. On the other side stood the decaying walls of a Roman fort, and behind the walls he could see the upper edge of another building he knew to be a Roman bath.

The men who had built the road they traveled on had built that as well, and Felix imagined that it, like the road, had been a marvel to behold in its day. It still was. He had spent nearly a full day there once, exploring what was left of that vestige of Rome. To the Romans, he suspected, it was no great thing. To him it was extraordinary. Even the Franks, whose towering stone cathedrals and palaces far outstripped those of the English, could not hope to do what the Romans had done.

And then they had abandoned it all.

Felix shook his head in wonder.

They approached the town itself and the Roman road under them seemed to fade away into dry and trampled dirt, making a wide swath between the clusters of houses. Here and there anxious faces peered out at the strange and marvelous parade passing by, but not so many as Felix would have expected, which reinforced his idea that the folk here had heard of the Northmen coming and had mostly fled.

He looked off to his right, toward the church that dominated the town. A low wall encircled the building and the cemetery that sprawled out from its east side. He could see no movement on the church grounds. He could picture the priests and the laymen loading the gold and silver chalices and reliquaries and candle sticks and crucifixes and communion service into carts and hauling them away at the first word of heathens in the neighborhood.

If the Northmen find nothing here, they'll certainly come to Winchester looking for it, Felix thought.

They arrived at last at the water's edge. Hamtun was situated at the north-west end of a stretch of water that looked more like a wide river than a bay, though it was not. Æthelwulf raised his hand and he and the rest stopped, since there was nowhere left to go. The king swung himself off his horse, and that was taken as a signal that the rest should do so as well, which they did.

Felix handed the reins of his horse to his servant, who had been following behind, and then walked stiffly up to where the king was standing. A press of men circled around Æthelwulf, hoping to be consulted, or at least noticed, and Felix had no chance of getting through them.

Nor did he want to. He had no interest in the opinions of that vainglorious mob, each man hoping to say something clever enough to get the king's attention. He knew that when Æthelwulf wanted his advice he would seek it out, so he turned his eyes toward the water.

Hamtun was a busy port. Trade to and from Frankia and Frisia and the Danes and the other North countries flowed though there. Several storehouses, much larger than the cottages of the town folk, nearly as big as the nave of the church, stood near the bank. Half a dozen long, sturdy wooden docks thrust out into the water. Eight or nine merchant ships lay tied to the dock, taking on or discharging cargo, and more were anchored just off the shore.

Now, along with those few merchant vessels, there were a dozen more ships of various sizes, each well-found, impressive and powerful looking. Felix knew them all. They were the fleet that he had helped assemble to carry Æthelwulf and the others across the water to the palace of Charles the Bald. Their size and number were calculated to impress Charles and to discourage anyone, Northmen in particular, from attacking them while they were underway. Felix felt sure they would do both.

He stared out over the bay, off to the south as far as he could see. No Northmen yet, but they would come, he was sure of it. There was nothing he and the rest of Æthelwulf's army could do but wait. Make ready and wait.

That notion did not sit so well with him. He felt a sort of disquiet in his gut. Then another idea flickered, half-formed, in his mind. He was just considering whether it was a decent enough notion to bring up when he heard someone near Æthelwulf speaking, loud and clear enough to hear. It was Leofric.

"Sire, I had a thought. If the Northmen come in their ships they can land here, and down there," he said, pointing to a place a hundred yards south of where they stood, "and there, and there," he added, pointing to various spots on the shore. "They can land wherever they wish and it will be hard for us to guess where that will be and be ready for them."

"Yes?" Æthelwulf said. "What of it?"

"Perhaps we should not let them land at all," Leofric said. "We have ships here, the ones meant to take you on your holy pilgrimage. Perhaps this is God's providence. Let us take to the ships and fight them on the water, where they will never expect us."

Yes, Felix thought. It was exactly the idea that had just occurred to him.

Chapter Sixteen

The sword shall
in sheath rest,
if one his brothers bane
he find tied up.

The Poetic Edda

It had always been Amundi Thorsteinsson's habit to be up well before *rismál*, the time of rising, when the sun was just showing itself. It was a habit instilled in him by a demanding father, and he had adhered to it all his life, and had instilled it in his own children. But he did not seem capable of rising at that hour anymore, not since his return from Grømstad. Not since his surrender.

The household was awake and already at work on the morning chores. He could hear them through the thin wall of his bed closet. He could hear the servants putting away the blankets and such, could hear them stoking up the fires. He could hear the soft clink of iron on iron as they set up a tripod and hung a heavy pot over the flames, filled, no doubt, with porridge of some sort. He could hear the muted sound of a barrel rolling over the packed dirt floor, the grunts of the men rolling it.

He was alone in the bed closet. His wife, Alfdis, had been awake for some time already. At least he guessed that she had been. She usually was. He had not heard or seen her rise. There was just an empty place beside him in the bed, an indent where her small body had been.

He sighed. He wondered what Alfdis made of his seeming inability to rouse himself of a morning. He had never asked her. He really did not want to hear the answer. So they didn't speak of it, just as they did not speak of what had happened at Halfdan's hall, except when there was no choice but to make reference to that recent history.

With a groan he sat upright, swung his feet off the side of the bed and set them on the floor. He sat there for a moment, conjuring the will to stand, which he did a few moments later. He pulled on his tunic and stepped over to the wash basin near the bed. He washed his face and ran wet fingers through his graying hair.

To have such a bed closet, big enough for a bed, a basin, and even chests for clothes and blankets and space on the walls to mount swords and armor, was a rare luxury indeed. Few men had halls large enough for such a thing, but Amundi did. There was a time when he was secretly proud of that, but he could hardly remember feeling that way now.

He opened the door and stepped out into the long hall. The servants who were bustling around bowed to him, shallow, obsequious gestures, at least those who could not avoid it, and he nodded to them in return.

One of the slaves, a young girl, pretty, stopped at his side and said, "Will you have breakfast, lord?"

Amundi thought about the question. "No," he said. "No breakfast." His appetite seemed to have gone the way of his habit of early rising. His leggings were already hanging loose at his waist.

He circled around the fire pit to the far wall. He lifted the latch on the heavy door and opened it and nearly collided with Thord, the overseer of his farm, who was rushing in as Amundi was reluctantly stepping out. Thord was a careful man, a man who did not speak much and did not get excited without serious provocation, but he seemed excited now, and not in any joyous way.

"Lord Amundi, there's a rider coming, and he carries a banner," Thord said. "Those with younger eyes, they say it's white and red. Long banner."

Long banner…red and white…Halfdan's banner. The mere suggestion gave Amundi a foreign and ugly sensation, a sensation of dread and humiliation, a desire to just lie down and wallow in self-pity and ignore all the world, let it care for itself.

He had been feeling this all along, but with Thord's words the feelings doubled, tripled. He had thought perhaps this turmoil in his mind would get better as the days passed, but it had not. He found himself returning again and again to that moment when he had stood, sword and shield in hand, at the head of his warriors, with the big oak gates of Halfdan's compound standing between him and an all but certain, bloody death. This desperate band — his men, and Odd's, and Vifil and Thorgeir and the rest — standing ready, refreshing the grip on their weapons, finding their footing with their shoes, ready for the gates to swing open, and for them to charge through.

Feeling alive with death so close at hand.

But the gates had not opened. Odd had called down to be ready, and they were ready, and then nothing. Time inched along. And then the sentry, confused, yelled, "Master Odd?" And then nothing. And then the sentry repeated his words.

"Master Odd?"

By the time it became clear what had happened it was too late for the men behind the gate. The sentry reported from above that Odd had gone down the wall and was walking away. Incredulous, Amundi sheathed his sword and climbed the ladder and saw for himself. Odd had climbed down the outside of the wall and was now walking, quick and determined, toward Halfdan and his men, who were riding in his direction.

"He's giving himself up," Amundi said out loud, even though there was no one close enough to him to hear.

Of course he is. Amundi cursed himself for a fool. If he had thought about it for one moment he would have realized that Odd would never have agreed to their plan, would never have allowed anyone to die because of his blunder. It had surprised him when Odd had acquiesced so easily, and now it was clear why he had. He had not really acquiesced at all.

Standing there, all but alone on the wall, Amundi had looked down at the men on the ground below. They were still ready for a fight, but the edge was gone. He no longer saw that complete willingness, even eagerness, to die then and there, fighting their way to freedom. He looked back at Odd and Halfdan. The riders had spurred their horses forward and now they were closing in on Odd on either side. It was too late. It was over.

When Halfdan approached the gate Odd was not with him. He had apparently been taken back to the camp, bound hand and foot, no doubt.

Is that the last I'll see of him? Amundi wondered. *Him walking calmly toward Halfdan's mounted guard? Yes, I suppose it is.*

Halfdan and his hird stopped in front of the gate just as they had several times before over the past few days, Halfdan a dozen feet ahead of the rest. The girl Hallbera was on the saddle in front of him.

"You made a wise choice, Amundi," Halfdan called.

"Odd made the choice, not us," Amundi replied.

"It doesn't matter. The right choice was made." It occurred to Amundi that they might still end up fighting for their lives. He had little confidence that Halfdan would keep his word, or that he could be trusted not to pull some trick or other.

"So, now what?" Amundi asked.

"Now all of you go home and allow me to live in peace in my hall."

Amundi paused, considering that. That could not be it, the end of it. He would need some guarantee that Halfdan would not attack them once they were clear of the walls. He was about to make that point when Halfdan spoke again, as if he had read Amundi's thoughts.

"I have the girl here, and I'll let her go, as I promised," he said, then lifted Hallbera under her arms and leaned over and set her down on the ground, where she stood, unsure what to do.

"Now I'll ride back to my camp," Halfdan continued. "Me, with my guard. We'll wait there until we see you've all marched off. We'll be under arms, of course, in case you get some stupid notion, but we won't advance beyond the edge of the camp."

Amundi looked up and off toward the camp in the distance. It was far enough away that Halfdan's men could not launch a surprise attack. If Halfdan did come for them, the freemen would at least have time to ready themselves for a fight. But it still seemed too easy.

"That's it?" Amundi asked. "We just leave?"

"Yes," Halfdan said. "Just leave. And I'll thank you not to steal any of my things, no more than you've stolen already."

Amundi did not answer right off. He sorted through the possibilities, the options, but there weren't many to sort through. Odd had given himself up and so far Halfdan had fulfilled his side of the bargain. He and the other freemen could remain in Halfdan's compound and face all the difficulties they had already considered: an overwhelming assault on the walls, starvation, a desperate fight to break free. Or they could trust Halfdan enough for them to open the gates, march out, and hope the king remained true to his word.

"What of Odd?" Amundi asked.

Now it was Halfdan's turn to remain silent for a moment, as if he was calming himself in order to speak. "Odd is mine now. He will be treated as a traitor should."

"Aren't we all traitors?" Amundi asked. "Don't you want to do as much to us?"

Halfdan shook his head. "You were led to this by Odd, that snake. I put no blame on you. Besides, who will pay taxes if I kill you all? You'll pay, I promise, but not with your lives."

Amundi thought back to what Ragnhild had told them all: *you're worth much more to him if you're allowed to live. Dead men don't pay tribute.*

"It's not my decision to open the gates," Amundi said. "I'll speak with the others."

"You do that," Halfdan said, and there was an edge to his voice that suggested his patience was running short, or, more correctly, he would not be able to maintain the façade of patience much longer. "My guard and I, we'll return to camp. You have until sundown to leave. After that, there are no promises anymore."

Amundi returned to the men on the ground, who had heard perfectly well the exchange he had with Halfdan. "Well?" he asked.

The discussion went as Amundi guessed it would. They cursed Odd for doing what he did. They were still more than willing to fight. But now, apparently, there was no reason to fight. What's more, with surprise lost, the slaughter would be even more complete. The men's honor would hardly allow them to just slink away, but did it make sense to die for no purpose and doom their families to starvation or slavery without them?

They did not have to talk long before that answer became clear.

It took until midday to load up food and drink for the journey home, for the men to sling their shields on their backs and push the big gate open. They stepped out, bold as they could. Amundi knew that each of them silently hoped Halfdan would attack and allow them to die with honor rather than slink off like beaten dogs, even though they all knew that slinking off was the right choice.

But Halfdan did not attack them. There was no discernible movement at all in his camp. Amundi and the other freemen and their warriors walked north along the hard-packed road until the walls of Halfdan's compound were lost to sight. Halfdan and his army made no move. It was as if they were carved out of wood.

More than a week had passed since that had all happened, and every day since returning to his farm Amundi braced himself for what would come next. Halfdan had kept his word about letting them leave, but Halfdan had also said they would all pay, but not with their lives. Amundi had heard the words then but had not given them their proper weight. Now he heard them again and again in his mind, and he was starting to appreciate what they could mean.

They would pay.

All of it — the worry, the shame — beat him down, filled him with a weariness he had never experienced before. The humiliation of surrender, marching off and leaving Odd to Halfdan's mercy, waiting to see just what Halfdan would do next.

Little Hallbera had come with him when he left Grømstad, and Alfdis had done her best to give the girl comfort, but she was still frightened and confused. But she was safe, and she would remain safe there until Signy could come for her.

When that might be, Amundi did not know, but he had good reason to think she would. Word had been sent to the waterfront. The people on the ships had been alerted to Halfdan's arrival while there was still time to get away. The men and women on board had slipped their anchor cables and taken up the oars and made for the open sea before Halfdan even knew they were there.

Amundi's ship, carrying Alfdis and the other women and children of Amundi's household, had parted company with Signy's ship and landed as near to the farm as it could get, just a few miles away. There was no word of what had become of the other ships, but also no reason think they had not gotten safe away.

Word would reach Signy that her young sister-in-law was at Amundi's farm, and she would send for her, Amundi had no doubt. Until then Hallbera would remain with them.

He glanced over at the girl, sitting on a bench fifty feet away. She was sitting with a handful of the other children and they were all employed shucking peas from their pods.

Odd sacrificed himself so that she might live, Amundi thought. It was a noble thing to do. The right thing to do. He knew that he himself had to keep going, if for no other reason than to honor Odd's sacrifice.

"Lord?" Thord said, pulling Amundi from his reverie, a waking dream state that was becoming all too frequent.

"Yes," Amundi said. "I guess this bastard is from Halfdan. We can do nothing but wait and see what he has to say."

"Yes, lord," Thord said and as soon as the words were out of his mouth they heard the hoof beats of the rider, coming close. The two men looked in the direction of the sound. The chief part of Amundi's farm — the hall, the smithy, the sheds, the smokehouses —was surrounded by a wattle fence about five feet high, as were most farms in that region. This was to delineate the boundary of the farm yard and to keep any wandering livestock out. It was not for defense, for which it was useless.

"Berg, open that gate!" Thord called and Berg, a farmhand who happened to be near the gate, swung it open just as the rider came up.

Will we hear of Odd? Amundi wondered. He thought of Odd often. Odd was like a ghost, haunting him. Indeed, Amundi wondered if that was more than just a feeling. He imagined Halfdan had killed Odd already and Odd's spirit might well be coming to him. It would not be so strange or surprising that it would.

Amundi did not care to think about what Halfdan had done to Odd, but he found himself thinking about it nonetheless. Halfdan was capable of great brutality. But Odd knew that when he gave himself up.

Well, it's over now. Odd's a dead man, Amundi thought. He had no way of knowing if that was true, but he very much hoped that it was.

The rider slowed as he came through the gate and approached Amundi and Thord, pulling the reins hard and stopping with a flourish as he did. He was one of Halfdan's hird. Amundi recognized him, though he did not know the man's name. Even if he had not recognized him, his armor and sword and fine horse would have marked him as one of the elite. Above his head the long white and red banner lifted and fell in the light breeze.

"Amundi," the rider said, a statement, not a question.

"Yes?"

"King Halfdan is on his way. King Halfdan and his party. He'll be here by midday and he expects you'll be ready to receive him. With proper honors."

Amundi nodded. "We will," he said.

This was completely unexpected. A royal visit was generally announced weeks ahead of time, but here Halfdan had given no more than a few hours' notice.

"Good," the rider said. He spun his horse around and headed back the way he had come.

And now we'll find out just how Halfdan intends to make us pay, Amundi thought. *Taxes? Gifts? Slaves confiscated, property confiscated?* Whatever price Halfdan put on treason, it would be high.

Amundi was still watching the guard ride off when Alfdis came up to him.

"What does he want?" she asked, nodding toward the rider. She did not have to ask who he was, or who had sent him.

"He says Halfdan is on his way. He'll be here by midday."

"Midday? Today? Why is Halfdan coming here?" Alfdis said.

"He didn't say," Amundi replied. "Only that we're to receive him with proper honors."

Alfdis was quiet for a moment. "How many in his party?"

"He didn't say that, either," Amundi said. "Many, I would think. Halfdan does not go abroad unless he's well protected."

"Nor should he," Alfdis spat. "Very well, I'll see that we're ready for the king's visit."

She turned and walked off and soon Amundi could hear her calling out orders, and could hear the bustle of the servants hurrying to their tasks. He wondered what he himself should do to make ready. He couldn't come up with any ideas, and he knew that even if he did he would not have the motivation to carry them out, so he shuffled over to a bench near the side of the hall and sat.

I will wait here, Amundi thought. He felt as if there was nothing else he could do. Indeed, there was nothing else he could do but wait there and see what new horror Halfdan the Black had come to visit on them.

Chapter Seventeen

[I]n the fleet's midst,
a king hard to make flee,
who has often
the eagles sated,
while thou wast at the mills,
kissing the thrall-wenches.

The Poetic Edda

They discussed what they would do next — Thorgrim and his men, Bergthor and his men — there on the beach on the south coast of Engla-land. And in the course of that discussion Thorgrim Night Wolf realized several things.

He realized that the masters of the ships in his fleet, men who had fought with him against Irishmen and Englishmen and the sea, had a powerful devotion to one another. It was something he had always believed, but had never really seen on display in such a way as that.

Certainly he had seen them standing side by side in a fight, overlapping their shields to form a shieldwall or charging screaming into battle. But that sort of thing he would expect of any warrior. What surprised him now was their unwillingness to break up the fleet. They did not think of themselves as separate things, any more than a man's arm would think itself separate from the rest of the body.

Thorgrim made it clear that he was willing to let any man or ship go its own way. His men made it clear they had no interest in doing so.

Bergthor and Geldwine explained to the others in some detail what they might hope to gain from raiding Winchester, and it was considerable. Seat of the king of Wessex, home of one of the grandest of the Christ churches: plundering Winchester could mean doubling the fortune they had spent the past year gathering. And the more Bergthor spoke, the more Thorgrim realized how very much he wanted him and his men to be part of the raid. He was not so much offering to let Thorgrim join as he was begging him to do so.

Thorgrim had the impression that the raiding had not been so good for Bergthor, who was not the luckiest of men. Now Bergthor seemed anxious, perhaps even desperate, to meet with some good fortune. It was possible that his men were ready to leave him if things did not change. When a man gained a reputation for being unlucky it was hard to convince anyone that it was not true, no matter what he said or did.

And, indeed, sometimes it was true.

But Thorgrim Ulfsson did not suffer that problem. He was known to be a lucky man. The fact that Thorgrim had made and kept a fortune in his younger days and turned that into one of the most bountiful farms in East Agder was proof enough for most. So was the fact that he had lived through all that he had lived through and was still alive, even now, when so many back in Vik had thought he was surely dead.

Thorgrim had to be a lucky man. He was the son of Ulf of the Battle Song, and Ornolf the Restless had seen fit to give him his favorite daughter as a bride.

Bergthor knew that, and most of the others did as well, and they believed it, even if Thorgrim himself did not think he was very lucky at all.

"So, there it is," Bergthor said to the assembled companies when he and Geldwine had finished their description of the riches to be found at Winchester. "If you wish to join us, you're welcome to do so. If not, we'll eat some more whale together and part company as friends."

Bergthor had make the raid sound tempting indeed, and easy as well, but Thorgrim had some time ago decided what his priority was. He had made it clear and he meant to make it clear again.

"We were on our way back to Norway," Thorgrim said, ostensibly for the edification of Bergthor's ship masters, but as a reminder to his own men as well. "We've been raiding some time in Ireland and England. We're heading home now."

He looked over at his men once again, expecting to see heads nodding in agreement, but instead he saw men exchanging uncomfortable glances with each other. And it was then that Thorgrim realized that the others did not necessarily share his burning desire to get home.

"What say you?" Thorgrim said, but no one spoke, not at first. Then Starri Deathless broke the silence.

"What's to be had in Norway, Thorgrim Night Wolf?" he asked. "A slow death. There's fighting to be had on these shores. A warrior's death." He looked around at the others but their expressions remained fixed. It seemed they were no more eager to follow Starri to a warrior's death than they were to follow Thorgrim to Norway.

"Lord Thorgrim," Godi said. "Sure, we're all eager to get to Norway. Those of us from Norway. The Danes and Swedes among us, they're probably eager to get back, too. That Frank, Louis, he thinks of nothing else. But… I think… and I could be wrong… but it seems to me that, me and the others, well, we think this raid on Winchester might be worth the effort. It's not so far from here, and wouldn't take so long. There and back and then underway for Norway once more, and richer to boot."

This time Thorgrim did see heads nodding and looks of relief, the men pleased that Godi at least was willing to say what the rest of them wished to say but did not dare.

"Of course, we'll do whatever you think best," Hardbein interjected. "If you don't think it's wise we go on this raid, then that would be fine with all the men here." Thorgrim looked around. Heads were still nodding in agreement, but more in resignation than with any great enthusiasm.

Thorgrim wanted to sigh, long and loud, but he kept it to himself. He wanted to grab Bergthor by the tunic and beat him senseless for showing up like this and throwing everything in disarray, but he did not do that, either. He wanted take *Sea Hammer* and sail off and forget all he had ever thought or said about not weakening the fleet, but he knew he could not do that, either.

In some situations — in most situations — Thorgrim was perfectly happy to issue orders and expect them to be obeyed without question. And almost always they were, because men did not generally cross Thorgrim Night Wolf. But this was not such a situation. This had to do with letting men choose their own destiny.

"You'll take a vote among you," Thorgrim said to his people. "And whatever the majority of the company wants, that's what we'll do. And while you vote I'll go find a cup of ale."

He left the ring and walked across the sand to where the stove-in barrels were resting by the smoldering remains of the bonfire. He drank a cup of ale, and then another, and when he felt he had given the men time enough to talk among themselves and vote he walked back to the circle. There he learned, to no surprise at all, that they would be going to Winchester.

But not immediately. They had been a few days on the beach already, enjoying their bacchanal and feasting on whale, and it would take a day at least to get everything back aboard and secured. There was still some whale meat to be had, despite the creature getting a little ripe, so a few men were set to butchering what they could and setting it to dry in the sun.

Thorgrim and Bergthor discussed plans for the raid, though there was not too much to discuss. They would make their way up the long bay to the place that Geldwine called Hamptun and go ashore there. And if there were English warriors waiting then they would fight their way ashore. And once there they would sack Hamtun and decide what to do next.

Simple.

It took the better part of the day to make preparations for getting underway, and the ships and men were still not ready by the time the sun had dropped far into the west. So once again the bonfire was lit, once again the mead and ale was passed around and once again the Northmen took their pleasure as if it was their last day on earth, which it might well have been. They were bound off for raiding in the morning, and there was every chance they would be in desperate battle before day's end. Every chancc that any of them might be wounded or dead.

No one found the notion particularly alarming, of course. They might be terrified to die the way poor Fostolf had died, twisting in pain inflicted by some malignant spirit, but dying in battle was something else altogether.

Thorgrim, too, ate and drank, though not as excessively as he might have as a young man. Not as excessively as Harald was. His son was standing at the other side of the fire, as conspicuously far from Thorgrim as he could get. Thorgrim was not even certain he was there, not until he stepped off into the dark and circled around the fire until he could see his son standing among his fellows.

Harald was smiling and laughing and had a cup in his hand and Thorgrim was glad to see it. Harald had not spoken to him since he had stripped the boy of his command, and he worried about what was going on in his son's head. He wanted Harald to learn a lesson, but he did not want the boy's spirit broken.

And from what Thorgrim could see now, it was not. Indeed, Harald was not just standing with the others, but the others seemed to be gathered around him, as if he was the center of their attention. They were all young men, near Harald's age, and they seemed to be attentive to anything Harald had to say.

Among them was Herjolf, who Thorgrim had just informed was the new master of *Dragon*. Herjolf did not seemed overly pleased by the news, but neither did he protest. Now, seeing how he hung on Harald's words, one would never guess which of them was the master and which was the man at the oar.

They still see Harald as a great hero for that whale nonsense, Thorgrim thought. Harald was a natural leader, Thorgrim had always believed that, and he was happy to see the others looking to him. But there was potential for trouble there as well. It would not be good if those young warriors looked on Harald as some great man, and it would be worse if Harald started to believe it himself. Thorgrim had seen that sort of thing before.

Harald's too level-headed for that, Thorgrim thought, and he hoped he was right.

He spent some time longer in the company of Bergthor and the others. The mood was jubilant, word of the coming raid having spread through the camp. Thorgrim had wondered if Bergthor's men would resent the newcomers, be unhappy about sharing any plunder with them, but that did not seem to be the case. They seemed as happy as Thorgrim's men did. Happier, maybe. They might have just seen their chances of success go up considerably.

Louis will not be so happy, Thorgrim thought. Of all the men on the beach, Louis the Frank was the only one as eager as Thorgrim to get home. And like Thorgrim he would not be happy about the delay that raiding Winchester would involve. But Louis, at least, did not have to agonize over his choice in the matter, as Thorgrim did. If Louis meant to get back to Frankia aboard Thorgrim's ship, which seemed his only option, then he had no choice at all.

The younger men seemed to be just warming up to their shouting and singing and drinking when Thorgrim decided it was time for bed. He bid good night to Bergthor, to Godi and Asmund and Hardbein and the others seated on the driftwood logs and headed off into the dark.

As he walked over the soft sand he looked up, craning his neck. The stars were arrayed in a great dome overhead, but only the brightest of them were visible through the thin clouds that had filled in. He smelled rain in the air, which would add more difficulty to the hard job ahead of them.

He stopped and turned until he found the North Star, then turned a bit more and looked out over the dark land. Somewhere beyond the land, beyond the water, was East Agder and his farm in Vik. If he was a bird he could fly straight in that direction and be home far faster than any ship could carry him. He could travel alone and not get waylaid by the plans of others. Then he smiled at his own foolishness and continued on to where he had made his bed.

He reached the dark patch on the beach that he knew was his furs and blankets. In the past he would have slept aboard *Sea Hammer*, even when she was pulled up ashore, but now the lure of the soft sand called to him. He reached down and undid his belt and felt the weight of Iron-tooth come off his hips. His eyes were adjusting to the dark after having been near the bonfire all evening. He thought he saw a lump under the fur that could indicate his bed was already occupied. And just as he noticed that he heard Failend's voice, soft and melodic.

"Good evening, Thorgrim."

"Good evening to you," Thorgrim said. He was never certain anymore if she would be in his bed or not. Sometimes she was, sometimes she wasn't. She seemed to decide at random, and when she did join him it was only to sleep. They had not made love in a long time. But even without that activity in the offing, Thorgrim was always glad to have her with him, and he was now.

He set Iron-tooth down on a blanket next to the pile of furs, off the sand and close enough for him to lay his hand on instantly. He pulled off his tunic and knelt down and slipped under the fur. He stretched out and luxuriated in the sensation of his taut muscles relaxing, his body pressed between the furs above and the blankets below, laid out on a bed of soft sand.

He felt Failend move beside him and then felt her drape herself across his chest, so light her weight added almost nothing to that of the fur. He felt her warm skin pressed against his and it felt good, good way down deep in him, and he realized that she was naked. He held her gently, just enough for her to know he was pressing her close.

"I've missed you," Failend said.

"I've missed you, too," Thorgrim said. He guessed that would be the right response, though he was not entirely sure what she meant.

She pushed herself a little further on top of him and rested her head on his chest, her long hair falling like silk thread across him. He ran his hands gently up and down her back and over the small of her back and over her rear end. For some time now she had been the only woman in the company of the Northmen. Thorgrim wondered if there had ever been a rear end so often stared at by so many as hers.

Failend made a soft sound, like a dove cooing, then said, "Wait...."

Thorgrim slowly ran his hands back up the her shoulders and rested them there. Failend pushed herself up so she was resting on her elbows and her elbows were resting on Thorgrim's chest, but her weight was too little for that to cause pain. There was just enough light from the stars and the glow of the fire some ways off that Thorgrim could make out her features, her lovely oval face, the gleam in her bright eyes.

"We're raiding Winchester?" she said. It was a question, but it sounded more like a statement.

"Yes," Thorgrim said. "It's what the others want."

"Not what you want."

"No," Thorgrim said.

"You could just tell them, you know," Failend said. "You could just tell them that the ships will sail to Norway and they would do as you say."

"I know," Thorgrim said. "But I won't do that." He hoped she would not ask why he would not, because he did not have an answer for that. Some decisions — many decisions, actually — he made because he felt in his gut they were right. And usually they were. Not always, but usually.

"I know you want to go home," Failend said. "Louis wants to go home. Sometimes I think of home."

"Ireland?"

"Ireland's my home. Was my home. I don't know," Failend said.

Thorgrim was quiet for a moment as he thought about that. It hadn't really occurred to him that Failend might miss her native country the way he missed his. In his mind she had become as much a part of their company as any of the men. She was just there, and always had been since he had first taken her prisoner. He assumed she would wish to go with him to East Agder, though he had not really thought about it very much.

"I'm sorry," he said at last.

She laid her head on his chest. "Sorry about what?" she asked.

Again he had to think about it. He was not sure. "Sorry about taking you from your home. Sorry about turning you into…a heathen."

She sat up again and he could see that she was smiling. "I'm only part heathen, you know. And you did not take me. Well, at first you did. But then I came with you on my own."

Thorgrim reached out and lifted the two silver ornaments that hung from the leather thong around Failend's neck, a silver cross and a silver hammer. Thor's hammer. "Part heathen, part Christian," he said.

"Like you," Failend said, touching the cross and hammer that lay on Thorgrim's chest.

Thorgrim smiled. "Your Christ God would not have me," he said. They were quiet for a moment, and then Thorgrim spoke again.

"Let me know what you want," he said. "I'll see you get it, if I'm able."

Failend nodded. "I thank you. What I want, I don't think you can give, but I thank you." She leaned her head down and kissed him softly on the chest, then shuffled closer and ran her lips up the side of his neck and then kissed him on the mouth. Thorgrim wrapped his arms around her and with little effort hoisted her up so that she was lying on top of him completely. He breathed deep, remembering the pleasure of losing himself in her, feeling that pleasure once again.

Chapter Eighteen

Thou art not a king
of wholesome counsel,
leader of people!
Thou hast let fire
the homes of heroes eat,
who evil deed
had never done thee.

The Poetic Edda

Amundi remained seated on the bench, staring out into the middle distance, waiting for Halfdan and his escort to arrive. How long he remained there he did not know. Time seemed like a strange and amorphous thing. He saw people passing back and forth, carrying cured meat and rolling barrels of something. Ale or mead, he imagined. He saw some of his men appear in mail shirts with swords and spears and he thought it would be nice if they were preparing for battle, and not turning out to do honor to King Halfdan the Black.

Alfdis appeared again. She had changed her clothes and was now wearing her finest white linen shift and over it a wool dress dyed a rich blue. The shoulder straps of the dress were fastened with large, oval-shaped gold brooches, with a half dozen strings of gold, silver and amber beads suspended between them. Grudging as she was to do Halfdan any honor, she knew better than to greet the king in anything less.

Behind her trailed one of the servants and in her arms were Amundi's finest tunic, a cape and his sword and belt, Alfdis having decided, apparently, that it was easier to carry these things out to her husband than to try to usher her husband back into the bed closet. On her orders Amundi stood and tugged off the tunic he wore and was helped into the finer one. The sword belt was wrapped around his waist and fastened and the sword adjusted to hang right. The cape was draped over his shoulders and fastened with a brooch. He felt like a child, or a decrepit old man, being dressed in that way, but he did not protest.

It was nearly midday, as the rider had predicted, when Halfdan's party appeared far off down the road, raising a cloud of dust as they marched. Amundi and the others could see the glint of sun off the helmets and mail of the hird, riding at the head of the line, and could make out more men behind, and wagons as well, though it was not clear how many there were. At least a hundred men, Amundi guessed, probably more. He did not think Halfdan would travel with less.

Alfdis and Thord gathered the people together, anyone of any importance, the warriors forming two lines starting at the gate and leading into the yard. They stood in loose order with spears straight up like a series of thin columns. There was no great uniformity in their equipment, but neither was it completely haphazard. Some of it they had provided themselves and some Amundi had provided for them so that the men who formed his own household guard would be able to make a decent appearance. And they did, with most of them fitted out with mail and helmets, and almost half with swords.

They were good fighting men, they had proven themselves in that regard, but Amundi had neither the wealth nor the inclination to fit them out to the standards of Halfdan's hird. Halfdan's men were warriors by profession; they had no work other than to protect Halfdan and fight for him. Amundi's men were farmers and smiths and woodworkers who turned out to fight when needed. And until recently they had not been needed to serve as warriors very often.

All was in readiness, and there was nothing left but to watch and wait as Halfdan's entourage approached. The man with the banner, the one who had come earlier, led the way. Next to him, on a horse that was several hands taller than the flag bearer's, rode Halfdan the Black. As they came through the gate, Alfdis leaned over to Amundi and whispered, "You watch your tongue, husband. We don't know what Halfdan wants, but it won't take much for him to decide to kill us all."

Amundi nodded but said nothing.

Halfdan continued to walk his horse closer to Amundi and Alfdis, and behind him his mounted warriors followed in two columns. They were led by Onund Jonsson, captain of Halfdan's hird, a man Amundi had once counted as a friend.

Amundi's men stepped back to make room for them as they passed. Behind the columns Amundi could see a few wagons drawn by lumbering oxen, carrying, no doubt, food and drink and tents. Not that Halfdan would need much in the way of provisions. He would expect those he visited to provide for him and his men, and to not skimp in doing so.

Behind the wagons came the foot soldiers, marching in two columns, spears held erect. Two or three hundred of them, at least. Amundi could not help but think of the food and drink in his storehouse that would be wiped out in feeding all these men. And that was not even considering what Halfdan would take with him when he left.

"Amundi, good day," Halfdan said as he stopped his horse twenty feet away. Amundi and Alfdis made shallow bows, as did the rest of the household.

"Good day, King Halfdan," Amundi said. "You honor us with your presence today."

"Indeed," Halfdan said, the word clipped. When last they had spoken, at Halfdan's hall, there had been an easy, almost casual quality to Halfdan's speech, as if he was not really taking any of it that seriously. Whether it was feigned or not Amundi did not know. But either way that quality was gone now. The king had spoken a total of four words and Amundi could already hear the hardness, the utter lack of empathy or consideration in his tone.

Halfdan looked around at the assembled people. "These are all the people of your household?" he asked.

"Yes, lord," Amundi said.

"All of them?"

"Well, not the slaves, lord, or the field hands or servants in the hall," Alfdis explained.

Halfdan nodded. "Get them out here. All of them. Children too. Every living body, get them out here."

Alfdis turned and said in a soft but urgent voice, "Go! Go!" gesturing to the servants behind her. "Go, get everyone, you heard the king." The servants hurried off and Alfdis hurried after them to be sure they moved with the alacrity she desired.

Amundi turned back and looked at Halfdan. He said nothing. Let Halfdan speak if he wished, but Amundi had nothing to say to him.

And apparently Halfdan had nothing more to say to Amundi. He turned and nodded toward Onund Jonsson and Onund half turned in his saddle and called, "Up here!"

From somewhere toward the back of the column three men came forward. They were not warriors; they looked more like the men who drove the carts and tended the oxen. Each had a shovel over his shoulder.

They walked past Halfdan and stopped half way between where he and Amundi stood, then without a word they arranged themselves in a circle and drove the points of their shovels into the ground. They pulled up heaps of brown dirt, deposited them in a small pile, then drove their shovels in again, enlarging the hole, while Halfdan and the rest looked on wordlessly.

For some moments it remained like that: fifty or more of the people in Amundi's household, three hundred or more of Halfdan's men, all standing in silence, the only sound the soft scrape of the shovels digging the earth. Amundi had no idea what Halfdan had in mind, but that ignorance did not stop him from feeling a profound and mounting dread.

Behind him he heard the soft sound of feet on the ground and Alfdis was at his side again. Halfdan ran his eyes over the assembled people but said nothing. The men with the shovels continued to dig.

Finally the men seemed to judge the hole deep enough. They stepped back and rested the blades of their shovels on the ground and leaned on the handles. When they did, three more men appeared through the press of Halfdan's men. They carried between them a wooden post, about eight inches thick and ten feet long. They set the end of the post into the fresh-dug hole, and one of them held it steady as the men with the shovels stepped up and filled the dirt back in around it, tamping it down when they were done.

Halfdan ran his eyes over Amundi's people. "This is it?" he asked. "This is all your household?"

"Yes, lord," Alfdis said.

"Very well," Halfdan said, then continued, speaking loudly enough for his voice to reach everyone watching. "You are all of you aware of the great treason that has been committed of late," he said. "You know who carries the most guilt, and who carries the lesser. But they are all guilty, all who took part in that heinous crime. And you also know how merciful I have been. But do not mistake mercy for weakness. There are limits to my mercy, and those limits have been reached. So I have come here to show you all what becomes of those I deem guilty. Heed this lesson, because next time my wrath will not be limited to one man alone."

He turned back toward his men and nodded once again. Amundi could see some bustling around the nearest cart, and then down the center of the two lines of mounted warriors came three men, half leading, half carrying another between them. Amundi sucked in his breath despite himself. He heard Alfdis give a muffled cry, and, from the others gathered around, gasps and soft wails.

It was Odd Thorgrimson, and though his legs were moving it was clear he would not have been able to stand on his own. His long hair was wild and ragged. One eye was bruised purple, red and black and swollen shut. His beard was streaked with dried blood. He seemed to have difficulty keeping his head upright as he was all but dragged forward.

Amundi felt his stomach turn. He heard Alfdis try to stifle a sob. Odd was brought up to the post and for a moment was allowed to stand on his own, which he seemed barely able to do, swaying as he stood. One of the men grabbed his tunic and pulled it up over his head as the others kept him from falling.

If they meant to flog Odd then it would not be the first time, Amundi could see that. Odd's back was already a crisscross of bloody red, brown and black lacerations. The wounds were no longer bleeding but they were clearly not very old. A few days, perhaps.

One of the men wound a cord around Odd's wrists and ran the other end through an iron ring that was made fast to the upper end of the post. He pulled it tight, jerking Odd's hands up, nearly lifting Odd off his feet. Odd let out a gasp, but no more. His eyes were closed, his head was back as if he did not have the strength or the will to hold it upright.

Amundi felt a certain madness wash over him. He felt he had to move but he could not, as if ropes were tied to his arms and legs and were pulling him in every direction with equal force. He wanted to kill someone. Kill himself, kill Halfdan, he was not sure. Both, perhaps. With Halfdan's men there, trying to kill the king would be as good as killing himself.

"Watch carefully," Halfdan called to the people. "Watch and learn the lesson. And if I see any one of you looking away, you'll be next at the post."

Another man stepped up, a big man with a brown tunic that was tight across his wide chest and over the muscles in his arms. He held a whip in his hand, a heavy braided and tarred rope that split off into four smaller ropes at the end, which, Amundi was quite sure, held weights of some sort. Hooks or barbs, perhaps. He clenched his teeth as if he was the one about to feel the impact of the blows.

The man with the whip looked at Halfdan and Halfdan nodded. The man brought the whip back over his shoulder and swung it down and around. It hit Odd's back and ripped across at a forty-five degree angle, opening up four straight, fresh lines of blood. Odd gasped loudly and arched his back. Amundi could only imagine how agonizing the blow had been. And it was only the first, and laid on top of near fresh wounds.

The whip came back again, and again it slashed at Odd's back, and again Odd gasped and twisted harder. He was hanging more than he was standing and there was little he could do to change position. Not that changing position would have helped him in the least.

The whip rose and fell over and over, and with each blow Odd's back became bloodier, his gasps louder, his moans held in until it was clear to Amundi that Odd was trying to not cry out, trying to not give Halfdan the satisfaction. But Amundi did not think he could keep quiet much longer.

Again and again, the smack of wet cordage on Odd's lacerated flesh, the writhing, the gasping. Then the whip bearer changed hands, shifting the whip from right to left. He brought it back over his shoulder, the motion as smooth and easy with that hand as it had been with the other. He tore the four weighted tails across Odd's back, opening up wounds crosswise to those already there.

Odd screamed that time. A short, sharp cry that he bit off as well as he could, but the pain was now too much for him to keep silent. Amundi looked over at Halfdan. The king had been expressionless up until then, but Amundi saw the edge of a smile creep onto his lips. But that was it, and then the impassive face was back.

The women all around Amundi were weeping openly now, as were the children. Amundi hoped that someone was shielding Hallbera from this but he did not want to look. He did not want Halfdan to think he was averting his eyes. Not because he feared a flogging himself, but because he did not want Halfdan to think he could not bear the spectacle.

Which was all but true. His face was as passionless as Halfdan's, but his thoughts were screaming and flinging themselves about like a madman. He wanted to beg Halfdan to stop, or to allow him to take Odd's place. He wanted to offer Halfdan his farm, his livestock, his slaves, anything just so he would cut Odd down. But he said nothing, because he knew that it was pointless to offer Halfdan anything he could just take if he so desired, and he knew that any pleading would have no effect save to add to Halfdan's pleasure.

The whip fell again with its sickening liquid smack but this time Odd did not shout out. He was hanging by his wrists and not moving and Amundi wondered if he was dead. He hoped that he was dead. It would not be the death that he or any man would wish, but it would be a relief none the less.

Halfdan nodded to someone else behind him and this man came up with a bucket of water in hand. He threw the water against Odd's back and Odd gasped and writhed and his eyes flew open. He was still alive, and Amundi did not know how to feel about that. He thought bitterly of how he had watched Odd walk off to surrender himself to Halfdan, how he, Amundi, had despaired of ever seeing Odd again. How he wished now that it had worked out that way.

The man with the bucket stepped back and Halfdan nodded to the one with the whip and the punishment started in once again. One blow, and another and another. Odd was not screaming now, but Amundi could see that it was not because he was trying to remain silent but because he no longer had the energy or the will to make a sound.

The whip came back again but this time Halfdan held up a hand and the man stopped and let the whip hang. Halfdan stepped over to Odd's limp body and with a look of mild disgust examined his face and his back. He turned and once again nodded toward the men behind him. Yet another stepped forward, also holding a bucket, but what was in it Amundi could not tell.

This is well rehearsed, Amundi thought bitterly. He wondered how often Halfdan had already inflicted this punishment on his prisoner.

The man with the bucket stopped near Odd and reached in and drew out a handful of salt, which he applied to the wounds on Odd's back. That drew a gasp from Odd, an arch of the back, but no more. The man smacked salt into the wounds again and again until at last all of Odd's back was covered.

Halfdan turned to Amundi and Alfdis and the crowd of people behind them. "I see to it that this traitor's wounds are dressed," he said. "And I'll give them some time to heal. It's important that Odd Thorgrimson live. Because I will be visiting every farm in Fevik, and there we will give this same demonstration, so that everyone in this country knows what happens when they betray their king. So I will not flog him to death. Not until the last farm is reached."

The men who had brought Odd forward now stepped up again and untied the cord that held him up. They eased him down and put his arms around their shoulders and dragged him off, upright. Odd made no effort to even appear to be walking on his own. Amundi doubted he could have made his legs work if he wished to.

What next? Amundi wondered. He did not think for a moment that Halfdan was done there. He certainly would not be leaving anytime soon. And still there was nothing that Amundi could do but wait for Halfdan to make his wishes known.

He did not wait long. Halfdan watched with apparently little interest as Odd was dragged away, then stepped around the post and up to Amundi. For a moment the two men just stood there, looking into one another's eyes, Halfdan waiting for Amundi to speak and Amundi forcing himself to not say those things that were fighting to leave his mouth. He heard Alfdis fidgeting beside him and he was sure she was terrified he would say what she knew he wished to say.

But he did not, and it was Halfdan who broke the silence.

"My men and I will be staying in your hall. Tonight, perhaps tomorrow night, I haven't decided. I also haven't decided what penalty you'll pay for your treason, so we'll search your hall and see what there is that will meet the price. You know, much like you did to my hall."

He paused and held Amundi's eyes, waiting for Amundi to speak. Daring him to speak. But Amundi knew better than to do that.

"Needless to say, we don't care to sleep in the company of thieves and traitors," Halfdan continued. "So you and your family and the others will sleep in the barn over there." He nodded toward the barn that housed the horses and the milch cows and the chickens, then met Amundi's eyes again.

"Will that be satisfactory?" he asked.

"Very. Lord," Amundi said.

"One thing more," Halfdan said. "Give me his sword. Odd Thorgrimson's sword."

"His sword?" Amundi said.

"Yes, his sword," Halfdan snapped. "Don't play-act with me. Blood-letter, the sword of Ulf of the Battle Song. Where is it?"

Amundi shook his head. "I thought you had it, lord," he said. "Odd was wearing it when he gave himself up to you."

For a long moment Halfdan stared into Amundi's eyes, looking for some sign of treachery, and Amundi held his gaze, expressionless and steady. Finally Halfdan spoke.

"If I find you're lying it will not go well for you. You've seen what I can do to liars and traitors."

"Yes, lord," Amundi said but by then Halfdan had already turned his back and was walking away.

The arrangements did not take long. Amundi's house servants were sent to get the hall prepared for the new guests, and to begin preparations for a grand feast that would include only Halfdan's men. The other servants and men, along with Amundi himself, were ordered to see to Halfdan's horses and oxen, to get them fed and staked out.

Afternoon was fading into evening when Amundi tossed the last fork-load of hay to Halfdan's mounts and checked that their hobbles were properly fixed. Alfdis came up beside him and laid a hand on his shoulder.

"You're done here, husband," she said in a soft voice. "Come and rest and eat."

The voices from inside the hall, muffled by the thick walls, were already loud and raucous, the sound of men enjoying themselves at another's expense. They would eat and drink as much as they could, and take as much, and damage as much, as they wished, and they would do it not only with the permission of their king, but with his encouragement. Amundi now understood that there was no one who could create a stew of physical and spiritual devastation, of terror and humiliation, like Halfdan could.

He allowed Alfdis to lead him into the barn. Most of the household were there, hunkered down in the long space that fronted the stalls. The air was thick with the smell of animals and hay and the candles burning in various lanterns hung from nails around the place. Fresh straw had been strewn on the ground and Amundi was all but certain Alfdis had ordered it. That would be like her, to try and mitigate the misery of the situation with whatever little thing she could do.

He sat on the floor and leaned back against one of the rough beams that supported the wall and roof. One of the slave girls came up and offered him a bowl of stew that had been cooked over a fire behind the barn, but Amundi shook his head.

"Please, husband, you should eat," Alfdis said but Amundi shook his head again.

"No, wife, I'm too weary," he said. "Too weary by far. But thank you."

He did accept a cup of ale, however, and drank that slowly as he listened to the various soft conversations around him and the sky outside grew darker.

Oh, I have failed, by all the gods I have failed, he thought as he looked at the people crowded in around him. *I thought to join with Odd's fight against Halfdan and I failed in that, and I failed Odd, failed to stand with him. Now Halfdan does what he wishes and I have failed my people.* Amundi felt a dark despair sweeping over him, just as the darkness was overtaking the farmyard outside the stable walls.

He sat there, awake, staring into the dark, as one by one the people around him fell asleep. The muttered conversations faded away, only to be supplanted by the soft rhythmic breathing of some, the coarse snoring of others. Alfdis lay down at Amundi's side and curled up and slept. She did not bother urging her husband to sleep as well. She understood, no doubt, that sleep was not likely to come to him.

But it did. Somewhere in the deep night sleep overcame Amundi at last, leaning against the post, his chin tilted down against his chest. It took him unaware, and when he woke he was surprised to find he had been asleep. And what had awoken him, he did not know.

Someone was shaking him. It took him a moment to realize that, a moment for his thick head to clear. The lanterns had been extinguished and it was very dark in the stable, but Amundi could just make out the shape of someone kneeling beside him and gently shaking his shoulder.

"What…?" Amundi asked.

"Pray, quiet, lord," the person said and Amundi recognized the voice of a girl named Unn who was one of the kitchen maids. Her tone was urgent, her voice so low it was just audible. He could hear the fear in it.

"What is it?" Amundi asked, speaking as softly as Unn had.

"Pray, lord, there's someone sent me to fetch you. Someone who would speak to you."

"Who is it?" Amundi asked.

"Please, lord, won't you just come with me?" Unn seemed afraid to even speak the man's name, as if doing so would conjure up some evil spirit. But Amundi could think of no reason not to go. This was not likely Halfdan's doing: if Halfdan wanted Amundi dead he would just kill him. If it was someone else plotting to kill him, well, Amundi did not really much care.

He stood, his muscles tight and sore after having been propped up against the beam for so long. He could just barely see. Unn was little more than a dark shape against a slightly less dark background, but he could see her walking slowly away and he followed her, stepping with care so he would not make any noise or step on any sleeping body.

Unn led the way out of the stable door, and with the stars overhead it was considerably easier to see, particularly as Amundi was familiar with every inch of that farmyard. He continued to follow as Unn led the way across the open ground, way from the long hall and toward the smith's shop, which was near the wattle fence to the east.

They came to the door of the smith's shop and Unn said, "Here, lord," then turned and raced off, seemingly desperate to get away, running as fast as she could and still not make any noise.

Amundi watched her go, then looked around him. He could see no one, nothing moving in the dark. He looked in the other direction just in time to see the dark shape of a man step around the corner of the shop. Amundi drew a breath in surprise and was about to speak when the dark shape spoke first.

"Amundi?"

Amundi knew the voice, and when he heard it he recognized the man as well, by his shape, his posture.

"Onund Jonsson," Amundi said.

Chapter Nineteen

With shields are your ships bedecked;
boldly ye bear yourselves,
few things ye fear, I ween:
tell me how your king is named.

The Poetic Edda

Thorgrim drifted off some time later with Failend, herself fast asleep, still sprawled across his chest. He slept so deeply that when he awoke he was not certain where he was, or what had woken him.

He opened his eyes slowly. It was not dark, not night-time dark, but it was not daylight, either. He looked out at the gray pre-dawn and realized there was water dripping on his head. The heavy fur was pulled over him nearly all the way, and stiff as it was it formed a sort of low roof and the water was dripping off that roof.

Is it raining? he wondered. He looked out over the beach. The air was thick with mist, just short of actual rain. The weather had been remarkably good since they had landed in Engla-land, with only a few days of rain on and off. Not at all like the miserable Ireland from which they had sailed. But it seemed that fine weather was going to desert them now.

He pushed the fur aside and sat up. Failend had moved in the night to sleep beside him, and had been entirely sheltered under the fur, but now he exposed her to the falling mist. She stirred, muttered something, then opened her eyes and looked around. She looked at the beach, she looked up at Thorgrim, she looked at the fur he had pushed off her.

"You damned cruel heathen," she said as she pulled the fur back over her.

"Daylight," Thorgrim said. "Or near to it. Time to go." He crawled out from under the fur, bringing his leggings with him. He pulled them on, balancing awkwardly and cursing himself for leaving his tunic on the sand rather than bringing it under the covers as well. He picked it up and pulled the cold, damp fabric over his head, then buckled Iron-tooth around his waist. Failend pushed the covers aside. Sometime during the night she had put her clothes back on, and so managed to keep them dry.

Together they rolled up the fur and the blankets while other men, scattered around the beach, did the same. They carried the bedding across the sand to where *Sea Hammer* was pulled up on shore, and handed it up to Vestar on board.

Bergthor came rolling up to them, his usual smile even wider now. "Ah, Thorgrim!" he said. "Beautiful morning for a raid, isn't it?"

Thorgrim looked around. The mist had turned to light rain and he knew it would soon turn heavier still. "It's a fine morning, Bergthor," Thorgrim agreed. "But I look forward to sleeping in an English home tonight, and eating English beef."

"Had your fill of whale meat?" Bergthor said. "So have I. Let's go visit the English, get our hands on something better."

Those men still asleep were roused to their feet by the encouraging shouts and kicks of their captains. Soon all the provisions and gear on the beach began flowing back aboard the ships. A fire was coaxed from the last of the embers and breakfast cooked.

Thorgrim and Bergthor and the other ship masters ate together on the ring of driftwood logs. Herjolf was with them this time, on Thorgrim's orders. He would have to hear the things they were discussing now.

"So, Bergthor, you trust this fellow, the Briton who you've taken on as pilot?" Asmund asked between scoops of porridge.

Bergthor nodded. "What he told us so far has been right, and I think he has no love for this king in Wessex. Yes, I think he'll pilot us as he said he would. Besides, he'll be on my ship, and he knows I'll kill him the moment I find he lied."

That seemed acceptable to the men in the circle. The Briton had a love of silver and a dislike of the king and a fear of his own death, and those things could have a powerful influence on a man.

"Good," Thorgrim said. "Bergthor and I will lead, we'll keep our ships abreast of one another. Let the next largest, *Blood Hawk* and…Bergthor, what is your next largest ship?"

"*Raven*, which is commanded by Steindor, over there." Bergthor pointed to one of his men sitting across the circle from him, a big man, beard halfway down his chest, the sides of his head shaved, a calmly lethal look on his face. He had not said one word this whole time. The sort of man Thorgrim liked.

"Then *Raven* will go with *Blood Hawk*. After will be *Oak Heart* and whatever ship is next largest for you, Bergthor."

"Lord Thorgrim," Hardbein said, hesitantly. "Can I ask why you're arranging the ships this way?" As master of *Fox*, one of the smallest of Thorgrim's ships, Hardbein and his men were bound to be near the end of the line, and to Hardbein's credit he seemed unhappy about it.

"There may be English warriors waiting for us," Thorgrim said. "We've been here on this beach so long word must have gone around the countryside by now. If the English form a line or a shieldwall we want the ships that carry the most men to land at the center of it. Each ship following will land as close as they can to the fighting and join in."

At that heads nodded. Even Hardbein could not argue with that plan. Herjolf, now commanding *Dragon*, which was as small as *Fox*, offered no opinion and made no effort to protest.

The mist was turning to drizzle by the time they finished, and every one of them was eager to move, to get underway, to do anything but sit there in the rain. They headed off to their various ships, which had crews aboard, gear stowed, shields on the shield racks and oars run out. A handful of men stood by the bow of each vessel to shove it the last few feet into the sea before climbing aboard. A little further down the beach the gulls screeched and circled and tore what they could from what remained of the whale.

Thorgrim climbed up over *Sea Hammer*'s side and made his way aft. He rested a hand on the tiller and looked forward to where Gudrid stood near the bow. Thorgrim nodded his head and Gudrid shouted to the men on the beach and *Sea Hammer* began to move, foot by foot, sliding back into the sea.

And then she was free of the shore and Thorgrim felt that familiar sensation in his legs as the motion of the ship changed, as she went from mostly floating to floating free. It was a good feeling, like the final bonds falling away.

"Back water, back water!" he called, and on the sea chests larboard and starboard the men leaned back, dipped their oars and shoved them forward, the inverse of their normal stroke, and *Sea Hammer* began to back away from the beach. Three ships down, Thorgrim could see Bergthor's *Wave Splitter* also making sternway as she left the land.

"Larboard, hold! Starboard, make way!" Thorgrim shouted and the men on the larboard side held the blades of their oars in the water while the men to starboard leaned back and pulled and *Sea Hammer* spun on her keel. Thorgrim looked for Harald in the place he would normally be when pulling an oar, a habit of old, but he saw Hall there instead and remembered that Harald was not aboard.

He had spoken with Harald earlier on the beach, given him the choice of sailing aboard *Dragon* or *Sea Hammer*, thinking he might not want to be aboard the ship which he no longer commanded.

Harald had not been very pleasant during their short talk, though he understood the limits of how rude he could be and still not receive a reprimand, or worse. He had come close, to be sure, but he had kept his attitude on the right side of tolerable. And he made it clear he did not wish to be aboard *Sea Hammer*.

Thorgrim looked from *Sea Hammer*'s bow toward the beach and then back again. The longship had turned nearly parallel to the shore, so he ordered all the men to pull together and the ship began to make headway. Next Thorgrim called for them to row easy, to allow *Wave Splitter* to come up with them.

Soon the two ships were side by side, with about two hundred feet separating them, and Thorgrim ordered a stroke to match *Wave Splitter*'s speed. He looked across the water. Bergthor, standing on the after deck of his own ship, raised a hand and waved and Thorgrim waved back. Then he turned his attention to the water and land ahead.

For days they had been looking up and down this long stretch of sand with no idea what lay beyond, so it was with great interest that Thorgrim watched the shoreline open up. The Briton, Geldwine, had said the land to the south was an island and Thorgrim could see that now. As they pulled away from the beach, the stretch of water that separated the island from the mainland opened up in front of them, several miles across. Beyond that the land was lost in the fog, but Thorgrim had a better sense for the geography now.

He blinked the rainwater out of his eyes and looked to the north. He could see the wide mouth of the river that Geldwine had mentioned, but that was not where they were bound. Instead they were aiming to pass the mouth of that river and round a point of land beyond, which presumably would open up into the long, wide bay leading to Hamptun. A tricky coastline, but nothing at all compared to the treacherous rocks and headlands and shoals of his native country.

It was raining harder now, and there was not a breath of wind and Thorgrim did not think there would be that day, which meant a long hard pull at the oars, and perhaps a brutal fight at the end of it. But it was nothing that the men had not done before, and the thought of the fight, and the victory, and the plunder and the warm, dry place they would find to sleep in Hamptun, once it was theirs, would make the rowing easier.

All morning they pulled through the rain, *Sea Hammer* and *Wave Splitter* side by side and two hundred feet apart, the rest of the fleet stretched out behind. *Blood Hawk* was right in *Sea Hammer*'s wake, and Thorgrim knew that if his eyes and the visibility were better he would see Godi's massive shape at her tiller astern. Beyond *Blood Hawk* came *Oak Heart*, then *Black Wing, Fox* and *Dragon.*

Thorgrim smiled. If Harald had still commanded *Dragon* then she would certainly not have been last. He would have made certain he was in front of *Fox* at least. But Herjolf did not seem to care, which was why Thorgrim hoped that Harald would learn some humility soon, enough that he could put the boy back in command.

It was near to midday, Thorgrim guessed, with the sun entirely hidden by clouds, when he called for the men to eat. Some of those not pulling oars broke out bread and dried fish and passed it around, and cups of ale as well, trying as best they could to shelter the food and drink from the rain. Once they were done eating they relieved the rowers so those men could eat and give their tired muscles a rest.

It's a strange thing, Thorgrim thought. *This rowing through the fog.* A dull, lifeless monotony, but yet it was carrying them to battle, where a man was most alive, where his body could pulse with the energy of the gods.

From overhead Thorgrim heard a voice call out, "Bergthor! Hey there, Bergthor! How much longer must we row?"

Starri Deathless was at his usual perch at the masthead. He had taken it upon himself to ask that question, and Thorgrim was instantly and profoundly irritated in that way that only Starri could irritate him. No one on Thorgrim's ship should be shouting anything except for Thorgrim, nor would anyone but Starri dare. Worse, Bergthor would most likely think that he, Thorgrim, had told Starri to ask that question though in fact Thorgrim would never had displayed such impatience. That misunderstanding made Thorgrim more irritated still, but there was no way he could undo it.

Bergthor took a moment to answer. "Eight miles or so!" he called back across the water. Thorgrim heard low groans from the men at the oars.

The starboard shroud began to shake and Starri came sliding down from aloft. He was still wearing his tunic: he had not stripped down to leggings for battle as was his custom, and he looked almost frail with the wet cloth sticking to him. He hopped to the deck and came aft and began to speak but Thorgrim cut him off.

"Starri. Don't ever again call to another ship. If I want information I'll ask for it," Thorgrim said.

"Yes, certainly, Night Wolf," Starri replied, and Thorgrim wondered if he had even heard the words. Reprimanding Starri was pretty much pointless, which further irritated Thorgrim.

"But see here," Starri continued, "I was thinking, this fog that we're in? The rain and the fog and the cold and wet? Well, this must be just like what Hel is like, don't you think? Can you imagine being in such a place as this until time ends?"

"Some say you'll be with your family in Hel," Thorgrim said. He thought of Hallbera, and his father, Ulf of the Battle Song. He would take great pleasure in being with them again. He might even be willing to trade his current life for that. In fact, he realized, he might do so that very day, whether he willed it or not.

"With family?" Starri said. "That makes it worse. No, give me Odin's Hall of the Fallen, where I can fight until Ragnarok. And when Ragnarok comes, I'll fight some more."

"You've been trying to get to the Hall of the Fallen since I've known you, and before that, I suspect. The gods don't seem to want you there."

Starri shook his head, a grave look on his face, and if he knew that Thorgrim was teasing him he did not show it. "No, Night Wolf," he said. "The gods have their fun with me, like they do with you. They test me. But the more I stand up to their tests, the more celebrated a warrior I'll be in Odin's hall."

That, Thorgrim knew, was Starri's deepest held belief, and it sustained him as again and again he suffered the disappointment of living through every battle.

They continued pulling into the long harbor that Geldwine had described, nearly silent in a near silent world, a wolf pack stalking prey. They kept half a mile off the northern shore, the land low and featureless, sand beaches and scrubby trees and brush.

I hope there's more to Hamptun than this… Thorgrim thought.

Off the starboard bow Thorgrim could see the mouth of a river. Not a huge river, a couple hundred feet wide, perhaps, one of several that Geldwine had told them ran into the bay. But a river generally meant sand bars pushing out beyond its mouth, and he did not care to go aground.

"Starri," he said. "There might be sand banks ahead. Up aloft, would you, and keep a look out?"

"Of course, Night Wolf," Starri said and turned and jumped up, grabbed the shroud and began to climb.

"And if you have anything to say, say it to me, not Bergthor," Thorgrim called after him, but Starri was already halfway up the mast by then.

The mouth of the river was drawing abeam and Thorgrim looked up to see if Starri was in place. And as he did Starri called out, "I see a long sandbar, Night Wolf! But it ends well over there!" He was pointing to the north shore. "We'll miss it easily on this heading!"

Thorgrim nodded. Good. He turned and looked behind him. *Blood Hawk* was there, the same distance astern that she had been all day, as if *Sea Hammer* was towing her. Beyond her wide hull he could see the rest of his fleet spread out behind. He looked forward again.

Can't be too much farther, can it? Thorgrim thought. He could not help but feel the anxiety and frustration that came with waiting, even though he would never give it voice.

And then the rain and the quiet were split by a loud cry from aloft, Starri's unique cry of joy and fury and blood-lust. A cry Thorgrim knew well.

"There, Night Wolf, there! Behind us!" he shouted. "Now they're coming out! Ha, a proper greeting!"

Thorgrim turned and leaned outboard and looked astern, past the ships in his fleet toward the north shore. There, just up the river and coming around a bend that had hidden them until that moment, was another fleet of ships. English ships. There were five in full view that Thorgrim could see and more coming. Through the rain he could see few details, but he knew well enough what a ship looked like when it was loaded with men and he could tell that the decks of those ships were well crowded.

And he knew what an ambush looked like, and it looked like this. The English fleet had timed it well, let most of Thorgrim's ships get past before launching their attack. They were moving now, pulling hard for the bay and the last ships in Thorgrim's fleet. The smallest. The most vulnerable. There at the end of the line because he had put them there.

Chapter Twenty

[B]ut thou nowhere canst
to the chief do harm;
iron forts
are around the prince's fleet;
knee-god may not assail us.

The Poetic Edda

Harald Broadarm was pulling an oar on *Dragon*'s starboard side, all the way aft, though Herjolf had not ordered him to do so. Indeed, Herjolf seemed unwilling to give Harald any instructions at all, even though he was now in command of *Dragon* and Harald was just one of her crew, no more or less. Harald was Herjolf's to order around as was any man aboard.

But Herjolf did not seem inclined to do so. He hardly seemed inclined to give any orders at all. So Harald took it upon himself to take up the oar. He could never stand by while others labored. If anyone was working hard, Harald felt compelled to work twice as hard. He had always been that way. He would die before he would let anyone think he was shirking his duty.

But there were other reasons Harald chose to row, reason of which he was only vaguely aware. He had achieved a certain status among the men, the younger warriors in particular, and he did not want to jeopardize that. His outrageous attack on the whale was already becoming legend. One day, Harald was sure, the skalds would sing songs of it.

The fact that he had been stripped of his command as a result was not looked on as a shameful thing, but rather as an injustice and a mark of honor. Harald had stood up to Thorgrim Night Wolf, commander of the fleet, former Lord of Vík-ló, warrior of renown, and on top of all that, his own father. Little wonder he was admired by the others.

But Harald also knew that the quickest way to lose the admiration of those men was to act as if he deserved it. Deciding to not pull an oar while the others did would not be looked on kindly.

Beside, Harald liked to row. He liked the rhythm of the work, the steady back and forth, the pull on the muscles of his arms and his back. It calmed his mind, and his mind certainly needed some calming now.

He had been in a quiet fury when he sat down at the oars, a fury directed at his father. The old man did not understand that, in going after the whale, Harald was making a display of leadership and courage. Thorgrim failed to appreciate how much good it would do as far as cementing the men's loyalty. And because he could not understand, he had taken away the command that Harald so coveted. And had so earned.

Harald had been rowing for half a day and he was calmer now. Even when Herjolf had switched out the rowers Harald had declined to give up his oar. And the work and the quiet and the chance to think had all worked their magic on his spirit. He had not forgiven his father, not even close, but at least his fury had ebbed away like the tide.

So entranced had he become with the steady pull of the oar that when he heard Starri's cry, far off but distinct and completely recognizable, he could not immediately place it. He frowned and looked off toward the shore and thought, *Now, what was that?*

It was then that he saw the fleet coming around the bend in the river and he felt the rush of comprehension — Starri's war cry and a gathering of enemy ships bearing down on them. And with that came the familiar sensations he always felt at such a moment: the tightening in his stomach, the energy like tiny bolts of lightning shooting though his arms and legs.

The image of an ax coming down and slicing him right where his neck and shoulders met.

It was a vision that was ghastly and frightening and for reasons he did not understand it always came to him in the moments before a fight. It filled him with fear, and the fear made him ashamed, but he pushed all those feelings down the way he always did.

The sudden appearance of the fleet was like a cold wave washing over him, one he had not seen coming. He was stunned for a moment by the surprise and the shock of it. And then the shock was gone and he began to think once more.

You bastards, you bastards, that was a clever thing, Harald thought. The English had let the big ships go by first, and that meant that *Dragon* and *Fox* and the rest of the smaller ships at the end of the line were in a bad place.

"What by the gods was that?" Herjolf all but shouted. He was looking forward, toward the source of the sound, Starri's unearthly cry.

"There, Herjolf, there!" Harald shouted, pointing as best as he could with his chin, unable to take his hands off the oar.

"What?" Herjolf asked. He was looking at Harald, not where Harald was gesturing.

"There! Behind us! Coming from the river!" Harald shouted and Herjolf turned and looked.

"Oh! Son of a whore!" Herjolf shouted, his back to Harald, his eyes fixed on the ships in the river. More and more of them were coming into view around the bend.

Harald pressed his lips together. *We need to arm, we need to get under arms!* he thought.

Thorgrim had planned to get the fleet closer to the town before the men donned mail and took up weapons and shields, and that made sense, since the arms were a hindrance when rowing. He would not have anticipated an attack over the water. None of them would have imagined the English would have so many ships at their disposal, and Harald wondered where they had all come from.

Behind him Harald could hear the shouts and curses of the other men at the oars as they, too, saw the approaching fleet. He wished Herjolf would stop staring at them like some paralyzed fool and order the men to take up arms, but he kept his mouth shut. It had been drilled into him from an early age that there was only one man on board a ship, or leading men in battle, who gave orders. Everyone else was to remain silent and listen.

But sometimes remaining silent was absolute torture.

Harald watched the lead ship of the English fleet turn until its bows were pointed right at *Dragon*, its banks of oars lifting and falling, the others astern of it turning as well. He realized two things. One was that his father had intended for *Fox* and *Dragon* and the smallest of Bergthor's ships to be last into the fight, but instead they would be first. The other was that his father had made a big mistake in arranging the fleet in that manner.

Both thoughts pleased him quite a bit.

As he pulled back on the oar he swiveled around and looked ahead, past the bow. The rest of the Northmen's fleet seemed to be reacting to the sight of the English, turning out of line, left and right, the fine parade of ships becoming a chaotic mess. There would be no unity in their defense, no coordination, while the English, Harald imagined, had planned their own attack quite well.

He leaned forward for another stroke and saw Herjolf look from the English fleet behind them to the rest of their own fleet ahead and back again. And still he said nothing.

Come on, come on… Harald thought, trying to will Herjolf into making a decision as he leaned back again for another pull. Then Herjolf looked forward again and his expression was more determined now, as if he had finally made up his mind. He pulled the tiller toward him and Harald saw the shoreline sweep past as *Dragon* began to turn.

Good, good, Harald thought. Herjolf was spinning the ship around to drive her first into the fight. But the men would have to get their weapons and shields, and get them quick.

Then the shoreline stopped sweeping past and Harald saw that Herjolf was not turning the ship all the way around. He was simply changing course to get clear of the approaching enemy, and despite himself and all his long-ingrained discipline Harald shouted out.

"Herjolf! Where are you going?"

Herjolf looked from the bow toward Harald and he still looked as determined as ever. "Your father said the big ships go into the fight first, and I'm getting clear of them!"

"That was when we went ashore!" Harald argued even as he pulled back for another stroke. "Not this! No one saw this coming!"

"Just row, do not argue with me!" Herjolf shouted back, sounding, for the first time, as if he meant to take charge. He lifted his eyes from Harald and looked over his shoulder, back at the English fleet, now directly astern. Harald felt his fury and disbelief and confusion boiling over. His duty, he knew, was to do as Herjolf said. And he did not care.

He leaned forward with the others, bringing his long oar back for another stroke, but unlike the others held it there. Brand, who was right behind him, pulled hard and tangled his oar with Harald's, and the next oar ahead became tangled as well, and the oar ahead of that and ahead of that until the entire starboard side was a flailing mess. Men were shouting and cursing and Harald heard at least one man fall right off his sea chest onto the deck. *Dragon* began to slew around as the larboard rowers continued to pull.

"You clumsy whore's sons, get those oars straightened out!" Herjolf called, trying to fight the pull of the larboard oars by pushing the helm to starboard.

"I'll get clear, I'll get clear!" Harald shouted and he pulled his oar in through the row port. The oar was considerably longer than the ship was wide at that point, but rather than lift the oar above the heads of the rowers on the larboard side, directly across from him, Harald ran it straight across the ship, starboard to larboard. The handle of the oar passed between two of the larboard rowers as they were leaning forward for the stroke. They cursed as they became entangled in the oar's handle, which Harald was swinging side to side like a long club, slamming into one man, then the other.

In an instant the larboard side was in as great a confusion as the starboard. The men cursed and shouted and *Dragon* slewed sideways as her headway dropped off and Herjolf stood at the useless tiller, his mouth hanging open.

Harald sprang to his feet. "We won't get clear now, Herjolf, we better get ready to fight!" *Dragon* was broadside to the oncoming ships, like a makeshift wall between the enemy and the rest of Thorgrim's fleet, and they would never get the oars straightened out before the English were on them.

"Run your oars in! Take up arms!" Herjolf shouted and the men obeyed instantly, because it was quite clear now that the English would be aboard them in moments and they had better be ready to receive them. Most of the oars came sailing in and were laid fore and aft, while the others were pushed out through the row ports and allowed to drop in the water. The men leaped to their feet and grabbed up shields from the shield rack and the spears and axes and swords that had been set down on the deck, ready for the fight.

Harald plucked the nearest shield from the rack and reached down and pulled his sword Oak Cleaver from its scabbard, the sword of his grandfather, Ornolf the Restless, a fine Frankish blade, and he relished the feel of the familiar grip in his hand.

"The deaths of these men, they'll be on your head, Harald Broadarm!" Herjolf shouted as he too adjusted the grip on his weapons and waited for the enemy bearing down on them. But Harald's spirit was singing now, every inch of him on fire, any thought of an ax blade splitting neck and shoulder long banished.

"You'll thank me!" Harald shouted back. "You have the chance to be a hero now, alive or dead!"

Herjolf scowled, then hopped down off the afterdeck and hurried forward to join the others. The forward-most English ship was close, one hundred feet away and coming on fast and it showed no inclination to avoid slamming into the smaller ship. There were men crowded on either side of its bow, helmets in place, spears held up like saplings, waiting for the two vessels to come together.

This is a big bastard… Harald thought. The ship had to be seventy or eighty feet long and might have a hundred or more warriors aboard. *Dragon* had thirty-six men in her company.

Should make for a fair fight, Harald thought. The English ship was driving at *Dragon*'s midsection and Harald wondered if her master meant to run right over *Dragon* and crush her and sink her. And then he wondered if he would be able to do so. And then he realized he was about to find out.

"Fight like furies, you men!" Harald shouted. "We have to hold them until the rest come up!" It was not his place to shout such things, but he was no longer thinking that way, nor did he care. They would all likely be dead in the next few moments, so the time for niceties was past.

Then the English ship struck, just a little forward of *Dragon*'s beam. She hit with the audible sound of crushing wood, but rather than drive over *Dragon* she lifted the smaller ship up, rolling her hard to one side, knocking some of *Dragon*'s crew off their feet. The English ship was perpendicular to *Dragon* when they struck, and as she drove forward *Dragon* began to pivot on the Englishman's bow. The big English ship was brushing *Dragon* aside on her way to fight the bigger of the Northmen's ships.

"Oh, no, you son of a bitch!" Harald shouted. The English were ignoring *Dragon* and Harald felt personally insulted by that. He tossed his shield aside and sheathed Oak Cleaver. He ran aft and grabbed up a grappling hook and walrus-hide rope, the same one he had used to catch the whale, and stepped up to the ship's side.

The big English ship was still driving right through *Dragon*, pushing her aside, pushing her clear, as she went after larger prey. Harald swung the hook once, twice, then sent it sailing across the water between the ships.

He saw the heavy iron grapple clear the side of the English ship and strike one of the oarsmen there, knocking him clean off his seat. He dropped his oar and it tangled with the one behind it and in an instant the English sweeps were in a garbled mess just as *Dragon*'s had been.

Harald heaved away at the rope and as he did he turned to shout an order down the deck, but he could see there was no need. Brand, forward, had already flung the other grapple. Harald saw it disappear over the side of the Englishman's ship and saw Brand and the men around him haul away quickly. The rope rose up out of the water as the strain came on it, just as Harald was putting a strain on his own line. And then a dozen men were swarming around Harald, grabbing up the rope and pulling hard, hauling *Dragon* up to the Englishman's side.

If the English ship looked big coming bow on, it looked considerably bigger broadside. Harald could see the great hoard of men crowded down her considerable length. He could see shields and spears in abundance, and the warriors aboard her were yelling and cheering and seemed as eager as Harald was for the two ships to come together.

There was twenty feet of water between them when the English spears started flying. A fellow named Vebjorn was standing ten feet away from Harald, right against *Dragon*'s side, shield in one hand, ax in the other, when the first of the spears struck him in the shoulder.

He roared in pain and dropped his ax and pulled the spear free from his flesh. One-handed, he spun the spear around and was about to fling it back when another spear caught him right in the chest, striking with enough force to knock him flat on his back. And that, Harald knew, was the end of Vebjorn.

"Pull! Pull!" Harald shouted. The only way to not be killed like deer in a pen was for them to get alongside and get aboard this bastard. And the others knew that as well. They heaved away, shouting as they did, some screaming for blood, some screaming from the spears that had impaled them.

Then the two ships came together, hitting hard enough to send a shudder through *Dragon*'s fabric. Harald wrapped the rope quickly around a cleat and turned to jump aboard the English ship but was met by one of the English warriors leaping aboard *Dragon*, which did not seem right. In his mind, Harald had pictured himself and his men boarding the Englishman, and somehow it had not occurred to him that the English might board them instead.

All this passed through Harald's mind in the instant it took him to pull his sword and knock the tip of the English warrior's spear aside, then drive Oak Cleaver straight at the man as he tumbled aboard. But the Englishman had his shield up in time, through luck or skill, and Harald's sword glanced off. The man fell the rest of the way, hitting the deck with his shoulder, and Harald could see it was an easy kill to be had.

He lifted Oak Cleaver over his head as the man on the deck swung his spear sideways as if he was threshing wheat. The spear hit Harald's legs at the knees and they buckled, and Harald felt himself going down. He hit the deck hard, flat on his back, and saw the other man leap to his feet.

No, no, no… Harald thought as he saw the man draw the spear back over his head. Harald had managed to land on top of Oak Cleaver, pinning the sword between him and the deck, and he was unable to get it free.

He braced himself, eyes on the spear tip, waiting for the right instant to move. The Englishman hurled the weapon straight down, right at Harald's chest, and as he did Harald twisted to one side. He felt the point of the spear nick his tunic as it went past, heard it make a distinct thud in the deck. Then Harald twisted back, pulling Oak Cleaver free as he did and slashing the Englishman across the thighs. He saw the man's legging open up and the flesh under them open as well, the instant pulse of blood. The man doubled over in pain and surprise and Harald kicked him to the deck then pushed himself to his feet.

He looked forward. This was not working out the way he had envisioned. Not that he had put a lot of thought into it. Or any, really. *Dragon*'s starboard side was lashed to the Englishman's larboard, but Harald could not see the rails of either ship under the press of men who were swarming aboard.

The cumulative roar of the battle was terrific, particularly after half a day of near silent rowing. The English were coming over the side in waves; the Northmen were wildly outnumbered, and unlike the English they had not been prepared for this fight and it was starting to tell. Beyond the English ship lashed alongside Harald could see more of their fleet pushing past to grapple with the other ships of his father's fleet, pulling straight and true and in good order.

He looked past *Dragon*'s bow. Thorgrim's ships and Bergthor's ships were turning to meet this new threat but they seemed to be in a great confusion, some ships turning to larboard, some to starboard, some still pulling ahead. It looked as if *Black Wing* and one of Bergthor's ships had managed to run into one another.

Harald snatched up the shield at his feet and put his arm through the strap and grabbed hold of the grip inside the boss. With a shout he ran forward, into the fight, but he did not have to run far. The English had overrun the ship and pushed the Northmen back from the rail — there were more of them aboard *Dragon* now than there were of *Dragon*'s crew.

He drove shield-first into the nearest of them, taking him by surprise, knocking him sideways and slashing down with Oak Cleaver. He felt the blade bite, saw the man scream — he could not make out the individual voice through the din — and saw him stagger back. Not dead, but wounded and out of the fight. Good enough.

A spear thrust at him through the press, though in the madness Harald could not tell who was wielding it. He felt the sharp tip jab into his side and he twisted as the weapon drove forward. He felt the point scrape along his side and was aware of the warm, wet sensation of blood running down flesh, but he felt no pain. He hacked with his sword, pushed with his shield, hacked again.

The noise was incredible, the deck of the ship so packed with men he could feel the very fabric of the vessel trembling under the weight.

There was no form, no organization, no thought in this sort of fighting. It was a just a brutal hack and stab, shield and mail against blade and point, and in fights such as that it was numbers that generally won. Even if these English were untrained men, timid men, it would be hard to defeat so many. And Harald could see they were not that.

Mail... he thought. He just noticed how many of the English had mail and swords. Less than half, to be sure, but even that meant they were better fitted out than he was used to seeing in any English army, or Irish or Northmen, for that matter.

Who are these men? Harald wondered, even as he was forced back a step, and then another. It did not seem possible that the English could have organized such an army, and a fleet as well, in the short time since he and the others had dragged the dead whale onto the beach.

He took another step back, swatting a spear point away with his shield in one direction, thrusting Oak Cleaver in the other. He felt the bite of a sharp blade on his shins and he shouted in pain and surprise and stepped back again. Someone had reached down under the shields and gone for his legs but in that crowd of men he could not tell who. Once again he felt the warm blood running over skin and he knew he would be in a lot of pain if he was still alive when the fighting was done.

Another step back, and then one more, and then Harald found himself pressed against the larboard side, driven right across the deck, and there was nowhere left to go. He tried to look forward, to see how the fighting was going down the length of the deck, but he could not see much beyond the men surrounding him, Northmen and English. Brand was on his right, two other shipmates on his left, and for all he knew they were the last four of the crew still alive.

Hope this was worth it... Harald thought. He did not mind laying down his life in bloody combat, but he hoped that by sacrificing his ship and crew he had given the others a chance to attack in some semblance of order.

Not my ship... he remembered and he felt that old rage, born of injustice, well up again. It should have been his ship; it was not fair that it had been taken from him. He roared and shoved his shield forward and knocked two of the English warriors off balance. He hacked down with Oak Cleaver and felt the blade bite and hoped it hit something worth hitting, but he could not tell in that melee.

From the corner of his eye he saw another spear coming at him and he slashed down with his sword and felt it knock the point away. He was bringing his sword up again when he felt the tip of a blade ripping into his upper arm. He shouted, twisted, and slashed in the direction from which the thrust had come.

We're done here… Harald thought. There was no place left for them to go and not nearly enough of the Northmen to drive the English back.

Then through the shouting and screaming and clashing of weapons Harald heard a long, piercing note, a horn cutting through all the confusion. He had no idea what it might mean. But the English did, apparently, because they began to back away, retreating back across *Dragon*'s deck as quickly as they could while still putting up a defense against the men in front of them.

It made no sense. They were retreating moments before they would have killed every man of *Dragon*'s crew. But suddenly Harald found himself with no enemy in front, just a stretch of blood-soaked deck between him and the retreating English.

He looked up. On the far side of the English ship, looming above the rail as if it was floating in air, was a sight he knew well: the leering, fang-bearing figurehead of *Fox*, run up on the enemy's far side, and one of Bergthor's ships just behind.

Chapter Twenty-One

And Æthelwulf, King of the Saxons, and his son Æthelbald, with the whole army, fought a long time against [the heathens]…after a lengthy battle, which was fought with much bravery on both sides, the most part of the heathen horde was utterly destroyed and slain…

Asser's Life of King Alfred

Felix heard King Æthelwulf make a snorting sound, a sound that indicated irritation and impatience.

They were standing on the afterdeck of the king's ship, the biggest in the fleet. Felix was standing a little in front and to the right of Æthelwulf, close enough to hear him, far enough that the king would not think he was hovering and grow annoyed. Just in front of them, along the edge of the afterdeck, stood two dozen of the king's finest warriors forming a human wall and fitted out in matching shirts of mail and shining helmets.

"Well, there goes Byrnhorn, driving right past!" the king said. "What does he think he's up to?" Felix had been expecting such a comment. Off the starboard side, the ship that had been astern of them, commanded by Ealdorman Byrnhorn, was now passing them by as it went after the Northmen beyond the bow of Æthelwulf's ship.

There was a good reason, of course, that Æthelwulf's ship was not pushing forward like Byrnhorn's. One of the smaller of the heathens' ships had lashed itself to their larboard side and the bastards likely thought they were going to board the king's ship and take it. Felix had to admire their guts, if not their brains.

The ship was a third the length of Æthelwulf's, with less than half the men aboard. Before one of the Northmen had set foot on the king's ship, the English warriors had broken like a wave onto the heathen's deck and driven them all back. Now they were butchering them in good order. It was a wonderful thing to see.

Felix flexed his shoulders to settle his mail shirt. The cumulative weight of the hundreds of interlocking metal links, the sound they made when he moved, had a very distant familiarity, something barely remembered. His hand, which once would have settled on the hilt of the sword at his waist with thoughtless ease, now had to search for it.

There was something refreshing about battle, he had to admit, something primal and basic: the armor, the weapons, the unambiguous objectives. It made a nice respite from the court intrigue that was now his lot, the careful manipulation of opinion and rumor, the subtle bending of attitudes.

Not that he could avoid the intrigue, even as they made ready for the sort of fight that involved iron, steel and leather rather than words. All of the ealdormen and important thegns of Wessex were there, each maneuvering for position, and he, Felix, royal gatekeeper, manipulator of the manipulative, had to regulate it, keep it all in order.

And other things besides. Now, for instance, he would have to placate Æthelwulf about his place in the battle and keep him from doing something too bold in the name of reclaiming his youth.

Leave boldness to the expendable ones like Byrnhorn, Felix thought.

But before he could turn and speak he heard Leofric speak first. Leofric of Dorsetshire, a wealthy thegn, old friend and, more importantly, old comrade in arms to King Æthelwulf. He had joined Æthelwulf aboard his ship, and Æthelwulf seemed glad to have him.

"Come now, sire," Leofric said, his voice loud, his tone jovial. "If you insist on taking the lead the way you did then you must fight whoever comes at you first, like this sorry whore's son who's tied himself alongside! And you have to leave some of these bastards for the others to kill, you know."

"I suppose you're right," Æthelwulf said and Felix silently thanked God for sending Leofric to him. Because, in this whole affair, Felix had only two goals in mind. One was to see that Æthelwulf had a big enough part in the battle to satisfy him. The second was to be sure he did not play so big a part as to risk getting hurt.

The day before they had allotted command of the various ships to the ealdormen and thegns who marched with the king from Winchester, and had spread the seven hundred or so warriors and men of the fyrd among them. They had cast off and rowed from the docks at Hamtun to a place up the River Hamble where they could not be seen from the bay, and there tied the ships to the banks.

Felix had suggested to Æthelwulf that his ship, the largest in the fleet, might be best situated at the end of the line, where the king could better see how the battle was playing out, and come into the fight where needed. It was a good try, and Æthelwulf had almost taken the suggestion, but in the end he could not resist being the first into the fight.

Scouts on horseback stationed at intervals down the bay had brought word of the Northmen's approach. At a council of war it was decided that they would let the heathens' fleet go past before launching an attack, and thus cutting off their escape. The goal was to crush the vermin completely. And Æthelwulf's big ship would lead the way.

So far the plan of battle had worked better than Felix dared hope. What Felix had not anticipated was the way the Northmen had arranged their fleet. The big ships had gone first, with the smallest making up the rear guard. And that meant that Æthelwulf's ship, largest of the English fleet, would be engaging the smallest of the heathens'. They could have their fight, destroy the Northmen and be done with it, with Æthelwulf never getting into the thick of the battle. And that was good because, ultimately, this was nothing but an enormous and unwelcome distraction.

For two years Felix had been organizing Æthelwulf's upcoming pilgrimage to Rome, and now, just as it was ready to begin, the Northmen arrived to make a mess of the whole thing.

Two years of work, Felix thought, *countless letters to Charles and to the pope, all the effort to get young Alfred to Rome and back, and now one unlucky blow from a heathen's sword and it will all be for naught…*

Felix turned to the king and gestured toward the heathen ship lashed to their side, and the fighting on its deck. "They're making short work of the heathens," he observed.

"Short work?" Æthelwulf snorted. "They're taking a bloody long time to make short work of them. Look, there goes Byrnhorn after that big fellow!" The king pointed to one of the others in the British fleet, pulling past, driving into the fight. "And…is that Ingwald? Yes, I believe it's Ingwald, going after the other. Get these men to finish up here so we can join in the real fighting."

In fact the men were fighting as well as they could, but before Felix had to take up the distasteful task of pointing that out Leofric jumped in again.

"Sire!" he said, and his tone remained jovial. "See there, those glorious whores' sons are killing the heathens as fast as ever they can!" He pointed to the larboard side where more than half of Æthelwulf's men had boarded the Northmen's ship and driven the enemy to the far side. It was hard to tell what was happening, but the sheer number of English warriors suggested that the Northmen were getting by far the worst of it.

Well done, Leofric, well done, Felix thought. He did not know if Leofric had the same idea as him — keep the king engaged but safe — but it did not matter. The result so far was the same.

Leofric had asked Æthelwulf if he might join him in the fight, and that had made Felix suspicious. Most of the other men of importance had campaigned for ships of their own to command, but not Leofric. He preferred to remain with the king, and Felix wondered what he wanted.

He caught snatches of their conversation through the morning hours as the ship remained tied to the bank. The talk consisted of reminiscing about battles past, interspersed with news from Dorset and rumors about the odd marriage of Ealdorman Nothwulf, who had command of one of the smaller ships, to his late brother's widow, and the friction that had ensued in Sherborne as a result.

Nothing of any great consequence, Felix was happy to hear.

Leofric's voice broke through Felix's reverie. "Ha! See here! Now you'll have your fighting, sire!"

Felix pulled his eyes from the heathen ship on the larboard side and turned to look at Leofric, but Leofric was looking out over the starboard side and pointing in that direction. Felix followed his finger. Two more of the smaller ships had peeled away from the heathen's fleet and were coming around to their unengaged side. Felix could see the hideous, open-jawed face of some fanged animal seated at the top of the long, curved stem of the lead ship, like some head on a pike.

The second ship was right astern, and the bows of both ships were crammed with warriors, a dense thicket of shields and helmets and furious, bearded faces. It was a sizable host, and Felix knew it was only a fraction of the men aboard — the bulk of them would be at the oars right up to the moment the ships hit.

He looked back to the larboard side. Most of the warriors who had come with the king were fighting the Northmen there; there were not nearly enough men still aboard to fight the starboard side.

"Ah, damn their eyes, we'll see to these fellows!" Æthelwulf shouted.

"We will," Leofric said, "but we could use some help."

Felix looked straight forward where the boy with the horn stood waiting for instructions. He met Felix's eye and Felix nodded. The boy put the horn to his lips and blew a long clear note.

They'll hear that, Felix thought. *Let's see if they obey.*

They certainly heard it. The men along the larboard side of Æthelwulf's ship, fixated on the fighting there, now turned just as the heathen ship with the animal figurehead was closing the last few feet. Felix could see the look of shock on their faces, but it did not last long. These men were used to this sort of work, and they immediately charged across the deck to meet the new threat.

The first of the English warriors was reaching the starboard side when the ships collided. The heathens had made no effort to slow and their bow hit a solid blow to the English ship's side. Felix stumbled with the surprising force of the impact and he saw half a dozen men go down, others staggering as they tried to retain their balance. They were still stumbling when the Northmen came over the rail.

They came swarming around the bow of their ship, climbing and leaping down to the deck of Æthelwulf's ship, shouting their devil's shouts with shields held ready and swords and axes and spears in hand. The first few went down under the blades of Æthelwulf's men, but soon there were too many Northmen, coming aboard too fast, for them to all be killed as they came.

Felix heard the sound of Æthelwulf drawing his sword. "Come along now," the king shouted, "let's be at these bastards! God is calling us to the fight!"

"Hold, sire, I pray," Leofric shouted. "Your guards are the best fighting men aboard. Let's wait to see where in the fight we can best be used!"

"We can best be used where the damned heathens are boarding the ship!" Æthelwulf shouted, but then he added, "Very well, we'll wait and watch a moment."

And it was an amazing thing to watch: the Northmen's ships to starboard and larboard, the fighting surging across the decks of the English ship and the smaller heathen ship lashed to the larboard side. Felix could see one fellow there, one of the enemy, broad and strong-looking, with long yellow hair, slashing wildly with his sword and fending off attacks with a half-shattered shield. He was bleeding from several wounds but seemed not to notice.

Along with him there was only a handful of the Northmen still standing, maybe a dozen or so. The rest lay strewn around the deck, their bodies tangled with the bodies of the English warriors they had taken down with them.

Once again Felix felt the ship shudder with the impact of another vessel, and he heard the deep thudding sound and the sharper cracking noises of two vessels coming together. The second of the Northmen's ships had hit the starboard side and the men were coming aboard as fast as they could. The English warriors were there to meet them, but they had to cover the whole length of the ship now, and their numbers had been much reduced by the fighting so far, and they were taking on the crews of two ships, not just one.

What had looked to be an easy victory at first was looking considerably more worrisome now. It had been Felix's thought that the king's men would board the heathens' ship and fight there. But now the heathens were swarming aboard Æthelwulf's ship. That was not how it was supposed to happen.

"Drive them back! Back aboard their own ships, fight them there!" Felix shouted and was immediately embarrassed by his own lack of restraint. No one fighting forward would hear him, nor was he telling them to do anything they were not already trying to do. It was just weakness on his part that he could not keep his mouth shut.

"We're surrounded now," Æthelwulf shouted, "so we can go forward and fight or we can stand here and die like frightened women! Let's go!"

Felix could think of no argument he might make. The heathens were closing in, and the best fighting men on the ship — the king's guards — were standing by watching as if this was some sport or dance. There was not much choice now.

He stepped forward, three steps, and grabbed the captain of the king's guards by the shoulder and leaned close. "We'll go into the fight! You and your men keep your wall around the king, hear? You fight as best you can, but your chief duty is still to protect the king!"

The captain nodded. He raised his sword, looked left and right. "Forward!" he shouted and the line that had stood like a palisade against the afterdeck began to move forward, quick but disciplined. Felix looked out over their heads. The English and Northmen were locked in close battle, a surging mass, hard to tell one man from another, or friend from foe. No one saw the king's guard advancing and that was good. Any advantage, no matter how small, was good.

"After them!" Æthelwulf shouted. Felix turned back and looked at the king. His face was split with a wide smile, parting his beard, grayer than black now, and revealing white and fairly even teeth. His eyes were bright, gleaming. He looked more alive than Felix had ever seen him. He looked like a man ready to enjoy a fight: brutal, decisive and unequivocal. He looked like a man who was remembering what it was like to be twenty-five and leading warriors into battle and liking it.

"Yes, after them!" Leofric shouted. He looked determined and serious. Not frightened at all, or hesitant, but not eager like Æthelwulf was. Leofric was not reliving the past, he was displaying concern about the present.

Then Æthelwulf stepped forward and to Felix's surprise rather than climb down from the afterdeck to the deck below, he jumped. And to Felix's further surprise he did not injure himself doing so. He and Leofric followed, jumped as well, and the three of them hurried forward in the wake of the king's guard.

The captain of the guard was the first of them into the fight and he chose his spot well, right at the aft end of the struggle, where the Northmen leaping aboard were threatening to come around the flank of the Englishmen and get behind them. The heathens did not see the guards coming until they were there, swords thrusting and hacking at the mass of men. Felix saw the captain's blade open up a long and bloody gash on one of the Northmen's arms. The

Northman turned toward the captain. He did not look hurt, only surprised, and he still looked surprised when the point of the captain's sword split his throat.

"At them!" Æthelwulf shouted as he came up behind his house guard. He thrust his sword between two of the men and Felix saw it deflect off the face of a Northman's shield.

"Stand aside, stand aside!" Æthelwulf shouted, struggling to get past his men and come to grips with the enemy, but the guards seemed not to hear him, and they did not let him through.

Felix stepped up next to Æthelwulf, sword held in front of him, and as he saw a space open between the guards he drove the point through the gap. He felt the sword stick into something that gave resistance, just for an instant, and then the blade drove further in and someone screamed. An old but well remembered sensation, like the feel of the mail shirt on his shoulders.

Somewhere close by Felix heard one of the English fighting men shout, "The king! The king is with us!" and suddenly a great upwelling of cheers and shouts and calls of "The king!" came rolling across the deck. And with it came a surge of energy, as if the crowd of English warriors were all one great beast and that beast suddenly roused itself to make a renewed push to drive this hated enemy off. They heaved themselves forward and step by step they drove the Northmen back.

The heathens were still shouting their devilish war cries, still fighting hard, but now they were all but drowned out by the enthusiastic cheers of the English. Felix saw some of the enemy host climbing over the rail of Æthelwulf's ship and back aboard their own.

"At them! Don't let the bastards live!" Æthelwulf shouted as he pushed forward with the rest. A spear reached out from the press of men and the king batted it away with his shield and countered with a thrust of his sword, a sword he had carried for four decades, that his father had carried before him. If it found a mark, Felix could not tell. Æthelwulf drew the sword back, raised it overhead and hacked down at the heathen line.

Good, good… Felix thought. He could sense the shift in momentum as the English warriors pushed forward. Leofric was on the king's other side and he and Æthelwulf were hacking away with abandon. There was no subtlety in fighting such as this: victory went to the most determined, and the most brutal.

Up and down the English line the cheering grew louder, the enthusiasm grew more palpable as the Northmen were hacked down or driven over the rail and back aboard their ships. Those English warriors who were unable to get close enough to the fighting to do any good hurled their spears over the heads of the others. Most missed, but here and there one found a Northman and sent him screaming and writhing to the deck, where he was trampled under the feet of the fighting mob.

The heathens were wielding their spears as well, standing on the sheer strake of their ship and thrusting or hurling them down into the English line. Felix could see the spears hit their mark, the men knocked back by the impact.

"We'll board their ships!" Æthelwulf shouted. "Board them and kill the lot, take the ships!"

No, we won't, Felix thought. Victory was almost in their hands now, as complete a victory as they could hope for. There would be no more risk to the king's life.

But victory was not won yet, and he and the king and Leofric were still hacking and thrusting at the enemy in front. Felix caught a flash out of the corner of his eye, heard a grunting noise. He turned and the king was not there. He looked down at the deck. Æthelwulf was lying splayed out on the boards, thrashing, eyes and mouth open, a spear standing up from his chest. The dagger point of the weapon, hurled with great force, had gone right through the king's fine chain mail and possibly out the other side.

"*Mon Dieu*, no!" Felix shouted. He grabbed the shaft of the spear and jerked the point free, not even considering whether or not that was the best thing to do. He dropped to his knee at Æthelwulf's side. Leofric was kneeling as well.

"My lord! My lord! Do you hear me?" he shouted. Æthelwulf looked at him, his mouth still open. There seemed to be a moment of confusion, and then he nodded.

"I hear you, Felix," he said, his voice stronger than Felix had dared hope. Another man knelt down beside the king and Felix saw it was the captain of the guard.

"Get your men around the king and get the ship clear of the heathens!" Felix shouted. "We must get clear so we can attend to the king!"

The captain nodded and was on his feet again. Half a dozen of the guard took their place forming a loose circle around the king and the two men at his side. Felix saw men hefting the long oars and pushing the heathens' ships away from their side.

He looked aft. The boy with the horn was standing there, white and frightened-looking. "Blow retreat!" Felix shouted. "Blow retreat, blow it loud!"

Felix, of course, was not the one to make such decisions; he had no such authority. But no one aboard that ship was likely to argue the point, and he hoped those on the other ships would take it to be the king's command.

The boy nodded. He put the horn to his lips. The first note was strangled and ugly, but the second came out pure and loud, very loud, loud enough, Felix was sure, to be heard on all the English ships in the fleet, even through the battle cry.

Enough of this nonsense, Felix thought. *We must attend to the king.*

Chapter Twenty-Two

[S]pear spilled
rivers of blood,
and it ran from
wound red on sword.

The Poetic Edda

Starri Deathless's war cry echoed around the fleet, followed right after by his announcement: *Now they're coming out! Ha, a proper greeting!* He did not bother clarifying, but any of the men who had sailed and fought with Starri knew right off what he meant. Enthusiasm like that could only mean there was an enemy coming to fight.

A buzzing ran fore and aft among the rowers, and those not on an oar leaned out over the side as Thorgrim had.

"Keep rowing, you bastards! Keep your minds on your work!" Thorgrim shouted, though his own mind was racing off in many directions at once. He could not let the English catch up with the smaller ships and crush them. It would be a slaughter. By the looks of it the lead ship alone in the English fleet might have a hundred men aboard.

Would Herjolf stand and fight, or would he get out of the way? If Harald was still in command then Thorgrim knew exactly what he would do: he would drive *Dragon* right into the enemy and fight as if he had no doubt he would win. But Herjolf? Thorgrim did not know him well enough to judge.

And which would he prefer that Herjolf do? Thorgrim was not sure of that either. It would not be smart of the little *Dragon* to take on that big English ship, but sometimes the smart thing was not necessarily the best thing.

Thorgrim saw Gudrid standing nearby and he called him over. "Take the tiller," he said. "Keep on this course. We'll be turning directly."

Gudrid nodded and took the tiller and Thorgrim stepped away. He had to turn the ship around, to go after the English fleet, but first he had to see what direction he should turn. He did not want his carefully organized fleet to turn into a chaotic mess, but he wasn't sure that he could stop it.

He grabbed hold of the tall carved sternpost, the wood slick with rain, put a foot on the sheer strake and heaved himself up, looking astern around the post like he was hiding behind a small tree. He was not pleased by what he saw.

The lead ship of the English fleet, the big one, was nearly up with the smaller ships at the end of the line. Thorgrim thought he saw *Dragon* turning away, trying to get clear rather than tangle with the more powerful vessel, but he could not be sure. All the Northmen's ships were turning at once, turning in different directions, looking to get into the fight, and Thorgrim had a hard time seeing through the ranks of hulls and masts and yards that stood between *Sea Hammer* and the enemy.

"Gudrid, turn to starboard!" Thorgrim shouted. Bergthor's ship *Wave Splitter*, two hundred feet away, was turning to larboard. Bergthor had sense enough to turn away from *Sea Hammer*, and not toward her, which would have put them in great danger of colliding.

The words had hardly left Thorgrim's mouth before *Sea Hammer* began to turn. Thorgrim dropped back down to the deck. No need to look astern: the other ships were abeam of them now and soon would be right ahead as Gudrid spun the ship around.

"There, Gudrid, keep this heading!" Thorgrim called as *Sea Hammer*'s bow pointed like an arrow at the mass of frantically maneuvering ships. *Wave Splitter* was now off their starboard side and also pulling hard for the fight. It looked to Thorgrim as if he and Bergthor had the same thought: *Sea Hammer* would come in on the left side of the fleet, *Wave Splitter* on the right, and the English would be caught between the largest ships of the Northmen's fleet.

The mass of vessels ahead was like a fog, sometimes an impenetrable wall, sometimes opening up to give a surprising view. Such a gap appeared, just briefly, between *Blood Hawk* and one of Bergthor's ships, and through it Thorgrim caught a glimpse of the big

English ship which was leading their fleet. *Dragon* had indeed engaged her. She was lying alongside and Thorgrim guessed they had grappled, and that even now the men of *Dragon* were storming over the Englishman's side.

Or at least he hoped that was what was going on. He was glad to see that Herjolf had taken the bold course, the way Harald would have done. He pictured the two of them, side by side, leading the men on the attack.

Then the gap closed again, with *Oak Heart* and another ship blocking Thorgrim's view as they turned toward the attackers. Thorgrim clenched his teeth with impatience and irritation. He had positioned the fleet so that *Sea Hammer* would be first into any fight. But now she was at the end of the line, and the smaller ships were already engaged.

Starri came sliding down from aloft. He hit the deck and pulled his tunic up over his head and threw it aside. His movements had a jerky, spastic quality and Thorgrim knew the fighting madness was coming on him. There was no talking to him now, and there would not be until the battle was done, assuming Starri once again suffered the disappointment of staying alive.

"Straight on," he said to Gudrid, then yelled forward, "You men who aren't rowing, get ready to board one of these bastards! Over the bow!" Men had been slipping on mail, putting on helmets, strapping extra weapons to their waists, whatever they could do in the short amount of time they had to prepare for the fight.

Thorgrim considered trying to get his own mail on and knew there was not enough time. His shield was near, and the helmet he sometimes wore, and those would have to do.

Up ahead the fog of ships broke up again, and Thorgrim saw a straight line between him and one of the Englishmen charging ahead. It and the rest of the English fleet had left the lead ship behind and were coming at the Northmen from either side, doing to the Northmen just what Thorgrim and Bergthor had hoped to do to them.

"There," Thorgrim said, pointing at the largest of the oncoming ships. "We'll go alongside those whore's sons, come right alongside and board them." He could feel the anger growing, the rage. The red madness, he used to call it. A fighting rage like Starri felt, if only a fraction as intense. Thorgrim, at least, was still able to think even when the fight was on him.

He opened his mouth to call for the rowers to be ready to pull in the oars when he saw Bergthor's ship turning fast, turning toward *Sea Hammer*, threatening to run into her starboard side if *Sea Hammer* did not turn as well.

"Bergthor!" Thorgrim shouted, more in frustration than in hope of being heard.

"Turn to larboard?" Gudrid asked with considerable concern in his voice.

"Hold," Thorgrim said, eyes on Bergthor's ship. *Sea Hammer* still had a straight and unimpeded course toward the big English ship, he did not want to throw it away, and there was still a chance he could shoot past *Wave Splitter*'s bow.

And then from behind *Wave Splitter* came another of Bergthor's other ships, not the biggest of them, but big enough, pulling hard for the same Englishman that Thorgrim was making for. They had driven past *Wave Splitter*, forcing Bergthor to turn out of the way, and were on a course to hit *Sea Hammer* next. Whoever was driving that ship seemed not to care who was in their way.

Thorgrim could see that *Sea Hammer* and this other would collide if he did not turn immediately. In truth it might already be too late. They were both driving toward a spot on the water where they would meet, bow to bow, with less than a hundred feet to go.

"Larboard, now!" Thorgrim called. Gudrid grunted as he pushed the tiller over. *Sea Hammer* began to turn, and as it did Thorgrim saw that it would do no good. Even if this other fool realized he was going to hit Thorgrim's ship it was too late to prevent it.

"Bastard!" Thorgrim shouted and spat out a mouthful of rainwater. "Get the oars in, now!" He could not avoid the impact but he could prevent his oars from being snapped like twigs.

The rowers pulled the oars in quickly, shouting and cursing the ship that was charging at them, not fifty feet away. In that final moment the master of the other ship must have realized the danger. Thorgrim saw his oars churning hard, pulling astern, trying to slow the momentum, a useless gesture. The ship slammed into *Sea Hammer* just forward of the starboard beam, its stem crushing the sheer strake as the men aboard *Sea Hammer* flung themselves out of the way.

Sea Hammer rolled hard to larboard with the sound of snapping and crushing wood and furious men. Then it rolled back again, doing more damage still to the starboard planks, but the two ships remained locked together, the bow of the smaller ship jammed into *Sea Hammer*'s side.

"You stupid whore's son!" Thorgrim shouted. In the tangle of men on the other ship's deck he could not see which of them was the master, but Thorgrim's every impulse screamed for him to leap aboard the ship, find the man and beat him to death.

It was only with some difficulty that he kept himself from doing so. The red madness had been creeping up on him before and this absurd collision only fanned that flame. It was bad enough that he was going to be the last into the fight: now he might not get into the fight at all, might have to watch, helpless and impotent, thanks to the stupidity of one of the captains of his own fleet.

You better have the good sense to die in the fighting, Thorgrim thought of the man, but that was all the time he could devote to him. He jumped off the afterdeck and ran forward. The bow of the other ship was looming up over *Sea Hammer*'s side like some monster come from the deep. A crowd of *Sea Hammer*'s men were clustered around, shouting and pushing against the smaller ship's stem, while men from the other ship leaned over the sides at the bow, adding their own pointless shouting to the chaos.

Thorgrim's men cleared a path as they saw him coming. He stopped where the other ship was wedged into *Sea Hammer*'s rail. He could see the shattered wood of the sheer strake and the two below it: still high enough above the waterline that they would not sink, unless the seas grew big.

"Any leaking?" he asked. A couple of the men had had the sense to pull up the loose deck boards and check.

"Not that we can see," Hall said. Thorgrim looked down into the dark space between the deck and the bottom of the ship. He could see water sloshing around, but there was always water there, just as there was aboard any ship. The important thing was that he could see no water coming in.

"All right, let's push these idiots free," Thorgrim said. Sometimes in a collision such as this the one ship was the only thing keeping the other afloat, but Thorgrim was pretty certain that both ships could still float on their own. At least he was pretty sure *Sea Hammer* could. He didn't much care about the other.

Like a distant cloud of noise he could hear shouting and screaming and the clash of weapons, the sea fight happening all around him while he dealt with a wound inflicted by one of his own. Hands reached up from *Sea Hammer*'s deck and pressed against the rain-slick stem and sides of the other ship, but there was not much space against which to push.

"Heave!" Thorgrim shouted, and every man who could lay a hand on the other ship pushed and strained, grunting, faces turning red with the effort. The bow of the ship moved an inch or so with a creaking protest, and then the men of *Sea Hammer*, as if on cue, stopped pushing and gasped for breath.

"Again!" Thorgrim shouted, and the hands went back against the ship's stem and sides. "Heave!"

Once again the men leaned into it, pushing and straining, guttural sounds coming from their throats, until it seemed as if their heads might burst. The bow moved another inch and stopped and the men stopped as well.

What by the gods is hanging this up? Thorgrim wondered. They had to get some oars down there, use them as levers to try to pry the other ship away. He was about to call for them when the deck under his feet seemed to shudder as if it was coming apart. He staggered and reached out for a handhold to steady himself but there was nothing to grab. He felt himself going down and saw other men falling as well, saw images of feet coming off the deck and arms flailing.

He hit the deck on his shoulder and felt the impact through his whole body. He grunted with the pain but pressed his palms against the boards and pushed himself up, still not certain what had happened. He heard shouting forward and turned to look in that direction.

There was a ship there, its forward end pressed alongside *Sea Hammer*'s starboard bow. A big ship, but it was lacking the elegant sweep of one of the Northmen's ships, and the high, proud stem topped with some frightening figurehead. There were men aboard the ship but they were climbing over *Sea Hammer*'s rails, shields and weapons in hand.

What is this? Thorgrim thought, and then the confusion brought on by hitting the deck hard cleared away and he understood. While they were all dealing with the aftermath of the accident, every eye aboard *Sea Hammer* directed at the ship lodged in her starboard side, one of the English ships had come surging through the fleet and slammed into them, unseen. And now the English warriors, many English warriors, were flooding over the side.

"On your feet! On your feet! We're boarded!" Thorgrim shouted as he pushed himself up. He had left his helmet and shield back on the afterdeck and there was no getting them now.

Thorgrim's men were still standing and retrieving weapons when the first of them fell to an English ax: Vestar, a young man who had been in Thorgrim's company for some time. More than a year, certainly. He charged right at the first of the English warriors, spear in hand. He thrust and the Englishman knocked the point aside with his shield and just as Vestar was raising his own shield the warrior raised his ax and brought it down on Vestar's head, a powerful stroke that split Vestar's skull and drove him straight down to the deck.

Thorgrim felt his stomach twist at the sight. Not at the hideous wound — he was well accustomed to that sort of thing — but for the terrible waste of a good man. A man he liked and trusted. A man who died because he, Thorgrim, did not have sense enough to keep his eyes on the sea around them.

The shouting and the clash of weapons grew louder as the English came aboard in waves and the Northmen, caught unaware, tried to grab up their weapons and hold the English back at the same time. Thorgrim could see the situation falling apart right before his eyes, getting worse by the second, when a sharp scream tore through all the other noise of the nascent fight and Starri Deathless came running down the side of the ship, leaping like a goat from one sea chest to the next, half naked, a long battle ax in each hand.

He came first to the man who had killed Vestar, who looked up at Starri with a mixture of surprise and horror on his face. He swung his ax but Starri shifted a few inches in his trajectory and the blade sailed past his legs. The Englishman raised his shield just as Starri jumped off the sea chest and came at the man airborne. He was still in midair when he swung the axes down. They went right through the man's shield, which seemed burst into a thousand slivers of wood, and did not stop on their way to his head and neck.

Good. Bastard, Thorgrim thought as he saw Vestar's killer fall.

Starri and his victim fell together, Starri landing on top of the man who was doubtless dead before he was down. The Englishmen on either side had frozen in surprise but they recovered as Starri and their fellow soldier dropped in front of them. Axes and spears came up and thrust and hacked down but Starri rolled out of the way as they did, and the weapons hit the dead man with a sickening sound.

Starri was back on his feet before the Englishmen could pull their weapons free. Thorgrim could see on their faces the expressions he usually saw on men confronted by Starri Deathless — surprise, fear, and in this case the horror of having accidently mutilated their dead comrade.

And, as usual, the expressions did not last long. Starri was on them with the axes going like threshing flails: snapping spears, shattering swords, lacerating flesh.

"Go! Go!" Thorgrim shouted to the men around him. Starri had bought them a few heartbeats' time, enough for them to get to their feet and get their weapons ready for the fight.

Thunder rolled overhead and a gust of wind blew across the deck and chilled Thorgrim in his soaked tunic. The rain, which had been just a drizzle, more like a heavy mist, built again into a genuine downpour as Thorgrim charged across the deck and into the line of fighting men.

Starri had hacked his way into the center of the packed Englishmen against the starboard side and was fighting in his manic and undisciplined way. The English, it seemed, did not know who to fight: the Northmen charging across the deck or the madman in their midst; and that confusion gave Thorgrim's men the one small advantage they had yet to enjoy.

Iron-tooth was in Thorgrim's hand as he reached the tideline of men. A battle ax came down at him and he raised the sword and caught the wooden handle of the ax with the blade, pushing it aside and sliding his sword down the shaft to slash the axman's hand. Thorgrim felt the blade hit fingers. He drew it back and saw the ax fall as the man shouted in pain and stumbled back. Thorgrim thrust but missed. He saw the point of a spear coming for his left side, and he swung the blade down to his left and knocked it aside.

I need a shield, Thorgrim thought. This sort of work did not go well without a shield. He could do without a helmet, a helmet was just protection, but a shield was as much a weapon as it was a means of defense.

He stepped up close to the man directly in front of him, grabbed the edge of the man's shield and jerked it and the man toward him. They were inches apart, too close for Thorgrim to use Iron-tooth, so he drove his fist right over the top of the shield and hit the man square in the face.

The Englishman's nose was at a strange angle, blood pouring over his face and mouth and turning a pale pink as the rain half washed it away. He was staggering, stunned. Thorgrim heaved on the edge of the shield and pulled it free from the man's arm, stepped back and slipped it on his own.

He was just in time. The English were pressing around to his left and he was set on by two men, both with swords and mail, elite warriors. The man on his left slashed down toward Thorgrim's head with a chopping motion, forcing Thorgrim to raise the shield, and as he did the other man lunged for Thorgrim's exposed side.

Thorgrim swung Iron-tooth down and to the right and heard it ring against the other blade, felt the vibration of iron striking iron. He pushed his shoulder into the back of his shield and drove it forward. He could not see the man he was pushing but he felt the shield slam into him and felt him lose his balance. Thorgrim continued to push.

The other one, the one who had tried to come under Thorgrim's shield, raised his sword for another blow, too fast for Thorgrim to fend it off with Iron-tooth — the English sword would cleave his head first. So instead he slashed low. He felt Iron-tooth's sharp blade sweep across the man's legs and saw the raised sword fall as the warrior staggered back.

Thorgrim gave one last push with his shield and the man in front of him went down. Thorgrim moved the shield aside to see him sprawled, wide-eyed, on the deck at his feet. He drew Iron-tooth back for the thrust that would finish him, and once again felt the ship stagger beneath him. He stumbled, tried to keep his balance, but his foot caught on the Englishman's leg and he fell forward, sprawled over the man he was about to kill.

Thorgrim shouted in anger and frustration. He pushed himself up. The Englishman had dropped his sword so he swung a fist at Thorgrim's jaw, but Thorgrim pulled back just enough that the fist only grazed him. He in turn punched the Englishman and the blow landed, not terribly hard but enough to give Thorgrim a moment to regain his feet.

He used Iron-tooth to help him stand. He was still not sure what had caused him to fall, but he saw it as he stood. A second ship, a second English ship, had rammed into their larboard side, and even now its warriors were coming aboard, catching Thorgrim's men between them and the Englishmen from the first ship on the starboard side.

That's the end of it for us, Thorgrim thought. Against the one ship there had been a fighting chance. But now many of the Northmen were down, and the rest were tired, and this second ship had sixty men at least aboard her.

"Larboard! Larboard! There's more of the bastards!" Thorgrim shouted, hoping his voice would cut through the sounds of the fight. He pointed with his sword and shouted again, then turned to meet the fresh wave of men as they crossed *Sea Hammer*'s deck to hit Thorgrim's men from astern.

Thorgrim held his shield at chest height, sword raised behind. He braced himself against his back leg, looking for grip on the wet deck, and realized he was alone, standing in front of this line of men pushing toward him. So be it.

They hit like surf running up on a beach, breaking around Thorgrim on either side while those directly in front ran into Thorgrim shield to shield. The English hoped no doubt to bowl him over but Thorgrim was ready for that, and the man who had hit him stopped as if he had hit a wall. Thorgrim dropped his shield, just for an instant, just long enough to thrust out over the other man's shield, long enough to feel Iron-tooth tear through the leather armor the man wore and send him reeling and staggering back.

To his left he caught the dull flash of a battle ax, poised, ready to come down. Thorgrim twisted and held his shield up to defend against the ax and as he did he felt the wicked point of a spear tearing into his side, his right side, just above his belt. It might have gone clean through him if he had not twisted, but as it was the point tore through flesh, a glancing cut but a deep one. The blood spilling out was warm against his cold, wet skin.

Thorgrim shouted in pain, or thought he did. With all the noise around him he could not be sure. Involuntarily he doubled over, holding his shield up as best he could, hoping it would ward off the next, fatal bow. But the blow did not come. Instead he found himself surrounded, not by the English but by his own men who had turned and pushed against this new threat, driving them back.

This won't last long… Thorgrim thought. His men were caught between the warriors of two ships, and more were coming over the rail.

He clenched his teeth and straightened and turned his shield in time to get it in front of a spear coming at him. He felt the point hit the shield's face, saw it tear through the other side. He jerked the shield to the left and it took the spear with it, exposing the spearman behind, and Thorgrim drove Iron-tooth into his chest. He pulled the blade free, cocked the sword back, and once again felt the deck shudder underfoot.

It was not so bad that time, not enough to even make him stagger or lose his footing, and he knew by then what it was. Another ship, run hard into *Sea Hammer*. More warriors pouring aboard. Toward *Sea Hammer*'s stern, he imagined, since he could not see the ship that had hit, and he was in no position to turn and look.

Let's be done with this, he thought. He did not imagine the fight would last much longer.

He heard shouting behind: the newly arrived warriors. He tensed for a renewed attack from the men in front of him, encouraged by this third line of attack. But instead he saw the English stepping away, glancing aft with expressions that did not look triumphant.

Thorgrim chanced a quick look over his shoulder. There was another ship alongside, run up against the starboard side aft, and Thorgrim knew right off which ship it was, because he recognized with just that quick glance *Wave Splitter*'s tall carved prow and the bundled red sail. The crew of Bergthor's ship was already coming over *Sea Hammer*'s side, and Thorgrim saw Bergthor leading the rush.

The Northmen's arrival seemed to temper the fighting spirit of the Englishmen, but it did not extinguish it. They took a step back, and another, angling themselves to meet the onrush, but they did not retreat any farther than that.

Bergthor's men were there in an instant, coming up on either side of Thorgrim and rushing into the fight on the starboard side as well. The shouting and clash of weapons rose like a building wind as the two sides pushed and hacked and thrust at one another. Men fell right and left, but the lines did not move, the two armies in bloody stalemate, the five ships drifting and locked together.

Then through the noise and the wind and driving rain Thorgrim heard a long, sharp note, a horn of some sort. It came from one of the English ships. It had to. It sounded like nothing Thorgrim had ever heard from any ship driven by Northmen.

He had no idea what it might signal, but the English did, apparently. The line of men who had stood unyielding began to back away. One of their number had climbed up on a sea chest and was shouting. The master of one of the ships, or captain of the guard, Thorgrim guessed. He seemed to have the air of a man in command, and the words he shouted sounded like orders rather than a mindless battle cry.

He kept shouting as his men backed away, and then suddenly he doubled over, mouth and eyes wide, as if he had been punched in the stomach, as if some spirit had struck him an invisible blow. Thorgrim frowned, puzzled, and then he saw the arrow jutting from the man's guts. He turned and looked aft. Failend was on the afterdeck, eyes moving over the crowd, another arrow already fitted to her bowstring.

He turned back. The English were climbing back aboard their ships, abandoning *Sea Hammer*, while those in the front ranks did their best to hold the tide of Northmen with the long reach of their spears. The Northmen pressed forward but with no great enthusiasm. They were too exhausted, too bloodied to follow up.

And finally the last of the Englishmen, the last who could still move, were back aboard their ships and shoving off as the oars came out through the row ports and the vessels pulled away. Thorgrim tossed his shield aside and let the tip of Iron-tooth rest on the deck. He closed his eyes and tilted his head back and let the cold rain run down his face and through his beard.

"Thorgrim! See here!"

Thorgrim tilted his head back down and opened his eyes and felt a sharp and agonizing pain in his right side, as if he had been skewered all over again. He sucked in his breath and clenched his teeth and when the worst of it had passed he looked beside him.

Bergthor was there, grinning, pointing with his sword past *Sea Hammer*'s bow. All of the English ships had broken off the fight and were pulling for the river from which they had come.

"See there!" Bergthor said. "They're retreating, the lot of them."

Thorgrim nodded. The English were retreating. "They didn't beat us, it seems," he said. "But sure as you and I are standing here, we did not win."

Chapter Twenty-Three

What new tidings
canst thou give
from Norway?
Why art thou, prince!
From the land driven,
and alone art
come to find us?

The Poetic Edda

The sun was up when Odd Thorgrimson came to. He was in the tent where they kept him when the army was in camp. In the gray, half-light inside the rough shelter he could see the canvas walls, the trampled grass on which he was lying.

He had been unconscious when they threw him in there, and so had no idea if it had been day or night then. And though he knew it was daytime now, he had no idea what part of the day —morning, midday, evening. He knew dark and he knew light and beyond he didn't know much else.

He was awash with pain, his entire body one great sheet of agony. The pain was like a heavy snow blanketing everything. He was on his back, had been put on his back deliberately, he guessed, and the pressure on the wounds was all but unbearable. He clenched his teeth, unwilling to make any noise, give any sign of the agony he was in, as he pushed himself slowly onto his side.

The motion made the pain redouble and he gasped despite himself, but once he came to rest, his back no longer on the ground, he felt the worst of it fade away. He was in a fever dream of torment and fear and humiliation, and had been since he had given himself up to Halfdan. He had no idea how long ago that was. He had no idea where he was or where he was going or what his fate would be.

He did know he was in the same tent in which he was always kept when the army was in camp. An old leaking affair, it offered just the minimum of shelter. Its purpose, Odd understood, was to provide enough protection to help keep him alive for as long as Halfdan wanted him alive, which would be just a little while longer. In his more lucid moments Odd could hardly believe he had not died already, after the punishment Halfdan had doled out. It made him marvel at the durability of the human form, and it made him shudder at the cruelty of the gods, that they could let such a thing go on.

But he also knew that his continued hold on life was no accident, no quirk of his own constitution. Halfdan seemed to have a canny sense for how close he could bring a man to death without actually killing him, how long his victim needed to recover before he could be subjected to such torment again.

In the dull light inside the tent Odd could see a wooden plate on the ground, a few feet away, a hunk of oat bread sitting on it, and beside it a cup of water. He reached out a hand, moving slowly to minimize the pain, but the fabric of his tunic was stuck to the dried blood on his back and it pulled against the wounds, causing him to gasp once again.

He lay like that for a moment, tortured by hunger and thirst but also knowing the agony that moving would bring. Finally he clenched his teeth and reached out, bracing against the pain as he gripped the cup and brought it to his mouth. It was awkward to drink that way, lying on his side, but trying to shift position would be worse, so he drank as best he could, spilling half the precious water as he did.

When the cup was empty he reached out again and took the bread. He bit off small chunks and chewed and swallowed slowly. This, he knew, would bring strength, such as it was. He had already endured more of these episodes that he could recall — waking in the tent after having passed out, struggling to take up the food and drink, feeling the slightest bit of rejuvenation sometime after.

Don't eat, just don't eat… he told himself, as he had often done. If he could just not eat, not recover his strength at all, then perhaps he would die and it would be over. But he could not bring himself to do it.

Weak…you're weak… he thought as he swallowed another bite. He did not have the courage or the will to just let himself die.

But it wasn't weakness, and he knew it. He thought of Signy and their children and that made him want to live. Sometimes, but not always. Sometimes it did little to move him, because he knew that even with all the courage and determination in the world he would not live to see them again. His life was in Halfdan's hands now, and Halfdan would allow it to continue just as long as he wished, and not a moment more.

Halfdan made that clear as soon as Odd had given himself up. They had met halfway between the walls surrounding Halfdan's hall and the distant camp. Halfdan came riding up, little Hallbera on the saddle in front of him, his hirdsmen behind.. The sight of Hallbera, at least, had been a relief to Odd. Halfdan, apparently, meant to keep his word, at least where his sister was concerned.

Odd stopped as Halfdan approached and Halfdan stopped as well, fifteen feet away. They remained there, Odd looking up at Halfdan, Halfdan looking down from his horse. Odd had no intention of speaking, and Halfdan did not look as if he could be bothered.

Then Halfdan turned to the men behind and nodded his head. Two men dropped from their horses and approached Odd on either side. They grabbed his arms, bound his hands with a long cord, then mounted again, one of the riders holding the bitter end of the rope. They spurred their horses and rode back to Halfdan's camp, keeping a pace that forced Odd to jog to keep up, which he was careful to do. He was pretty sure that if he fell they would not stop, but rather drag him the rest of the way.

Back in the camp they tied him to a post set up near Halfdan's tent. When Halfdan returned he climbed down from his horse and stepped over to where Odd was bound. He stood a few feet away and looked into Odd's eyes and Odd met his stare.

Then Halfdan moved, so fast Odd did not see it coming. He swung his fist in a tight arc and slammed it into Odd's face, snapping Odd's head to the side. Odd could feel the blood, warm in his mouth. A tooth was loose, he was pretty sure. He spat blood onto the dry ground and looked back at Halfdan, but Halfdan was already gone, heading for the door of his tent. He had not said a word, and since that moment he had still not said a word to Odd. There was no point, no need.

That had all happened before Odd was lost to the fever dream of agony. He remained tied to the post that night, and the next morning he had been untied and shoved into a tent, not tall enough for him to stand in. He was aware of the goings on around him then, the routine of the warriors in the camp, the changing of the guards outside.

Not long after that they had broken camp and returned to Halfdan's hall. There Odd had been locked in a small, sturdy building that must have been built as a jail. How long he was held there he did not know. It was dark in the cell and Odd lost track of day and night and the unreality began to assert itself. It was torture, waiting on what would come next. He knew that Halfdan had planned it that way. It was perhaps the worst torture Odd had ever endured, the worst he could imagine.

He had no idea what was to come.

It was dawn some days later when they finally moved. Odd was dragged from the cell and pushed into the back of a cart, hands and feet bound, but not before he saw the three hundred or so warriors standing ready, some mounted, some not. Halfdan's best men. They rolled out of the compound and marched for all that day, setting up camp that night, where Odd was once again put into his tent, a cup of water and a hunk of bread left for his dinner. The next morning they were underway again.

Odd thought he recognized the country around them though he could not see much, bound and lying in the cart as he was. But he could see the hills far off and occasionally a distinct outcropping or rock and he was pretty sure they were on their way to Hakon Styrsson's farm, which was the closest of all of them to Halfdan's hall.

And soon Odd was certain of it. The army halted its march and the wagon came to a creaking stop. Odd could hear voices off toward the head of the column but he could not understand what was being said. Then he heard another sound, familiar, but he could not identify it at first. And then he did.

Shovels, he thought. *Shovels digging in the earth. Now what could that be about?*

They had visited three farms since then, but after the brutal flogging at Hakon's, a beating that Odd was sure would kill him, his sense of time or place was smothered by the all-encompassing pain. A bloody beating, salt in the lacerations, tossed back in the cart, back in the tent, it had grown more unreal, more completely nightmarish with each passing day until Odd hardly knew if he was alive or dead and cared even less.

And yet he clung to life. A bite of bread, a cup of water, and the spark was back. Weak, sputtering, but it was still there. For how much longer he did not know. One more beating? Two? He did not see how it could last beyond that.

He rolled a bit more on his stomach and felt something hard dig into his thigh. He thought it was a rock, or a root, but somewhere in the back of his mind was the notion that it was something else, something important that was now lost to memory. He puzzled over it for a minute but he could not make his mind function with enough clarity to remember or understand.

Slowly he reached his hand down, moving with care so that his tunic did not rip at his wounds with any force. His fingers inched along the fabric. Whatever it was was under his tunic and maybe under his leggings as well. He found it with his fingertips and ran them over the length of the object. It was round like a spear shaft but only a foot or so long.

Knife… Odd thought, and the tide of memory began to flood. *Knife…*

He had been in the back of the cart and they had been bumping and jolting over the battered road to the next farm, two days out from the last. His wounds had stopped bleeding, a hint of strength returning to his body. Life would not leave him, and he would be strong enough to be beaten down again.

He heard a soft thump on the floor of the wagon just a few feet from his head. He twisted his neck so he could see. The knife was lying there, right behind the seat on which the two drivers sat, right next to the box of tools that was shoved in a corner of the wagon's bed. Odd recalled one of the drivers fishing it out of the box when he was mending a leather strap, part of the oxen's harness. He must have set it back on top of the box and left it there, and the jarring motion of the wagon had shaken it off.

For a long moment Odd just looked at the knife. What use he might make of it he did not know, but somehow the sight of it gave him more optimism than he had felt since surrendering himself to Halfdan. It was, truly, just the faintest glimmer of hope, but it was hope none the less.

His hands were bound at the wrists but they were not tied to the wagon. Not since the first flogging had the drivers bothered to do that, since from that time on he could barely move, and the idea of his climbing down from the wagon and running was absurd.

He rolled a little more on his back, enough that he could see the drivers on the seat in front of him, taking shallow breaths though clenched teeth against the pain. They were paying no attention to him so he shuffled forward a bit and paused, eyes on their backs. They had not seemed to notice. Again he moved forward and paused, and now he was within reach of the knife.

The wagon rolled over some pothole that made the whole vehicle shudder so the driver and his partner had to grab on to steady themselves. They cursed but still they did not look back. And the knife, Odd saw, had been knocked just a little closer.

He reached up and his fingers found the handle and he snatched it up. He brought the knife down to his waist and curled his body around it to hide it from view. Then he lay still for a moment, in case his movement had attracted attention, and to let the pain subside.

He heard nothing from the men on the seat, and soon the pain had dulled enough for him to think and act.

Now what?

He could do nothing with the knife just then. If it was to be of any use it would have to be used with stealth. In the dark. So he had to hide it until then.

Under my tunic… he thought, but he knew that would not work. There was too much chance of its being seen. So it would have to be hidden in his leggings.

A length of the rope that bound his hands was hanging free, and after some fumbling he managed to use the knife to cut it away. Awkwardly he lifted the hem of his tunic and slipped the knife down his leggings, thankful that the ox cart drivers did not keep their blades as sharp as the warriors did. Once the knife was laid against his thigh he wrapped the length of cordage around his leg as best as he could with wrists bound, pulled it tight and tied it off, so it held the knife in place under the cloth. Then he pulled the hem of his tunic down over the cord.

The task was exhausting in his condition, and he felt drained and sick. He thought he might throw up, though he knew he would bring up bile if he did and nothing more. There was nothing else in his stomach. He lay still and after some time the sick feeling subsided, and after some more time, despite the shaking and jarring of the cart, he passed out again.

All of that all came back to him as he lay in the dim light of the tent, feeling the knife through the cloth of his leggings.

Tonight… he thought. *I'll use it tonight.* There was no point in waiting. He had no way of knowing if one moment would be better than another.

He left the rest of the bread on the plate and concentrated on untying the line bound around his thigh, holding the knife in place. It took some effort, fumbling awkwardly with the knot, but at last he felt it fall away. He paused and let his breath settle, and once he had recovered from that effort he worked his hands down his leggings, found the handle of the knife and pulled it out.

It was an ugly affair, a thick iron blade with a patina of rust and a rough wooden handle. But it would do for his purpose. He tucked it under his body, hidden until the time came to use it. He felt his head swimming and he closed his eyes.

When he opened them again it was dark, near absolute blackness in the tent with just a whisper of light coming in from around the flap, the vestiges of a fire somewhere in the camp. Odd's stomach was twisted with hunger and he reached out carefully and felt the ground in front of him until his hand landed on the bread. He grabbed it up and ate as quickly as he could.

Bread gone, he felt around for the cup and when he found it he brought it to his lips and tipped it back. It was all but empty, though he still managed to get a few drops, enough to cut the terrible thirst he felt.

He let the cup fall with a dull thud on the ground and then he remained completely still, staring into the dark, listening. At first he could hear nothing, but as he concentrated he began to hear the distant sound of insects in the long grass and the occasional pop of a log in a fire or the soft whinny of a horse. But no singing or laughing or even soft talk in muted voices.

It's late…very late… Odd thought. Past the time where even the hardiest in camp would still be awake, or dare make noise enough to wake Halfdan.

Time to go.

Odd pulled the knife from under him and laid it aside, then rolled partway onto his stomach. Every move brought a tearing, cutting stab of pain. He could feel warm blood running down his back where the pull of his tunic had opened half-healed wounds. He clenched his teeth hard. He could not make a sound now, for reasons greater than simply denying his enemies the satisfaction of hearing his pain.

He pushed himself up on his knees and picked up the knife. He rested for a moment as he considered his next move. The tent was not tall enough for him to stand upright, and if he did stand there was every chance his legs would buckle under him. Very well, he would remain on his knees for now.

He took a step forward and then another. With his left hand he reached out and grabbed the pole that supported the front end of the tent. He took another step and reached out with the knife and with the blade eased the tent flap back.

There was the last of a fire burning in a fire pit some ways off, casting the light that had crept into his tent. That same light was falling on the guard standing just a few feet to Odd's right. Odd could see the back of his legs and the bottom edge of his mail shirt. The butt end of a spear shaft rested on the ground next to him, like a spindly third leg. Odd looked to his left. A second guard was there, but a little farther away. He, too, wore mail and leaned on his spear, enduring the dullest duty a man could pull.

Odd looked back at the man on his right, the one who was within reach of his knife. He had not moved in the slightest, was still unaware of Odd's presence. He was the one Odd would have to take out first, and since Odd could not possibly get to his feet in time, he would have to bring the guard down.

He took another shuffling step forward, drew the knife back and lunged, driving the point into the back of the man's thigh. Odd let out a stifled cry of pain as the impact of the knife against the guard's leg sent a shudder through his body. He could feel how utterly weak and ineffectual the thrust had been.

His hope had been to bring the guard down so he could kill him on the ground, but he did not even come close. Instead the guard let out a cry of surprise and spun around, bringing his spear up as he did. Odd gripped the tent pole and pulled himself to his feet, holding the knife in front of him. He had had one chance at this, and he had failed completely.

But it didn't matter. Odd had never honestly believed he would escape. His primary hope, he knew, was to die with a weapon in his hand, to go down fighting.

"What…?" the guard said as he leveled the point of his spear at Odd's chest. Odd could see the look of surprise on his face change to something more like amusement and it made him furious. He wanted to drive the knife through his heart, but he had not even had the strength to drive it into his leg hard enough to slow him down.

Even as Odd was considering his move — knock the spear point aside, lunge for the man's throat — a hand came down from his left and clapped on his arm just above the wrist. Odd tried to fight against it but he could not move his arm in the slightest. He felt like a child as the second guard plucked the knife effortlessly from his hand, then jerked him off balance and kicked him to the ground.

Odd fell in a heap and the pain shot through him from a hundred places. He gasped and rolled on his side and looked up at the men standing over him. The first guard, the one he had stabbed, was drawing his spear back so he could drive it right through Odd's heart, and there was nothing that Odd could do but watch.

The spear paused in the instant before the thrust, but before it could reverse direction a voice called out from the dark, close by, harsh but quiet.

"Hold there! Hold!"

The guard stopped and looked over in the direction from which the words had come. Odd pushed himself to a kneeling position. He thought it was the second guard who had spoken, but as he looked to his left he saw it was someone else, coming toward them with hurried steps. Odd heard the soft rustle of the man's mail shirt as he came to a stop five feet away.

"What by all the gods do you idiots think you're doing?" the man demanded. Odd could barely see him in the weak light but his voice was familiar, a voice he had heard very recently, but his head was swimming and he could not put a face to it.

"He was trying to escape," the guard said. He reached down and touched the wound on his leg, held his bloody fingers up for the man to inspect.

The man glanced at the bloody fingers. "Where'd he get the knife?" he demanded.

"Don't know," the second guard said. "But you see, he was ready to kill us to get away."

"Kill you?" the man said. "He can hardly stand up. And you thought you had to kill him to save yourselves?"

The guards had no answer to that because there was no answer. They had nearly killed Odd because they wanted to, not because he was a threat.

The man took a step closer. "You can thank the gods I showed up before you killed him. What Halfdan would have done to you if you had…it would make what he's done to this man look like a spanking."

Then Odd recognized the voice. Onund Jonsson, captain of Halfdan's hird. Which was why the guards showed him so much deference.

"It was Halfdan sent me here now. Get him to his feet," Onund said, nodding toward Odd. The two guards said nothing as they set their spears down, stepped quickly up to Odd's side and lifted him up under his arms. Odd gasped in pain but said nothing beyond that.

"Bring him along and come with me," Onund said next. "Halfdan has something special in mind for this one."

"What, now?" one of the guards ventured.

"Don't you dare question!" Onund said in his harsh whisper, then seemed to relent a bit. "Yes, now. Something that just came to him, apparently. Something that can't wait."

Onund headed off and the guards followed, with Odd half walking, half being carried between them.

Something special… Odd thought. He knew whatever it was would not be good, but he was beyond the point where he could manage to care.

They walked past rows of tents, just visible like dark shadows in the dark night. Now Odd could hear the sound of men snoring and rustling about, but there seemed to be no one awake save for the four of them.

They were heading for the edge of the camp when the guard on Odd's left said, "Halfdan's tent, sir, is over there." He nodded to a spot over his left shoulder.

"I know where Halfdan's tent is," Onund snapped. "What Halfdan intends, he does not intend to do in camp. Not in front of all the others."

The guard grunted but said nothing more. Odd's head was swimming and he could not make any sense out of what he was hearing, beyond a feeling of mortal threat.

Soon they had left even the tiny bit of light from the camp behind and they walked out across the dark field, lit only by the impressive spread of stars overhead. Odd felt his weak legs growing weaker still and knew he would collapse if the guards were not holding him up.

A few feet ahead of them, Onund raised a hand and said, "Hold, a minute." He stopped and the guards stopped as well. It was quiet, save for the sound of the insects. Then Odd heard a rustling of grass from in front and behind, men closing in on them.

Dark shapes loomed up on either side of Onund and Onund turned toward Odd, drawing his sword as he did, and Odd wondered if this was it, if it would end here, and what would come next if Onund cut his throat. But Onund held the tip of his sword under the chin of the guard holding his right side, and the man to Onund's right held the tip of his sword under the chin of the other guard.

Behind him Odd felt two other men taking him under the shoulders as Halfdan's men were pulled aside, the sword tips never leaving their necks. The man on Onund's right, who held his sword to the guard's neck, looked very much like Amundi Thorsteinsson, though Odd no longer trusted anything that he saw or heard or thought. The whole scene had the unreal quality that had marked all of Odd's life for the past weeks, but threefold.

More men appeared out of the dark, stepping up on either side of Halfdan's guards and snatching the helmets from the men's heads. Odd could see the uncertainty, even fear, on the men's faces. He saw movement in the dark, the hum of something coming through the air, and each of the guards, at the same instant, took the blow of a club on the side of their heads. They were knocked sideways into each other, an almost comical move, and then they went straight down like sacks of grain dropped from a wagon.

Odd felt hands on his face and he turned and looked down. In the starlight he saw a face looking up at him. The face was crying, tears coming down cheeks, and it looked very much like the face of Signy, his wife, and it made Odd wonder if he was in fact dead, and if not, what all this could mean.

Chapter Twenty-Four

High state and place, kindred, a wealthy crown,
Triumphs, and spoils in glorious battles won,
Nobles, and cities walled, to guard his state,
High palaces, and his familiar seat,
Whatever honors his own virtue won,
For love of heaven hath left, and here retir'd…

Epitaph for Caedwal,
King of the Saxons

The fighting was still going on, the battle fully involved: men shouting, screaming, killing and dying, weapons clashing, the splash of men and gear falling into the brackish water; but all of Felix's world had closed down to the twenty square feet around the king.

"Lift him, lift him! Careful there, you clumsy *imbécile*!" he shouted, directing the house guards in how to lift the old man by shoulders and legs. In the intensity of the moment he had to remind himself to speak English, not Frankish. "Bring him back to the afterdeck, quickly now! But be careful, damn you!"

Æthelwulf gasped in pain as the men lifted him, and then, to Felix's relief, he began to curse and protest in a strong voice as he was carried aft over the blood-slick deck. At the break of the afterdeck they laid him down. Felix knelt beside him and leaned close to examine the wound that the spear had left.

"Get me some water!" Felix snapped. "And see if that priest is still alive, the one who knows the practice of medicine!"

The king's mail shirt was torn in the wake of the spear point, a mess of silver links and bright red blood, and through all that chaotic damage Felix could not really see what sort of hurt had been done.

He gently lifted the edges of the torn mail and pulled them aside, but there was nothing to see but blood-soaked cloth and flesh and more glints of silver. Blood still pulsed from the wound, but slowly. It was not spurting out in great bursts and Felix knew enough about medicine to know that was a good thing.

"Water, lord," one of the soldiers said, holding out a bucket.

"Pour some, there, over the wound, gently now," Felix said and the man did so, washing the blood away and revealing the torn flesh below. And something else. A heavy silver cross the king generally wore around his neck, and apparently had been wearing between his mail and his padded tunic. Felix could see where one of the arms was bent, where, he suspected, the point of the spear had hit and deflected off, much reducing the power of the thrust.

Thank you, Dear God, Felix thought, and he made the sign of the cross.

"What the hell are you doing, Felix?" Æthelwulf said, and his voice was strong, though Felix could hear the pain in it. "Are you administering extreme unction? Get a priest for that! But I reckon you're a little early." He tried to sit up and grunted in pain and the men at his shoulders eased him down again.

Someone knelt at Felix's side, a young man in mail and a helmet, which he removed and set on the deck. Felix recognized him as Father Aelfgar, who had a reputation as a skilled hand in healing, so Felix stood and stepped away to give the priest room to work.

He turned toward the bow, his attention back on the wider world, and was surprised to see how much things had changed in the few moments he had been attending the king.

Leofric had taken command of the king's ship and had apparently led the men in driving the heathens back aboard their own ships. The ropes binding the cluster of vessels together had been cut and there was twenty feet of water between them now.

"Oars! Get to the oars, damn you!" Leofric shouted. The men seemed to be staggering around, unsure what to do, as if they had each taken a hard blow to the head. But some at least heard Leofric's orders and understood and began lifting the long oars and thrusting the blades through the row ports.

The deck was a vision of hell. Dead and dying men were tossed around in every part of the ship. Some had strength enough to crawl and beg for help, some had strength only to reach out feebly or move their legs in a useless manner. Most were not moving at all. English and heathen, they were all scattered together.

And the lion shall lie down with the lamb… Felix thought. But the dead and wounded were in the way of the rowers now. Felix was about to say something when Leofric beat him to it.

"Get those wounded out of the way! Get the Englishmen out of the way!" Leofric called. "Throw the damned heathens over the side."

More and more of the survivors regained their senses, and they worked in pairs to get their fellow Englishmen clear of the rowing benches and toss the heathens into the bay. Knives were out, leather pouches or purses on the heathens' belts were cut free before the whores' sons were dropped over the side.

Felix watched as a couple of the house guard grabbed up one of the brutes, a big man with a braided beard, head lolling, eyes wide and fixed, and with some effort they tossed him over the sheer strake. The dead man hit the water with an audible splash that sent spray back aboard. The two grabbed up another of the heathens, one who still had life enough in him to wave his arms in a weak attempt at defense, and he too went over the side.

Felix lifted his eyes to the water beyond Æthelwulf's ship. The king's vessels seemed to be drawing off from the heathens, oars coming out, bows turning toward the shore. The long note of retreat that the frightened young man had blown on his horn had indeed cut through the fight, and the others had heard it, recognized it, and obeyed.

We'll sound the horn again, Felix thought. The ships seemed to be retreating toward the river mouth, but he could not tell for certain. He looked forward, searching out the young man with the horn. He saw him on the larboard side, jammed up against the second rowing bench forward. His face was white as fine linen, his eyes and mouth open. Blood had formed a neat, round pond on the deck under him.

Maybe not, Felix thought.

Someone dragged the dead horn player clear as a rower took his place on the bench, thrusting the oar through the hole in the ship's side as he did. Leofric called an order and the men already at the oars, more than half of them, leaned back and pulled and the ship began to move. Stroke by stroke it gained momentum, pushing past the smaller heathen ships.

Felix surveyed the Godless enemy as they passed close by. The heathens seemed to have no interest in continuing the fight. Felix could see the same stunned look on their faces that he had seen on the English warriors. He could see the heaps of dead and wounded, the damage to the bow and rails of the ships. No one aboard the Northmen's ships was moving very quickly, and most were not moving at all. Those still standing were simply watching the big English ship gather way.

Leofric stepped up beside him. He nodded to the heathen ship slipping past. "We may be the ones breaking off the fight," he said. "But those bastards got the worst of it, by far."

Felix nodded. "We did what we had to do, I think. We did great slaughter to them. And we kept our own army together. Which means the pilgrimage may go on." Of course, he did not really know that. That statement was as much hope as fact.

The last of the heathens' ships, drifting and broken, was left astern and there was nothing but water between Æthelwulf's ship and the mouth of the river from which they had come. The rain that had plagued them all day had eased off to a fine mist, relieving them of that constant irritant. Toward the middle of the bay the other English ships were also gathering way, oars driving them through the scattered heathen vessels, forming a line as they followed the king's ship in.

Felix took a few steps toward the ship's stern. Æthelwulf's mail shirt had been removed somehow and the king was sitting up, his back against the ship's side. Father Aelfgar was kneeling beside him, pressing a bloody cloth against the wound in the king's chest. Around the wound the padded tunic hung in shreds.

The spear seemed not to have done as much damage as it first seemed, and for that Felix thanked God. But it could still go putrid and kill him quickly enough, as so often happened.

"Sire, how are you faring?" he asked, squatting down opposite of Father Aelfgar.

Æthelwulf scowled at him. "A heathen just ran a spear through me, how do you think I feel?" he said and Felix took delight in the strength of the king's voice and spirit. "What's happening? Where are we going?" From where he sat on the deck Æthelwulf could see little beyond the ship's sides.

"We've broken off the fight, sire," Felix said. "The heathens are all but done for. We did great slaughter. No reason to lose any more of our own men."

Æthelwulf grunted, but he did not protest, and Felix was glad of it. It had been he, Felix, who had ordered the retreat with no real authority to do so. It was a decision he would have to answer for if it turned out to be the wrong one.

They pulled into the mouth of the river and continued on until the wider bay was lost from sight. Soon after they reached the place where they had tied up the night before, and once again eased against the bank and ran lines ashore. Behind them the other ships came up the river in random order and each in turn tied up broadside to the land.

The train of wagons with all the supplies for the campaign, tents, rugs, portable beds, food, drink, cooking equipment, had been left in Hamtun, to which they had intended to return. Leofric gave orders that a makeshift tent be set up for the king on shore, and soon a ship's sail and a dozen oars had been lashed together in clever fashion to form a tolerable shelter.

Guards were posted at the perimeter of the naval camp, and others were sent farther afield to see what the heathens were doing. The English fleet had launched a very successful surprise attack on the Northmen, and they did not need the Northmen returning the favor.

Once the king had been moved ashore and settled, the wounded attended to, and what food and drink they had aboard doled out, the ealdormen and thegns began to gather in Æthelwulf's tent. They were men who had survived a bloody and exhausting battle against a tough, skilled enemy, and they looked it. Some of the nobles sported bloody bandages around arms and legs, some limped, some carried their arms in slings. Their hair was matted with blood and sweat. Many had great rents in their mail.

They would none of them dare show up looking unscathed, Felix mused. If they'd received no wounds in the battle they would have wounded themselves before showing themselves to the king.

Not all of the ealdormen or thegns were there, of course. Several had been killed, several more wounded and unlikely to survive. Which meant that those who still lived would be maneuvering for the lands left lord-less, the shires in search of new ealdormen. Soon the real battle for Wessex would begin.

But there were more immediate decisions to be made, plans to be formulated, business on hand that needed attention. They had won the day, or so it seemed, but they had not driven the heathen host away. The wolf was still among the flock.

Æthelwulf sat enthroned on a chair made of barrels covered over with blankets. He still wore his blood-soaked padded tunic. His face lacked its usual color, his movements their old vitality, but for the most part he seemed strong enough as he congratulated the men on their victory and asked for opinions as to what action to take next.

Ealdorman Byrnhorn led off. "The heathens are still here, but they're reeling. Badly hurt by that brilliant attack, led by King Æthelwulf. I say we strike again, and fast, while we have the army assembled."

Felix watched heads nod, but none with any blatant enthusiasm. It was not that these men did not want to fight, they simply did not want to express their opinion one way or another. Byrnhorn might be old enough, and close enough to the king, with a long history between them, that he did not worry about such things, but most of the others would not offer any suggestion until they knew Æthelwulf's thoughts on the subject.

"We may be getting ahead of ourselves," Ealdorman Alhmund offered. He, too, had fought with Æthelwulf in the younger days and that gave him more leeway than most of the others enjoyed. "We don't yet know where the heathens are, if they've gone to Hamtun or headed back to sea. Or maybe they all sank."

That suggestion made Æthelwulf chuckle and so the others laughed as well. But Alhmund had a point: they could hardly make plans until they knew what the Northmen were up to.

Happily a rider appeared just then, one of the scouts who had been given a horse and sent off to keep an eye on the enemy. He made his way into the king's makeshift tent, not bothering to ask for leave to enter, knowing how much the nobles and thegns of Wessex were waiting on what he had to say.

He bowed to his king. "Sire, I've just come from the mouth of the River Itchen," he said in a sure voice. "I could see the heathen fleet well, sire. They made their way up the bay, but they did not land in Hamtun. They landed on the south side of the River Test, sire."

Of course they did, Felix thought. *They may be Godless heathens, but they're not fools.*

The English camp was south of Hamtun. About four miles north of them the River Itchen and the River Test joined to flow into the bay, and the town of Hamtun sat on the triangle of land where the rivers met. If the heathens were in Hamtun they would be very vulnerable to a quick attack by the English army, the very attack that Byrnhorn was advocating. But instead the heathens had gone ashore on the far side of the river. Now the English army would have to march miles out of the way, along the banks of the Test, to come to a place where they could cross. There would be no swift counterattack now.

Let us withdraw to Winchester, Felix thought. That was the thing he most wanted to do. Any sort of military engagement entailed considerable risk, and Felix did not care for risk, not with everything that hung in balance. Æthelwulf had nearly been killed once that day already — they did not need to chance it again.

But Felix kept his mouth shut, because he was not an ealdorman, or a thegn. He was not even English. He was the king's secretary, sent from the court of Charles the Bald, and even if he had a vastly better sense for the grand picture of world affairs than did these provincial nobles, he was in no place to offer an opinion.

Byrnhorn, however, did not feel the need to remain quiet, and the news from the scout had not tempered his desire to fight. "This makes our business harder, I'll grant," he said. "But an attack is still the best course. Hit them hard, now, while we have the men, I say. Let us stamp them out."

This had heads nodding again, more vigorously now, as they could see Byrnhorn's speech seemed to meet with the king's approval.

"There's an old Roman bridge, only a mile or so up the Test," Ingwald offered. "When last I saw it it was in good repair. That would take us around to the south shore fast enough."

More heads nodded, and Felix could see that the enthusiasm was building for Byrnhorn's plan. "Lords," he said, loud enough to get everyone's attention. "If I may be so bold. I can't question your judgement in such things, obviously. You know far more about this business of war than I do. But…as secretary to our beloved king…I dare say, with his late wound, he'll be in no position to lead this campaign. He for one must be given time to recover. But if you feel that this fight may proceed without the king in command, then I would not deign to argue the point."

He looked around at the faces of the gathered men. He waited to see which of them was willing to suggest that Æthelwulf was not needed in the coming fight, that they would be fine without him. They were all thinking it, Felix knew, but he waited to see who might dare say as much out loud.

No one spoke. Finally Byrnhorn cleared his throat, breaking the grave-like silence. "Perhaps we'd best to go back to Winchester, then? See to the defense of the city?"

Heads nodded again.

Chapter Twenty-Five

Thence sent messengers
the potent prince
through air and water,
succours to demand.

The Poetic Edda

King Halfdan's face showed no expression. It was fixed, immobile, like that of a dead man. He had never been one for expression. Joy, sorrow, anger, amusement, boredom, he felt them all, as any man did, but they did not show on his face.

He had always been that way. And it served him well. His face was a mask, unchanging, despite what was going on behind it. Still, he guessed that Skorri Thorbrandsson, standing in front of him, needed no hint to guess at the rage that was roiling behind the façade.

Skorri's face, half lit by the various candles burning in Halfdan's big tent, also showed little expression. Halfdan suspected that Skorri cultivated that trait. It made him seem competent and fearless, and Halfdan's feelings were mixed when it came to that. He liked men who were fearless. But not entirely fearless. Not so fearless that they were not afraid of him.

"Dead, lord," Skorri said.

"Dead?"

"Yes, lord. We found them out in the tall grass, about a quarter of a mile off." Halfdan had just asked Skorri about the guards who had been standing outside the prisoner Odd's tent.

"Their helmets were off and lying beside them. Their throats were cut," Skorri added.

Dead… Halfdan mused. *Just as well...*

If the guards had allowed Odd to escape through their incompetence they would certainly have run off rather than stick around to see what he, Halfdan, would do to punish them. The example he was setting, punishing Odd the way he was, was having a wonderful effect on those who would rebel against him, and it was having the same good effect on his own men as well.

But now Odd was gone, though not for long. He would be found and those who helped him would be found and then there would be even more men at the whipping post.

"So…" Halfdan said, "at least we know that the two guards weren't part of Odd's escape."

"Yes, lord."

"And Onund Jonsson?" Halfdan asked.

"Ah, yes…" Skorri said and now there was some inflection in his voice, some note of hesitancy. No one liked to bring Halfdan bad news, and that was doubly true if the news suggested some mistake on Halfdan's part. Such as misjudging a man's character.

"We have not found Onund, lord," Skorri went on. "I thought he might have been killed along with the guards. We looked all around the field, followed the trails left in the grass, searched the camp, but found no sign of him."

Halfdan said nothing. It was clear that this treachery had begun with Onund, but Skorri did not want to say as much, because Halfdan had trusted Onund and clearly he had been wrong to do so.

For a long time Halfdan just stared at Skorri. Most men would have been profoundly uncomfortable under Halfdan's gaze, but Skorri remained as still as a carving. Halfdan took note of that, though his thoughts were not on Skorri. They were on Onund. And they were not good thoughts.

Onund, who knew the people of Fevik well. He was a friend of Odd and Amundi and even of Thorgrim Night Wolf. And he was a man whom Halfdan had trusted. A man Halfdan had put in a position of great responsibility. Onund had earned that trust several times over. He was the one who had told Halfdan about Odd's sister, who had facilitated Halfdan's bloodless capture of Odd.

But now? Onund, apparently, had changed sides. Betrayal of any sort was intolerable, but betrayal by one who had been so trusted and so rewarded was something else entirely. And it made Halfdan furious indeed.

I saw this a long way off, Halfdan thought. He had had misgivings about Onund, once this business with Thorgrim Ulfsson's farm had begun, but he ignored them. He thought Onund's connections to the people of Fevik would be an asset. Now he saw it for what it was — the seed of treachery.

"How much of a head start do they have?" Halfdan asked.

"The guards were cold, lord, and their blood was not running. They'd been dead some time. Killed somewhere in the very late night. After all was quiet in the camp."

The sun was just rising now, which meant the fugitives might have been running for half the night already. Skorri, making dawn rounds of the camp, had been the first to see Odd's tent unguarded. He sent men off to search even before alerting Halfdan that the prisoner was gone, no doubt hoping to have Odd back before telling his king what had happened. Halfdan couldn't blame him for that.

"And now?" Halfdan asked.

"My men are searching, lord. My best trackers. The trail leads off in one direction, but I have men searching in all directions in case the trail we see is meant to deceive."

"Good," Halfdan said and he felt a fresh rush of rage sweep through him. He wanted to leap up, to draw his sword, to drive it through the nearest man. He wanted to have the guilty men before him — the guards who had let this happen, the men who had plotted to set Odd free — and he wanted to kill them as slowly and patiently as could be done. He felt as if only the screaming and the blood and the expressions of suppressed horror on the faces of the onlookers could soothe the burning fury.

But he had no one to punish. Not yet. He let the surge pass over him before he spoke again.

"There is nothing…nothing…of greater importance than capturing Odd and the men who came to his aid," he said at last. "You understand that?"

"Yes, lord."

"I'm sending you to make that happen. You understand?"

"Yes, lord."

"How many men do you need?"

"Three dozen, lord, if I may pick them myself," Skorri said.

"Very good," Halfdan said. "Go. Come back with Odd. And his compatriots. Alive." He considered adding that if Skorri could not do that then he had best not come back at all. But he did not say as much. He did not have to. Skorri knew it perfectly well.

*　　　　*　　　　*

It took Skorri Thorbrandsson precious little time to round up the three dozen men he meant to take with him on the hunt. They were the men who had come with him when he joined Halfdan's household, the men who had ridden with him for much of his long, effective, bloody career as hirdsman to various jarls, as a soldier for hire, a killer for hire, and now sœslumadr for King Halfdan the Black, the greatest leader he had ever known.

Most of Skorri's men were already on the fugitives' trail. He sent them out the very moment he discovered Odd and the guards missing. He sent men to rouse Onund Jonsson, though Skorri had been pretty certain they would not find Onund in his tent. Skorri saw Onund's hand in this business from the first: Onund had divided loyalties and Skorri had never trusted him.

Skorri's horse was waiting just a few dozen yards from Halfdan's tent, saddled and ready, the reins in the hand of Kolbein Thordarson, who was mounted as well. Skorri took the reins and swung himself up into the saddle.

"What of the others?" Skorri asked.

"Those you sent to the west and south, they came back. Found nothing. They're waiting just beyond the camp. Those to the north, they have not returned."

Skorri nodded. The dead guards and the tracks though the tall grass were off to the east, and that was most likely the direction in which the fugitives had gone. But Odd was a clever one, Skorri knew that, and whoever had helped him had to be clever as well, so it was important that nothing be assumed.

"Very good. I'm going to the east. Get the rest of our men and follow."

Kolbein nodded and jerked his reins, spinning his horse to the left as Skorri spun his own horse to the right. He put the spurs to its flanks and charged off, covering a stretch of ground he had already covered several times that morning, the few hundred yards of open field between the camp and the two dead guards.

The track was a wide swath of trampled grass leading off to the east. Made by the two guards walking side by side, and most likely supporting Odd between them, because Odd certainly did not have the strength to walk on his own.

Onund had been with them, Skorri was certain. There was no indication that the guards had been forced to go. They must have been ordered to take the prisoner and follow. And the only men in the camp with the authority to give such an order were himself, Halfdan and Onund.

Skorri came to the place where the guards lay dead. Their bodies were just as they had been found, one man on his side, one on his back, deep rents in their necks, black with dried blood, eyes wide open, dark patches below their heads where the blood had soaked into the ground and coated the weeds and grass.

Skorri came to a stop and slid down from his horse. There was no one else there — he had ordered the others to follow the trail, to hunt down Odd and whoever was helping him. He stepped closer to the dead men, looking close to see if there was anything he had missed. Their spears and seaxes were gone, no doubt taken by the men who had killed them. No reason to leave good weapons behind. The leather pouches on their belts had been clasped shut when Skorri first saw the bodies that morning, but now they were open. It must have been his own men, helping themselves to the spoils. Skorri smiled. That was fine. He hoped there would be even more plunder coming their way.

He heard the sound of horses coming and looked up to see Kolbein Thordarson leading a dozen horsemen down the trail. Skorri mounted his own horse again, swung it around and led the way east, the rest of his men following behind. There was nothing more to be learned from the dead men.

They continued on, following the path of trampled grass. Skorri would have been able to follow the trail even if it was not so easy to pick out. He was a good tracker. He was good at most everything he did. It was that inherent talent and native intellect and brutal and remorseless ambition that had taken him from third son of an impoverished farmer to the man he was now.

He was fourteen years old when he took his father's sad smattering of weapons and the family's only horse and rode off to make himself into something his father and grandfather had never been. A man of power, position and respect. The weapons and horse were not a gift. He had just taken them. And even at fourteen he was a man his father dared not challenge.

From there it had been a long, inexorable and bloody uphill climb to where he stood today.

The field over which the fugitives had run sloped down for half a mile or so until it terminated at a gravel beach where the sea lapped gently back and forth. Here and there outcroppings of granite broke free from the ground, and stands of woods made little dark patches on the green countryside. Just offshore a smattering of small rocky islands were scattered like a broken wall between the land and the open ocean beyond.

Skorri's men were down by the water, some mounted, some standing by their horses. They had orders to track the fugitives only so far, and then to wait for him. As much as he relied on his men Skorri didn't really trust anyone besides himself to do things right. Certainly not when it came to something as crucial as this. A great deal of Skorri's future now rested on how well he carried out Halfdan's orders.

He reached the water's edge where the others were waiting and climbed down from his horse, and Valgard Arason, Skorri's second in command of the men, stepped over to him. Valgard had long hair and a long beard which received little attention from him, grooming-wise, and so was generally a tangled mess. But what Valgard lacked in aesthetics he made up for in loyalty and strength. He was smart as well, but not too smart, which was what Skorri wanted in a second.

"We tracked them this far, Skorri," he said, pointing to the ground. "I figured here we had best wait for you."

Skorri nodded. He looked down at the ground where Valgard was pointing. The path madc by the men in flight ran down through the tall grass and onto the beach and then headed north along the shore, though the footprints were hard to see in the gravel. Skorri knelt down beside the trail, where the grass yielded to stone.

"Any of our men walk here?" he asked, gesturing toward the track.

"No. I made sure they kept clear. The tracks are just from those whore's sons we're after."

Skorri nodded. *Good,* he thought. He could learn something from a trail that was undisturbed.

He let his eyes move slowly over the ground. He could see where something had been dragged and he guessed it was from Odd's feet as they half carried him away, trying to move fast. Two men had helped him walk, and there were more beside that. Half a dozen people, maybe? That seemed about right.

He looked next at the point where the trail ran onto the beach. The fugitives would have known they could be easily tracked through the field, so they went down to the water's edge where their tracks would be much harder to see. Skorri could see the trail running off north, moving in and out of the water. They would have tried to step though the surf where their tracks would be completely obscured, but it was probably not so easy in the dark.

"Looks like they headed north there," Valgard offered. Skorri nodded, though he had no interest in the man's opinion. But Valgard was right. Odd and his rescuers had headed north, following the edge of the sea. If they were on foot they could not have gone far. If they had horses waiting then they would be easy to track.

Skorri stood, his eyes still on the ground. "We'll follow along the shore, but send some men out…" He stopped, something catching his eye, some oddity, something out of place. He walked slowly toward the water's edge and squatted down. There was an indent in the shingle beach, like a heel print. Not heading north like the rest. It looked more as if it had been made by someone walking south.

He moved his eyes slowly along the line where the sea met the shore. He could see more prints at various intervals stretching away. Barely visible, so faint they might not have been prints at all, might have been some naturally occurring depression in the beach. But Skorri did not think so.

Once again he stood and slowly he began to follow the beach south, moving in the opposite direction from the more obvious tracks. He could hear Valgard and a few others following behind, but they would know better than to interrupt him as he scanned the shore.

Fifty yards down the beach he found it. A sharp cut in the gravel, a deep groove that seemed to emerge from the water. Around it, the prints of feet that had dug deep into the beach. It was the place where the bow of a boat had been run up ashore, where men had struggled to shove it back into the sea.

Oh, may the gods strike them down, Skorri thought, but furious as he was he was impressed as well. A clever trick. They had almost fooled him.

He looked out over the water, but there was nothing to see save for islands and the distant sea.

"Find a boat, now. Now!" he said to Valgard. This business had just become vastly more difficult.

Chapter Twenty-Six

By land and water
the king's fleet is safe,
and the chief's men also.

The Poetic Edda

Thorgrim Night Wolf stood on the raised deck at *Sea Hammer*'s bow as the men came ashore, all the men who had just fought so desperately. Men limping, men with arms hanging uselessly or tied in slings, men supported by their fellow warriors or carried by their fellow warriors and eased over the sides to waiting hands ashore.

Sea Hammer and some of the other ships were tied up to the docks that jutted out into the river, others were run up onto the mud banks. When the English fleet had withdrawn, breaking off the fight and making for the river down which they had come, it left Thorgrim with a choice — continue on to Hamtun or flee back down the bay to the safety of open water.

That was the choice but really it was no choice at all. The English had already served out more humiliation than Thorgrim cared to eat in a lifetime. He would die, and he would lead his men to their deaths, before he would compound their shame by running off.

The hard rain had turned to a mist, engulfing them like a wet smoke as they pulled north. The town of Hamtun, or what Thorgrim guessed was Hamtun, came into sight at last off the starboard bow. A cluster of thatched houses, boats pulled up on the shore. Nets set out to dry, which they would not do that day or for some time to come, Thorgrim guessed. A few docks reaching out into the water. They could see the roof of a church rising above the other buildings and set back from the water, but overall it was a sorry looking place.

It was not Hamtun they had come for, of course, but the promise of Winchester, somewhere off to the north. Winchester, seat of the king of that country, with Christ churches filled with silver and the homes of rich men to plunder.

Winchester better have more to it than this pig sty, Thorgrim thought as he watched the town of Hamtun materialize out of the fog. He shook his head slowly, disgusted with himself. One mistake after another. He had little experience with the English and he had underestimated them and that was the most foolish mistake of all.

But he would not do it again. The docks and the village off the starboard bow were tempting, but the English army that had met them on the water might well be on shore by now. If Thorgrim landed his fleet in Hamtun there would be nothing stopping the English men-at-arms from launching another attack against his own bloodied army. And Thorgrim did not think they could survive another such assault.

With a sharp order he instructed the helmsman to turn *Sea Hammer* to larboard and as the ship turned the rest of the fleet followed astern. They would land across the water, putting the head of the bay between the English warriors and his own men.

There were no orders given, no council of the lead men, as one by one the ships came ashore. It was clear to everyone what had to happen next. The wounded had to be tended to. The dead had to be sent off to wherever they were bound. Vessels had to be repaired. Vengeance had to be meted out. They would not be leaving that place for some time.

If Hamtun was nothing too impressive, then the village across the water was even less so. There was the same cluster of houses, only fewer, the same boats, the same nets. And there was a larger building, just as there was in Hamtun, which Thorgrim guessed was also a church, and he was pleased to see it. Not for any hope of plunder: if that church had ever held anything of value it would have been carried off by now, though Thorgrim doubted it had ever housed anything much worth taking. Nor he did not care about that. It was a big place, a dry place, and it would serve as shelter for the wounded men of the fleet.

He turned and looked inboard again, down at *Sea Hammer*'s deck. He opened his mouth to shout an order and then stopped, catching his words. He was about to call for Harald, he realized, just as he was so accustomed to doing. But Harald was not there. He had been aboard *Dragon*. And now he might well be dead. Thorgrim recalled how Herjolf had boldly turned the little ship toward the fighting.

He felt a twist in his stomach. He wanted to go and see for himself, or at least send someone to find out, but he refrained. He would not treat Harald differently from any of the other men, for all his aching desire to do so.

"Vestar!" he called, the first trusted man who came to mind. But the name was just leaving his mouth when he recalled the ax splitting Vestar's head and driving him to *Sea Hammer*'s deck. Those thoughts were stumbling around Thorgrim's head when Hall called forward.

"Vestar's dead," he said. "Can I help?"

"Get some men and go see that building over there is clear," Thorgrim called, pointing toward the church. "And the houses around it. We'll start getting our wounded in there."

Hall nodded and called to a few men around him and together they headed for *Sea Hammer*'s side. The deck was wet with the rain and mist, which had mixed with the blood to form an odd reddish sheen on the boards. There were still a few dead men lying at strange angles around the ship. The living had looked to the wounded first, getting them over the side where they could be better tended. The dead would get their turn.

Starri Deathless was sitting on the deck, his back against the mast, his face turned up to the gray sky. His bare chest and face were covered with striations of blood and water as the rain ran in lines down his skin. He looked to be in agony. Not physical agony, not suffering from any wound caused by an English weapon, but in moral agony at being still among the living. Once again, Thorgrim was certain, Starri had come through the fight with not a scratch to show for it.

He heard a voice behind him. "Thorgrim?"

It was Failend. He knew it as soon as she said his name. There was certainly no other person in the fleet with a voice like hers, high and slightly musical with her Irish accent. Thorgrim turned and looked down at her. She had a bright red line across her cheek where a blade had evidently left its mark, and a bandage wrapped around a thigh.

"You're hurt," Thorgrim said.

"It's nothing," Failend said. She nodded toward Thorgrim's waist. "So are you."

Thorgrim glanced down at the rent in his tunic, the torn fabric dyed pink with the blood and the rain. It had hurt terribly once the fighting had stopped, but as he concentrated on the fleet's next move and his own failures the pain had subsided. He felt it flare again as he remembered that the injury was there.

"That's not anything either," he said.

"Hmm," Failend said, doubtfully. "But I came to tell you, I went by *Dragon* and Harald is alive. He's wounded…we're all wounded, I suppose…but not bad. Not as bad as you. He's helping with the men there."

Thorgrim gave Failend a smile. He had not asked her to check on Harald. He would not have asked her to do that. But she knew that he was worried about his son, whether he would admit it, or show it, or not.

"Thank you," he said. He reached out and squeezed her shoulder. At another time he might have hugged her. Or kissed her. But not then.

"Let me see to your wound," she said.

"No," Thorgrim said. "I have to see to the others first."

Failend nodded. She did not argue. She knew full well he would not allow himself to be tended to until the others were looked after.

Hall and his men came back and reported the church, the neighboring houses, and indeed all of the town were deserted. Thorgrim issued orders that sent the men of the fleet in to take possession of the empty structures. The wounded came flowing off the ships and were carried to the church, and those who could still walk with help were supported by their shipmates as they hobbled along.

The dead were laid out along the waterfront. Thirty-six men lost, and many of the wounded would join them over the next few days. And for that Thorgrim had won possession of a miserable village on the shore of some miserable bay.

As those men who were still mostly whole saw to the dead and wounded Thorgrim called Gudrid and Hall to him one more time. "Get a couple of boat crews together and find some boats. Plenty all along the water's edge here. Hall, you take your boat down to the river that the English fleet came out of. Get as close to their ships as you dare, see what they're about. Gudrid, you take men across the bay to Hamtun and see what's going on there. You're not going to fight or to raid, just to see what the English are doing. Report back to me once you know something. Understood?"

The two men nodded and turned away and Thorgrim knew they would do as instructed. They were good men, dependable men. He was glad they had not died under some English blade.

Thorgrim did not remain aboard *Sea Hammer*. He stepped up onto the sheer strake and then across to the dock to which they were tied. It was well worn, slick with the rain, but heavily built and felt sturdy enough. He walked along toward the shore, calling to the captains of the other ships he passed, hearing reports of the number of men they had lost, the damage they had suffered. It was not good, any of it.

The smaller ships, *Fox*, *Dragon* and *Black Wing*, along with some of Bergthor's vessels, were run up on the shore. Thorgrim paused at each, speaking with the master or some of the men of the crew, hearing what they had to say of the fight, encouraging them as he could, though he was not in the mood to summon up much in the way of optimistic speech.

He stopped near the bow of one of Bergthor's ships, a bow he knew well from having seen it rammed into *Sea Hammer*'s side. He could see the damage to the ship's stem where it had collided with his own ship, thanks to the master's blind stupidity. He looked up at a cluster of men near the bow.

"Who's the master of this ship?" he asked.

"Kotkel Skidason," one of the men replied. "Or he was. Dead now. The bastard English took his head clean off."

Thorgrim nodded. *Good*, he thought. *Saved me the trouble.* He left them and continued on.

He came to *Dragon*, which was the next to last ship on shore. He could not see Herjolf and imagined he was dead or wounded or off seeing to his wounded men in the church. Harald was amidships, helping set up a lanyard on the forward shroud that had somehow been cut through in the fighting.

"Harald!" Thorgrim called. He saw the boy look up, saw the cloud of resentment pass over his face as he saw who had called his name.

"Hello, father," Harald managed and then went back to his work, which made Thorgrim angry in turn.

"Harald, get down here," he called and Harald, with a grand look of exasperation, left off what he was doing, jumped over the low side into knee deep water and waded ashore.

"Yes?" he said, stopping a few feet from Thorgrim, arms folded across his chest. The anger had not dissipated, it seemed. Thorgrim had hoped maybe the violence of the battle would have washed it away, but it had not. If they had been fighting side by side, like before, than maybe it would have done, but as it was Harald's attitude seemed not to have changed.

Thorgrim looked him up and down. There was a tear in his tunic at the shoulder and twin rips in his leggings across both shins, the obvious result of a sword passing by. The cloth was shredded and dull red, soaked with blood and rain.

"You're wounded," Thorgrim said. "You should have those bound up."

Harald shrugged.

"Where's Herjolf?"

Harald shook his head. "Off seeing to our wounded, maybe?" Thorgrim did not reply, just fixed Harald with his gaze. Harald met his eyes, held them for a moment, then looked away.

"You fought well, you men aboard *Dragon*," Thorgrim continued. "I saw the ship turning out of the line. I thought you were getting clear of that big English bastard. I wouldn't have faulted you if you did. But Herjolf was bold, took the ship right into the fight. I was pleased to see it."

Harald nodded, but with no enthusiasm. "Yes," he said. "Herjolf is a bold one."

Thorgrim searched his son's face for some expression or meaning behind his bland words but saw none. Various replies sifted through his head, shadows of things he wanted to say, but none of them formed into anything as solid as words.

"Good," he said finally. "Good. See to your men."

He turned and walked off with an uneasy feeling, an incomplete feeling. He wanted to think about what had just happened. This was new ground for him. Certainly Harald had been angry with him in the past. Harald was his son and Thorgrim had punished him many times over the years for any number of transgressions. But he was a man now, a man coming into his own. He seemed to feel this punishment more deeply than he ever had, and was holding on to it in a way he never had.

Well, then, he should not have been such an idiot in the first place, Thorgrim thought, and he got no further into his analysis when the next interruption came.

"Thorgrim!" Bergthor came pushing up, a bandage wrapped around his head and covering his left ear, where it was marked by a wide flower of blood.

"Bergthor," Thorgrim said. "Is your wound bad?"

"Whore's son English took my ear right off, son of a bitch," Bergthor said, though in truth he did not seem so terribly upset. "Well, no matter, there's nothing around here worth listening to anyway. Are you hurt bad? Lose many men?"

"I'm not hurt bad," Thorgrim said. "I don't know how many men I lost. More than I cared to lose."

Bergthor made a grunting noise. "Yes, we all did that," he said. Thorgrim could sense the man was about to ask what they should do next, or what Thorgrim had in mind, but Thorgrim was even less in the mood for discussion than usual, so he spoke before Bergthor could.

"We'll get the wounded into the church over there where we can tend to them. We might as well have men go through the houses here, see if there's any food or drink or anything worth taking. I doubt there will be. And we'll see to the dead. Too many to bury. We'll get them into one of these houses and send them off with fire."

Bergthor was nodding at this, and it seemed he would have sense enough not to speak.

"I sent some of my trusted men off to see what the English are doing," Thorgrim said. "I would just as soon they stay put. We're not in much shape for more fighting today."

Bergthor nodded again.

"Send men to find some cattle we can use for the funeral ceremony," Thorgrim continued. Then, as he spoke, another idea came to him. "And find horses," he added. "A dozen or so. With saddles and bridles, if that's possible."

Bergthor nodded again and said, "I'll see to it, Thorgrim," which was all Thorgrim wanted him to say.

"Good. Thank you," Thorgrim said. "And…your men fought well. Thank you for that."

Bergthor smiled, just a bit, and hurried off. Thorgrim continued his inspection of the men, the fleet and the town. The wounded in the church were being well cared for. Straw had been located and mounds of it set up as beds, various robes and such found in trunks had been torn into bandages. Food and ale were being served out. There was nothing there that required Thorgrim's attention, so he left and returned to *Sea Hammer*, where repairs to the sheer strakes and other damage was well underway.

He was watching Ulf and a man named Raud, one of the better shipwrights in *Sea Hammer*'s crew, fitting a new section of planking when Failend found him. She had a small leather bag in her hand, a bag he recognized.

"Time to sew you up," she said.

Unconsciously he reached down and touched the rent in his tunic and the throbbing wound underneath. He felt the warm, wet blood on his hand. It had stopped bleeding earlier, but his recent activity must have opened it up again. He sighed. There would be no putting Failend off.

He carefully tugged his tunic over his head and tossed it aside, then leaned against the side of the ship. Failend knelt in front of him. She drew a needle and thread from her bag and started in stitching him up, pinching the wound closed and running her needle through the flesh on either side. Thorgrim gritted his teeth against the pain: it was like being stabbed repeatedly by a tiny dagger.

Thorgrim had been stitched up many times before, by many different people, but almost always by fellow warriors, men more accustomed to killing than healing, men with big and clumsy hands. Failend, a woman of breeding, had been trained to needlework, and her stitches were small and even and elegantly done. Painfully, but elegantly done.

When she finished she washed the wound and wrapped a bandage around Thorgrim's midriff. She found another tunic in Thorgrim's sea chest and helped him put it on, then took the first to wash and mend with the same fine stitching she used to mend Thorgrim himself.

As the sun set, those who could gathered around the cottage in which the dead had been laid out. Bergthor's men had rounded up three cows which were slaughtered. Thorgrim used Iron-tooth to slay one of the animals. He raised the sharp blade high and as he did so he felt all the anger and frustration and fury at himself come boiling over, like leaning over the glowing coal of a forge.

He swung the blade down and it cut through the animal's neck and the cow dropped as if the sword had pushed it to the ground. Blood ran free from the great rent in its neck and Starri Deathless stepped up and thrust a bowl under to catch as much of the warm liquid as he could.

Starri held the bowl and followed behind Thorgrim as he walked around the house, dipping the leaves of a severed tree branch in the blood and sprinkling it on the walls and thatch. He called to the gods to look kindly on the brave lives and honorable deaths of the men inside.

This was the funeral ritual that Thorgrim had made his own, over many years of performing such rites. He knew others did not send their dead off the way he did, but he guessed his way was as pleasing to the gods as any. The living stood watching, quiet and solemn. The dead did not complain.

When that was done the house was set on fire, lit from the inside. The rain and mist had stopped but the world was thoroughly wet and Thorgrim did not fear that the fire would spread to the other houses.

Soon the flames filled the doorway and the few windows of the house, and soon after that the tendrils of fire began clawing their way through the thatch on the roof, which was bone dry on the inside. Moments later the house was completely engulfed in flame, and the men inside were off to wherever the Valkyries deemed they should go.

Thorgrim was standing a ways back, watching as the roof collapsed, sending up a great shower of flame and embers when Bergthor stepped up, Hall and Gudrid beside him.

"Thorgrim? See who's returned," Bergthor said and it took Thorgrim a moment to remember that he had sent them off in the first place.

"What did you find?" Thorgrim asked.

"Not much," Hall said. "I didn't just approach the English ships, I climbed aboard one of them. They're deserted. Tied to the river bank and deserted. Not a man aboard them, or anywhere near, that I could see."

"Gudrid?" Thorgrim asked.

"The village was deserted, too," Gudrid said. "We saw no one from the water so we landed and moved farther and farther from the river, and not a living thing did we find. We went about a mile beyond the village. There were signs the army had been there, and not so long before, but we saw nothing of them."

Thorgrim nodded slowly as he considered this. Certainly the English could claim a victory in the fight on the bay, even if they had been the ones to leave the field. Did they think their work was done, that they would withdraw the army back to Winchester, or wherever it had come from? Would they not follow up on the beating they had given Thorgrim and his men?

"I can call together all the ships' masters," Bergthor suggested. "Call a war council, make some plan of what we'll do next."

"No," Thorgrim said. "No council. I know what I'm doing next." He was done with talking. Now he would act, and he would act as he saw fit.

Chapter Twenty-Seven

It was a whirlwind,
when together came
the fallow blades
where men together fought:
ardent for battle,
disdaining flight;
the chieftain
had a valiant heart.

The Poetic Edda

Skorri Thorbrandsson was pleased with the boat that Valgard found. A fishing boat, about twenty-five feet long and heavily built. It had six oars and a short mast to carry a square sail, much like a longship in miniature. Skorri would be able to cram fifteen of his warriors aboard if he was not concerned about their comfort, which he was not.

He was less pleased with the amount of time it took Valgard to find the vessel. Half the morning had been eaten up waiting while he and a handful of men searched the coastline for some suitable craft. Skorri was not a patient man in the best of times, and this was hardly the best of times.

But he was not an unreasonable man, either. He knew even as he was giving Valgard the order to find a boat that it would not be done quickly. There were only so many boats, and most would be out fishing at that time of the day, despite the growing threat of weather. Or because of the growing threat of the weather. The fishermen would want to haul their nets one more time before Thor and Njord conspired to keep them land-bound.

This forced idleness gave Skorri time to think: to think about where Odd and his rescuers might have gone to elude pursuit and what he might do to run them to ground. To think about how far his service to Halfdan might take him, the wealth and power he might accrue in the service of the king.

And conversely, what might become of him if he failed to bring Odd back. Skorri did not care to admit it, but the example that Halfdan had made of Odd left a deep impression on him, as it had on all the men who had seen it, those who were in Halfdan's service and those who were not.

"Alf!" Skorri called to one of his men sitting nearby. All the men under his command were hand-picked, good, reliable men, but of them Alf was the most dull-witted and perhaps the most expendable. He had been chosen for his strength, which was considerable, and not for his cleverness, which was less so.

"Lord?" Alf leaped to his feet.

"Ride back to Halfdan. Tell him we have not yet found Odd or Onund. Tell him we're on the trail but we might be gone the night. He should look for our return tomorrow. I doubt before that."

"Yes, lord," Alf said, and it was clear by his tone and expression that he did not relish this task.

"Wait…" Skorri said as Alf turned to go. Alf looked back hopefully. "Tell Halfdan our return might be the day after tomorrow."

"Yes, lord," Alf said with even less enthusiasm. He looked afraid. Not terribly afraid, but more afraid than Skorri had ever seen him look. He hesitated for a moment and it seemed as if he might speak again. But he didn't, and instead jogged off to fetch his horse.

I can't go to Halfdan myself, Skorri thought. *Valgard might return any time with the boat. I can't be away.* And it was true. Every word. But it was also not the chief reason he did not want to bring this bad news to Halfdan in person.

Coward… Skorri chided himself.

Alf, however, had not yet returned by the time Valgard and the others arrived with the boat, and Skorri took that to mean he had made the right decision. It would have only delayed them further had he gone to see Halfdan in person.

Maybe Alf never went to Halfdan at all, Skorri thought as he watched the boat coming in toward the beach, its square sail set and drawing, four men on the thwarts, Valgard aft at the tiller. *Maybe he ran off, too afraid to talk to Halfdan.* If that was so, then Halfdan would think Skorri had never sent word, and he would not be pleased about that.

Stop it, you whore's son coward... Skorri thought. He was not, and never had been, a man given to fretting and second guessing. Except when it came to serving Halfdan the Black.

The halyard was let go and the sail came down in a jumble and the boat covered the fifty feet to the beach with the last of the way it carried. The bow ground up onto the shingle and Skorri's men grabbed hold and pulled it farther up.

"I'm sorry, Skorri, we were gone so long," Valgard said. "We saw boats on the water, but to find one on shore we...."

Skorri held up his hand and Valgard stopped. "I know you moved quick as you could," he said. "Now we have to go."

He turned back toward the other men. In the time Valgard was gone, Skorri had done more than just worry. He had made the men empty their bags of any food they had and bundle it all up to take in the boat. He had decided who of the men would go with them and who would stay and keep searching the shore.

"You men I named off for the boat, get aboard," Skorri said, and those designated began to climb over the side of the boat and find places on the thwarts and up in the bow. Skorri turned to Valgard. "You know what to do?"

"Yes, lord," Valgard said.

Skorri was all but certain Odd's rescuers intended to take to the sea and get as far away as they could, as fast as they could. But they had already proven themselves to be clever, and it was quite possible they would double back and come ashore. Under Valgard's command the handful of men Skorri had left would split up and patrol the coastline, north and south, riding back and forth over the miles until they found Odd and the others, or they were recalled, or they died of old age.

Spears and shields and the bundle of food and a small cask of ale were handed to the men aboard the boat, and then the rest clambered in over the side and squeezed in where they could. Skorri climbed aboard last and threaded his way to the stern, taking his seat beside the tiller. He nodded to the men on shore and they grabbed onto the sheer strake and shoved the boat back into the water, splashing out waist deep to get the heavy-laden craft well clear of the bottom.

Awkwardly the men on the thwarts lifted the oars and set them in the tholes and began to row. Their efforts were much hampered by the number of men on board, but at least they would not have to row long. There was a breeze blowing, and once they were clear of the shore, once Skorri had decided the course they would take, they could pull the oars in again and set the sail.

Skorri pushed the tiller over and swung the boat off to the east, heading directly away from the beach. He looked over his shoulder. The men on shore were already mounted and riding off, half to the north, half to the south. He nodded to himself. *Good men,* he thought. All those hc commanded, they were all good men because he had picked them and trained them himself. Together they would find Odd and bring him back.

And one day those men would be his hirdsmen, his private warriors and guard, when he was something much greater than King Halfdan's sœslumadr.

He moved his eyes up from the beach, toward the jagged line where the sky met the land. The hint of pending storm had not gone away: indeed, the clouds had grown darker, the sky more looming and ugly.

He turned his eyes back out to sea. The coast here looked just as it did in much of Norway, an irregular shoreline of rocky, pine-covered peninsulas jutting out into the sea, small humps of granite islands scattered at random, some so close you could throw a rock to them, some a mile or more off shore. It was a jagged, broken coast with hundreds of places for a small boat and its crew to hide. The chances of catching up with Odd and those who had helped him were frighteningly small, but the thought that he might fail did not even cross Skorri's mind.

"Get the sail on her," Skorri called and he could sense the relief as the men pulled the oars in and others cast off the lashing that had been put around the sail and yard. A moment later the sail was hoisted up, snapping and flogging in the breeze. Then the sheet was pulled aft and the sail filled. The boat heeled to leeward and the note of the water running down her side rose in volume as the men on the thwarts leaned toward the weather side.

Skorri felt the tug on the tiller as the boat tried to round up into the wind. He pulled it toward him a bit and settled on a course for open water. He had already put considerable thought into what direction he might go. Now, very soon, he would have to commit.

He scanned the horizon, south to north. There were a half dozen or so boats out on the water, fishing boats much like the one they had commandeered. He let his eyes settle on each in turn. None of them appeared to be making any attempt to flee. None of them was really moving much at all. They seemed practically fixed where they were and Skorri imagined they were hauling nets. A few were moving slowly under sail or oars, searching out the schools of herring. Not the actions of men trying to put miles between themselves and possible capture.

Somewhere off to the south lay Grømstad, the seat of Halfdan's kingdom. To the north lay Fevik, Odd's homeland, a place where he would be more likely to find shelter and help. But the wind was out of the north and west, which meant sailing north along the coast would not be easy.

Odd was in bad shape. They would not want to subject him to the beating he would take on a small boat banging along to weather, spray coming over the rail. On the other hand, they would not much care to head to Grømstad and the den of the wolf.

They'll want to tend to him, Skorri thought. Odd was near death. There were not many men who could have survived as long as he had, and Skorri had come to grudgingly respect the strength of the man. But Odd was the son of Thorgrim Night Wolf, grandson of Ornolf the Restless and Ulf of the Battle Song. He came from good stock.

Still, strong as he might be, there were limits to even his endurance. The rigors of the escape might have been enough to kill him. It seemed most likely that his rescuers would want to find a safe place to come ashore and tend to his wounds. Get him fixed up before they continued the flight.

Skorri scanned the horizon again, ignoring the boats, looking instead at the islands. If Odd and the others were in a boat and wanted to briefly go ashore, then they would go to an island. They would not return to the land where they might be found by Halfdan's patrols. If they did that, they would piss away all the advantage they had gained by taking to the sea.

From his vantage point, his eye level just a few feet above the water, it was difficult for Skorri to tell how many islands there were.

He did not know those waters, and it was not clear what was one island and what was two, overlapping, or if there were other islands hidden behind the ones he could see.

Then something caught his eye, a smudge, a discoloration against the gray sky. He frowned and squinted and leaned forward. The wind was steady and brisk and that made it hard to tell if he was seeing what he thought he was. But yes, he was seeing it. He was all but certain. A thin column of smoke lifting up off an island somewhere ahead, a mile and half away.

"You men," he said, "any of you see smoke from any of the islands?"

The men all turned one way or another, scanning the horizon, looking from one outcropping of land to another. It took a moment, but finally a man named Kolbein Thordarson, who was probably the most experienced sailor aboard the boat, spoke up.

"There, lord," he said, pointing in the same direction that Skorri had been looking.

"Yes, I see it," said another. "Wind's blowing it away fast as it rises, but yes, I think I see it, too."

"Good," Skorri said. He pushed the tiller away, turning the bow toward the base of the smoke column. "Ease that larboard sheet some, and take up on the starboard."

The sail was bellied out and straining, filled with the stiffening breeze. The boat was pitching a bit, its bow hitting the seas and tossing spray back. They were moving fast, as fast as they were likely to go with a boat as heavy laden as it was. The vessel could bear the weight, Skorri knew. It was built to stay afloat with the bottom loaded feet deep with fish. Hundreds of years of the experience of boat builders trying one thing then another had gone into her lines, her scantlings. She would not sink, even with fifteen men aboard. But neither would she sail terribly fast.

Skorri looked through the crowd of men forward toward the island beyond their bow, a hump of granite a quarter mile long with a cap of pine trees. The smoke was coming from the far side, or so it seemed. In truth Skorri did not know if it was coming from that island or one behind it. And he would not know until he had rounded the island's west end and seen what was there.

"You think that's them, lord?" Kolbein Thordarson asked, and the question surprised Skorri. It took a great deal of courage and an unbearable curiosity for Kolbein to have spoken up that way.

"Yes," Skorri said in a tone that did not invite further questions. But he had spoken the truth: he did think it was them.

If Odd and the rest had tried to escape by boat — and Skorri was all but certain they had — then they would not have dared go far while it was still dark. Too many things to wreck on in those waters. They would have waited until first light, but it was not long after that when Odd was discovered missing and Skorri and his men tracked them down to the water. There had been no boat close to shore, no boat in sight save for the few fishing vessels off in the distance. Which meant the fugitives had stopped somewhere.

It had to be the island. They would have wanted to tend to Odd's wounds, get some hot food in him. Get him warm. It had to be the island.

Skorri pulled the tiller a little more toward him. His eyes were on the island's granite shore, his body was motionless save for the small movements of his arm shifting the tiller side to side. But his mind was hard at it as he envisioned the various ways this might play out, the most effective approach he might take.

Land on this side of the island? Attack them overland?

It had its merits. The fugitives would have no warning, unless they had a lookout in the trees watching them at that very moment.

There might be more than one island, Skorri thought next. It seemed that the smoke was coming from the island just ahead, but he knew that could be deceptive. The fire might be burning on some bit of land behind this one, and he would look foolish indeed if he came ashore on the wrong island.

No, there was no choice. Sail around the west end of the island and come ashore as close to the fire as possible. The men who had masterminded Odd's rescue might have thought an island was a good place to hide, but it had a downside as well. On an island there was only so far you could run.

The boat pounded along, driven by the taut sail. The water beyond the island came into view and Skorri could see there was no other island there: the fire was burning just around the point of land they were rounding. Odd and the rest were almost within arm's reach.

"We'll come around this point and come ashore near as we can to where the fire's burning," Skorri said to the men. "Get ashore right off, round up anyone you can find. They'll probably scatter like rats but we can round them up. Try not to kill any of them, but absolutely do not kill Odd. Do you hear? I'll kill the man who kills Odd Thorgrimson."

Heads nodded. The men amidships fished out the spears and the shields and the helmets, no easy task in the crowded boat, and passed them out to their owners.

Skorri's eyes were still on the rocky shoreline as it passed down the boat's larboard side and more and more of the far side of the island came into view as they rounded the point. They came into the lee of the land and the boat sat a bit more upright as the gray ledges partially blocked the wind.

The column of smoke was more visible now, but Skorri still could not see its source. He pictured Odd and his rescuers sitting around the fire, maybe watching a pot of porridge swinging from a chain on a tripod. He pictured their shock when they saw the boat crammed with warriors come into view. He imagined them leaping to their feet, feeling the impulse to flee, and then realizing they were trapped.

The image gave him a deep sense of satisfaction. They might be clever, these men who had rescued Odd, but they were not more clever than Skorri Thorbrandsson.

He pulled the tiller closer as the boat cleared the western point of the island. Now Skorri could see all of the south side of the island that had been hidden from view, the quarter mile of long gray rocky shore, interrupted by a small gravel beach, a perfect place to land. He could see the fire from which the smoke was rising, a tall stack of logs, more a bonfire than a cooking fire, burning intensely, sending its thick cloud of smoke aloft like a signal fire.

But he could not see Odd or his rescuers. And, more crucially, he could not see their boat pulled up on the beach. And just as he was considering those facts, wondering where the boat might be, a realization came into his head as if the gods had whispered in his ear.

They had fooled him again.

"Bastards!" Skorri shouted and he saw a few of the men jump in surprise. "Man those sheets, we're going about on the other tack!"

He could see the looks of confusion on the men's faces but they were well trained enough that they did not ask questions, simply grabbed up the sheets that held the corners of the sails and made ready to trim them in any way that Skorri saw fit.

Skorri clenched his teeth in suppressed rage and pushed the tiller away. The boat began to turn hard, turning away from the island, and the sail began to flog as the wind took it from the wrong angle. The men on the thwarts hauled on the sheets, turning the yard overhead, elbows thumping into neighbors as they tried to work in the tight pack of men. But no one protested, no one spoke.

The boat came around until it was pointed in the direction they had just come, going back over the water they had just covered, or as near to it as they could get on the opposite tack. Skorri's face was set in a scowl, his squinting eyes looking out to the horizon, but the island was still in the way.

Everything he had thought was correct. They would not have gone far in the boat. They would have wanted to stop, and they would have stopped on an island. But they would not have built a fire. Of course they would not have built a fire. It would give them away. Skorri thought it had given them away. But he realized now it had been meant to draw him to the island. Why else would the fire have been built so big, built to send off so much smoke?

"Bastards!" Skorri shouted again.

It was not long before they had left the bulk of the island astern and once again they could see out to the open water. Skorri moved his eyes slowly along the horizon. The fishing boats were all pretty much where they had been, some shifted a few hundred yards this way or that as they chased their catch. None of them were moving with any particular speed.

Save for one.

Skorri could see it now, off to the north, a mile and a half away, maybe a little less. Like his own boat it had a square sail set and drawing and it was racing off up the coast, the only boat in the fleet that seemed at all eager to make distance. North, toward Fevik. Where Odd's people lived.

"Lord…?" Kolbein said, his voice sounding timid, and timid in Kolbein sounded strange. Skorri looked away from the distant boat and at his men crowded forward.

"They fooled me," Skorri said, willing to admit the truth, at least to these trusted few. "Bastards fooled me into going one way, while they're going another. You see that boat to the north? With the sail set, running off for the horizon?"

Heads swiveled, nodded, turned back toward Skorri. "That's them. I'll fall on my sword if it isn't. And we'll run them down and we'll bring them to Halfdan and we'll enjoy watching them die, and I reckon Halfdan will see that enjoyment lasts a good long time."

He saw eyes dart off to the west, to the dark and ugly clouds that seemed to be building up from the land itself.

"We'll run them down," Skorri said again. "Or we'll die trying. Because we'd be better off dead than going back to Halfdan stinking of failure."

Chapter Twenty-Eight

'Twas night in the dwelling, and Norns there came,
Who shaped the life of the lofty one;
They bade him most famed of fighters all
And best of princes ever to be.

The Poetic Edda

They rode north through country that seemed as if it had been swept by the most virulent plague. There was nothing amiss: houses were standing intact, some with coals still glowing in their hearths, fences had not been torn down, the small kitchen gardens were undisturbed, as were the larger fields of barley and oats. But there was not a living creature to be seen. Not human, not animal, nothing moving save themselves and the birds that flitted through the trees and the fields.

"It seems word of our coming has spread," Louis de Roumois said dryly. "Bad luck, Thorgrim. I image the people took all their gold and silver with them when they ran."

Thorgrim made a grunting noise, the closest to a laugh he could manage. They had passed the hovels of fishermen and the sagging cottages of poor farmers and a few large, timber-built churches. Any miniscule treasure the churches might have housed would have been moved to safety at the first sign of Northmen. As to the others who lived in that miserable place, it was unlikely any would have owned a single piece of gold or silver.

They had used caution riding through Hamtun, alert for any surprise the English might spring on them, but the village was deserted just as Gudrid had reported. The doors to houses, the gates to pens, were all gaping open. Of course the people there would have been quite aware of the bloody fight that had happened on the water just a few miles south. They would have fled their homes out of fear that the Northmen had won and would be coming for their spoils.

Actually, they might have fled regardless. Any army meant drunkenness, looting, rape, even if it was an army of your countrymen.

The village of Hamtun grew more sparse as they moved away from the water, fading at last into open country, and still there was no one to be seen. It was clear that an army had moved through there, and not long before. The muddy road was deeply pockmarked by the passage of hundreds of men on foot and horseback, and dozens of heavy-laden carts.

It was something less than an army that Thorgrim was leading in their wake. A dozen people, no more. Gudrid, Hall, Godi, Vali, Failend. The warriors he had come to trust as much as he trusted himself. There were not many. And Louis de Roumois, as well.

Starri was there, of course. Thorgrim would have asked Starri to join them anyway, but he did not have to because Starri was going to come no matter what anyone said to him.

Harald was also with them. Thorgrim had wrestled with that choice. Under normal circumstances there would have been no question, but Thorgrim was still not pleased with Harald's behavior, not happy that Harald seemed to take no responsibility for his own mistakes, showed no sort of remorse. The younger men still seemed to look on Harald as if he was some kind of champion and Harald still seemed to believe it was true. The Norns who controlled the fates of men did not much care for hubris.

But Harald, of all the men there, was the one who Thorgrim most trusted, even when he was playing the ass. And for the final weight on the scale, Harald, with his surprising knack for language, was the only one among them who could speak passable English.

Thorgrim had not asked Harald to come. Rather he told him he would be coming and he told Harald he might bring one of *Dragon*'s crew if he wished. Thorgrim had guessed he would ask Herjolf, with whom he seemed to have struck up a friendship. Herjolf had just shown himself to be a brave fighter, throwing his small ship in the path of the big English longship.

But Harald had asked someone else, a young man about Harald's own age named Brand, who had an active, intelligent quality about him, so Thorgrim agreed.

A few others of *Sea Hammer*'s crew rounded out the dozen, and that was all that Thorgrim wished. This whole raid, the passage up the bay, the intention of landing in Hamtun, the bloody sea battle, had come about because Thorgrim felt he owed it to Bergthor and to those of his men who were still eager for plunder. They had made for Winchester because the Briton Geldwine had convinced Bergthor there were riches to be had there. They had been attacked and they had been beaten and now they did not even know where their enemy had gone.

Thorgrim was done.

Done listening to the suggestions of others, done considering anything save for the safety and riches of his own men, and his desire to get back to his farm in Vik. He was done learning second and third hand about what was happening around him. Done hearing about the wonders of Winchester. It was time for him to go and see for himself, to decide for himself, based on what he saw with his own eyes, whether it was worth spending one more drop of blood on this quest. Then he would make a decision, and the others were free to agree with him or not.

Bergthor seemed happy enough to do what Thorgrim told him. Along with rounding up the cattle for the sacrifice for the dead, he and his men had come up with twenty horses, and all but four had saddles and bridles. They had all been gathered up within five miles of where the Northmen had come ashore. Some had been left behind as their owners fled the invaders. Some had been given up after their riders were convinced it was in their best interest to do so.

There had been no council of war, no meeting of the ships' masters. Thorgrim simply gathered Bergthor and the other ships' masters and told them what he would do and what they would do.

He would take his small band and ride north to Winchester and see how promising it looked, see if they had any hope of sacking the place, see what had become of the army they had fought on the bay. The rest would see to the wounded and send those who died off in a proper way and repair their ships and repair their weapons and wait for Thorgrim's return, at which time he would tell them what would happen next.

There were no objections. Nor had Thorgrim thought there would be. The Norse army was in no shape to do anything but lick its wounds. And Bergthor seemed happy to not have to make any decisions.

So they rode north, and they rode mostly in silence, their eyes alert for signs of an ambush or someone tracking their movements, but they saw nothing. They followed the wide dirt road and soon it became something more than just a muddy stretch of ground battered by the passing of an army. There were stones, carefully cut and fitted to make a road thirty feet wide and amazingly flat and straight. The borders of the road were likewise lined with cut stone, but longer and standing proud, like a short wall to hold the others in place.

The road even seemed to be rounded, just a bit, in such a way that rain would run off to the sides rather than settle in pools. At first Thorgrim thought that was an accident, the result of the particular contour of the land, but as they rode on and he saw that the slight arch did not vary at all he realized that this had been done on purpose.

But astounding as the road might be, it did not seem new at all. There was a quality to it that suggested it had been built ages before. In sundry places he could see where it had been repaired by men not nearly as skilled as those who had built it.

"Louis," he said at last. It took a great deal of curiosity for Thorgrim to ask Louis anything, being as it was a tacit admission that Louis might know something he did not. "What do you know of these roads? Did the Britons build these? Or the Saxons?"

"The Romans," Louis said.

"Romans? Who are the Romans? They live in this country?"

"They did," Louis said. "They lived everywhere. Frankia, Germania, Engla-land. They conquered it all. Many, many generations past. We have such roads in Frankia, and other things the Romans left behind. They conquered all the world at one time."

Thorgrim considered that. *Romans.*

"They did not conquer Ireland," Failend said.

"No," Louis said. "The Irish were too great a bunch of lunatics for the Romans to conquer."

"I don't think they conquered our country," Godi said. "We have no roads such as this. I've never heard any speak of the…Romans."

Louis sighed. "I meant to say they conquered all of the civilized world."

They rode in silence for a bit more, then Thorgrim asked, "These Romans, they worshiped your Christ god?"

"No," Louis said. "Not at first. They were the ones who killed him. The Romans worshiped many gods."

"Of course," Godi said. "How could any people become so powerful if they worship only one god?"

Failend made a sound that was somewhere between a laugh and a snort of contempt. "One god is enough," she said, "as long as he's the right god."

They continued on for some time more, the ancient road over which they passed making the going easy. Thorgrim felt certain they were traveling in the right direction. If Winchester was as important a city as the Briton had said it was, then this road must lead there. Still, he would have liked to question some local person, but so far there was not a person to be seen.

The road ran through low, open country, and every once in a while through a cluster of small houses gathered where a lesser road met up with the Roman way to make a crossroads of sorts. Sometimes there was a larger, heavy-timbered, two storied building among the smaller ones which Thorgrim guessed would be an inn of some sort. If there was anyone inside they were keeping hidden.

It was lucky for them, Thorgrim mused, that he had only an army of twelve with him. If all the Northmen had been marching past they would not have been able to resist plundering the place for anything they could carry off.

They rode all through the morning hours then stopped to have their midday meal at a spot where a tumble of large rocks would make comfortable seating, though once they dismounted none of them felt much like sitting again. The fields of waist-high grass ran off for a mile or more in any direction, which meant they would have ample warning of anyone approaching unless they were crawling on their bellies.

With groans and other guttural noises they stretched and then fished out the dried meat and bread and cheese and skins of ale they had brought in the bags hung over their saddles. They ate leaning against the rocks, somewhere between standing and sitting.

"Might finally see some people," Harald said as he chewed, one of the first statements he had made that day.

"Why do you say that?" Godi asked.

Harald nodded in the direction where the road led. "Some smoke up there. House or a smith or something. And I'm pretty sure I saw some folk off in the distance."

"Well, all of Engla-land couldn't have fled in terror," Gudrid said. "I suppose we'll meet up with someone eventually." That met with a few grunts of agreement and they continued eating for a while longer. Harald's companion, Brand, was the next to speak.

"Do you think they're watching us?" he asked. "I've been keeping lookout, but I haven't seen anyone."

"Neither have I," said Hall.

"I haven't either," said Thorgrim. "But I'll wager they are, and are just good at keeping hidden. They know we're in Hamtun, and they'd be fools not to watch the roads from there to Winchester. And those men who surprised us on the water, they were no fools."

They finished their meal in silence, then mounted again to continue on their way. Thorgrim looked over his small band as they swung themselves up into their saddles. They were mostly outfitted with mail shirts, and all had helmets they were not currently wearing. They carried round shields on their backs or hanging from their saddles. Anyone seeing them would know they were warriors, but they would not necessarily know they were Northmen. They would appear little different from English men-at-arms, and seeing as there was only a dozen of them, Thorgrim did not think they would cause much alarm in the countryside.

The poor folk, the farmers and laborers, would not be eager to approach any warriors at all, and Thorgrim expected they would keep a wary distance. He counted on it. If the king or whoever ruled in those parts had sent men to watch the road, it would not be entirely clear to them if the dozen riders were Northmen or not. He guessed they would be able to ride all the way to Winchester without anyone being certain of who they were.

At least he hoped that would be the case.

A few miles on they began to see folk for the first time, farmers mostly, off in the fields some distance from the road. They would stop in their labors and watch as the riders approached, alert for any threat, and only when the dozen had passed by and shown no interest in them did they resume their work.

Once they came upon a small house near the road. A woman there was running back and forth in a panicked rush, herding her children inside. It was almost comical. As they rode past Thorgrim imagined the woman huddled in a corner, shielding her children, the ax she used for splitting kindling held in her trembling hands. He wondered how long she would stay like that before daring to come out again.

By midafternoon the broken patchwork of fields past which they had been riding all day seemed to grow more regular, more carefully laid out, the houses scattered around more numerous. There were more people, too, men working in the fields and men working in makeshift shops in the yards outside their cottage doors. It was clear they were approaching some sort of central and well-populated place.

We must be nearing Winchester, Thorgrim thought. *If Winchester is a real place, then this must be it.*

He heard hooves behind him, and Louis de Roumois drew alongside. "Have you see them?" he asked.

Thorgrim nodded. "Not for a while. But they made little effort to hide themselves before."

There were other riders nearby, men on horseback just a half mile or so ahead. They were not on the road, they were moving through the fields and the stands of trees, keeping just ahead of Thorgrim's band. They were doing a decent job of concealing themselves, but not a perfect job. Thorgrim had caught glimpses of them from time to time, and he had a good idea of who they were. Poor farmers did not ride. Simple travelers did not avoid the road.

"What do you make of them?" he asked Louis.

"There are five or six that I can see," Louis said. "But they're not riding together. They have shields on their saddles. Sometimes I think I see mail, but I can't be sure from so far off."

More hoof beats and Starri Deathless drew up on the other side. Despite the rain of the day before there was still a fair amount of dried blood in his long, tangled hair and scruffy beard. His tunic, however, was clean, since he always went bare-chested into battle.

"Are you talking about the riders ahead?" Starri asked. Starri had the keenest sight of any man in the fleet. Thorgrim trusted Starri's eyes more than those of anyone else, but he did not so much trust Starri's interpretation of what he saw.

"Yes," Thorgrim said. "What do you make of them?"

"English warriors. Half a dozen. They're trying to keep hidden while they spy on us, but they're doing a piss-poor job. I've been watching them since just a little after our midday meal."

"They must suspect that we…you…are Northmen," Louis said. "But they can't be certain. They might take us for some wealthy man's hearth guard."

"Which is why they don't attack us," Starri said. "Which is why we must attack them."

"No," Thorgrim said. He could just imagine the dozen of them chasing these English bastards all over the countryside. "Let them wonder. We're just going to Winchester to have a look."

The watchers did not leave them, but they were better able to hide themselves as the number of farms and clusters of homes and wayside inns became more numerous.

And then, finally, they could see it. Still several miles off, still mostly hidden, but they could see the spires of a church, the roof of a large building that looked to be a great hall, various other tower buildings, thin columns of smoke rising up from dozens of small fires.

"That must be Winchester," Godi said, putting words to the others' thoughts.

"Must be," Hall said. "Biggest village we've seen yet in all Engla-land."

That was certainly true. They had been months now in that country and had seen only small fishing villages huddled up to the sea. Hamtun was the largest of those, and it was certainly larger than most such villages in Norway, but it was still of no terribly impressive size. But this town up ahead, this looked like a truly large, truly important place.

Winchester…

"Ha! Look at that whore's son!" Starri called out. He was pointing off to their left and Thorgrim looked in that direction. One of the watchers had come out from behind a byre and was riding off hard across the field, heading toward Winchester, it seemed.

"I reckon soon enough all Winchester will know we're here," Gudrid said.

"I hope so," Starri said. "I hope the cowardly bastards try to do something about it."

Thorgrim watched the man ride off. He was surprised they had not been challenged yet, despite their ambiguous appearance. He would have thought one of those scouts might have come close enough to enquire as to who they were. One spoken word would tell any Englishman that Thorgrim's band was not English. Instead, they had just kept watch from a distance, and made a poor effort at hiding themselves.

"What now, Thorgrim?" Louis asked.

"We keep going," Thorgrim said. "This changes nothing. We see what Winchester is about, and then we ride back." That was as much as Thorgrim meant to explain, and it was also about as much as he had thought through.

Just ahead of them a dirt road crossed the Roman way at a right angle, the deep ruts in its surface, left behind by generations of cart wheels, making a sharp contrast to the well-ordered bricks over which the Northmen traveled. There was a scattering of houses at the crossroads, just as they had seen at others, and one larger building, two storied and heavily built with timber frames and wattle and daub walls, the way the English seemed to build their more substantial structures. There was a stable and a fenced-in area and a few outbuildings: smith, kitchen, latrine. An inn catering to the travelers going to and from Winchester.

There were no people there, at least none nearby. There were some off in the fields, a couple of men driving a team of oxen that dragged a plow in their wake, some others sowing seed, apparently. More at work farther off. But no one in the houses, no one at the inn.

They rode slowly past, keeping a careful eye on the buildings as they did. The doors were shut, the windows shuttered. Nothing moving. There was something almost eerie about it. Thorgrim heard the whinny of a horse coming from the direction of the stable, the only sign of any creature there. It was a familiar sound but seemed out of place in the strange silence.

Then they were past, continuing on, Winchester becoming more visible in the distance, the clusters of houses scattered around the open country more numerous. It was as if a big town like Dubh-linn had been broken up and the bits tossed around the hills and fields.

Thorgrim was looking at those things but he was not thinking about them. He was thinking about the horse's whinny that he had heard, coming from the stable at the inn. There was nothing at all strange about a horse being in a stable. Indeed, it would be more odd to find such a stable that did not have at least one horse in it. But he could not shake the idea that something about it was not right.

You're becoming a foolish old man, frightened of shadows, he chastised himself, but even that could not drive off the uneasy feeling he had. He could not dismiss what he felt. He was no stranger to such things, the gods whispering warnings in his ears.

Then another thought came to him, another hint from the gods. The scouts might not have been doing a poor job of concealing themselves. They might have been quite clever, in fact. They might have been keeping the Northmen's attention on them, while others set up a surprise attack.

"Listen, the lot of you," he said, loud enough to be heard without turning around in his saddle. "I think we're about to be set upon. From that inn we passed. I may be wrong, but make ready for it anyway. Get helmets on and get your shields and weapons ready. But easy. If they come, let them think they're surprising us."

He heard a shuffling and thumping behind him as his warriors did as he said, settling helmets on heads, taking shields off their backs or their saddles where they hung. He heard Starri make some strange sound, something like a whimper, a strangled note of eager anticipation.

Thorgrim reached down with his right hand and grabbed Iron-tooth's hilt and pulled the sword out, just an inch or so, just enough to know it would draw easily. He untied the cord that held his conical helmet hanging from his saddle and settled the helmet on his head. He unhooked his shield from the other side of his saddle and was just putting an arm through the leather strap when the English launched their attack.

The quiet of the afternoon was shredded in an instant by the sudden pounding of hooves, the shouting of men who hoped the noise would surprise and disorient an unprepared foe. Thorgrim jerked his reins to one side, making his horse spin in place, just in time to see twenty or more riders come pouring around the corner of the inn, spears in some hands, swords held high in others. Fighting men, they wore mail and their helmets were shining.

Thorgrim kicked his heels back hard and his horse plunged forward and Thorgrim drew Iron-tooth from its scabbard. Now he was shouting, too, and Starri was screaming his battle cry, more disconcerting than anything the English could hope to produce. All the Northmen were turning their horses together, like dancers performing some choreographed move, and they were building speed as they charged to meet the enemy head to head.

Failend was near the back of their group and that meant the English would be on her first.

"You bastards!" Thorgrim shouted as he kicked his horse again, his eyes on Failend. She had her helmet on, and her shield on her left arm, her seax in her right hand. She looked like a child set against the men around her. She had been riding toward the enemy but now she pulled her horse to a stop and braced herself for the attack coming at her.

Thorgrim made a loud, guttural sound of frustration as he tried to get to Failend's side before the English did. She was a good warrior, she had proven herself many times, but the bow was her weapon. Practiced as she was with her seax, her weight was slight and her reach was short and there was nothing she could do to change that.

Thorgrim was still fifty feet away when the first of the English riders came up with her. He was a spearman and he held his weapon level, right at Failend's shield, and Thorgrim knew if it struck with all the force behind it, it would likely go right through. That, or if the man was skilled, he would shift the point just a few inches to go under or around the shield and drive the wicked point right through Failend's small frame.

He gritted his teeth as he saw the two come together, saw the point of the blade dip to go under Failend's shield. And he saw Failend drop the edge of her shield to meet the point. The spear tip impaled the wood and Failend pushed it aside, knocking the spear out of line, as she lunged with her seax.

Now the rider's momentum worked against him as he rode right onto Failend's blade. Thorgrim saw the point of the short weapon drive through the spearman's mail as the two horses collided and Failend and the Englishmen were knocked clean off.

The two fell from sight and Thorgrim could spare them no more attention. The other English riders were breaking around Failend's and the spearman's horses and charging toward them, still shouting as loudly as they could. But they had not taken Thorgrim and the others by surprise, and now the Northmen were shouting as well and charging to meet them.

Starri had managed to get his tunic off and his two battle axes in hand and had let go of the reins as he urged his horse forward. He drove past Gudrid and Hall, who were also racing into the fight, forcing them to swerve out of the way. Starri's horse seemed in a blind panic now, as out of control as Starri himself. It careened into the two English warriors leading the way, checking their momentum, making their horses twist and buck in fright.

In one fluid move Starri leaped up into a crouching position on his saddle and flung himself from his horse to that of the nearest Englishman, axes flailing as he flew through the air.

But Starri's madness did not slow the other Englishmen as they rode around the terrified mounts and met the Northmen coming at them. Harald and Brand had turned their horses and were going in side by side, Brand swinging a long battle ax and Harald with Oak Cleaver in his hand. They met two of the English head-on, coming up on either side like ships in a sea-fight, hacking down with weapons, meeting shields with shields, bringing the weapons back and hacking again.

Thorgrim was still not in the fight. He urged his horse forward once more but the animal balked, turned part-way back around, tossed its head, and Thorgrim could see it was near panic. The English were riding mounts trained for combat, the Northmen were not. And Thorgrim's seemed to be the shyest animal of them all, and that would not do.

"Come on, you stupid beast!" he shouted as he pulled the reins back, trying to make the horse turn, but he could see his efforts were only pushing the horse into greater terror. Then one of the English riders broke through the swirling fight ahead, spear leveled, riding right for Thorgrim and the horse he could not control. Thorgrim felt his aggravation crest like a wave and break.

The rider was fifteen feet away and closing fast when Thorgrim slipped the shield off his arm and flung it, edge-first, at the man. It sailed neatly through the air and hit the Englishman hard on his own shield, hit with the combined force of Thorgrim's throw and his horse's forward momentum. The rider was knocked back in his saddle and his carefully aimed spear was knocked out of line, but the horse under him kept coming.

Then Thorgrim's horse finally, accidentally, did what Thorgrim wished it to do. It turned to the right, coming hard against the spearman's horse. The man's shield was still on his arm and Thorgrim reached out with his left hand and grabbed it, pulling hard. The rider, already off balance, was jerked forward. Thorgrim brought the pommel of Iron-tooth down on the back of his neck and the rider continued on down, tumbling off the horse and under the stomping hooves as Thorgrim swung his leg off his own horse and onto the animal just vacated by the English warrior.

Even as his feet found the stirrups Thorgrim could tell this mount was a breed apart from the last. There was no hesitancy, no sense of panic in the way the animal moved. Thorgrim whirled the horse around in a half-circle. Godi had two men around him who were just trying to keep clear of his long ax.

Louis was engaged with another. Thorgrim watched the Frank's quick blade parry a thrust and get in past the man's shield. He saw the Englishman's eyes and mouth fly open wide with surprise and Thorgrim knew that was it for him.

Another rider was coming along side, screaming, sword raised, a big man with a massive red beard, more like a Northman than an Englishman, Thorgrim thought. He was mounted on a horse that was white with random patches of black, as if it had been haphazardly daubed with tar. The man brought his sword around hard and Thorgrim raised Iron-tooth to stop the hacking blow from the weapon.

Thorgrim had no shield now, but that was not a problem: indeed it seemed on horseback he was better off without it. He turned the sword aside and thrust, but the Englishman's shield was there to deflect the blow. The Englishmen cocked his arm back and thrust at Thorgrim's belly but Thorgrim knocked the point aside with his mail-clad arm.

He dug his heels into the horse's flank and the horse drove forward, right into the other horse, well within reach of Iron-tooth's point. Thorgrim thrust for the man's neck, hidden behind the red beard, but the man twisted and the tip of the sword drove into his shoulder. It was not enough to kill him, but enough to put him out of the fighting.

Good horse, Thorgrim thought and just as he did he felt the horse going down, its front legs buckling under it. He felt himself pitch forward in the saddle and as he did he saw the shaft of the spear that had been driven into the horse's chest jutting out. The horse hit the bricks of the Roman road and it started to fall sideways and Thorgrim was tossed right over the horse's neck. He hit shoulder first on the unforgiving surface of the road. He felt the impact in his shoulder and back and then through his whole body as he came to rest.

His first impulse was to just stay put, to remain as he was until he was certain he had not shattered his entire frame, which he felt he had done. But a voice in his head was shouting for him to stand and with a groan he rolled onto his side and pushed himself to his feet. His helmet was gone but from long practice he had not lost his grip on his sword.

He held Iron-tooth up and in front, ready to fend off the next attack, and then he realized there would not be one. The English men-at-arms were scattered on the ground, some moving, some not. He could see three others, including his red-bearded adversary on the white and black horse, riding off as fast as their mounts would take them. In the distance he saw a handful of the riders who had been watching them. They had apparently been coming to join the fight, but on seeing how the surprise attack had played out they too turned and headed for Winchester.

Starri was off his horse and looking frantically around for someone else to fight. Harald and Brand and the others were still on their horses, and Louis was just sliding down from his. They were all there, all apparently unhurt.

Save for one.

"Where's Failend?" Thorgrim asked, and he could hear the sudden worry in his own voice.

Chapter Twenty-Nine

Their horses shook themselves,
and from their manes
there sprang dew into the deep dales,
hail on the lofty trees,
whence comes fruitfulness to man.
To me all that I saw was hateful.

The Poetic Edda

Failend was on the ground. She could hear the fighting going on around her. From her supine position she could see the wild dance of horses' legs, hear the shouting, see others standing or lying on the stone road. But for her the fight was done.

She had experienced quite a bit in just a short few moments: surprise, then fear, then any thought or emotion shutting down as training and instinct took hold.

The English men-at-arms seemed to come out of nowhere, but she was ready, as ready as she could hope to be. Somehow Thorgrim had seen it coming. His wolf's sense, the pagans might say, but she would not say that. She did not believe in such things.

But neither could it have been the hand of God. God would not help the heathens in such matters. She did not know what it was, or how Thorgrim could have known the attack would happen. She only knew that he did, that his unnatural sense was a real thing. She had seen it before in him.

So when Thorgrim said they were about to be attacked, that they should don helmets and get weapons ready she, like the others, did not hesitate. Helmet on her head, shield on her arm, her seax in her right hand which held her reins as well.

She could feel her stomach twist, a sheen of sweat on her forehead and her back under her padded tunic. It was the fear she always felt as she stood on the edge of the fight. The Northmen did not feel fear, or so she thought — she had never asked one of them so she did not know for certain — but she felt fear abundantly, and she was not afraid to admit as much. Or would not be afraid to if anyone ever asked, which they never did.

The English men-at-arms came charging around the corner of the inn, just as Thorgrim had seen they would. They came riding hard and shouting, hoping to bring with them shock and fear, to throw their enemy off balance. Failend jerked the reins over, spun the horse, felt the fear melt away like a snowflake on warm skin. It occurred to her that she was now at the head of the Northmen's line, the first point of the English attack. That fact was a curiosity, no more. She was beyond being afraid.

She kicked her heels into her horse's flanks and the horse charged forward and somehow that only made Failend even more aware of how small she was. The rider at the head of the English charge was a spearman, his weapon leveled at her, his mouth open in a battle cry as he came on. If they hit with their combined speeds and the spear found its mark it would go right through her shield, right through her mail and her chest and out her back. She had seen it happen to other men, men who were much more substantial than herself.

With a jerk of the reins Failend stopped her horse and prepared for the impact, her eyes fixed on the point of the spear. Everything seemed to move slowly now, the rider coming at her moving like he was under water, the sound of the hoof beats and the shouting dull in her ears. Her world closed down to the tip of the spear, the wicked black point carrying death right to her.

There was no thought now, no feeling, nothing. As the spear point came at her she saw it dip and thrust at her belly, under the edge of her shield, but it still seemed to be moving too slow to be of any concern. She dropped her shield three inches and felt the tip of the spear hit the canvas-covered wood. She swung her arm left, directing the trust of the spear aside and stuck her seax out, straight-armed, right at the rider's chest.

The Englishman was wearing mail and a helmet. Failend's eyes flashed from the point of her seax, inches from the man's chest, up to his face, his eyes. They were very blue, wide with surprise and the intensity of battle. He was looking at her, their eyes fixed on one another, not two feet separating them as they came together.

Failend felt the tip of her seax hit the man's mail and she locked her elbow against the shock. She felt her arm pushed back, her body twisting from the force of the man against the blade. And then the point broke through the iron links and the resistance seemed to disappear as the rider rode right onto her weapon.

The Englishman's horse slammed into Failend's with an impact that made her gasp and threw her forward in the saddle. The Englishman was knocked back, Failend's blade still in his chest. Failend's hand was locked on the hilt as if she would fall to her death if she let go.

The spearman started to tumble down and Failend felt herself dragged along with him. The shield came flying off her arm and she was lifted out of the saddle and she had a passing thought that a bigger person would not have been pulled from her horse that way.

Failend was dragged off her horse, dragged over the man's saddle and over the far side of his horse as together they rolled off their mounts. They twisted as they fell, the Englishman's arm coming around her as if he was trying to hug her. Then they hit the ground and Failend felt as if she had been punched by a hundred fists at once. The breath was knocked out of her and for a second all she could do was kick and gag and thrash as she tried desperatly to fill her empty lungs.

With a gasp she sucked in air, and she felt the panic subside. She was flat on her back and the English soldier was lying face-down, half on top of her. Her hand, she realized, was still on the hilt of her seax which was still driven into the man's chest. She pulled at it, trying to slide it free, and the man gasped and jerked as she did.

Failend shouted in surprise. She turned her head and she was face to face with the Englishman, inches away. His eyes were open, those startling blue eyes, open very wide. His skin was smooth, with just a short stubble of beard, and his cheeks were red from sun and exertion. She could hear the thumping of horses' hooves all around her, the frightened mounts now riderless and unsure what to do, but she was transfixed by those eyes, that face, so close, like the face of a lover when the act was done.

Is he dead? Failend wondered, but then the man's mouth opened slowly, as if he was trying to speak. Failend could feel his warm blood washing over her hand as it spilled down around the blade she was gripping. She was no longer trying to pull the blade free, no longer trying to squirm out from under him. She was looking into his eyes and she felt as if she could do nothing else.

A hoof came down inches from Failend's head, but she did not move. She was aware of their horses moving away, aware of the sounds of the fighting, the shouting, the clash of weapons, the whinnying of the horses. Starri Deathless's frightening battle cry. She heard it all but she was not able to move. The man's eyes held her.

Then the Englishman gasped, like one last desperate attempt to hold onto life. His body shook and seemed to settle and the breath eased out of him. Failend could feel it warm on her face. And then his eyes changed. Not the shape, not the color, but something went out of them and Failend knew the man was dead.

And still she did not try to get out from under him. The fighting was swirling all around her, loud and urgent; her people, the people with whom she'd lived and fought for two years and more, were battling for their lives, but Failend did not move.

She couldn't move. Not because she was hurt, or pinned under the dead man. Those eyes kept her there, as if they had cast a spell, the way those spirits that lived in her native Ireland could do. Those blue eyes, those eyes she had watched go from living to dead, held her, along with the sound of that last gasp, the feel of that warm, final breath on her face.

Failend had seen many men die over the course of her bloody career as a warrior. She had killed any number herself. But it had been with her bow, mostly, or stabbing and slashing in the passion of battle, turning to the next opponent without even seeing the work her weapon had done. She had never experienced anything like this. She had never watched a man, inches away, die on her blade.

Her breathing was normal again, her mind coming back to the present, but still she could not make sense of the strange mix of feelings in her. Sorrow, horror. Victory. Gratitude that it was him and not her. Guilt that she felt that way.

The men she had killed before were just…men-at-arms. Enemies. They were not men with blue eyes and ruddy cheeks and warm breath.

She had a sense that the tone of the battle had changed, that things had settled, the same way the Englishman's body had settled on top of her as the spirit left him. She knew she could not remain as she was forever, but still she could not bring herself to do anything else.

Suddenly the Englishman began to move as if he was trying to stand, a dead man coming back to life. Failend gasped in horror. Then she looked up, and there was Thorgrim Night Wolf pulling the man off her. The Englishman's arms hung down as if he was reaching for her and she shuffled out of the way of his reach and then Thorgrim tossed the man aside as if he weighed no more than a sack of bread.

"Failend, are you hurt?" he asked. His eyes met hers, then his gaze moved down her body. She realized she was still holding her seax, that Thorgrim must have lifted the Englishman right off her blade. She looked down as well. She was bathed in blood, the copious blood that had run out around her weapon.

"No," she said, sitting up. "No, I'm not hurt."

Thorgrim reached down and grabbed her under the arms and stood her up as if she was a child learning how to walk. She felt dizzy and she swayed in place and Thorgrim put his arm around her to steady her.

"You're certain you're not hurt?" he asked.

"Yes. This blood is his," she said, nodding toward the dead man on the ground. She looked around for the first time. Some of the Northmen were still mounted, some were standing. A few were lying stretched out on the road, as were a number of the English men-at-arms.

"What happened?" she asked.

"We beat them, mostly," Thorgrim said. "We drove them off, anyway. About half a dozen rode off. The rest are dead. Or will be soon." Failend did not know if he meant that they would die of their wounds or be killed for being English, and she did not ask.

"You had best see to the others," Failend said and Thorgrim gave her a half smile and nodded and walked off. He called for the men to see who of theirs were wounded or dead, to get the horses under control, to keep a lookout for more English riders coming.

One of the Northmen was dead, a man named Aud who had joined them back in Vík-ló. Vali had taken a spear thrust to the arm, his right arm, and did not have the use of it. Gudrid and Brand held wads of cloth torn from the Englishmen's tunics over bleeding wounds, but they insisted the wounds were not bad enough to send them back and Thorgrim did not argue.

"Can you ride, Vali?" Thorgrim asked.

"Yes, lord, if someone can help me mount."

"Good. We'll put Aud's body on a horse and you can go back with him," Thorgrim said. "We'll stash the English dead in the inn over there and continue on."

"Continue on?" Louis asked, and as usual he sounded curious, no more. "I have a feeling the English know we're here now."

"I'm happy to hear it," Thorgrim said. "Maybe they'll send us food and drink. But we came to see what this Winchester was, and we'll do that whether they know we're here or not. Brand!"

Brand, who had been examining a long tear in his tunic, looked up. "Yes, lord?"

"You fought well. I saw you. You and Harald." Thorgrim pointed to the Englishmen who lay on the ground, dead or nearly so. "You can have your pick of any of the mail these men wear, and any of their helmets and swords if you wish."

Brand looked down at the men on the ground. Mail and swords were not easily come by, and these men seemed to be outfitted well with each.

"Thank you, lord," Brand said. He surveyed the Englishmen sprawled on the ground, walking slowly along as he did. Failend wondered if he would take the mail from the man she had killed, but that man, she guessed, was not one of the wealthy ones. He was just a spearman. There would be better mail shirts to be found.

And just as she guessed Brand knelt down beside one of the men at the edge of the battlefield and fingered the hem of his mail shirt. He looked up at Harald, who had joined him, and nodded and the two of them began tugging the shirt off the lifeless figure.

But it turned out he was not as lifeless as he appeared. As they pulled the mail up the man gave a strangled gasp and waved an arm. Failend jumped in surprise, even from a distance, and she saw Harald and Brand do the same.

"Lord Thorgrim!" Brand called. "This one's just had a knock on the head, I think. Not too hurt."

"Lucky him," Thorgrim said.

"But, lord, I think he might have been in command here," Brand said. "Better sword and mail than the rest. Silver trim on the helmet. Good shoes."

No wonder it was his mail you wanted, Failend thought, but she would not begrudge Brand the best of the spoils.

Thorgrim walked over to where the man lay on the ground. By the time he got there the man was starting to move a bit. For a moment Thorgrim just looked down at him and said nothing.

"He looks like a man of means," Thorgrim said. "He might be of value. Information, or ransom. " He looked up at Brand and Harald. "Get his mail and sword and whatever else you want. Bind his hands. We'll take him with us."

The two young men turned to it, and as they did, the others relieved the rest of the English of weapons and mail and the purses that hung from their belts. Several of the men-at-arms were dead, the rest wounded to various degrees, and they moaned and made feeble gestures as their valuables were liberated. The ones who could still ride had ridden off, apparently, leaving these behind.

Finally the Englishmen were dragged through the front door of the inn and deposited on the floor. Failend was happy to see that Thorgrim only meant to leave them to die, not to actively bring about their ends.

By the time they mounted their horses again and continued north, Thorgrim leading them off the road and through the open country, there was little sign that a battle had taken place. They rode through fields planted with oats and barley and across grassy meadows where cattle grazed. They kept a sharp eye out as they made their way north, but they saw no one save for a few farmers who kept their distance.

Failend rode at Thorgrim's side but she did not try to engage him. Her gaze was fixed on the towers rising up above the fields.

Winchester.

But in her mind she saw the eyes of the man-at-arms, looking at her. And behind that she saw all of her life, stretching back to her girlhood in Ireland. And in particular she saw the last few years. As Louis de Roumois's lover. Warrior. Thorgrim Night Wolf's lover. Part heathen, crossing the seas in a Northman's ship. How very strange it all seemed.

She thought of a moment almost two years ago now, maybe more. She had stood with sword drawn, her husband, bleeding and enraged, standing in front of her. And also in front of her, a choice: drop her blade and her life would go off in one direction, thrust it into her husband's throat and her life would go off in another.

She had made her choice then. She remembered it well and she thought about it now. Because now it was time to choose again.

Chapter Thirty

It would beseem thee better
thy sword to redden,
than to grant peace
to thy foes.

The Poetic Edda

Thus far, Onund Jonsson had been honest, and he had been correct. Amundi had to admit as much. He hoped Onund would continue to be those things, but he was still wary.

It had been Onund's suggestion that they might free Odd Thorgrimson, a suggestion made on that dark night, standing by the door of Amundi's smith's shop. Amundi had barely heard Onund's words, and he had understood them even less.

Amundi was still moving in a dream world then, struggling to make sense of what was going on around him. Trying to understand how Halfdan, how any man, could act in the way he had, so utterly brutal, so utterly uncaring. He heard Onund say *Odd Thorgrimson* and Amundi's mind was filled with images of the horror he had just witnessed and he could not think beyond that.

"Do you hear me, Amundi?" Onund said, his whisper harsh and as loud as he dared. "If you'll work with me, we can free Odd from this. But we have to work fast. Odd does not have much time left. No man could live through much more of this."

Amundi nodded, then realized Onund could not see the gesture in the dark. "Very well," he said. "But how?"

Onund outlined the plan. He said it would work. Indeed, he said it would not be terribly hard because of the place he held in the hierarchy of Halfdan's army. There was no one who would question Onund's orders, no one who could countermand them save for

Skorri Thorbrandsson or Halfdan himself, and those two could be avoided.

Amundi listened to the plan, and as he did he started to feel more connected to the things around him, more aware, more able to act, like a man slowly shaking off a deep sleep. He was done drifting on the tide. He was ready to act.

But he could not act immediately. It was another two days before Halfdan left Amundi's hall. It took Halfdan that long to sufficiently indulge himself at Amundi's expense, to loot Amundi's farm for whatever he wished. And all the while Amundi and his household lived in the stable and were fed porridge and water.

Finally the army was ready to move on to the next farm, the next flogging, the next ostentatious plundering. When they left, Onund took one of Amundi's slaves for his own. He did not hide the fact. Indeed, he made it clear that he, too, was extracting plunder from the traitor Amundi, and Halfdan heartily approved that decision.

The slave, whose name was Oleif, was a smart, active young man, and loyal, and Amundi had chosen him as the one for Onund to take. Oleif, stealthy and quick, had traveled regularly and unseen between Halfdan's camp and Amundi's farm, bringing word back and forth, carrying plans as they were crafted: find Signy and some of the others, send Amundi's people to safety. Wait until Halfdan went into camp near the sea, then come with a fishing boat to carry them to safety. They would need only an hour on a dark night to bring Odd off and spirit him away.

Amundi had been suspicious at first, and Alfdis his wife had been doubly so. But finally they succumb to the simple logic that had led Amundi to meet with Onund in the first place: it was not a trick because Halfdan had no need for subterfuge. If he wanted Amundi dead he would just kill him. If there was one thing Halfdan had proved it was that he did not care in the least about men or laws. And that alone was reason enough to risk setting Odd free, and to risk fighting back against the king.

There was another reason, of course, that Amundi agreed to help Onund, one which Amundi would admit only to himself. He could not continue to live as he was anymore, having seen what had become of Odd, and knowing his own part in it. He would much rather die fighting Halfdan than continue to live with that shame.

It was not more than a week after Halfdan's army marched away from Amundi's farm, the horrible wagon bearing Odd creaking along somewhere in the middle of the line, that all the elements of the plan came together. Oleif arrived in the dark of night with word from Onund: it was time to act.

The following day, around midday, Amundi loaded Signy and Alfdis into the fishing boat, along with his overseer, Thord, Oleif, and a dozen of his best hands, his most skilled warriors, who volunteered for the task. They rowed and sailed to the spot where Onund had arranged to meet them. By sundown they were a half a mile from the shore, with most of the men hiding on the bottom of the boat and the rest pretending to haul nets, just in case they were seen, but as far as Amundi could tell they had not been.

They came ashore in the dark, met Onund at the beach and followed him up the field to where he told them to wait. In all of their efforts to free Odd, that time was the worst. Amundi and Signy and six of his men stood in silence, with only the sound of a soft breeze in the grass, and they waited. They waited for Onund to return with Odd. They waited for Onund to return with Halfdan and two dozen warriors. They waited for what would happen next, and they had no idea what it might be.

It turned out to be Onund, true to his word, with two of Halfdan's men and Odd between them. It had worked out just as Onund said it would. Easier, as it happened, since the men guarding Odd had been caught doing something stupid, and as a result they were even less apt to argue when Onund gave them orders. They did as they were told and it cost them their lives.

Amundi's men half carried Odd down to the water, his arms slung over their shoulders. It was not clear if Odd was even aware of what was happening. They laid him down on the bed they had prepared on the bottom of the boat and waited while Onund and a half dozen others made a false trail to the north, then came splashing back along the water's edge. They climbed aboard and pushed off and drifted away in the dark.

"We should get the oars out. Row away from the shore," Onund said. His voice was calm but Amundi wondered how much fear he was hiding. What Halfdan had done to Odd would be a joke compared to what he would do to Onund if he caught him.

"We can," Amundi said. "But we must row easy. There are ledges and rocks hereabouts. It wouldn't do to hit one if we were making any speed." The easiest thing would have been to raise the sail to the breeze, but that would be even more dangerous as they went blundering around in the dark.

Amundi looked up at the sky. It was overcast. Not a star to be seen. They had been drifting for several minutes, the shoreline lost in the dark, the boat probably spinning as it floated away. Amundi no longer had any idea as to which direction they were pointing.

"Very well, get the oars in the tholes. Quiet now," Amundi said and the men forward, barely visible, lifted the oars and set them down with care between the wooden thole pins. They held the blades just above the water and waited for word. They were warriors and farmers, but there was not a man among them who was not intimately familiar with ships and boats as well.

Amundi cocked his head and listened for any sound that might come out in the night. He heard a soft murmur off the starboard side. The wash of small surf over the pebble beach, perhaps. He felt the breeze on the back of his neck. While they were still ashore he had noted it was blowing out of the north-west. That meant their starboard side was parallel to the shoreline. Most likely.

"Now, give way," he said softly and the men dipped the oars and pulled back and the boat began to gather way. Amundi held the tiller over, just a bit, turning the boat ninety degrees to larboard. That was the best he could do to set a course. It would have to do until first light gave them a hint as to where they were.

Now what? Amundi thought. Making plans was his problem now. Onund had promised to do no more than free Odd and help them escape as best he could, but once Odd was free their escape would be up to Amundi. Amundi knew that country and he had friends there. Onund had been too long in Halfdan's service to hope for any help or trust from the folks thereabouts.

The boat pulled carefully through the dark, the only sounds the small creak of the oars in the tholes and the occasional soft moaning from Odd, followed by gentle words from Signy or Alfdis, kneeling beside him. Amundi considered their situation. By first light, or maybe before that, the people in Halfdan's camp would realize that Odd was gone, and it would be like a rock thrown into a bee hive. They would be able to follow the trail through the grass easily enough, even in the dark. But with luck Onund's false trail would fool them. In any event, they would not be able to see the boat until the sun was nearly up.

We do not want the boat near shore when the sun comes up, he thought.

His plan had been to grab Odd and head straight out to sea, but the place Onund chose to free him was a more treacherous stretch of water than Amundi had anticipated. They had nearly wrecked the boat several times the day before, even with the sun well up, as they threaded their way through the islands and the rocky hazards that lay just under the surface. He did not dare to go charging seaward in the dark.

Island, Amundi thought next.

There were several islands nearby. If they could get close to one, then at first light they might be able to get around the far side before they were seen from shore. If the false trail on shore worked they could hide on the island for a day or two, then make their way up the coast.

He saw movement in the dark and then Signy was in front of him, kneeling on the floor boards. He could barely see her, but her face appeared drawn and he thought he could see the glimmer of tears on her cheeks.

"Signy?" he said. "How does Odd do?"

"Not good, Amundi," Signy said, and he could hear the fear and the tension in her voice. "Not good at all. I…it's hard to see how bad he is, in the dark. And it's wet on the bottom of the boat. He's dry now, I think, on the furs, but they'll soak through. We must get him ashore, Amundi, as soon as we're able. Get some hot food in him, see to his wounds in the daylight." The words spilled out of her, carried by her desperation.

"Very well," Amundi said. That decided it. "We're going to get as close as we dare to the island to the south, and once we can see something we'll go ashore there."

Signy was quiet for a moment. "Thank you," she said.

Thank me if we live, Amundi thought. *Thank me if I don't order my men to kill us all before Halfdan gets his hands on us.* But all he said was, "Of course, my dear."

They continued to pull in a direction that Amundi guessed was south-east. Every now and again Odd would make a low, moaning sound, and Signy or Alfdis would comfort him and Signy would stifle a sob. Amundi sent one of the men up to the bow to keep a lookout ahead, though he doubted the man would see any rock or ledge until the boat ran up on it. Still, it gave the others some hope.

It was impossible to tell how long they rowed through that netherworld, the men barely putting any effort into pulling the long oars, the hull of the boat making the softest of sounds as it moved through the water. It felt to Amundi as if they had been there for days, though he knew it had been only a small part of the night. He could hardly fathom how much longer this would go on, or if Odd would live, or if they would all go mad before dawn.

Sleep was coming over him as he leaned on the tiller, his eyes starting to close, when he felt a kick to his shin, not hard but insistent. He opened his eyes and sat upright with a twinge of embarrassment.

"Dawn's coming," whispered Thord, who was pulling the oar nearest Amundi.

Amundi looked off to the east and saw that the sky was indeed lighter than it had been. It was not dawn yet, but not far from it. He could see the soft glow of the sun lighting up the clouds as it began to make its climb over the horizon beyond the sea.

He looked around in every direction. He could still see nothing but night, but it was a softer night than it had been.

There was still a breeze, and Amundi said, "Unship your oars and get ready to set the sail." Forward he could hear men moving around, and he could even make out their shapes against the sky. He heard soft grunts of orders passed around as the yard and sail and rigging were straightened out.

Then he looked up and he was startled by what he could see. The dark gray sea stretched away from them in every direction. The shoreline was still hidden from sight but right ahead, and not so far away, the dark hulk of the island stood out against the ever-lighter sky.

"Get the sail on her," Amundi said, and with those words a glimmer of possibility began to mitigate the despair he had been feeling, in the same way that the rising sun was replacing the night.

Hands pulled on the halyard and the sail went flapping up the mast and soon it was set and drawing. The boat heeled a bit to larboard as it gathered way, and the sun continued to reveal the sea and the island ahead.

Amundi steered for the west side of the island. They had come that way the day before, and the route had seemed clear of hazards, but that did not mean there were none, just that he hadn't seen them. He realized he was tensing up, his whole body tight and waiting for that awful sensation of the boat slamming into a rock or a ledge, and he tried to relax.

The sun was up, though hidden behind thick cloud, as they skirted around the point that formed the island's western end. Amundi ordered the men to scan the horizon and the distant shore, now visible, for any sign of movement, but they could see nothing. The only things moving in those first few moments of the day, beside the boat that carried them, were a few gulls wheeling around in search of dagmál, their morning meal.

They ran the boat ashore on a small beach on the south side of the island, sheltered from the breeze and from sight of the mainland. They built as large a fire as they dared, which was not large at all, and carried Odd ashore. They carefully removed his tunic and Signy fought down the tears and the sobs as she tended to his wounds. Odd groaned at her touch and said a few things that might have been words. Some of the others warmed broth over the fire and Signy spooned it into his mouth.

Amundi and Onund took a few of the men and crossed over the small island, pushing their way through the narrow stand of woods to the granite ledge that made up the north side. From there they could see the shoreline from where they had left, a good mile and a half away, but they could make out no details. If the sun had been out they might have seen more, but under the overcast sky everything was rendered in shades of gray and black and it all seemed to meld together.

"They'll know by now that Odd's gone," Amundi said. "And you gone as well."

"That they will," Onund said.

"Will Halfdan himself come looking for us?" Amundi asked.

Onund shook his head. "No. He'll send Skorri after us. If he goes himself than there's no one else to blame for failure."

Amundi knew who Skorri was of course. Halfdan's administrator for the district, his sœslumadr, who had taken over that duty after Einar Sigurdsson had run off in disgrace. But he did not know much about him.

"Is Skorri clever?" Amundi asked.

"He's clever," Onund said. "Cunning might be a better word. He's smart and skilled and as vicious as Halfdan, at least. Maybe more."

"And he's motivated," Amundi said. "If he succeeds in bringing us back then Halfdan will reward him well. If he fails, then…well…I suspect his life will not be worth much to him after that."

"You're right, Amundi," Onund said. "So we had best make sure he doesn't succeed."

They left a few men to keep lookout as best they could, though Amundi did not think there would be much to see. He certainly hoped that would be the case. They crossed back to the camp that had been set up around the small fire. Some of the men were eating, some sleeping. Odd was lying on his side, his lacerated back slathered with bear grease and various healing herbs. He was asleep. Signy and Alfdis were kneeling beside him.

"How does he look now, in the daylight?" Amundi asked, though he could see for himself, and what he saw was not encouraging.

"He's not good," Alfdis said, standing. "But he's not as bad as we feared. He's a strong man. He was even able to speak a few words before the sleep overtook him. He thanked us."

Amundi nodded. "Even if we fail, he'll die a better death than he would have as Halfdan's prisoner. I think that's true for all of us. We won't carry our great shame into the next world."

It was not the best encouragement he could offer, but it was all he had.

Much as he wished to remain awake, Amundi could no longer ignore his own exhaustion. *You are not a young man anymore,* he thought as he lay down on a patch of grass near the fire and rested his head on a rolled up cape. He was asleep before another thought could come to him.

And then someone was nudging him awake. He forced his eyes open, not at all certain of where he was, but the memory of the recent past came back to him quickly. He sat up. Oleif, who was one of the men left on lookout, was kneeling beside him.

"Oleif? What news?"

"There's a boat," Oleif said. "You had better come. You and Onund."

Amundi pushed himself to his feet while Oleif went off to rouse Onund, and the three of them made their way back through the stand of trees to the north side of the island. The other lookouts were there, including one of the younger men who had managed to climb up to the top of a tree.

"There are fishing boats, out there," Oleif said, pointing out toward the east. "They showed up soon after we got here." Amundi could see them, though just barely. A smattering of small boats, probably much like the one they were in, spread out over the water. They were hardly moving. Amundi guessed they were casting and hauling nets.

"And there's another boat, there," Oleif continued, pointing now toward the shore, pointing in the general direction they had come after getting Odd off the beach. Amundi could see that boat as well, just barely. It was far off and harder to make out against the dark line of the land. If its sail had not been set then Amundi probably would not have been able to see it at all.

"Hmm…" Amundi said.

Onund looked up at the man in the tree. "What can you see from there?" he called.

"The boat's been keeping near the shore, making for the beach we were on," the man called down. "I think I can see riders on the shore, but it's pretty far off…oh, the boat just dropped its sail."

"Hmm…" Amundi said again. He looked back toward the shore, but with the sail gone he could see nothing of the boat. "What do you make of it, Onund?"

Onund was frowning and looking out over the water. Finally he spoke. "I think Skorri was not fooled by our false trail. I think he figured out we went by boat. Now he's getting a boat of his own to come after us."

"But how can he find us?" Amundi asked. "There are a thousand places we could have gone."

"Maybe," Onund said. "Or he might guess at the decisions we made. Might guess we wouldn't want to be seen when the sun came up, and the best way to avoid it would be to get to an island. Nearest one. This one."

"That would take a very clever man to think that through," Amundi said. "You think Skorri's that clever?"

"I do," Onund said. "I wish I didn't. I wish I knew Skorri for a fool, but I fear he is not."

Amundi looked up from the shoreline to the sky above. It was dark, and not just because of the early hour. There were ominous clouds building there, layers of cloud against cloud. There was no immediate threat, he could see that, but that would not last.

They crossed back to the south side of the island and told the others that they would have to get underway again. Amundi could see the hesitancy in Signy's face. She did not want to move Odd, not yet. But Amundi did not give her or anyone a choice, and so without complaint they loaded everything back into the boat, setting Odd gently down on the bed of furs again.

"I thought of something," Onund said to Amundi as the last of the people headed for the boat. "Since we're leaving, we want Skorri to look for us here. Because we won't be here. We want him to come here while we sail away."

"Yes, we do," Amundi agreed.

"Let's build the fire up. Get it so it's making a lot of smoke. Skorri will see that, and he'll guess it's us and come here. I hope."

Amundi could see the reasoning in that, so he called to the men standing nearby to gather up any driftwood or any downed limbs or small trees they could find in the forest. They built the flames higher, stick by stick, until the small fire, barely alight, had grown into a respectable blaze reaching as high as the height of a man. They continued adding larger and larger pieces of wood, limbs and logs, until the fire was too big and too hot to approach. Then they made their way back to the boat, climbed aboard and shoved off.

"Set the sail?" Thord asked. He was already kneeling over the lowered yard but Amundi shook his head.

"No," he said. "The sail's too visible. We row."

The men took up the oars, dropped them between the thole pins and pulled. They pulled with a will now, because they could see where they were going and they were eager to make all the distance they could. Amundi steered them around the east end of the island and then straight out to sea, keeping the island between them and Skorri back on shore. That was not their final course, but he wanted to get out to sea a bit, get to a place where they could mix in with the other fishing boats, attract no undue attention.

They continued on in silence, leaving the island astern, the motion of the boat becoming more pronounced as it met with the swells coming in from the sea. Once they were far enough out Amundi turned the boat north and steered a course parallel to the mainland.

Oleif was the first to speak. "That boat there, lord," he said, pointing over the larboard side. "That's the boat that went to the beach, I'm all but certain."

Amundi shifted around until he was looking back toward the shore. A boat had put off and it was just setting its sail. At that distance it was little more than a light-colored smudge against the dark of the land, but Amundi had seen enough boats from enough vantage points that he knew what he was looking at. And he was quite certain of who it was — Skorri Thorbrandsson with a crew of well-armed and determined warriors. The question now could only be, where would they go?

"Pull easy, pull easy," Amundi called forward. The men had been leaning into the oars, trying to make distance, but that might look suspicious. None of the other fishing boats were working that hard. Amundi could see questioning looks on the faces of the men, but none of them spoke; they just slowed the pace of their rowing.

Amundi turned back toward the shore. The boat was still putting off from the land, and the sail seemed to be driving it along, driving it out to sea. Driving it straight at Amundi and his men.

No one spoke. All eyes, save for those of Odd, Signy and Alfdis, were trained over the larboard side, locked on the distant sail. It was nearly two miles off and hard to see, but it certainly appeared to be on a course right for them. Time passed, measured in strokes of the oars, and every man waited for the boat to turn and set a course for the island on which they had built the fire. The plume of smoke was obvious enough, even with the growing breeze.

"Maybe they don't see the smoke," Amundi said after some time.

"Or maybe they do," Onund said, "and it's not fooling them."

Amundi looked toward the north. There were half a dozen boats scattered over the water, some rowing, some hauling nets. Skorri would not be able to tell their boat from any of the others. So he might just search them all. Under sail he would be much faster than they were under oars. At some point Amundi would have to admit he had not fooled Skorri. He would have to set the sail and try to outrun his hunter.

"There, lord!" Oleif said, so loud it made Amundi jump. Once again Oleif was pointing toward the shore. "They've changed course now, lord!"

Amundi followed Oleif's arm. The boat was there but the shape was different, the angle of the sail different. Skorri's boat had turned now, and it was running south. Sailing for the island, lured by the column of smoke.

"Good, good!" Amundi said. "Now, we'll wait until they go around the island, and once they're out of sight we'll set our sail. With luck they'll waste time searching around the island for us."

The tension in the boat lifted like morning fog. Men talked back and forth in low tones. Skorri's boat was still in sight, but it was sailing away from them now. Soon it would be lost around the island.

It did not take long. With the wind rising, Skorri's boat was making impressive speed. Amundi could see nothing beyond the small dot of a sail, but he could imagine the boat heeling over, banging into the choppy seas, spray coming back over the bow.

And then it was gone, lost around the west end of the island, lost to Amundi's sight, which meant that Amundi's boat was lost to theirs.

"That's it! That's it! Get the sail up, quickly now!" At some point Skorri would realize that Odd and his rescuers were not on the island. He might even realize they had tricked him. When he did he would take up the hunt once more, more determined than ever. Before that happened, Amundi hoped to put a significant distance between them.

As fast as they were able the men pulled the oars in and laid them across the thwarts. Amidships, Thord cast the lashing off the sail while eager hands laid onto the halyard and the sheets. Once the sail was free Thord nodded and the men with the halyard hauled away. The yard climbed quickly up the short mast, the sail flogging below it, until it was hoisted all the way and the sheets hauled tight.

The boat responded instantly, heeling over to starboard. The wind billowed the sail out and the mast and shrouds creaked under the strain. Heavy and unwieldy as the boat was, it seemed to spring ahead like an eager colt. The bow rose and fell and slammed into the sea and threw spray aft. Amundi waited for Signy to protest, to say that Odd could not endure that sort of jarring, but she did not speak.

She knows, Amundi thought. *She knows if we don't sail as hard as we can it won't just be Odd who dies.*

"Oleif," Amundi called. The young thrall was proving to have very good eyesight. "Keep an eye on the island back there, let me know when you can see Skorri's boat again."

Oleif shifted position to get the best view aft while Amundi turned his attention to the set of the sail and the course of the boat. "Ease off that weather sheet a bit," he called and the men on the larboard side eased the rope a foot or so until Amundi declared it correct. It had been a long time since Amundi had driven a small boat under sail. He had forgotten how much he loved it.

With the sail trimmed just right there was nothing more for Amundi to do but make minor adjustments of the tiller, keeping the boat plunging ahead, making northing as fast as they could, leaving Skorri astern. Soon they were among the fishing boats which were scattered around over a few miles of ocean. Under oars Amundi's boat would have looked like all the rest, but now they were under sail, the only vessel there driving hard on the wind.

"There, lord!" Oleif called. "Skorri's boat's back, coming around the west end of the island!"

That didn't take long, Amundi thought. He knew that time would seem compressed with the intensity of their escape. But even taking that into consideration he was sure that it had only been a short time since Skorri disappeared behind the island.

"He must not have gone ashore at all," Onund said, speaking aloud what Amundi was thinking. "He must have turned around once he saw there was no boat on the beach. He's a clever one, like I said."

"I suspect you're right," Amundi said. He half turned and looked astern. He could see the smudge of the sail behind them, around a mile and a half away. It was a race now, and they would soon find out which was the faster boat.

Amundi felt a burst of wind strike them, colder and stronger, the precursor of a storm. The boat heeled over farther and the men eased the sheets a bit to make it stand more upright. He looked off to the west. The skies which had been threatening all morning seemed ominous now, like something conjured up by the gods. Astern of them, Skorri's boat drove on, its bow pointed right at theirs.

Amundi looked forward again, past the taut sail, out toward the open sea to the north, and quite involuntarily he did the one thing he least expected to do in that circumstance. He smiled.

Chapter Thirty-One

What men cause a ship
along the coasts to float?
Where do ye warriors
a home possess?

The Poetic Edda

Winchester was still about two miles off when they came to a farm of respectable size, with a hall and stables and storehouse. Failend followed Thorgrim in as they rode through a wooden gate in a wattle fence that surrounded the farmyard, a fence to keep wandering livestock out, no more.

Two women came out to greet them, one young, just of marrying age, the other older. Mother and daughter, perhaps. They seemed curious as they stepped out from the hall, but that look changed to one of genuine concern as they looked up at the well-armed and blood-covered riders.

"Harald," Thorgrim said. "Ask them where the men are."

Harald slid down from his horse and took a step toward them and they took a step back, clutching one another. Harald held his arms out in something like a welcoming gesture, and he looked considerably less threatening on foot, so the women stopped their retreat and waited. Harald spoke to them, his words halting. The women shook their heads and Harald spoke again, and that elicited a response.

"They say the men are all off to the king's hall. They were called up as men-at-arms. I think," Harald said.

Thorgrim nodded. "Tell them we'll leave the horses here for the night. And some of our men. If they feed us and see to the horses and don't tell anyone we're here they'll get silver. If they betray us, it won't go easy for them."

Failend doubted that Harald, even with his facility for language, would be able to translate that, but he seemed to get the meaning across, in any event.

"They understand," Harald said.

"Good," Thorgrim said. There was an odd sort of formality between the two. It was not so bad now as it had been — the fighting seemed to have knocked some of the stubbornness out of both of them — but still their relationship was not what it had been.

Failend knew full well what was going on. Some of it Thorgrim had told her, and some of it she had heard from others and some she had seen herself. And some of what Thorgrim told her she had to see for herself in order to know the truth. When it came to people and emotions and such, Thorgrim's understanding was not always entirely correct.

They climbed down off their horses and the women took the animals away and soon there was food brought out from the hall and passed around, and servants rolled out a barrel of ale. The women, apparently, did not want the heathens to go into the hall, but Thorgrim did not seem to care. Failend knew he had no interest in plundering such a place, and he did not intend to stay long.

The prisoner they had taken from the battlefield seemed to have recovered pretty well. They had tied him to his saddle to keep him from falling off, and now they untied him and tried to help him down but he refused their help, sliding down to the ground on his own. He hit the ground and staggered a bit, then recovered and was able to stand upright without help. He was even able to manage a look of defiance as he stared around him.

"Failend, Harald, come with me," Thorgrim said. "Godi, you too." He led the four of them over to where the prisoner stood. They formed a semicircle around him, while he attempted to maintain the defiant look, not so easy with Godi looming over him.

Starri Deathless joined them, uninvited, though with his blood-streaked face, remnants of the day's battle, and his wild hair and the mad look that was always in his eyes, Failend could see he did as much as Godi to intimidate the prisoner.

Thorgrim had been right about the man's status. His mail shirt was gone, Brand's property now, and under it he had been wearing a tunic of fine-woven wool with elaborate embroidering around the cuffs and neck. His leggings were bleached white linen, their quality obvious even soiled with dirt and blood. This was no foot soldier, or even a member of a house guard. He was the sort who had a house guard of his own.

"Harald, ask him if that's Winchester," Thorgrim said, nodding toward the distant town. "Is the king's hall there?"

Harald turned to the prisoner and spoke in the strange-sounding English. Failend could hear that the words were halting, but the prisoner seemed to understand. He replied, just a few words.

"Yes," Harald said. "That's Winchester. The great hall is there. The king's name is…" Harald frowned. "I don't recall what he said. I can't pronounce it anyway."

"Ask him how many men the king has under arms," Thorgrim said and Harald translated.

"He says a thousand men," Harald said.

Thorgrim smiled. "A child could lie better than him," he said.

"There's something familiar about this one," Harald said. "I have to say. I've seen him before, I could swear it."

"Where?" Thorgrim asked.

"I don't recall," Harald said. "It was not so long ago." But there was no time for further speculation. Thorgrim had Harald ask a few more questions, about the defenses, about the church and the wealth stored in the king's hall. He received no answers that were very satisfying or credible, but that did not matter much, at least not for the moment, so he let the prisoner rest, and his own men as well.

The sun was well into the west when Thorgrim stood and ordered the men back to their feet. "We'll walk to Winchester, near as we can get. We'll attract less notice than if we ride. Find some place we can hide ourselves, see what we can see. Maybe we'll enter the city in the night, if that seems the best plan."

They headed off across the open country, leaving the prisoner behind with four of the others to guard him and the horses. They no longer had to guess if they were going in the right direction because Winchester was in sight now, standing proud from the rolling hills like the clearest of landmarks.

The road, the one the Romans built, was off to their right, running straight and true to the city gate. There was considerable traffic on it: riders and men and women on foot and carters driving their teams of oxen in front of awkward, lumbering wagons, heavily loaded with the great wealth of goods and food needed to keep both a royal household and what must be one of the biggest towns in Engla-land supplied.

Soon they could see the wall that surrounded the city, a stone affair, fifteen feet high or so. Not an impassable barrier, but one to slow an army down. One that could create a killing field at its base.

"There," Thorgrim said, pointing to a farm about a quarter of a mile away, halfway between themselves and the walls of the city. "We'll go there, keep a watch from there. See what we can see."

The others nodded. They were tired of walking. It had been a long day. They were ready to sit. So they trudged the rest of the way and once again they came upon a hall, not quite as large as the last, peopled with women and servants who were quickly made to understand the benefits of cooperating with the Northmen, and to understand as well that they did not really have much choice.

This time Thorgrim insisted on entering the hall and they were met with only muted, grudging protest. They stepped into the dim interior and shed their helmets and mail and leaned their shields against the wall.

Failend's mail shirt was still well coated with the dried blood of the spearman she had killed, and as she tried to pull it off she felt her tunic coming with it. She ran her hand under the mail, separating the iron links from the cloth, then pulled the mail off over her head.

She looked down at her tunic. The blood made an odd pattern on the cloth where it had come through the chain mail. She stared at it for a moment, thinking she wanted to wash it away, and also thinking that doing so would wash away her last connection to the young man with the blue eyes.

The others sat at the big table and drank ale and Failend joined them there. Then Thorgrim and a handful of men went outside to keep an eye on the city and the country around, alert for any sign that they had been found out, that men were being sent to hunt them down.

Failend stayed with her fellow warriors at the table and sipped at a cup of ale and looked down at the table top, worn smooth by generations of elbows and trenchers and pots. But she was not thinking about that. Her mind was still sorting out the myriad thoughts that had sprung from the one moment when she found herself looking into that dying man's eyes.

What have I been doing? she thought. It had all seemed so natural, running away with Louis, joining in with the Northmen, becoming a warrior, becoming a raider, becoming Thorgrim's lover. She had never even questioned it, really. She had killed her husband, stolen his hoard of silver and thought little of it. She had just flowed from one thing to another, like the waters of a brook running into a stream then running into a river then into the sea.

And now she could not even recall what she had been thinking, and she wondered if she had been thinking at all.

She stood up from the table and stepped outside. Thorgrim was sitting on a bench by the stable a few dozen yards away, looking out over the city, and she sat beside him. The roofs of the houses and the towers and spires were lit up orange by the setting sun. They looked like embers glowing in the bed of a fire. The two of them were silent for a moment, watching the amazing play of light, and then Failend spoke.

"What do you think? Of Winchester? Is it a place you will go? Is it a city to raid?"

"I think perhaps it is," Thorgrim said. "I think it's what the Briton said it was. Tomorrow we'll get closer, look at the walls, what buildings we can see. See if we might take it without too great a loss. The woman spoke of a king's hall. Probably where those square towers are. And you see that very tall building? Do you think that's a church?"

"No," Failend said. "Yes…I mean, it's a cathedral. More important than a church. Bigger."

Thorgrim made a grunting sound of acknowledgement and Failend was suddenly sorry she had said that. Sorry she had given Thorgrim more reason to raid Winchester.

Why am I sorry? she wondered. *Because I think Thorgrim and the others might be killed if they try? Maybe. But not entirely.*

No, that's not it. Not at all.

She really did not know, except that she was too tired of fighting to think about it anymore. Tired of raiding. She did not want to do it and she did not want anyone else to do it.

They remained like that for some time, Failend leaning against Thorgrim's shoulder, the two of them watching as the light faded from the earth and Winchester and the countryside were slowly swallowed up by the dark. Finally Failend stood and stretched.

"Let me fetch you some ale," she said and Thorgrim looked up, and in the failing light she could see him smile.

"Thank you," he said.

Failend left him there and stepped into the barn. There was just light enough still to see the stalls where a few animals stood, the wooden posts that held up the thatched roof, a big pile of fresh hay to be fed to the hungry livestock. From there she made her way into the hall where the rest of the men were still at the table or sleeping on a raised platform against the wall. She found a cup and filled it with ale.

"Godi," she said. Godi was one of the few still awake.

"Yes?"

"Will you take the watch outside? Thorgrim is near dead with exhaustion but he will not admit it. If you're there I might be able to convince him to rest."

"Certainly," Godi said, lifting his massive frame off the bench. "Brand, come with me," he called and Brand leaped to his feet. "We'll take the watch and then have some others relieve us later."

"Thank you," Failend said. "Thorgrim's out by the stable but you might as well take your place just outside the hall here. I'll tell Thorgrim you're here and see if I can get him to sleep a bit."

Godi and Brand headed for the door. Louis was sitting at the table a little apart from the others as was his wont. She sat down next to him.

"You weren't hurt today?" she asked. She spoke in Irish, one of the two languages they shared. Failend sometimes wondered if Louis even remembered how to speak Frankish.

"No. The English…they are not fighters, no matter how they dress themselves." He turned and looked at her. "You? I saw you and that spearman go down off the horse."

Failend gave a little smile. "No," she said. "A little bruised, but that's it."

"Good," Louis said.

For a moment they just looked at one another and did not speak. Failend searched Louis's face. He was still as handsome as he had been when she first welcomed him into her bed, though he looked older. More worn. She had slept with him first out of boredom and a need to defy her husband. But it had become more than that. And then they had been taken by the Northmen and…it was more than Failend could fathom.

"Do you miss the mass?" she asked and Louis squinted as if he had not heard her correctly.

"The mass?" she said again. "You remember. The prayers, the chanting? The incense? The sacrament of reconciliation?"

"That's an odd question," Louis said.

"No," Failend said. "We've been a long time among the heathens. Sometimes I wonder if I've become a heathen myself."

"I'm not sure either of us would get the abbot's blessing for what we've been about these past years," Louis said. "The mass? I wasn't the best Christian back in Frankia, I'll admit. In Glendalough, at the monastery, they were pretty insistent I change my ways. You know better than most how well that worked out. No, I can't say I miss the mass."

They were silent for a moment more. "Do you?" Louis asked.

Failend shrugged, and she did so with a sense of irony, since that was Louis's preferred gesture. Then she gave a little smile and stood, picked up a candle and walked to the far end of the hall. The women and servants were nowhere to be seen and she guessed they were hiding in one of the chambers off the large central room. But she had seen a chest against the wall and now she found it in the light of the flame. She lifted the lid and looked inside.

There were wool blankets and what seemed to be a cloak, and on top of those a white linen shift and a wool gown to go over it, and a cloth to use as a head covering the way she had seen the English women wear. She guessed that these were the clothes that one of the women saved for special occasions, high feasts and the like. They were nowhere near as fine as the clothes Failend had worn as the daughter and then wife of wealthy men back in Ireland, but they were good enough. She grabbed up the clothes and one of the blankets, shut the lid and hurried out of the hall.

Thorgrim was still on the bench. Failend could see his outline in the fading light. She stuffed the clothing she was carrying behind a barrel that was against the wall of the stable and slipped up beside him, handing him the cup of ale.

"Still awake?" she asked.

"I think so," Thorgrim said, taking the cup. "But I thought you must have fallen asleep."

"I'm sorry I was so long with the ale. The others were in a talkative mood."

Thorgrim tilted the cup back and drained it. "Are you tired? You've had a hard day."

"I think I'm just waking up," Failend said. "I saw Godi and he insisted that he and Brand take the watch. They can't bear for you to not get any rest. They're down by the hall now, keeping lookout."

"That's good of them," Thorgrim said. "But they should have spoken with me."

"I think they were afraid to," Failend said. "But they know what needs doing, what to look for. And you need rest. Here, come with me." She took his hand and tugged and Thorgrim stood as if she had pulled him to his feet. With another tug she led him along to the door of the stable, barely discernible in the dark. Inside they could hardly see at all, but Failend knew where the pile of fresh hay was and she led Thorgrim there.

"Here…here's clean hay," she said. "If it's good enough for the cows to eat it should be good enough for a heathen to lie in. Pray, take off your weapons and lie down here."

She thought she could see Thorgrim nod and she could just make out the movement of his arms as he unbuckled his sword belt and set Iron-tooth down on the hay. Failend's eyes were getting accustomed to the light in the barn, and now she saw him kneel down and feel the hay, then turn and lie back. She heard the crunching of the hay under him and heard him give a deep sigh.

"Ah, that's good, thank you," he said.

"You're welcome," she said. She undid her own belt with the seax hanging at her side and laid belt and weapon down, then pulled her tunic, stiff with dried blood, up over her head. With a quick, practiced motion she shed her leggings and shoes. She stood there for a moment. The cool night air raised tiny bumps on her bare skin and the sensation made her shudder. She looked down at Thorgrim but she could not see him against the hay. She wondered if he could see her. If he was still awake.

Her hand found Thorgrim's tunic as she knelt and she guided herself down until she was lying nearly on top of him. She felt his rough hands on her shoulders, sliding down her back, brushing her long, black hair aside.

She heard him make a little grunt of surprise. Apparently he had not seen her disrobe. She scooted up a bit until her face was near his and she kissed him. She felt his hands come up so that they were pressed against either side of her face and he held her that way and kissed her back, a gentle but demanding kiss.

She reached down and grabbed the hem of his tunic and pulled it up a bit, more a suggestion than a real attempt to get it off. And Thorgrim took the suggestion, sitting up a bit and pulling it up over his head and tossing it aside.

He lay down again and Failend ran her hands over his strong, muscled chest and kissed him on the neck and the shoulders. She could feel the cloth wrapped around his middle, holding a bandage over his latest wound, courtesy of an English spear. She could feel the irregular scars that crisscrossed his skin, some from wounds she had seen, some from wounds delivered before their paths had crossed.

Thorgrim was not a big man, not like Godi, but he seemed to exude power and strength and she always felt very vulnerable and small when she was on top of him that way. With another man that might have been an uncomfortable feeling, but with Thorgrim, after all this time and all these miles together, it felt safe.

She continued to kiss him, softly, careful not to put pressure on his wound. She moved down his chest and down his stomach and her hands found the ties of his leggings and her fingers deftly untied them. Thorgrim needed no further suggestion to pull them down and kick them away. Failend climbed up on top of him, straddling him, still careful to avoid his wound. Her mouth found his again and they kissed again, but with the passion building between them, their breathing growing heavier through mouths pressed together.

Soon Failend could stand no more and she sat up and eased herself down. Thorgrim twisted a bit and suddenly he was inside her. She made a sound deep in her throat as they moved together and the sensation overwhelmed her.

They remained like that for a while, indulging in one another, relishing the steady rhythm, then Thorgrim grabbed her around the waist and rolled over as if she weighed nothing at all. She felt the hay making tiny sharp pinpricks in her back as Thorgrim's weight pressed her down. She bit her finger to keep from screaming, which she knew would bring Thorgrim's men running. She felt that familiar pressure building, building inside, and then the sudden, jarring, lightning bolt of release. She gasped for breath, her eyes wide and staring up into the dark, and a moment later Thorgrim followed in her wake.

For some time they lay like that, letting their breathing settle. Failend was sweating despite the cool night. *Like a horse that's been ridden hard,* she thought, and she almost giggled.

Finally with a groan Thorgrim rolled over and Failend rolled on her side and pressed herself against him. They lay there, silent, motionless, and Failend knew if she wanted to speak she had to do so soon. Thorgrim would quickly fall into a deep sleep, as he always did, which is what she wanted him to do, but not just then.

"Thorgrim?" she said in a whisper.

"Yes?"

"Thank you."

That was met by silence for some time. "Thank you for what?"

Failend sighed. She wasn't sure. Thank you for being the man she needed when she needed him? Thank you for the protection and the weapons and the training and the chance to run wild like an animal for as long and as far as she wished?

"Thank you for being kind," she said, and even as she said it she was struck by the irony. How many Irish had ever said those words to a Northman? Not many, she would guess.

"You're welcome," Thorgrim said and she could hear the sleep in his voice. "But I don't think I've been kind. Not at all the way I should have been. And I'm sorry."

Failend pressed herself closer and did not respond. There was nothing more she had to say, and nothing more she wished to hear from Thorgrim Ulfsson. Thorgrim Night Wolf.

It was not long after that Thorgrim's breathing became rough and even and she knew he was asleep, and she knew from experience it was a deep sleep. She slowly pulled away, peeling herself off of him. She stood with care so as not to make a crunching sound in the hay, grabbing her clothes, shoes and seax as she did.

She remained still and listened. Thorgrim's breathing had not changed, and even after she was certain he was still asleep she remained, listening to the sound of his breath. Then she turned and moved carefully to the door of the stable and out into the night.

Again she stood motionless, feeling the cool air on her sweat-damp skin and shivering a bit. She looked around to see if anyone was coming, but she could see little in the dark, and that meant no one would see her. Her ears caught nothing but the insects in the field and the muted snoring of the men in the hall.

She found the clothes she had stashed behind the barrel and pulled them out, then hid her old clothes in the same place. She held her seax for a moment, enjoying the familiar feel of the grip, the weight in her hand. She debated bringing it, then leaned over and tucked it out of sight along with her tunic and leggings. With some difficulty she managed to get the shift and gown correctly oriented and pulled them over her head, then secured the shoes on her feet. She wrapped the head cloth around her neck, leaving her head uncovered for the time being.

The rest of Thorgrim's men were in the hall or keeping watch just outside of it, so Failend headed off in the other direction, picking her way carefully through the dark yard. At last she came to the wattle fence that encircled the place. She paused there and looked back, though she could see nothing save for one tiny prick of light, a candle seen through a window of the hall.

She felt like saying something, saying it soft, to herself, but nothing would come. So she just looked back in the dark and let the images move through her head. She felt the tears running cool down her cheeks, tickling her skin. She turned and hopped over the fence and walked out into the night.

Chapter Thirty-Two

There are also in the same parts many other nations still following pagan rites…

Venerable Bede,
Ecclesiastical History
of the English People

There was no moon, but the light of the stars was enough to provide some visibility, enough to create lighter and darker places, enough to allow Failend to navigate over the dark country.

It felt odd, walking in a shift and gown and not the leggings and tunic to which she had become accustomed in the past few years, but she was not really thinking about that. Mostly she was concentrating on making her way toward Winchester, which was marked by a few spots of light too low down to be stars: lanterns in high windows, perhaps, or small fires tended by the watchmen on the walls.

Once she stumbled over a rock jutting up from the ground, stubbing toes through her soft leather shoes. She cursed under her breath and continued on, ignoring the pain. Soon, off in the distance, she was able to make out the smooth, straight expanse of the Roman road and she headed that way, knowing that the going would be easier.

Fifty feet from the edge of the road she stopped. She turned around and looked back toward the farm where Thorgrim and the others were hunkered down, now lost to sight in the dark. If they had discovered her gone and were making an effort to find her, she would see the pinpricks of light from lanterns and torches swirling like fireflies, even from that distance, or so she imagined. But there was nothing to see save for darkness, and the only pinpricks of light were the stars.

She continued on and soon she reached the road, and the bricks felt smooth and permanent through the soles of her shoes. The road was nearly straight and it stood out against the darker grass of the fields through which it ran, and Failend was able to easily follow it toward the few distant lights that marked Winchester.

There were no other travelers on the road that she could see, no sounds save for the insects in the grass and an occasional owl or the sharp cry of a nightjar. Even her shoes were silent on the smooth pavers. Her senses were sharp, eyes and ears and nose all searching the night, but there was nothing she could pick out that was not as it should be.

Soon she could make out the hulking presence of the town ahead, the high stone walls and the tops of the buildings beyond. No details, nothing distinct, just the darker, more solid looking blackness ahead. There would be gates, of course, and they no doubt had been shut up at sunset. But there would be a sally port certainly, and a guard standing there. A small woman alone, such as herself, would look particularly unthreatening. A young, pretty woman could usually talk a guard into doing as she wished.

She stopped suddenly, stood straight and frowned as a thought came to her.

I can't speak to a guard, she thought. *I can't speak to anyone…*

For most of her time with the Northmen she had still been in her native Ireland, where she spoke the language. As she became more fluent in the Norse tongue she had even served as translator during those times when Thorgrim wished to speak to the people with his words rather than his sword.

She had not been long in Engla-land and during that time she had been solely in the company of Thorgrim and the others. Over the past day her thoughts had been roaming far afield, and it only now occurred to her that she had no way to communicate.

I'll think of something, she decided as she continued on. *In the church they'll understand what I want.*

She looked up at the sky as she walked. She saw no hint of dawn, and had no sense for how far off it was. But she figured there was no reason to arrive at the gate before then, and probably good reason not to, so she searched around for some place to hunker down. About fifty feet off the road she saw a spot where some high brush made a natural screen. She walked over to it, lay down and made herself as comfortable as she could.

I can lie here and rest at least until daylight, she thought. It was the best she could hope for. She knew she would not sleep.

She woke sometime later to the loud clatter of a cart's wheels on bricks. She sat up and looked around. She could not see the road through the brush that concealed her, but overhead she could see that the sky was the palest of blue, and she knew it was just a little ways past dawn.

Good… she thought. *Good.*

She stood slowly, looking around as she did. The cart that had woken her had rumbled past already, heading for the gates of Winchester. Her eyes moved past the cart and onto the town itself. She had been looking at it from a distance all the day before, but now she was just half a mile away. The stone wall looked more formidable than it had, and the towers and roofs of the great hall and cathedral rose up behind it to impressive, commanding, almost frightening heights.

Failend pulled her eyes from the walls and towers and swept the countryside all around. There were clusters of houses in every direction, huddled close to the city walls and spreading out from there, something she had not realized walking that way in the dark. She was surprised she had not stumbled into one. She could see the smoke from fires rising up from each as embers were stoked into flames. She could hear roosters far off, giving their morning alarm. She could see cows moving slowly in the fields. She could see nothing else. No people.

Do they know I'm gone? Failend wondered. She could imagine Thorgrim thinking she had left the stable and gone back to the hall, and the men in the hall thinking she was still with Thorgrim, and it taking them some time to sort it all out.

Then what will they do? she wondered next. *Come looking for me? Shrug their shoulders and forget I was ever with them?*

She shook her head, as if trying to shake those thoughts free, and told herself it did not matter what the heathens did. She brushed the grass off her wool gown and wrapped the cloth around her head the way she had seen the English women wear it. She pushed through the brush and across the field and back onto the Roman road. The cart was well ahead of her now but it was the only thing on the road, so she followed in its wake.

The closer she came to Winchester the more frightening the town seemed, the walls looming higher and higher, the towers more menacing. She could see there were indeed massive wooden gates in the wall: the Roman road ran right up to them. As the ox cart leading the way came up with them the gates swung open, giving Failend a glimpse of buildings inside, and the cart rolled through without pausing in its lumbering progress.

Failend could see now that there were guards, men standing on either side of the gate with spears and helmets and green tunics with red crosses on them. She took comfort in seeing the symbol of the cross once again, to see it and know she had not come to plunder God's house. She had been very long and very far from the church in which she had been raised.

She approached the gate, trying to walk with a confidence she did not quite feel, trying to navigate all the conflicting tides in her mind. She could not help but think she was stepping into danger. She reached down to rest her palm on the handle of her seax, an unconscious gesture after all that time of wearing it on her belt. But her hand found nothing there and she remembered that she no longer had the weapon. She felt thrown off balance by that truth.

Must I stop for the guards? she wondered. She did not know if the guards would demand she give some reason for entering the town or just let her walk right past. They did not look terribly attentive or even interested in their task. The cart had not stopped, but then the guards might well know the carter. It might happen every morning that he drove his cart through the gates.

Just walk through, bold as can be, she decided, and that plan worked well for the next half dozen steps. She had another six steps to go before she was through the gate when one of the guards lowered his spear to the horizontal, blocking her way.

She stopped and looked at him and smiled as coyly as she could. The guard had a quizzical look on his face, and Failend guessed it was as unusual for a young woman to be walking alone in Engla-land as it would have been in her native country. He spoke to her, a string of words that might as well have been an animal grunting. She continued to smile, unsure what else to do.

The guard frowned and squinted as if that might give him some insight into who she was, but Failend could see he was no more than mildly curious. She crouched down as if genuflecting and made the sign of the cross, touching her forehead, stomach and shoulders. Then she pointed through the gate in the general direction of the cathedral.

With that the guard seemed to relax. He stood and smiled a bit and raised his spear, gesturing with his head for her to enter. She smiled and nodded and walked through the gate as casually as she could, wondering what the guard must think.

Does he think I'm a mute? Do they get so many folk here who don't speak English, so that it attracts no notice? That would be a useful thing to know.

And why was he so certain I'm no threat? she wondered next, aware that she was slightly offended by that.

She kept walking, stepping along with feigned confidence, but as her eyes took in the town of Winchester that attitude became harder and harder to maintain. The massive stone wall ran off in either direction until it bent around and disappeared, so that it seemed as if it must continue on forever. Within its confines, houses built of heavy wooden planks with high-peaked thatched roofs, some two stories tall, rose up around her, separated by muddy streets that twisted and disappeared between the buildings. Fenced off yards were crammed with the tools and materials of the craftsmen's trades: blacksmiths and woodworkers, bakers and coopers and potters.

The streets were not empty, not even at that hour. Women in coarse gowns and aprons were already bustling around, baskets or bundles in their arms or sacks on their shoulders. Some were tossing grain to chickens in the yards or the contents of chamber pots into the streets. The men were ambling out into the yards, some staring at their tools as if seeing them for the first time, other settling down to work.

It was stunning, like nothing Failend had ever seen. She had always considered Glendalough, her home, to be an impressive place, a monastic city that had risen up around the great stone church founded hundreds of years before. She figured that it must rival in grandeur almost any place in the world. But now she realized that her understanding of the world was completely wrong.

The towers of Winchester that had guided Thorgrim's band across the countryside now guided Failend through the city. She walked along past the houses that crowded up to the streets and past the yards with their workshops, delineated by low wattle fences. Men and occasionally women would look up and watch her pass, but she seemed to attract no undue notice, and she was happy about that. She scrutinized the clothes the women were wearing, and as far as she could tell her own clothes did not differ in any important way.

She continued to move toward the towers, like a headland seen from the ocean. Sometimes they were lost from view, and then she would pass one of the larger houses and there they were again, getting closer each time.

Finally the press of houses and shops seemed to come to an end, as if they were pushed against the shore of a lake, and in the open space that was left stood a massive building, with walls and gates of its own and towers at either end and a great hall that was longer than any building Failend had ever seen, rising thirty or forty feet in height.

The king's hall… Failend thought as she walked slowly past. Ireland had many kings, and as a result few of them were terribly grand. She had been to the halls of several of them and had not been much impressed. But this was something different. Whatever king occupied such a place as that must be a powerful man indeed.

She continued along, skirting the royal compound, her destination the building now hidden behind the hall but marked by Winchester's highest tower. The cathedral, or so she guessed. She could not imagine what other structure might rival the king's hall in size and height.

Failend skirted the wall of the king's enclosure and soon the cathedral came into view. It was stone built, unlike the king's hall, but bigger and more impressive in every way. Failend walked toward it, slowly, as if she was approaching something that might do her harm. As if she was approaching the Holy of Holies. She stopped fifty feet away and looked up.

The walls stood to an impossible height, fifty or sixty feet at least, all made of stone, some of it much like the stones that made up the Roman road. The roof, shingled in slate, made a steep angle up to its peak. At the far end a square tower rose up even higher than the roof of the nave, and on top of that a conical spire reached higher still, with a massive cross perched at its tip.

All along the length of the nave were tall windows with rounded tops. The bottoms of those windows were about ten feet above the ground, and higher up, near the top of the nave, were more windows, smaller versions of the lower ones. Each window was complete with glass panes. Failend stared for a long time at that. She had seen glass panes only a few times in her life. She would never have thought that one church could boast so many.

She looked down at the heavy wooden door that was set into the side of the building and she swallowed hard. She would have to go in through that door, but the majesty and size of the building filled her with trepidation. She was certainly aware of how ridiculous that was — over the past years she had charged headlong into many battles, and it was unlikely that anyone in the church would be as great a threat as an English spearman on horseback, or a man-at-arms with a sword and shield.

Failend took a deep breath and began walking again, crossing the open ground that encircled the church. She reached the door and grabbed the big iron door pull. It occurred to her that it might be barred from the inside, but as she tugged it swung open easily on its hinges, never making a sound.

Slowly she stepped through, putting her feet down softly so as not to make a sound. She walked into the nave, down the length of the massive space. It was lit by the weak sunlight coming in through the windows high above and lower down, and from dozens of candles, but still the light seemed swallowed up by the great building. The walls were smooth with daub and painted white which helped to make the space lighter. Far overhead an elaborate structure of wooden beams supported the wood-and-slate roof.

It was very quiet. Failend was the only person in the cathedral at that hour, as far as she could see. She continued walking slowly toward the sanctuary where the altar stood, and behind it the tabernacle with the Holy Eucharist. She was almost halfway there before she remembered to bow and make the sign of the cross, which she did.

I truly am a heathen, she thought. *Or nearly so.*

With careful steps she continued toward the front of the church when she heard a bang, like a door being shut, and she jumped in surprise. A young priest appeared from the side of the sanctuary. He wore a long brown hooded robe, and a line of light brown hair delineated his tonsure. He held a bunch of candles like flowers in his hand. He knelt and crossed himself and then began to replace the stumps of candles in the many candleholders with the new, taller ones.

Failend stood motionless, watching the young man, not sure what she should do. She wanted to call out, but she did not want to startle him. She wanted to get his attention, and she also wanted to remain unseen.

But then the priest turned and stopped in mid-movement and looked over at her and she could see the surprise on his face. He apparently did not expect anyone to be there. But then he seemed to relax as he saw she was just one person, and a woman at that. Strange as it might be to have a woman, alone, come sneaking into the church at that hour, he did not, apparently, regard her as a threat.

He came down the steps from the sanctuary and walked over to her, a trace of a smile on his face. He stopped and spoke, and his words were the same incomprehensible jumble that the guard had spoken. She could hear traces of the Norse tongue in them — the languages were similar in some ways — but not similar enough that she could make sense of them.

"I'm sorry, I don't speak English," she said in Irish, hoping the young priest might know that language. After all, many priests studied in Ireland and then were sent to churches all over Engla-land and Frankia and beyond. But the priest just frowned and looked at her in an odd way and shook his head.

Failend frowned as well. She would not try Norse. There was little chance he would speak Norse, and she did not care to reveal that she did, so she was not sure what to do.

Then the young priest seemed to brighten. He held a finger up which Failend took to mean she should wait a moment, and she nodded. The young priest nodded as well, then turned and disappeared the way he had come.

The cathedral fell silent again, a silence deeper than that of a still night or an empty house. A silence that felt to her as if there was nothing there at all, nothing save for her and God.

Then the door banged again and the young priest was back with another, a bit older than him, with a kind-looking face and dark hair that must have been an unruly mop before the bulk of his head was tonsured. They approached Failend together, and then the new priest said, in Failend's native tongue, "Do you speak Irish?"

It felt to Failend like clouds parting to reveal bright sunlight. She had not heard Irish spoken in some time, and certainly not spoken by a young and kindly-sounding priest, a man of God. She smiled and nodded.

"Yes, father," she said. "Yes, I speak Irish. I am Irish."

She nearly added that she was from Glendalough but she held her tongue. She was wanted for murder and other crimes in Glendalough, and it was possible the priest had heard those tales and might guess at her identity.

The priest nodded and turned and said something to the other, and he nodded as well, smiled at Failend, and then went back to replacing candles at the altar. The dark-haired Irish priest regarded her with a curious look. "Well…welcome," he said. "I'm Father Conall. What brings you here, child? Alone and so far from your home?"

Failend had her story ready. She did not want to lie, certainly not to a priest, but she saw no choice. So she planned to say that she had been taken by Northmen from her native country, and they were taking her to Frisia, she guessed, to the slave markets there. She had suffered horribly at their brutal hands, but had managed to escape when they landed at the town to the south a few days before. Surely the priest had heard that the Northmen were raiding just to the south.

She opened her mouth and another thought came to her.

"Father, will you hear my confession?" she asked.

"Of course, of course," the priest said, nodding. He gestured toward a chair that stood by the near wall and led Failend over to it. The priest sat in the chair and Failend knelt in front of him, her hands clasped in supplication. She could feel the cool, hard stones of the floor through her shift and wool dress. She bowed her head, and then looked up again.

"Father…?"

"Yes?"

"The sacramental seal binds my confessor…you…doesn't it?"

"Of course." Father Conall smiled his half smile. "I cannot break that seal. I can never reveal anything I hear in confession. I would be excommunicated if I did. So have no fear. But see here, I can tell by the way you speak you're a lady, a woman of quality, and not some poor, sorry creature. I'm hard pressed to think a young woman such as you would have anything so terrible to confess."

Now it was Failend's turn to smile, just a bit. She glanced over toward the altar. The other priest was gone now. She made the sign of the cross and said, "Forgive me father. It's been…years since last I confessed…"

And with that she set in and let the story spill from her lips. The fornicating, the murder of her husband, running off with Louis, joining with the Northmen. She told Father Conall about falling in love with the leader of the Northmen's band, of joining with them in battle, raiding and plundering.

The tears started in, just a minor leak at first, but soon they were running unchecked down her cheeks. Her voice trembled and stammered. She felt as if she had been smothered in layers and layers of blankets and now they were being lifted off of her, one by one. She let the entire tale come up from her bowels and spill out onto the hard stone floor. And finally she was done. She looked up at the young priest. She could see the surprise— the shock — that she knew she would be there. But not so much shock as she had thought she would see.

"That is…quite a story," Father Conall said. "You're certain it's all true?"

"I'm certain," Failend said. It seemed like an odd question, but an understandable one.

"And you forsake that? You are truly penitent and mean to give up that life?"

"Yes, father," Failend said.

"Well, then," the priest said, reaching out and putting his hand on Failend's head "Through the ministry of the Church may God give you pardon and peace. And I absolve you from your sins in the name of the Father, and of the Son, and of the Holy Spirit." Failend made the sign of the cross as the priest said those words. She felt light, she felt free, she felt new-born.

Now what? she wondered.

Behind the alter the door banged again and Failend and Father Conall looked over. The first priest was back, leading a much older man behind him. The older man was a bit portly, a bit stooped, but he moved with vigor. He wore a white gown, intricately embroidered, and there was nothing kindly about his face. Nothing kindly at all. Four young priests followed behind him, like wolves behind the pack's leader.

"This is the bishop, Bishop Ealhstan," Father Conall said. He stood and Failend stood and the bishop hurried over toward them. "Seems word of your presence has spread and it's made others curious."

Father Conall bowed and Failend bowed and the bishop began to talk. Failend had no idea what he was saying, save that he was talking about her, since he nodded and pointed at her as he spoke. Father Conall was apparently answering questions, making Failend more afraid with every word.

"Father, you won't say what I confessed, will you?" Failend interrupted.

"No, of course not," the priest said and the bishop snapped out some sharp words, and Failend guessed he did not care to have them speaking Irish in his presence. She could see the old man was getting angrier at every exchange between himself and Father Conall.

"What's the matter, Father?" Failend asked. She could feel the fear mounting.

"The bishop is suspicious of you, I think," the priest said. "People are on edge, with the heathens so close. He knows I can't say what you confessed but he's not happy about it."

This fresh exchange in a language the bishop did not understand only seemed to make the man angrier still. He turned to one of the priests behind him and the priest stepped around the bishop and over to Failend. Failend glanced at her confessor, hoping he might come to her rescue, but the man just looked on, silent and helpless.

The priest reached out and tugged the cloth around Failend's head loose. Failend felt frozen in place, unable to move. Terrified. She felt his fingers grab the cord around her neck and tug it up from where it was hidden under her shift. She heard gasps from the others, a smug and knowing look on the bishop's face, as they saw the two silver pieces hanging from the cord's end: the cross of Jesus and the hammer of Thor.

Chapter Thirty-Three

I am sorely
by afflictions stricken.
Has the sea him deluded,
or the sword wounded?
On that man
I will harm inflict.

Poetic Edda

Amundi was nearly overwhelmed by the rush of sensations, and surprised by his reaction to them.

He could feel the wind on his cheek blowing harder, making the men's hair and the women's hair whip around to leeward. He could smell the tang of the salt water and the heavy, wet air. The spray blowing back from the bow made sharp pricks of cold on his exposed skin. The boat rose and fell, bucked and twisted in the mounting seas. The wood of the tiller was warm where he had been holding it against the pressure of the rudder.

It was not a comfortable situation. His tunic and cloak were soaked with the spray, and the wind on the wet cloth chilled him. The motion of the boat was increasingly violent. Sometimes the stern would lift and then come down hard with an impact that jarred him right through. His arm was growing tired from steering, his whole body cramped from sitting in the same spot and bracing against the pitch and roll of the boat.

But Amundi felt the energy coursing through him, like the first effects of a deep draught of wine. He felt strength in his arms and his legs, despite the weariness. He felt bold and reckless in ways he had not felt in many years. Not since he had been a young man in the company of other young men, raiding, fighting, drinking and feasting, before he had wife and children, an extensive farm to oversee, a position in the community that required him to be staid and respectable.

I've lost it all, all that I have, he thought. *It's all been taken from me.*

Halfdan the Black had come to deliver a message. He had come to show what happened to those who would rebel. But more than that, by helping himself to whatever he wished from Amundi's stores, by housing himself and his men in Amundi's hall, and making Amundi and his people sleep in the stable, he had made it clear that Amundi owned nothing. There was nothing he had that Halfdan could not take at will. Amundi was as much a slave to Halfdan as Oleif was slave to Amundi.

Halfdan had meant for that message to cow Amundi and to cow all of Amundi's neighbors who received a similar visit. And at first it had. At first Amundi had been paralyzed by the realization. But then something happened that Halfdan had not counted on. Amundi had been set free.

I have nothing, Amundi thought, but the thought was not grief or self-pity. It was freedom. He had no farm, he had no people, he had no place in the community. There was nothing but the boat and the people in the boat and Skorri Thorbrandsson in their wake. It was clean and pure and unambiguous and it made Amundi feel alive.

"Seems these fishermen don't much care for the weather," Onund said. He was sitting a little forward of midships and looking out toward the mainland, about a mile and a half off the larboard side.

Amundi's eyes had been moving between the sail and the seas ahead and the point of land to the north-west that jutted far out from the shore, but now he twisted around to look in the direction Onund was looking. The smattering of boats that had been chasing schools of fish in their slow and deliberate way had all given up on that. They were heading for the shore now, sails set. They looked almost comical the way they tossed and bobbed up and down in the waves. There was a small fishing village just south of the headland and Amundi guessed it was there they were headed.

He looked at the sky to the west, the dark clouds reaching up from the horizon, chewing up the softer gray overcast in their menacing advance. He felt the wind rise again, pressing the boat down a little farther to leeward, and another burst of spray came flying aft.

No wonder they're running, Amundi thought. The wind was cold and it had an ugly feel to it. He could tell that it had risen considerably since they had first rounded the island where they had landed, and the sky to the west suggested it would continue to rise. The boat they were sailing could live in the wind and seas as they were at that moment, but it could not take much more.

"What do you think, Amundi?" Onund asked, speaking loud to be heard over the wind, the creaking of the rig, the thump of the hull against the water. "Should we follow their lead? Head to shore?"

Onund had asked the question, but every person aboard the boat was listening anxiously for the answer. They were each of them familiar enough with boats to judge their present danger, and to understand how much worse it would get, and how soon.

Rather than answer, Amundi twisted around the other way and looked astern. The boat in their wake had not turned, was not heading for shore like the others. Its course had not changed at all. It was about a mile astern and still driving as directly at them as it could go. If there had been any question that Skorri was in that boat, then that answered it.

In his mind Amundi saw the geometry of the situation, the triangle formed by his boat, Skorri's boat, and the village ashore. He considered the relative distances, the relative speeds, the courses that the boats could sail with the wind as it was.

"If we head to shore now we'll be sailing right into Skorri's arms," Amundi said. "We have to get around the headland there, off the larboard bow. If we can get around that ahead of Skorri, if he loses sight of us, then hopefully we can find a place to go ashore. Maybe lash the tiller and let the boat sail off on its own, hope Skorri follows it."

Onund nodded but did not say anything. Amundi looked at the others, at Signy and Alfdis and Thord, at Oleif and the rest. Their faces were grim, their mouths set. A few of them nodded their heads, almost imperceptibly. But on one spoke, no one objected. They all knew he was right. The only way to escape from Skorri was to get around the headland.

The question, of course, was could they do it, or would the storm roll over them and drive them under before they were able? And the answer was that it didn't matter. They were dead if they went down and they were dead if Skorri caught them, and of the two, the watery death was preferable.

A gust of wind struck and rolled the boat further to leeward, far enough that the sheer strake dipped into the sea, scooping a good barrel-full of water into the bilge before righting itself. The water was inches high in the bottom, rushing fore and aft like a tidal race. It soaked the fur bed that Odd was lying on and soaked the arm of his tunic as well. Odd had managed to fall asleep, but with the shock of the cold water he moaned and rolled his head to one side.

Signy and Alfdis grabbed the edge of the furs and hauled to windward, pulling Odd away from the water sloshing back and forth. The women looked back at Amundi, Signy's expression pleading, Alfdis angry and accusatory, but there was nothing Amundi could do.

"There's a bucket, get that water out of the boat, quick as you can," Amundi said. "And there's a cook pot, use that as well."

Thord grabbed the bucket and began to bail. One of the other men pulled the cook pot free and Oleif found a drinking cup and they began to fling water over the leeward side. Amundi felt the boat heeling farther to leeward, threatening to dip the lee rail under again.

He looked at the sail. It was bellied out taut, the windward shrouds that held the mast up quivering with the strain, the yard that held the sail bowing in the middle. They were right on the edge, and if the sail blew out or the yard broke or the shrouds parted then it would be over. Skorri would be on them while they were still sorting it out.

"We'll have to shorten sail," Amundi said when the last of the water that could be got out of the bilge had been flung over the side. A series of short ropes were rove through holes in the sails, parallel to the bottom edge, so that the bottom of the sail could be gathered up and tied in place, reducing by a third the amount of cloth exposed to the wind. As much as he did not want to do it, Amundi knew they had no choice. They could not push the rig that hard. And in truth the boat would probably sail faster if it was sailing more upright, not heeling over so far.

There were no arguments about that decision. Amundi pushed the tiller over and the boat turned up into the wind. The sail began to flog as the wind spilled out of it and the men who were closest to the foot of the sail grabbed onto the canvas and knotted the short ropes together. Thord lowered the yard down a bit to accommodate the new, shorter sail and Amundi pulled the tiller back, turning the bow away from the wind until the sail filled again.

The entire maneuver had taken very little time, but when Amundi looked back over his shoulder he could see that Skorri's boat had closed another hundred yards or so, close enough that Amundi could see the white water curling around its bow, the fine burst of spray it flung up with every violent pitch. The boat still had its full sail set and yet was not heeling over too terribly far. And it was going very fast.

He'll have to shorten sail too, soon enough, Amundi thought, though he knew, unfortunately, that it was not necessarily true. Skorri's boat might be more stable, more heavily built, the rig might be stouter or better balanced, the sail newer. Some boats were just faster than others, more able to endure the kind of punishment they were experiencing. And if that was the case, if Skorri's boat was the stronger and faster, there was nothing much he could do.

Amundi looked forward again. The men had finished with shortening the sail and were crowded up on the windward side, sitting as low as they could to get out of the spray flying aft. It was more comfortable on the high side, less chance of being soaked if they scooped another wave, and getting the weight to windward helped keep the boat on a more even keel, which in turn would make it sail faster.

And it was all about that now. It was a boat race. Amundi and his people trying to get around the headland and out of Skorri's sight before Skorri and his men came up with them. The prize was life or death.

The blackness in the west continued to reach overhead, blotting out the more benign gray clouds, spreading its menace. Amundi thought he could see sheets of rain coming down, off to the west, and it would not be long before it reached them.

"Signy," he said, having to speak quite loud to be heard over the volume of noise made by the boat and the storm. "We'll have rain soon, I think. We should find something to cover Odd. I don't know if there's a tarpaulin in the boat, or what we might have."

Signy nodded, but before she could move some of the others crawled toward the bow where bundles of various things were stored: nets, small barrels, worn, stained canvas sacks. There had been no time to empty the boat out, and they had no idea what the fishermen had left behind. Now they rifled through the gear, looking for something that would be of help. There wasn't much. An old blanket, a fragment of a torn sail. They pulled them out and covered Odd as best they could.

Amundi looked astern once again. Skorri's boat was driving hard, bucking in the seas. Closer. Noticeably so. The sail was billowed out solid — Amundi could practically feel the strain on the cloth and the rig.

He'll have to shorten sail, Amundi thought again. He didn't understand how Skorri's boat wasn't already lying on its side in that blow.

And then he thought of Skorri's men. Skorri would not have come in pursuit with some meager handful of warriors. He would have brought as many as he could, because he did not know how many Amundi had. He must have crammed twenty or so men on a boat that size, big men, with weapons and even mail, perhaps. Twice as many as were aboard Amundi's boat. In light wind they would have slowed him down, but in this blow, with all those men huddled up on the weather side, they would keep the boat on a fairly even keel despite the strength of the wind. It would drive Skorri's boat much faster than theirs.

How can his rig take that? Amundi wondered. With the sail full and all those men holding the boat flat it would be putting a tremendous strain on the sail, the yard, the mast and the rigging. If Skorri's rig did blow out it would do so in a spectacular way, he imagined, the yard shattering, the sail shredding in the wind, the mast collapsing. But so far it showed no signs of doing any of that.

Once again Amundi tried to ignore the boat astern as he directed his eyes and his attention ahead. The point of land they were steering to round was off the larboard bow and a mile or so away. Amundi nudged the tiller, trying to put the boat on a more direct course. But as he did so he saw the leading edge of the sail start to curl and he knew he could not steer any more directly into the wind. He was sailing as close toward the headland as he could, and as fast as he could, and there was nothing more he could do.

It was not long after that the rain started in, a few drops at first, indistinguishable from the spray. Then it started coming down harder, sweeping in sheets over the water, soaking already wet clothes, running down beards and down the necks of tunics. The women adjusted Odd's covers, then sat in the bottom of the boat hugging themselves as the rest pressed against the weather side and did the same.

When Amundi could stand it no longer he turned once more and looked astern. The shoreline was lost in the rain but Skorri's boat was still visible, plowing along toward them. It was so close astern now that Amundi let out a gasp of surprise, which was happily inaudible to the rest. The rig was still standing, the sail still full and drawing. He could see the men lining the weather side of the boat, a crowd of men, just as he had imagined, like shields on a shield rack.

He looked back toward the headland off the larboard bow. Once again he saw the geometry of the situation in his mind. And he knew they would not make it. They would not get around the headland before Skorri's boat was up with them.

Should I say anything? he wondered.

But before Amundi could decide whether or not to speak, Onund, also looking astern at Skorri's boat, said, "This will be a close thing." That was met with grunts of agreement from the others. They understood the situation as well as Amundi. And they all knew that it would not really be close at all.

For some time more they plunged on through that purgatory of rain and cold and the violent motion of the boat, the spray coming over the bow, the tension of knowing that the entire rig could come down at any moment. And astern, Skorri's boat clawed its way closer and closer.

"We had better get ready with what weapons we have," Amundi said at last. "Skorri's coming up to leeward of us. Let's be ready."

With that the men pushed themselves off the high side and dug around for what weapons they had: some swords, a few spears, a couple of battle axes. They had come with the intention of escaping, not fighting. They had understood from the onset that they would be greatly outnumbered by their pursuers, which would make fighting pointless, so they had brought only the weapons they would normally carry as a matter of course, and no more.

"Don't know what that bastard Skorri thinks he'll do in these seas," Thord said. Skorri might be able to overtake them, but with those big seas running it would be madness for him to even try to come alongside Amundi's boat, never mind attack it.

"This won't stop him," Onund said. "He'll try to board no matter what, even if he takes us all to the bottom. He's more afraid of Halfdan than he is of drowning out here."

No one said anything to that because no one doubted it was true. They found their weapons and resumed their places at the weather side and waited.

They did not wait long. Soon Skorri's boat was all but up with them, just a hundred feet or so astern. He was coming at them from downwind, which meant there was no direction Amundi could sail that would not just bring the boats closer.

They could see Skorri in the stern, hand on the tiller, his blond hair and beard looking black, soaked through as they were, his eyes fixed on Amundi's boat. There was no question now as to what he intended. His men were crowded in the bottom of the boat, weapons in hand, ready to make the treacherous leap from one boat to the other once they had closed the last few feet. Twenty men, at least, just as Amundi had guessed.

He looked away from Skorri's boat. He looked at the headland off to larboard. He looked to windward, he looked astern. He looked for some way out of this, some escape, some clear path, but there was nothing. The only course available now was one that led right into the arms of Skorri's overwhelming force.

Amundi felt a strange mix of emotions roiling like the chaotic sea in his mind: anger, resignation, a wild recklessness. *Very well,* he thought.

"Cast off those braces, cast them off!" he shouted. The braces held the yard from swinging side to side: casting them off would allow the yard to be moved if they wished to change direction. Which no one expected Amundi might want to do.

The order was met with looks of surprise and confusion, but Amundi did not feel much like explaining. He pulled the tiller toward him and the boat swung wildly to starboard, heeling harder as it turned away from the wind, tossing wildly as it came broadside to the seas. Alfdis shouted in surprise and Amundi saw men grabbing for something to hold against the violent, unexpected motion.

The bow swung in a wide arc, pointing out to sea, and the land and Skorri's boat were lost from view behind them. And it kept turning, sweeping around in a nearly complete circle. The yard swung around with the turn because Onund and Thord had had the presence of mind to cast the braces off.

Directly ahead and only fifty feet away was Skorri's boat, now right under their bow, close enough that Amundi could see the looks of surprise on the warriors' faces and on Skorri's face. The seas moved under Amundi's boat and lifted it and flung it forward with tremendous force. Then it passed under and Amundi's boat was starting to go down in the trough and Skorri's boat was starting to lift right at the moment they hit.

The gods, it seemed, were with Amundi. The heavy-build oak stem of his boat that formed the very bow slammed into the more vulnerable side of Skorri's boat nearly amidships. The impact threw Amundi and the others forward, half of them landing in the bilge. The mast shuddered in a way that flashed terror into Amundi's heart, terror that the rig would go by the board. Over the rain and wind he could hear the sound of cracking, snapping wood.

The force of the impact had tossed Amundi to his hands and knees on the bottom of the boat. He looked forward toward the bow. His view was partially blocked by the gear stowed there but he could see no obvious damage, no water spewing in around shattered planks.

With a hand on the sheer strake he pulled himself up. He sat down on the thwart and grabbed the tiller that was swinging wildly. The bow of his boat was still pushed hard against Skorri's, but the point of impact was below the rail and Amundi could not see if they had done any damage.

Skorri's men had been tossed to the bottom of the boat just as Amundi's had, but there were more of them and therefore a bigger pile of thrashing arms and legs to untangle. Skorri was shouting something. Amundi could hear the words but could not make them out. The fury in Skorri's voice, however, was unmistakable.

For a moment it seemed as if all the world was standing still, as if all the wild motion and roaring noise and driving rain had stopped, just for a heartbeat. Amundi looked at Skorri just as Skorri looked over at him. Their eyes fixed on one another. Neither spoke, neither moved.

Then everything started again. The sea lifted Amundi's boat up and the wind filled the sail and drove it forward as the sail of Skorri's boat was flogging and coming aback. Amundi's boat surged forward, pushing Skorri's aside, pulling the bow free from where it had struck. Amundi could see the damage now. Several planks had been stove in, buckled so far that he could see clean through the gap. Not below the waterline, but close enough.

As Amundi's boat drove past Skorri, rising stern-first on the following sea, he saw Skorri bend over, reach down into the bilge, and come up with a spear in his hand. The move so surprised Amundi that he did not react, did not move, just watched as Skorri braced his legs and drew the spear back to throw.

Two things happened at once. Amundi saw a blur of motion to his left. He turned his head in time to see Oleif getting to his feet, the iron cookpot in hand. He brought his arm back and flung the pot at Skorri the instant before Skorri flung the spear.

The pot hit Skorri square in the chest and the spear flew wildly off to the right, missing the boat entirely. Skorri fell backwards, and for a moment Amundi thought he was going over the side, but instead he fell against the sheer strake and slid down to the bottom of the boat.

And then they were past, running nearly straight downwind, and Amundi knew he had to get his boat under control. "Take up those braces!" he called. "We're going around again!" He could not see the distant shore through the driving rain, but he knew it was out there somewhere, and it was not where he wanted to end up.

He looked astern at the waves coming up behind. He waited as the stern of the boat dipped down into a trough, and as it began to rise again he pushed the tiller away. The boat spun round on the top of the wave while Thord and Onund pulled on the braces and hauled the yard around.

Skorri's boat was already fifty feet away, broadside to the seas and drifting. The pressure of the sail coming aback had finally done for the rig. The mast and yard and sail had come down and were now dragging in the water as the boat drifted out of control. He could see men bailing like mad, using buckets and helmets. One of them was using the pot that Oleif had flung at Skorri.

Amundi looked forward. Thord and Onund had trimmed the sail and made the braces fast and the boat was once again on course to round the headland, which was once again off the larboard bow.

He looked astern. Skorri's boat was a few hundred feet away by then, rising on the waves and then nearly disappearing into the troughs. It was impossible to tell how badly the side was stove in, how much water it was taking on. Amundi did not know if they would make it to shore or not. He just knew they would no longer be giving chase.

Chapter Thirty-Four

On a wolf rode,
at evening twilight,
a woman who him
offered to attend.

The Poetic Edda

Thorgrim woke, gasping, his hands clutching something not quite solid. He was naked and covered in a sheen of sweat. His eyes were wide, staring into the semi-darkness. He did not know where he was, or who he was.

He sat motionless and his breathing began to subside. He felt tired, as if he had been running, and running hard. It started coming back to him: moving through the night, moving silently down narrow streets, a place unlike any place he had been. The smells were strong, smells of fire and horses and chickens and pigs, mud and dung and people.

Wolf dream... he thought. He had had a wolf dream. It had been some time since he had had one, and it had not been foreshadowed by his usual foul temper, an inability to endure the presence of anyone at all. Save for one person.

He turned halfway around in one direction and then the other. It was hard to see inside the dark building, though streams of sunlight were coming through the door and the gaps in the walls. They looked almost solid as they passed through the copious dust.

Starri Deathless was not there. Usually the berserker kept him company, sitting close by, silent and protective, while Thorgrim was in the depths of one of his wolf dreams. Those were the times when some part of Thorgrim — his mind, his spirit, he did not know what — left him and moved around the countryside. It allowed him to see things others could not see. It had happened since he was a young man, though it was happening less and less often of late.

You are getting old... Thorgrim thought, and just as the wolf dreams were coming less frequently, that thought was coming more so. Things did not work the way they had always worked, either with his body or his dreams. Even his mind, his emotions.

He worried about Failend, and the feelings that seemed to be pulling at her. He wondered whether he was making things worse or better for her. He would make things better for her if he knew how, but he was not sure.

He worried about Harald. He found Harald's stubbornness and his grudging obedience annoying in a way he would not have done before. In earlier days he would hardly have noticed it, and he would have cared even less. But now he wanted it to stop. He wanted Harald to understand how grave a mistake he had made, to admit it and learn from it.

So far the boy had shown no inclination to do so.

Thorgrim pulled his wandering thoughts back to the present. He looked down. It was hay he was gripping, handfuls of hay from the haystack on which he was sitting. He frowned and looked at the hay and slowly the night started to come back to him. Failend, forcing him to take his rest, easing him down onto the soft bed, then coming to him. His surprise to realize that she was naked. They had not been together in that way for a long time.

Failend seemed to be wrestling with feelings that were stirring things up in her like a wind will do when it's blowing against the tide. Almost everything she did now came as a surprise to him.

His mind wandered back through their time on the haystack, and the wonderful feeling of it all, which went beyond the physical. There was a connection between them that had not been there in a long time, as if Failend's uncertainty had vanished and something had settled in her mind.

Now she was gone. The blanket that had covered them was bunched in a heap, and there was a slight depression in the hay where she had been sleeping. Thorgrim looked at the blanket and the dent in the hay and he felt his mood start to shift, his thoughts start to move off in a direction not so pleasing as the memories of the night before.

Wolf dream. It was starting to come back. He remembered visions of moving over the countryside, past clusters of farms. He remembered streets, tight streets with houses pressed up close. He remembered Failend. He remembered danger, terrific danger.

He looked up again, staring into the half light, and the gasping fear that had woken him in the first place was back again. He leaped up and snatched his leggings and pulled them on, then his tunic and then he buckled Iron-tooth around his waist. He hurried out of the stable. The morning light was blinding and he blinked and felt the tears run down his cheeks as he hurried across the yard toward the hall.

Hall and Gudrid were standing watch and they turned as he approached. They were smiling, ready no doubt to needle him for sleeping late after his night with Failend, but when they saw his face their expressions changed in an instant.

"Where's Failend?" Thorgrim demanded. "Has she come by here?"

The two men shook their heads. "We haven't seen her, lord," Gudrid said. "And I don't think she's in the hall. We thought she was…" His voice trailed off.

Thorgrim pushed past them and into the hall. Most of the men were at the big table eating porridge and bread and they looked up as Thorgrim came in.

"Is Failend here?" Thorgrim demanded, and the men, more confused than helpful, glanced around, glanced at one another, and shook their heads.

"Isn't she with you?" Starri asked. "She was last night, there was no question about that. Not sure how any of us were supposed to sleep."

Thorgrim shook his head. He was in no mood for Starri's silliness. "No," Thorgrim said. "She's not with me. She's gone, and I've seen she's in danger. Great danger."

This brought more silence and confusion from the assembled warriors. It was Starri, once again, who spoke, but his tone was much different now.

"You…saw this?" he asked.

"I did," Thorgrim said.

"Wolf dream?"

"Yes."

Starri nodded. "Strange I didn't see it coming," he said. Starri, more than any of the men there, believed in the truth of the wolf dreams. Berserkers were known to have a connection to the gods that other men did not have, and Starri was certain that Thorgrim's wolf dreams were a gift from Asgard. He did not question them. It was why he was so loyal to Thorgrim, and why he wanted to be close by when Thorgrim was in the midst of them. And likely why Thorgrim could tolerate his company.

"Where is she?" Harald asked. "Do you know? What danger is she in?" The wolf dreams had been part of Harald's reality for all his life, but to him they had always been something to fear: his father in a foul mood, his father gone in some other-worldly way.

"She's in Winchester, I'm sure of it," Thorgrim said. "I don't know how she got there. Walked, I suppose, in the dark. And I don't know why. But she's in danger now."

Again there was silence and Thorgrim was sure each man was considering the same thing he was: why had she done that, and how could they possibly help her now?

"Has she betrayed us?" Gudrid asked. "Why would she do that?"

"No," Louis said, "she's not betrayed us. When we got to this place, she was talking about…" He stopped and frowned. "I don't know what you would call it in your language. The church. The Christian church. She said she missed it."

That brought another moment of confused silence. "Why would she miss it?" Thorgrim asked. "If she wants to honor her gods she can honor them anywhere. Why would she miss a church?"

Louis shook his head. "There's only one God, and we don't worship him the way you heathens worship your gods. To do it right we must have a man of God to help with the worship." Louis had been a long time in the company of the Northmen, and he spoke the language passing well, but Thorgrim could tell he was having trouble finding words that would make sense. There was a divide here that was wider than just language.

"It doesn't matter," Thorgrim said. "Whatever her reason, she's gone to Winchester, I know it, and she's in danger."

"Then we must get her," Harald said. There was none of the sour, grudging tone he had used since his command was taken from him and Thorgrim was pleased to hear it. Failend was well liked by all of them, and apparently a threat to her life was enough to make Harald forget the injustice he felt had been done to him.

"The city gates will be open, and probably not too many guards there," Starri said, his voice tinged with growing excitement. "It would be nothing to get into the city."

"And then what?" Thorgrim asked, knowing that the others were thinking it. "We don't know the city, we don't know where to look for her. And we're less than a dozen men." It was cleverness that was called for now, not strength of arms.

"The prisoner we took yesterday," Harald said. "The one I've seen before. He's a man of wealth. Part of the king's court, maybe. He must know his way around Winchester."

That was met with nodding heads, Thorgrim's included. He felt half-formed ideas coming together, spinning into something more solid, definite, with substance enough for him to act.

"Gudrid, Brand, Harald, go back to the farm where we stopped before," Thorgrim said. "Bring the horses and the prisoner here. Also, all the mail and helmets and such that we took from the dead English. Be quick, now."

They left, heading out so fast that even Thorgrim could not grow impatient. The rest donned their mail and helmets, settled weapons in place, slung shields over their backs and headed off in the opposite direction, making their way over the country toward the walls of Winchester, easily visible even to Thorgrim's not so young eyes. They stopped at the crest of a small hill, unseen by any but the cows that milled around, and for some moments looked at the city. No one spoke.

From where they stood they could make out the guards walking along the top of the wall, no more than small glinting points of light from that distance, and not too many of them. They could see traffic on the Roman road: ox carts and travelers on foot and people driving livestock before them and men-at-arms on horseback, a great flow of traffic to and from the city.

"Everyone going about their business, it seems," Hall observed.

"They must know we have a dozen ships full of warriors, just a day's march away," Starri said. He sounded as if he took offense at the Englishmen's calm, and Thorgrim guessed that he did.

"I reckon they have enough warriors of their own that they're not too afraid of being sacked," Thorgrim replied. "I doubt they have the thousand men the prisoner said they did, but they have enough."

That was met with a few grunts of agreement. None of the men there were likely to forget the beating they had just received in their sea battle with the English.

They remained where they were for a short time more, watching in silence, but it was clear there was not much to learn, so they trudged back to the farm to wait for the others to bring the prisoner and the horses. They ate, sharpened weapons, and soon the sound of drumming hooves alerted them that Harald and the others had returned.

Thorgrim stepped out of the hall and into the bright daylight of the farmyard just as Harald was reining to a stop and sliding down from the saddle. Gudrid and Brand were still mounted, and behind them each was a string of six horses, saddled and bridled. There was one horse tethered to Harald's mount, and on it sat the prisoner, his fine tunic looking a bit less fine, his face pale and drawn, his hands bound together and tied to the saddle. He looked wary. Maybe even afraid.

Good, Thorgrim thought. He turned to Godi and Hall. "Get the prisoner down, sit him on that barrel over there."

The two men dragged the prisoner out of his saddle, pushed him over to the barrel Thorgrim indicated and sat him roughly down. Thorgrim let him remain there for a few moments, flanked by the two Northmen. Let the uncertainty and fear build. Finally he gestured for Harald to follow him. He grabbed another barrel and walked it over in front of the prisoner and sat facing him, with no more than three feet between them.

"What's your name?" Thorgrim asked, his eyes holding the prisoner's while Harald translated. For a moment the prisoner remained silent, and then he seemed to decide there was no advantage in doing so. He spoke, two words.

"He says his name is Lord Nothwulf," Harald said.

Thorgrim nodded. "You look to be a man of some importance, Lord Nothwulf," he said. "We mean to ransom you."

Harald translated and Nothwulf replied.

"He says he's no one," Harald said. "Not worth ransoming."

"Then I suppose we'll kill you," Thorgrim said. "You're no use to us."

Harald translated and Nothwulf tried to keep his face free of expression as he realized he might not have played that well. He made no reply, probably afraid he would make things worse.

"However," Thorgrim continued, "you may buy your own life. You can help us instead. Best I can do."

Harald translated and Nothwulf made a short reply. "He says he'll never help us," Harald said.

Of course he did, Thorgrim thought. He nodded and smiled just a bit. This Nothwulf was so predictable it was as if Thorgrim had told him what to say. He slowly drew his seax from the sheath on his belt, fourteen inches of honed and polished iron.

"Tell him he will help us," Thorgrim said. "Tell him he most certainly will."

Evening was coming on when the small band of warriors rode toward the gates of Winchester, Lord Nothwulf, their ostensible commander, at the head of the two columns of six. Behind him rode Thorgrim on his left side and Harald on his right. They each held spears upright like banner staffs, but the weapons could be leveled in an instant and driven into Nothwulf's back at the first sign of betrayal. Nothwulf was aware of that because Thorgrim had made certain he was. From the set of his shoulders Thorgrim could tell Nothwulf was bracing for a spear in the back at any moment.

We're not going to kill you until after you've helped us, you English blockhead, Thorgrim thought, though he was happy to have the man think his life was in constant peril.

They were all wearing mail, Thorgrim and Harald and the men riding behind them. But it was not their own mail. Rather, it was the mail they had taken from the dead and wounded Englishmen after the fight at the inn. They were wearing English helmets as well, and had the Englishmen's shields hanging from their saddles or slung over their backs.

Nothwulf, too, wore his mail shirt, his helmet and sword and shield, which had been borrowed from Brand, their new owner. In the soft, late-day light they would be indistinguishable from any small English patrol. Even in full daylight they probably would not have drawn any notice.

They approached the gate at a walk like weary riders returning to their barracks, thinking only of a meal and ale and their beds. There were half a dozen sentries posted outside and they seemed not in the least alarmed at the arrival of the armed band.

Nothwulf held up a hand and reined to a stop and Thorgrim and Harald and the rest behind stopped as well. A sentry stepped up to Nothwulf's horse and said something and Nothwulf replied, just a few words. Thorgrim studied Harald's face, but there was no expression there, no sign that Harald sensed Nothwulf was raising an alarm.

It was possible, of course, that Nothwulf was doing so in words Harald could not understand, but if so there was nothing for it. If Nothwulf betrayed them, Thorgrim felt certain there would be time enough to drive a spear into him before he and his men were taken down, and that gave him some comfort.

The sentry stepped aside and made a gesture for Nothwulf to continue. Nothwulf nodded and flicked his reins and headed for the gate, the Northmen behind. Thorgrim tried to keep his eyes ahead, his face devoid of interest, but it was not easy. Winchester was unlike any place he had ever seen.

He had been to the big trading centers at Hedeby and Birka. He had spent months in Dubh-linn, which nearly rivaled those places, but none were like this. The streets of Winchester were lined with houses and workshops, some two stories high, and crowded with people and animals and carts. He could see the great tower of the church rising above the buildings, and the towers of what must be the king's residence as well. The narrow streets ran like streams between the buildings, and the entire thing was surrounded by a great stone wall.

Incredible…

He looked over at Harald and Harald met his eye and raised his eyebrow, just a bit, and Thorgrim knew his son was thinking just the same thing that he was. This place, Winchester, was a wealthy and formidable place. Very formidable indeed.

And with that thought, Thorgrim felt his first twinge of doubt. Somehow he had thought it would be easy to find where Failend was being held. Or, if not easy, than at least not impossible. He had questioned Nothwulf on the point, the tip of his seax hovering near Nothwulf's eye, and the young lord had been quite forthcoming. If

Failend was taken prisoner, Nothwulf told him, then the king and his men would wish to know, and would wish to speak with her, and she would undoubtedly be held somewhere in the king's great hall.

It all seemed quite straightforward, sitting on the barrel in the farm yard. Now it looked considerably less so, but it was too late for a change of plan. Thorgrim had told Nothwulf to take them to the king's hall, to wherever the men-at-arms would be expected to go. Once they were there, the foxes among the hens, he would figure what to do next.

The light was fading quickly as they emerged from one of the narrow streets into open ground surrounding what Thorgrim guessed was the king's compound. There was a separate wall around the place and towers and the roof of a great hall rising above them.

Nothwulf, clearly familiar with the place, did not pause as he headed his horse toward the gates in the wall where torches were already burning, throwing their light on the guards who stood nearby.

Good, good, Thorgrim thought. The dark was good. It was hard to make out faces in the light of torches, particularly faces half-hidden by helmets. They might still get in undetected.

Once again Nothwulf stopped a dozen yards from the gate and one of the sentries approached, but this man did not look as bored as the one at the main gate had. He and Nothwulf exchanged a few words, then the sentry stepped back and shouted up to another man on the top of the wall.

Thorgrim adjusted the grip on his spear to make certain he could bring it down and thrust it forward in an instant. He glanced over at Harald.

"He's telling the man on the wall that Nothwulf has returned," Harald said, as loudly as he dared. "Telling him to open the gate."

Thorgrim nodded and then heard the groaning sound of the big oak doors swinging open. The sentry stepped back and Nothwulf continued on, and the Northmen followed behind. Thorgrim felt a great wave of relief. They were through, they were in the king's compound. They were drawing closer to Failend with every step of their horses' feet.

Then Thorgrim realized that men were still yelling: the call from the sentry on the wall had been taken up by others and it seemed to bounce around the courtyard, building in volume.

He leaned toward Harald. "What are they yelling about?" he asked.

"Saying Nothwulf's back," Harald said. "It seems to be big news."

Thorgrim scowled. Of course it would be. They probably had word of the fight, probably thought that Nothwulf and his men were captive or dead. This sort of attention they did not need.

He looked side to side, as much as he dared, as much as he could without seeming overly curious. There was a massive hall in the center of the walled-in area, two stories, with the towers on either end. There were other buildings as well, barracks, Thorgrim guessed, and a kitchen and stables. Whoever this king was, he was not like the petty rulers they had known in Ireland or even the jarls of Norway. This man ruled a kingdom of some genuine significance.

Where would Failend be? Thorgrim wondered. He did not know. Sometimes, in the wolf dreams, he saw things clearly, so clearly he could find them again when he was awake. But the dream he had the night before was not like that. It had told him of Failend's danger, and nothing else.

There were men coming out of the hall now, and more coming from other directions to meet the new arrivals. Some held torches aloft to light the way for the weary riders. Behind him Thorgrim heard the creak of the big gates closing again.

There were men gathering around Nothwulf now, shouting up to him, asking, no doubt, what had happened. Others were closing in on the mounted Northmen, who they still took to be their fellow English men-at-arms. Thorgrim held the spear tighter. He felt a twitching in his arms and legs that told him he would have to do something, and soon.

He looked down to his left. There was a man there, holding a torch, looking up and smiling. A big man with a big red beard. The warrior from the inn. The one who had been mounted on the white and black horse.

Their eyes met and Thorgrim saw the man's smile freeze and hang there on his face for just an instant and then turn to a look of confusion. He frowned and his eyebrows came together.

Well, that didn't work, Thorgrim thought. *Now what do we do?* But he knew there was no one who could answer that, save for himself, and he was pretty much out of ideas.

Chapter Thirty-Five

I have no host in battle him to prove,
Nor have I strength his forces to undo.
Counsel me then, ye that are wise and true;
Can ye ward off this present death and dule?

The Song of Roland

Louis de Roumois was riding somewhere in the middle of the file of horsemen, Gudrid to his right. He had no idea what was going on, but he still had a bad feeling about it.

It had been that way for some time, really. At least since they had first approached Winchester, riding English horses with the English lord leading the way.

Failend was gone and Thorgrim had sent Harald to get the horses and the prisoner. When they returned Thorgrim spoke to the Englishman, seax in hand, the point often hovering near the prisoner's face. That made Louis think it was not a particularly friendly conversation.

It was only after that that Louis had his first hint of the plan. Thorgrim gathered the men around him and laid it out. He meant for them to ride into Winchester in the guise of English men-at-arms, the prisoner leading the way. Once inside the walls they would locate Failend, who Thorgrim believed was in danger. That belief was based on one of the absurd wolf dreams that Thorgrim claimed to have and the ignorant pagan Northmen took as gospel. They would free Failend and then the lot of them would make their escape.

This is a very bad plan, Louis had thought. *It's not even a plan at all.*

It was, in fact, ridiculous. The chances of getting into Winchester undetected were tiny at best, and even if they made it that far, the chances of then finding Failend were all but nonexistent.

But the Northmen all nodded their agreement with Thorgrim's intentions. Louis, though certain that the idea was ludicrous, nodded as well.

It never occurred to him not to join with Thorgrim and the rest. He, too, was worried about Failend. Very worried. If the English guessed she had been with the pagans than she was done for. What's more, Louis's refusing to go might be construed as cowardice, rather than good sense, and that Louis could not tolerate.

And, as much as he dismissed Thorgrim's wolf dreams for the heathen superstition they were, he had witnessed their surprising accuracy on occasion. They were no doubt a gift from Satan, and Thorgrim would repay that gift for eternity, but when it came to helping Failend Louis was willing to accept a gift from wherever it came. And Louis could think of nothing better to try.

So when evening came on and the Northmen donned the plundered English helmets and mail and mounted up, Louis did the same. He rode in silence with the rest, and when they reached the gates of Winchester waited as the prisoner jabbered with the guards in the barbaric tongue of the English, as bad as that of the Northmen. Then with the others he rode slowly through the gates and into the city.

Abandon hope, ye who enter here, he thought as they rode deeper into Winchester.

They approached what had to be the king's great hall, which was walled, like the city itself. Louis guessed that all of this, the crowded streets of the city, the high walls, the stone church looming over them, must seem quite magnificent to the English, and to the pagans it must seem like something out of their fantastical tales, hardly to be believed. But to Louis, who had been raised in the palace at Roumois and had been to Paris many times, it seemed little more than a pathetic attempt at civilization, an effort by a lesser race to imitate the grandeur of Frankia.

At the wall around the royal compound the prisoner once again jabbered with the sentries and once again the gates swung open to welcome them into the next circle of their fate. They rode through unmolested, and Louis, magnanimous and sensible as he was, was willing to admit that thus far things had worked out just as Thorgrim planned.

As he was admitting as much to himself he heard the gates close behind them, which was not unexpected, but still it was an ominous sound. Men were shouting from various quarters, and soon, as they rode slowly toward the great hall, they were surrounded by Englishmen who turned out to greet them. A few of them carried torches against the failing light, illuminating the prisoner at the head of the column and the others behind.

There was nothing hostile at all about the crowd surrounding them. Louis could tell, even without knowing what was being said, that the English were happy to see the men who had ridden through the gates, men who were ostensibly their brethren.

The exact moment when the English realized the truth was not entirely clear, but it happened fast. One instant the men were crowding around the riders, laughing and calling out, and then suddenly the laughter changed to shouts of alarm. Louis saw a fellow with an impressive red beard take a step back, point up at Thorgrim and shout, and the shout was taken up by others. Louis could not understand the words, of course, but he did not need to.

Oh, merde, he thought.

The English prisoner at the head of the column had spun his horse around and was shouting and pointing back at Thorgrim and the rest. Thorgrim brought his spear level and tried to hurl it at the man but a dozen English hands reached up and pulled him sideways, down off the horse, and the spear fell uselessly to the ground.

Damn these bastards, Louis thought. He pulled his sword from its scabbard and jerked the reins of his horse sideways, making the animal twist in place as he hacked down at the men suddenly coming for him. He had a vague thought that it was pointless, that he could not escape even if he managed to cut his way through the men surrounding him. There were hundreds more English warriors there, and the gates were closed.

He swung his blade at the closest of the Englishmen and kicked his horse hard in the flanks. If he could break free, he thought, if he could drive his horse out of the press of men, then maybe something would come to him, some idea or opportunity. He kicked again and felt hands grabbing at his legs and his mail shirt. He hacked down with his sword and more hands grabbed his arm, too many for him to fight against, and he felt himself dragged from the saddle. There was shouting all around, none of which Louis could decipher, save for the unearthly shrieks that he knew were coming from the throat of Starri Deathless.

"Bastards!" Louis shouted and his foot jerked free of the stirrup and he fell with a painful thump to the ground. He thrashed and kicked and tried to strike out with his sword, but his arm was held tight and he felt the sword pulled from his grip. He tried to get his arms or his legs under him, to push himself up, but it was no use. Every limb was pinned as Louis was pressed face down into the soft ground.

Finally exhaustion and a sense of futility took hold and he stopped struggling. He lay still, gasping for breath, but the hands did not let go, the force pushing him down did not ease.

"Let me up, you stupid English bastards!" he shouted. He was yelling in Frankish, which was pointless, he knew, but he felt that he had to say something. If they understood him or not he did not know, but in either case no one let him up.

His arms were pulled around behind his back, crossed at the wrists, and bound tight with cordage that cut into his flesh. Only then did the men around ease off. More hands grabbed him under the arms and lifted him like a child to his feet. He was shoved forward, the crowd of English warriors parting for him, revealing in their midst Thorgrim and Harald and the rest, all similarly bound, helmets and weapons gone.

Starri was lying on the ground and Louis thought at first he was dead, but then he saw he had been bound hand and foot. Blood covered his face and matted his hair, and still he was kicking and twisting in pointless rage.

The guards formed a circle around the Northmen, their spears leveled, like the teeth of an animal looking for a reason to bite. The crowd of Englishmen was considerably bigger now: hundreds had come running at the sound of the fighting. Most were in tunics, and some just leggings, having been surprised in whatever they had been doing.

Orders were shouted back and forth. The man issuing the bulk of the orders was not wearing a helmet or mail, though he seemed to be in command, calling out, pointing here and there. He was fifty feet away when his and Louis's eyes met. They held each other's gaze, just for an instant, then the man looked away and started calling orders again.

Do I know you? Louis thought. The man looked familiar, as wildly unlikely as that would be.

Another pushed through the crowd and Louis recognized him as the prisoner, the English lord they had taken at the inn, the one who had been made to lead them into Winchester. He spoke to Harald, a few sharp words, and then Harald turned to Godi and they exchanged a few words. Then Godi leaned over and grabbed Starri Deathless and hefted him up and over his shoulder as if he was a mattress stuffed with straw.

Starri shouted and kicked but it seemed to make no impression on Godi, who stood stoically by. Starri was not a big man in any event, but draped over Godi Unundarson's massive shoulder he looked more like a child.

Another word from the Englishman, gestures with the points of spears, and the Northmen and Louis, the prisoners, walked off in the direction indicated, still surrounded by English men-at-arms. Louis wondered if Thorgrim and the others would go peacefully, or try fighting their way free, which would be tantamount to killing themselves. Starri certainly would, if he was able. The Northmen had a terrible fear of dying a dishonorable death, which the English were likely to give them, and soon. But dying with hands bound might not be much better.

No, Thorgrim's too clever for that, Louis thought. Thorgrim would not throw away his life and the lives of his men, not then, not when there was still a chance for escape or death with a weapon in hand.

They were marched past the king's great hall, past the barracks farther off and the other, smaller buildings, until they came at last to a small house built right against the wall that surrounded the king's compound. Like the wall, it was made of stone, with a slate roof, a single, heavy, iron-bound door and a massive lock hanging from a hasp, and Louis guessed it had been purpose built to house prisoners. The door was pulled open ahead of them and one by one they were driven into the lightless space, and when the last of them was inside the door was closed with authority and they heard the click of the lock being shut.

For a long moment there was nothing more to be heard but the sound of men breathing. Then Thorgrim said, "Anyone wounded? Badly wounded?" His words were met with silence and a few grunts. No one spoke.

"Harald, come here," Thorgrim said next and Harald made a guttural sound and pushed his way through the men toward the sound of his father's voice. "There's a knife at my ankle, under my leggings. They didn't find it. Can you get it out?"

Again Harald grunted and that was followed by a few moments of rustling and shuffling. Louis pictured Harald, in the dark, sitting on the dirt floor, trying to extract a hidden knife from under Thorgrim's leggings with his hands tied behind his back. The image was comical and Louis smiled despite himself.

And then, to his surprise, he heard Harald say, "I've got it."

This was followed by more rustling and murmured communication and then he heard Thorgrim say, "There. Cut now, hard as you can." A moment later Thorgrim was pushing his way through the others, cutting their bonds away, accompanied by sighs of relief and the sound of rough hands rubbing raw skin.

"Feel around the walls, high as you can. Along the floor," Thorgrim said. "See if there's some possible way out of here." More shuffling in the dark, but Louis did not move. It was pointless. He knew there was no way out of that stone building and he suspected Thorgrim did as well. Thorgrim just wanted to keep the men busy, to see they didn't have time to ponder their situation. But he could not keep them occupied forever.

And indeed he did not. Soon each of the men spoke up in the dark and reported that they could find nothing that seemed remotely like a way out. That done, they lapsed into silence, and even Thorgrim did not try to find anything more to distract them.

Louis felt his way to a wall and sat, leaning back against the stone. For some time he remained like that, though how long he had no idea. Long enough for some of the Northmen to fall asleep, their snoring loud and ugly-sounding in so confined a space. Louis wished that he, too, could fall asleep, if for no reason other than to pass the time, but he knew that was not going to happen.

He was still staring out into the dark when he heard the sound of men approaching the prison. Quite a few men, heralded by the clinking of mail and the thump of weapons and the tread of many feet. He tensed and listened as intently as he could.

Yes, they were certainly coming toward the prison.

He opened his mouth to speak but before he could he heard Starri Deathless say in a sharp whisper, "Listen! There are warriors coming!"

This caused a stirring among the men who were still awake and a grumbling from those who were waking up.

"On your feet, on your feet!" Thorgrim said. "Get ready!"

Ready for what? Louis wondered, but he was sure that Thorgrim did not know either. Ready for whatever horror would come next.

The men-at-arms stopped on the other side of the door and someone pounded on the oak planks with some hard object and called out a few words. There was a shuffling movement among the Northmen and Harald, who had worked his way to the door, replied. He and the man on the other side went back and forth a few times, speaking in short bursts, then Harald spoke in his native tongue.

"This bastard says he's going to open the door. He says we're to stand against the far wall. There are spearmen there and anyone who goes through the door will be killed."

This led to more grumbling. Every man there understood the situation. They might hope to rush the Englishmen, but they could only go through the door one at a time, and they could easily be cut down as they did.

After a moment Thorgrim said, "Very well. All of you, back against the wall." They all moved back, stumbling into one another, cursing, until at last they were all pressed against the wall that formed the back of the prison and Harald called out to the man at the door.

The lock clicked and the door creaked open and the light from a half a dozen torches spilled in, looking bright as the sun after the absolute blackness of the prison. A man stood framed in the doorway, appearing as no more than a black figure with the flames behind him. He took a step forward and spoke.

"Louis de Roumois? Is Louis de Roumois among you?"

Louis did not reply. He was so stunned to hear his name called out he did not know what to say. He did not even realize at first that the man was speaking Frankish. He was no Frank — the accent was clearly English — but he was speaking Louis's native tongue.

"I am Louis de Roumois," Louis replied at last.

"Come with me," the man said and Louis saw the silhouetted arm waving him over. For a moment he did not move. It was too dream-like for him to act on it.

"Come on," the man said, more insistent and less patient than before. Louis pushed himself off the wall and walked toward the light, as if he had just been killed and was going to his final reward.

This may be the first step on that road, he thought. He had no sense at all for what might be happening.

He stepped out into the night and stopped. A half a dozen spears were leveled at him. Behind him the man shut the door and locked it once again, then stepped up beside Louis. He was an older man, a warrior, captain of this guard, no doubt. He had probably seen a lot of campaigning, maybe in Frankia, maybe where he learned the language. Louis had a hundred questions to ask, but the old campaigner did not look like a man much ready to answer, so when he gestured for Louis to follow, Louis did so without a word.

The odd little parade crossed back over the ground they had covered on the way to the prison, but then they veered off to the left and made for the great hall. The sentries there opened the door as they approached and Louis and the captain stepped through, followed by two of the guards.

Still the old man said nothing as he led Louis down the length of the massive building. A fire was burning in a wide hearth at one end and the flames illuminated the space up to the carved rafters some fifty feet overhead. There were tapestries on the walls and fine chalices and plates and such set on the long table. Louis looked around as they walked and he found that the king's great hall met with his approval.

He was not impressed, but he approved.

They crossed to the far side of the hall and Louis could now see there was a door there, wide and tall, that apparently led to yet another wing of the building. The captain led him through it and down a hallway, also hung with tapestries, and with thick rugs covering the stone floor. They stopped at one of the doors which opened onto the hall. The captain knocked and Louis heard a voice from inside call, "*Entrez!*"

The captain had already opened the door half-way before Louis realized that that order, single word though it was, had been spoken in Frankish. And this time without the adulteration of an English accent.

The door swung open the rest of the way to show a room well-lit with candles standing on tall iron candleholders variously positioned.

There was a bed and several trunks and a big table pushed up against one wall with papers scattered over its surface and a man sitting at it, back to the door. He was scratching away with a pen, but he set the pen in an ink well and turned, a slight smile on his face.

"Ah, Louis," he said.

Louis frowned and squinted and tried to make sense of what he was looking at. He opened his mouth, then closed it. Then opened it again and said, "Felix?"

Felix smiled wider and stood. "Here I thought you did not recognize me!" he said. "I wasn't sure I recognized you." He stepped close and grabbed Louis's shoulders and kissed him on both cheeks, then released him and took a step back.

"I was directing the heathens be sent off to the jail," he continued, "and I thought for certain I saw you among them! Couldn't imagine how, but here you are!"

Louis shook his head, astounded. He did recognize Felix, but just barely. If he had seen the man in the court of King Charles of West Frankia, where he was accustomed to seeing him, then he would have known him instantly. Felix was probably ten years older than Louis, and had served Charles for as long as Louis had been going there in company with his father, which was several times a year at least, for most of his life.

He and Felix had never been more than acquaintances, but amiable ones, companions when Louis was at court. They had shared many meals together in the company of others, and many cups of wine. There had always been a mutual respect between them, Louis felt, even affection.

"Yes," Louis said. "Yes, of course I recognize you. Or would have. It's been some years and....I was surprised...to see you here."

"Of course you were," Felix said. He nodded to the captain of the guard and the man bowed and exited. He closed the door behind him and Felix gestured for Louis to sit. When he had, Felix handed him a cup of wine.

"Fear not," Felix said, sitting as well. "It's Frankish wine I brought with me. Not the effluence that the English call wine."

Louis took a sip. It was good. Frankish. He hadn't tasted its like in some time. "So...how...?"

"How do I happen to be here?" Felix asked. "Charles sent me to help out in King Æthelwulf's court. Thought the English could use someone of sense. And you know, Æthelwulf will be visiting with Charles soon. On his way to Rome. Would have been off by now, but he was wounded fighting the heathens."

"Wounded?" Louis asked. "Badly?"

"No, no," Felix said, "It looked bad, and I feared for his life, but he's recovering well now. But tell me, how do you happen to be here? It's been years since I've seen you. I heard you had gone off to an Irish monastery, after your father's death."

"Yes," Louis said. "Yes, I did. Not through any choice of my own, mind you." He told Felix the story, starting with his brother's jealousy of him, his fear that Louis would usurp his position after their father had died, how he had shipped Louis off to Glendalough in hopes he would stay there and rot.

The words kept coming from Louis's mouth, building momentum, forming a narrative he had never really put together as a whole thing before. He told of how he fought the Northmen to defend Glendalough, how the Irish had turned on him, how he had been taken captive by the Northmen, escaped, been taken captive again. How he had thrown in with the Northmen because it seemed the entire world was his enemy and he wanted nothing but to return to Frankia and avenge himself, and it seemed the Northmen were the most expedient means of doing so.

Through all this Felix just listened, arms folded, head cocked to one side. He asked a few questions here and there and listened closely to each answer. "So now you are in Hamtun with this…Thorgrim?" Felix asked at last. "You fought with the heathens in the battle on the bay?"

"Well, yes," Louis said. "Heathens, English, none of them are any friends of mine. Or of Frankia."

Felix nodded. "And how do you happen to be here? I mean here now, in Winchester?"

Louis had not told Felix about Failend. It seemed unnecessary, and the tale he had told was convoluted and strange enough without the addition of a love affair: his, hers, Thorgrim's. "One of Thorgrim's people, they came into the city and did not come back. Thorgrim wanted to find them, so I agreed to go with him."

"I see," Felix said. "And this person, was it a woman? A young woman? Pretty? Actually an Irish woman, not a Northman?"

Louis was not able to hide his surprise. He knew it showed on his face, making it pointless to lie. "Yes, that's right. An Irish woman. From Glendalough. She and I are…close…"

Felix nodded again and pressed his fingertips together and for a long moment he was silent, just staring at Louis, until Louis began to feel uncomfortable. He was about to speak, but Felix spoke first.

"Tell, me, Louis de Roumois, is there anyone you won't betray?"

Louis was silent for a moment, not certain he had heard right. "What?" he said at last.

"I'm wondering," Felix continued, "if there is anyone you won't betray? First you try to take the place of your brother Eberhard, who is rightful heir to your father's estate." He held up his hand to stop the protest on Louis's lips. "Don't try to deny it, we've had the entire story from him. Then he shows you mercy and allows you to take your place in the church, yet you betray your vows and run off. And not just run off, you join with the heathens, Frankia's greatest enemies. Enemies of all Christendom.

"You assist them in battle, take up arms against King Æthelwulf, a pious man, a friend of our King Charles. A battle that nearly kills the man I serve. And here you are, sneaking into Winchester like a thief, a thief in service to the Godless butchers. And don't tell me they forced you to join them. This sort of thing, this sneaking into the city in disguise, is not something a man does unless he does it willingly. Eagerly, even."

"Are you…?" Louis tried to begin, but there was too much trying to come out. The outrage was all jammed up in his head and would not fit through his mouth. "I never…surely you must be…"

It was as far as he got. Felix picked up a bell that was sitting beside him and rang it, a small musical sound. It sounded out of place in that room.

Louis heard the door open behind him and the old captain came in with the two guards behind him and two more behind them. Louis was still sputtering as they grabbed him by the arms and lifted him from the seat. He twisted and jerked away but they held him tightly with their considerable strength.

"Damn you, Felix, can you possibly believe I have betrayed anyone?" he managed to shout. "My brother, that bastard, he sent me…I never…"

Felix nodded toward the door and the guards half dragged Louis away, his heels kicking at the soft carpet. "Damn you, you bastard!" he shouted, but before he got the words out the heavy oak door was shut tight once again.

Chapter Thirty-Six

So might be heard,
when together came
the tempest's sister
and the long keels,
as when rock and surge
on each other break.

The Poetic Edda

With every violent roll of the boat, water came shooting in through the shattered planks like high surf hitting a rocky cliff. Six or seven men were frantically bailing; the rest were still lying on the bottom where they had fallen, looking on stupidly.

Skorri Thorbrandsson was one of those looking on stupidly. He was up near the bows, too stunned to move. The blow from the iron pot had stunned him. The speed with which he had gone from having Amundi and Odd in his hands to being on the verge of drowning stunned him.

He pushed himself to his feet as the boat took another roll. He staggered and grabbed the sheer strake before he went down again. He knew he had to live. As long as he was alive he could still drag Odd and Amundi before Halfdan and reap those rewards, and that was reason enough. But if the idiots he commanded were left to act on their own they would all be dead by the time another three sets of waves passed under them.

Before he moved forward Skorri looked out to windward and saw what he dreaded seeing, but what he knew he would see. Amundi's boat was intact, the rig still standing, the sail still drawing. They were clawing their way north, rising and falling in the seas, and unless something went very wrong they would weather the point of land and escape.

"Ah, you bastards!" Skorri shouted, furious at the ill luck that had befallen him. Amundi could not have planned to do what he did, he could not have intended for his boat to hit Skorri's so perfectly. He had been lucky, the gods had favored him above the others.

But Skorri knew what the gods wanted — bold and ruthless action — and he knew how to give them that.

"Move aside, you fools!" Skorri roared and he let go of the sheer strake and stepped across the boat, timing his steps with the wild rolling underfoot. The mast had snapped a few feet above the bilge and gone over the leeward side in a great tangle of spars and rigging and sail. It was half on the boat and half dragging in the water now, but that was not the most immediate concern.

One of the men was standing right in Skorri's path and Skorri shoved him aside, tumbling him back into the bilge as he made his way forward. "Get out of my way, you idiot!" he shouted and as his words registered the other men began to back away.

He stopped a few feet from the stove-in planks, holding the shattered end of the mast for balance. Two of the strakes were buckled inward far enough that he could see through the gap to the foaming sea on the other side, and a third plank was cracked and threatening to go completely. The hole they made was a few inches above the waterline, which meant that the water was not flooding in, just jetting in when the boat rolled to starboard.

The men who had not moved out of Skorri's way were still bailing like mad.

"Don't just bail, find something to stuff in that hole!" Skorri roared. He turned around and grabbed the corner of the sail that was draped over the thwarts and pulled it toward him. He drew his knife and stabbed it down through the heavy linen canvas and began to slice sideways, then up and back until he had cut out a square section, three feet on either side. That done, he cut four pieces of rope from the tangled rigging and tied one to each corner.

He turned back to the men at the shattered planks. Some were trying to work a bundle of cloth into the hole, while the others continued to bail.

"Lambi!" he shouted, handing his canvas and rope lash-up to the man. "Take this and spread it out over the hole, from the outside! Let two of the lines snake under the boat!"

Lambi nodded and took the canvas from him. The others stepped back as Lambi turned and leaned far out over the edge of the boat. He tossed two of the lines to windward in hope that they would be swept under the boat, then leaned farther still, spreading the canvas over the shattered planks as he did.

"Someone see if those lines are under the boat, grab them up from the larboard side!" Skorri shouted. If they could get the lines under the boat they could effectively tie the canvas in place over the hole, and it would greatly reduce the amount of water gushing in.

The boat rolled off to larboard, lifting Lambi and the starboard side high. Then it dipped down again and as it did a breaking crest slammed against the bow. The boat shuddered from stem to stern and Lambi shouted in surprise. His arms flailed for something to grab but there was only air. He pivoted head first over the rail, feet high, screaming as he hit the water.

"Son of a bitch!" Skorri shouted. "Grab that canvas, grab it before it gets away!" He leaped for the rope lying on the bottom of the boat but it snaked over the side before he could put his hand on it. He watched it go, and as he followed its path he saw Lambi in the water, ten feet away. Just his head and mail-clad arms were visible, his mouth open, his eyes wide with terror as he thrashed at the sea around him.

Wonder if he can swim… Skorri thought. He saw a rope go flying out over the water, one of the other men tossing a line to Lambi. It landed just a foot away but in the same instant Lambi slipped below the surface, first his head and then his flailing arms, then hands and then he was gone.

Guess not, Skorri thought.

He pushed himself back onto his feet. "Any of you bastards grab that piece of canvas?" He turned fore and aft. The others were just looking at him, saying nothing, and he knew they had failed.

"You sons of whores!" he shouted. Now he would have to waste time making another canvas patch. "Keep bailing! And take your mail off, you fools!"

With that he unbuckled his belt and dropped it, then pulled his own mail shirt over his head and tossed it aside. Balancing against the roll of the boat, he strapped his belt on again. He grabbed another part of the sail and pulled his knife and cut out another square, and then a length of line.

When he was done he handed the canvas to a man named Hrolf. "Spread this out like Lambi was doing, but hold onto it and don't fall overboard like an idiot!" he shouted over the rain and the wind. Hrolf took the canvas and nodded.

"And some of you others, hold onto Hrolf's belt like you should have done with Lambi!" Skorri shouted next. In truth he had not thought about holding Lambi's belt either, but he was not about to admit as much.

Hrolf leaned over the side while two others took a firm grip on his belt. He streamed two of the lines under the boat and Kolbein on the larboard side grabbed them up and tied them off. Hrolf spread the canvas over the hole and when he had done Kolbein grabbed the other two lines and made them fast as well, holding the canvas in place over the shattered planks. The water that had been gushing in was reduced to a trickle.

"All right, let's cut this rig away!" Skorri shouted next. "Just cut it free, toss it over the side!" The men drew knives and went at the tangle of ropes and canvas and broken poles, shoving what was still on board into the sea. It drifted away and the boat began to roll more violently still, with the drag of the wreckage gone.

And with that there was nothing more to do. It was pointless to try and row against those forces, and the wind and sea were driving them toward the shore in any event, pushing them in the direction they wished to go. The men sat as low in the boat as they could get, where the motion was less violent, but Skorri resumed his place in the stern, looking west through the rain. If there was land anywhere near, he could not see it through the storm, and if the waves were breaking he could not hear them.

"Are the oars free to be used, if we need 'em?" Skorri shouted over the wind. They couldn't row against the gale, but they might be able to gain some control over the boat as they went ashore.

The oars were in the bottom of the boat and the men were leaning or sitting on them, so they began to shuffle and move and pull the oars free. Skorri looked along the sheer strake. He could see two of the thole pins that would hold the oars in place were broken and one was missing.

"See if there are any spare thole pins on this miserable dung-heap of a boat!" he called next, and a few men began to rummage around in the bow to see what they could find.

Skorri was watching the men rifling their purloined boat when another sound caught his ear, something that stood out from the constant monotony of the driving rain, the slam of waves against the hull. He turned quick and looked aft. The wind and sea were driving them stern-first toward the shore and now, through the gloom, he could see a gray, undulating form, a rolling, surging mass, like something alive but in its death throes.

"Breakers! Breakers!" Kolbein shouted. Skorri had not been the only one to hear the sound, and to recognize the dim shape made by waves slamming into something immovable. Granite ledge, most likely.

"Get the oars in the tholes! Get ready to pull, you bastards!" Skorri shouted, and the men who a second before had been sitting miserable and despondent in the bottom of the boat suddenly began crawling and stumbling in every direction. The oars were passed up from the bilge and others took them up and dropped them between the thole pins that were left, and still others took seats on the thwarts and grabbed the handles of the oars and began to pull.

"Come on, pull, pull, pull!" Skorri shouted. If they could keep the boat off the rocks they might be able to work their way along the shoreline until they found a beach or some place they could safely land. But there were thole pins for only three of the six oars, two to starboard and one to larboard — not enough. Even with all the oars in action it would not be easy to buck that wind and tide.

"Pull!" Skorri yelled. "And find some more rutting thole pins!" Three men dove forward to resume their search as the rowers leaned back and pulled hard. Rainwater streamed down their faces and Skorri could see the exertion as they put every bit of remaining strength into the task. He grabbed the tiller and pushed it to larboard. If they could make any headway against the seas then he would be able to steer them away from the rocks.

He braced his feet to turn and look back, to see if they were making any progress, when one of the men in the bow shouted, "Thole pins!"

Skorri looked forward. The man was still on his knees but he was holding up a half dozen thole pins in one hand, a look of triumph on his face. And then the boat hit rock.

The stern rose up under them in the same way it had with every passing wave, rising high and then sinking in the trough as the wave passed under. But there was no trough this time. The aft end of the boat came down on solid granite, engulfed in an explosion of spray.

Skorri was once again knocked off his feet, and as he went down he saw the boat actually bending in the middle, forming an odd angle, the planks splitting and shattering as it did. He heard men shouting and wood cracking and water rushing all around them. He grunted as he hit, his body like a dead weight, but his brain was screaming at him to stand, to get off the boat, to get to shore, get to shore.

The next wave lifted the boat and slammed it down again and Skorri could see it was indeed coming apart in the middle. A third of the men were aft of where it was breaking in two, the rest forward. Underfoot Skorri could feel the planks grinding against the ledge, and he could see the wet rock over the side of the boat.

"Come on, come on, get ashore!" he shouted. There was a coil of rope lying on the bottom of the boat and Skorri snatched it up and stood. He could feel the boat lifting again as he flung himself over the rail. His feet came down on the rough, wet granite just as the wave hit. He held onto the side of the boat and the water slammed into him like a fist, rushing around his legs up to his waist, trying to toss him free.

Then it rushed back and Skorri let go of the boat and took a dozen steps along the ledge, moving higher on the rock. He stopped and looked back and saw four of his men crawling up after him, and beyond them the shattered boat and the men still clinging to it as the next wave rolling in to break it further apart.

Skorri grabbed the end of the rope in his left hand, the coil in his right, just as the four men reached him. "Get ready to tail onto the rope, we'll see if we can't pull some of these bastards ashore!" he shouted as he cocked his arm and flung the coil away.

The rope spun through the air, unwinding, and dropped across the disintegrating boat. "Grab ahold, grab ahold!" Skorri cried but he did not think they would hear him over the roaring all around them.

Hear him or not, the men in the boat saw the rope and they knew what it meant. A lifeline, a chance. One by one they grabbed it and rushed aft, hand over hand. The first man on the rope, Kolbein Thordarson, reached the stern and climbed over onto the ledge, as did the man behind. Skorri tossed the tail end of the rope behind him and the four men there grabbed it up, and together they heaved away, pulling the others in as much as they could, aiding their efforts to climb.

There were still six men left in the forward end of the boat when the next wave rose up under it. Three of them were grabbing for the rope when that half of the vessel twisted free, ripped completely away from the stern end and rolled over in the breaking surf. Skorri saw, just for an instant, the looks of shock and confusion, and then the forward half of the boat lifted and turned over and came down again, the seas piling up on the vessel's rounded, glistening bottom.

"Heave!" Skorri called. Six men gone, but that was better than losing them all. "Heave!"

One by one the men on the rope reached the high place where Skorri and the others stood, high enough that each surging wave came up to their calves and no higher, high enough that they could keep their footing with only a little difficulty. The surge was bringing with it shattered planks and oars and broken thwarts now as the last of the boat fell apart forty feet away.

Skorri dropped the rope. It could not do any more good. "Let's get off this miserable rock," he said. He pushed his way through the men and continued along the ledge, beyond the reach of the sea, and finally the rock yielded to scrubby brush and dirt. The driving rain still pelted them, but they were finally clear of the killing sea.

They stopped there, breathing hard, silent, as if they were all trying to make sense of what had happened. All save for Skorri. For him the wreck of the boat, the death of the men, was already history, forgotten. His mind was on to something else.

Bastard Amundi…must have got around that point. But he wouldn't stay in the boat…no, he'd get ashore quick as he could.

If Odd was still alive, which Skorri had to think was unlikely, then Amundi and the others would want to get him ashore and get him to some place where they could tend to him. Even if he was dead, Amundi would want to get his people ashore before they suffered the same fate that Skorri's men had.

"Let's go," Skorri said and moved past the gaggle of men and headed off inland, across an open field. The day was getting late, what little light there was was starting to fade, but Skorri had no intention of stopping for anything: not dark, not the storm, not the battered condition he and his men were in. Nothing.

There was nothing but open country as far as Skorri could see, though he could not see terribly far. There were no farms or clusters of houses that marked some sort of village. Wherever those other fishing boats had gone when they ran to shore in the face of the storm, it was nowhere near there.

But he guessed there would be a road. That part of the country, Fevik, had enough people that there would undoubtedly be a road running roughly along the shoreline. He would find that and head north, because he imagined that Amundi would take that road as well.

The men followed behind and no one spoke. Skorri would tell them where they were going and what he planned to do once they reached the road, and not before. They might be surprised when they learned he had no intention of returning to Halfdan's camp empty-handed.

But then again, they probably would not be so surprised.

It was not long before they saw it, a dark band rising and falling with the hills a little farther inland, the road that Skorri had guessed must be there. He thought of Amundi and his people somewhere along that same road. They would have a significant head start. It would be no easy task to catch up with them, even assuming they did not leave the road and head off for some other shelter.

Skorri walked through the last of the knee-high grass and stepped onto the road, now a puddled and muddy swamp, the ruts from cart wheels like rivers running down the edges. Once they were all standing there, shoes sunk a half an inch into the mud, they stopped and Skorri looked down the road, south, then up the road to the north. Nothing. No one moving. He had not imagined there would be. Not on such a day.

He turned to the others. "We go north," he said. "We're still hunting Odd, and we won't stop until we have him."

He could see the lack of enthusiasm on their faces, the sense of exhaustion and defeat they felt, and he did not care at all. And he had no intention of explaining or arguing or even saying one more word about it. They would follow him without question and he would kill anyone who did otherwise.

Once again Skorri led the way with the men now walking in a single file at the very edge of the road where the going was easiest. Skorri could hear the squishing sound their feet made in the mud as they walked. He looked up. It would be night soon. He hoped there would be a moon behind those thick clouds, one bright enough to give just a bit of illumination to the sky. Without that it would be hard going in the dark. Even with that it would be hard going.

They had covered a mile or so when Skorri heard a sound he did not recognize immediately: not an unknown sound, just one he had not heard for a while. His mind had been far off as his feet had carried him along. He was thinking about Amundi. He was thinking about how pointless this all might be. If they had horses then there would be a chance that they might overtake the fugitives, but on foot the chances seemed very slim indeed.

And even if they did find them, they had lost most of their weapons and all of their mail when the boat had wrecked. If Amundi and his men were well-armed, then taking them might not be as easy as Skorri had assumed.

He heard the noise again and this time he stopped and raised his hand and the others behind him stopped as well. He stared off into the rain and cocked his ear. And there it was. A horse's whinny.

"Riders coming," he said, and suddenly he saw the possibility of the horses he had been dreaming of. Now, he thought, the gods might be rewarding his bold recklessness.

"Off the road," he said, just loud enough to be heard. "Half of you on the far side, get down in the grass. Hide yourselves. Wait 'til you hear me yell and then you leap out at them, drag every one of the bastards down off their horse. Go!"

The men divided up, half to one side of the road, half to the other. Skorri found a place in the high grass and lay down, feeling the mud soft under his body. He would not be seen from the road, he was quite certain, but that also meant he could not see the road himself.

They waited and listened and soon the beating of hooves could be heard, soft and slow. The riders were not moving fast, which was lucky. They would be wet and tired and the shock of more than a dozen men bursting from the grass would throw them into confusion.

The sound of the horses drew closer and Skorri felt his body tense, his muscles pulse, his teeth press together. He wanted desperately to look over the top of the grass and see where the horsemen were, but he resisted.

A moment more, a moment more… Skorri thought, and then he saw the first rider, his head appearing just above the top of the grass and almost even with where Skorri lay. Skorri pushed himself to his feet, charging forward even before he was fully up, a wild cry bursting from his mouth as he raced through the twenty feet of grass to the road ahead.

There were five horsemen but Skorri's eyes were on the lead rider, a big man, a bearded man, his eyes wide with shock at this sudden attack. He hauled back on his reins and his horse reared and came down and the man shouted, two words, and not the words Skorri expected to hear.

"Lord Skorri?"

The man's horse shook its head and half turned as the rider struggled to keep control, but his eyes remained on Skorri as Skorri burst out of the grass and came to a halt.

"Vermund," Skorri said. "Where have you been, you lazy bastard?"

Chapter Thirty-Seven

Would it be for you both
in battle to engage,
and the eagles gladden,
than with useless words
to contend,
even if hate
is in chieftain's hearth.

The Poetic Edda

Failend sat half on the edge of the wooden bed frame, half on the straw-stuffed mattress that was doing little to support her weight, insignificant though it was. She stared at the floor and the strange zigzag patterns of the mortar between the flat stones. They stood out sharply, illuminated by the small flame of a single oil lamp, the only light in the windowless space. She wondered if this was how it looked to a bird, flying over hilly country, looking down at humps of land intercut by streams and rivers.

This detail of the floor was pretty much all she had left to look at. The cell she was in was tiny, perhaps eight feet by ten feet. It was not a jail, she did not think. More like a monk's cell or some such.

She had already explored every bit of the space, walking the perimeter of the walls with the oil lamp in her hand. There was nothing much to see. Stone walls on four sides, and wooden beams supporting wooden planks for the ceiling. The door was wood as well, with a heavy iron latch. She tried it, of course, but it would not move. She recalled seeing a bar on the outside just before she had been pushed into the cell. She recalled hearing the bar drop into place.

She knew for certain that the cell was in the king's hall. They had taken her there from the cathedral, after they had discovered the truth of her. After the priest, on the bishop's order, had pulled the necklace out of her shift, the necklace she had forgotten about, that physical manifestation of her divided loyalties.

They had argued at first: the bishop and Father Conall, the priest who had heard her confession, and then several others who had arrived after. Failend could not understand a word of it, but she had an idea they were fighting over who should take charge of her, where she should go. The bishop seemed to be arguing one point, Father Conall another, and doing so with an impressive amount of vehemence, considering whom he was arguing against.

Father Conall, of course, knew Failend's story, her entire story, and she guessed he had sympathy for her, both as a man of God and an Irishman. But he could not tell that story to the bishop. Failend considered telling the bishop herself, but she thought in that instance it might work against her. The bishop did not seem to be a man much given to sympathy.

In the end it was the bishop who decided what would be done with her, or perhaps the decision was made for him by the men-at-arms. They arrived in the cathedral while the discussion was still on-going, twelve men in mail and carrying spears and led by a captain who looked as if he knew his business. There was not much talk after that.

Failend's hands were bound behind her back and she was led off, the spearmen flanking her on either side. She looked back over her shoulder as she was marched away, back toward Father Conall, the Irish priest who had heard her confession, who had been so kind, and she could see the genuine despair on his face.

They led her out of the cathedral and into the bright, mid-morning sun. The streets which had been waking up before were now crowded with men and women and children and carts and animals and barrows, and it seemed as if everyone was shouting and no one was listening. But as the ring of armed men passed, surrounding a woman whose hands were bound and whose head hardly reached the top of the shortest man's shoulders, the people stopped and watched, their curiosity piqued.

Failend wondered how different it would look if she had been wearing her mail and helmet, seax on her belt, bow and arrows over her shoulder.

That would make them curious indeed, she thought.

The men-at-arms led her back the way she had come, around the corner of the wall that surrounded the king's great hall. They did not bring her through the main gate but through a smaller door flanked by two guards who held it open for them. They led her across the open ground, past the cluster of buildings that formed the royal residence within the walls of Winchester.

They came to the east wing of the great hall, with the rest of that magnificent building stretching off to their left, the two towers rising to impressive heights above. They marched her through another door and into that wing and there was not much impressive there, save for the fact that it was made of stone. There were no tapestries or carpets or any touches of comfort or refinement, and Failend guessed it was quarters for religious, maybe the priests and monks who served in the royal chapel.

The big open room at the entrance to the wing led to a long hall with doors lining either side. The doors were close together, suggesting that the rooms behind them were not large, and the unadorned space suggested they were not particularly comfortable. The captain led the way down the hall and stopped in front of one of the doors, nodding to one of the men to open it. There was nothing hesitant about the captain's manner. The man had been clearly instructed as to what to do with his prisoner.

The door swung open, the room inside dim lit with the small flame of the oil lamp, and Failend was pushed inside, a gentle push, but a push nonetheless. Someone stepped up behind her and untied her wrists, then the door was shut behind her without a word and the bar fell into place.

For a long time she just stood, silent and unmoving, listening, but once the men-at-arms had marched off she could hear nothing through the thick stone walls. She picked up the oil lamp and examined the room, though she had no idea what she was looking for. A way out, perhaps, though she certainly did not believe she would find one. In truth she knew she was looking simply because there was nothing else to do.

When she was done with that she sat down on the bed and stared at the floor. She let her mind wander back over the years. She had not thought much about it until that morning, really, but now the dam was broken, the memories allowed to flood out, and she could not stop them. All the twists and turns: she could see them now, as if from above, the same way she was seeing the twists and turns in the mortar between the stones.

But it was only the turns behind her that she could see. She had come around another bend now, taken another turn, but there was no seeing what lay ahead. She had decided to abandon her sinful, pagan ways, and now she might well die because of that decision.

She lay down on the thin mattress, aware of how uncomfortable it felt, but also aware of how exhausted she was. She had walked through much of the night, had slept briefly behind a bush before covering the rest of the distance to Winchester. It had been a trying day already, and it was not yet noon.

And beyond the physical she felt drained spiritually. She had seen men in battle suffer from pulsing wounds, when some great vein was severed, allowing them to bleed out in minutes. Now she felt as if her soul had received such a wound, as if it was pouring out of a rent in her flesh and pooling on the floor. She didn't know if she could die from such a thing, but she felt as if she might.

Sleep came over her at some point, sneaking up unseen, and when she woke again she had no sense at all for how long she had been in its hold. She felt as if her body was pressed down into the mattress, as if she had not moved in a very long time, semi-permanently fixed like something cast up on the beach and half buried in the sand as tide after tide washed over it.

She did not move, except to open her eyes, but there was nothing that she could see that gave her any idea of how much time had passed. The oil lamp was still burning with its tiny flame, still the only light in the room. It had been full daylight outside when she was put in the cell, and it might still be. Or it might be fully dark. Or twilight. Or dawn. She had no idea.

There were sounds from down the hall, voices calling, a rustling like some struggle going on, and she guessed that was what had woken her. It was the first thing she had heard since the guards had left her. She pushed herself up onto her elbow so that both ears could be turned toward the noise.

Are they coming for me now? she wondered.

She had no idea what the English might do to her, an Irish girl they probably assumed was a spy for the heathens. Maybe they would just leave her in that cell to die of thirst, but she doubted that. Before they killed her they would want to hear everything she could tell them about the hated Northmen. After that, who knew? Beheaded? Burned at the stake? Drawn and quartered? Any of those seemed likely.

So as she listened to the sound of the men coming closer she wondered if they would drag her from her cell and do whatever they had to do to extract the truth. And if so, would she tell them the truth? And if she did, would it make things better or worse? Or could she hope to lie her way out of it?

No… she thought. *That's not it.*

She could hear struggling and shouting. It sounded as if another prisoner was being brought to a cell, one who was far less cooperative than she had been.

A door opened in the hall, from the sound of it one of the doors near hers, and then more shouting and then the door closed again and a bar fell into place. Failend sprang to her feet and crossed over to the door of her cell and pressed her ear against it, listening to this new man pounding and shouting in words Failend could not understand.

The voice, however, she did know. Or at least she thought she did. She waited until she heard the door at the far end of the hall slam shut and the man behind the other door fall silent. She pressed close to her own door, lips near the wood, and called as loud as she dared, "Louis?"

There was no answer at first, and she was about to call out again when she heard the reply, across the width of the hall and through two heavy oak doors. "Failend?"

She smiled. It was a voice she knew so well. A voice that had seduced her once, then given her the chance to embrace a savage part of life, the life of a warrior, something she had not even known she craved. A voice that had been present through every possible emotion: desire, terror, rage, love, exhilaration. Louis de Roumois. How did he happen to be there?

"Yes, Louis, it's me!" Failend shouted, louder this time. "How are you here?"

"We came looking for you," Louis said, speaking loudly in his Frankish-tainted Irish. "Thorgrim and some of the others. We were all taken. Foolishness. It wasn't my idea," he said, and then added, "But I came, of course."

Failend stared at the grain of the wood in the door and tried to understand what Louis had said.

They came for me?

She would not have thought that would happen. How did they know she was here?

"Is Thorgrim there with you? Or in one of these other cells?" she called.

"No," Louis called back. "Just me. They're still in the prison. I think. Somewhere on the far side of the great hall. I don't know where, exactly. There's nothing we can do for them." He paused, then added, "Or for ourselves, I imagine."

There were a hundred things Failend wanted to ask, to understand, but it was hard to shout through the thick doors. Louis was speaking as loud as he could, she could tell, but she could still just barely hear him, and she imagined he could hardly hear her at all. She sighed and stepped away from the door. She would give her throat a rest and try again.

She paced back and forth in the dim light of the single flame, her mind moving fast and far, though her body was confined to that tiny space. She thought of Thorgrim and the others coming for her. Which others? Harald, certainly. Godi. Starri. Starri would never stand for being left behind. And Louis, who seemed to think that the whole thing was madness, but he came anyway.

They had come to save her. Had Thorgrim just guessed that she had gone to Winchester? How would he guess that, and how would he know she was in trouble?

Wolf dream?

Failend stopped as the thought came to her. Is that how he knew? At the thought of it she made the sign of the cross. She was about to call to Louis once more, to ask if that was it, when she heard another sound, the sound of the door opening at the far end of the hall. She had heard it several times now and she recognized it, and it made her stop in her pacing. She stood motionless, listening.

Is this it now? she wondered. She heard steps in the hall, the soft footfalls of leather shoes on the unyielding stone. The steps came closer and finally stopped, not too far away. She heard a voice. "Failend?"

"Father? Father Conall?" Failend called. "I'm here!" She banged on her door and heard the steps come closer, heard the heavy bar lifted from the door. The door swung open and in the light of the lanterns lining the hall she saw Father Conall standing there in his long brown robe, a bundle in his hands.

"Ah, yes, you are!" Father Conall said and smiled. "You're not hurt?"

No," Failend said. "No." She stepped out into the hall. The priest had not invited her to do so, but with the door open she could not stand to remain in the cell a moment longer. "What are you doing here?" she asked.

"I've come to give you the Eucharist," he said. "After such a confession as you made. That's what I told the guards."

"Oh," Failend said. It was something she wanted, of course, the body of Christ, but somehow she had thought there was more to the priest's arrival.

"And I've come to get you out of here," Father Conall went on. "You have to get out. They'll…" He shook his head. "I don't want to think what they'll do to you."

"I guessed it would not go easy for me," Failend said. "So I've been thinking about how I might make it better. And I thought, what if I told them the truth? Confessed to the bishop, the way I confessed to you?"

Father Conall shook his head. "No," he said. "Even if the bishop believes your story, he'll have no sympathy for you. A fornicator. A killer. A woman who chose to join with the heathens. Chose to fight against King Æthelwulf."

"But I've been forgiven those things."

"Yes, in the eyes of God," Father Conall said. "Not in the eyes of the bishop, I wouldn't think."

Failend opened her mouth, ready with her next thought, but the priest cut her off. "And you can't lie to them. They'll know it if you do, and it will be worse for you. No, you have to run. I have to get you out of here. It's the only way. I brought this."

He held up the bundle in his arms and Failend could see it was a brown robe like the one Father Conall was wearing. Failend looked at the bundle and then up at the priest. And then she remembered they were not alone.

"Louis!" she called in a sharp whisper. "Louis, where are you?"

"Here," she heard his voice through the door across the hall from hers and down one. She stepped over and lifted the bar that secured the door and pulled it open. Louis was there, framed in the doorway. Failend hugged him, buried her head in his chest, and wished for that fleeting second she could just remain like that, pressed against him, with no other considerations in the world.

"Failend, what's this about?" Father Conall asked. Failend released Louis and turned. The priest was staring at them and Failend could see the suspicion in his eyes, the concern on his face, the fear he had made a grave misjudgment.

"This is Louis..." Failend said. "Louis de Roumois. He's a Frank. A Christian. He was an acolyte in the monastery at Glendalough. He was with me when the Northmen took us."

Father Conall nodded and seemed somewhat mollified by this explanation.

Failend turned to Louis. "Father Conall has come to get me out...get us out," she said.

"I have only the one robe," Father Conall said, holding it up. "I don't know how..."

"You meant to dress Failend in that?" Louis asked in his accented Irish. "Walk her out of here?"

Father Conall nodded.

"Aren't there guards down there?" Louis asked, nodding toward the door at the end of the hall.

"Yes. Two," Father Conall said. He spoke with hesitation, as if he knew the question that would come next.

"How did you mean to get past them?" Louis asked. "You come in here, one man, but two leave?"

Father Conall did not reply. It was clear to Failend that he had no plan for that. That he was relying on divine intervention of some sort. And maybe it had just arrived.

"Two guards," Failend said, turning to Louis. "Is that a problem?"

Louis shrugged. "A problem for them, maybe."

It took only a few moments to prepare. The three of them went to the end of the hall, taking care to make no noise. Failend and Louis positioned themselves on either side of the door, backs against the wall. Father Conall then opened the door and called to the guards in English, something urgent-sounding, and he held the door open for them as they hurried past. As they did, Louis grabbed the shoulder of the second man through and spun him around until they were face to face.

The guard held a spear, an unwieldy weapon in those close quarters, and wore a mail shirt and helmet, which meant that most of him was pretty well protected against attack from an unarmed man. Most, but not all. His face was still quite vulnerable, and that was what Louis drove his fist into, connecting with the guard's left cheek, snapping his head around and sending him reeling against the stone wall.

The sound caught the attention of the first guard, who turned quick, his mouth open to shout in surprise. He was looking at Louis when Failend whirled the iron lamp in her hand around as fast and as high as she could and crashed it into the side of the man's head.

His helmet absorbed much of the blow, but it still sent him stumbling. He dropped his spear as he tried to keep his feet and Louis snatched the helmet off and drove a fist into the man's temple in one swift and smoothly executed motion.

The guard made a grunting noise as he dropped and Louis turned to the first man, who was near recovering from the punch in the face. He whipped that man's helmet off too and dealt out the same punishment, and he, too, dropped with a grunting sound. For a moment there was nothing to hear but Louis's huffing as he tried to recover his breath.

"They're…they're not dead, are they?" Father Conall asked.

"No, no, they'll be fine," Louis said but Failend was not sure that was true. They would not die from the blows Louis had given them, but what might happen to them for letting the prisoners escape was another matter.

Louis knelt down over the guard who was closest to him in size and began tugging his mail shirt off, and Failend knelt beside him to help.

"What are you doing?" Father Conall asked. "We should go."

"You only have one robe," Failend said. "Louis needs this mail and helmet so he can look like one of the guards." Father Conall made no reply to that, and soon Louis and Failend had the belt and mail off the guard and Louis slipped it on over his head, strapped on the belt and set the helmet on his head.

There was a knife and a small purse hanging from the guard's belt, and a purse on the other guard's belt as well, so Louis pulled his newly acquired knife from its scabbard and cut the other purse free.

Failend wondered if Father Conall would object, but if he noticed he said nothing.

"I've spent so damned much time in English armor of late," Louis said, "I'm practically an Englishman now."

Next Failend pulled the robe Father Conall had brought her over her head and settled it down. It was a good fit, made for a boy, Failend guessed. The three of them dragged the semi-conscious guards into the nearest cell and barred the door, then stepped out into the big room at the entrance to that wing of the hall. There was no one there, happily. Father Conall opened the door out to the yard beyond and they stepped out into the night, and still they could see no one.

Failend breathed deep and looked around. In her cell she had lost any sense for the time of day, but now she could see it was very late at night, or, more likely, very early in the morning. There was no bustle of anyone at work, no indication that anyone in the whole world was awake. She imagined there were guards walking the top of the wall, but she could not see them, and she was sure they could not see her or Father Conall or Louis.

"There is a door, just over there," Father Conall said to Louis, pointing across the dark ground. "Used mostly by servants and such. There may be a guard there, but I doubt it. You should be able to walk right through."

Louis nodded. "I know you didn't come to help me, Father," he said, "but I'm grateful that you did."

"Of course," Father Conall said, though it occurred to Failend that she had not given him much choice in the matter.

Louis turned to her. "Come along, Failend, we need to go," he said. "They'll find out about our escape soon enough."

"Ah…" Failend said, and she felt her heart turn over. She had put considerable thought into what she would do next, and had arrived at some difficult decisions. But she forgot that Louis was not privy to them.

"Umm…I'm not going with you, Louis," she said.

That was met with a brief silence and then Louis said, "Not going with me?"

"No," Failend said. "I'm done. This…all this…this life as a warrior. This was what I needed. Back, a long time ago. In Ireland. And then we had no choice, you know. When we met with Thorgrim, and we were his prisoners. And then…well…I wanted one thing and you wanted another, but for our own reasons we stayed with Northmen. But now I have to be done with that. Now I need my life to be different."

Louis nodded and seemed to be considering those words. Failend wondered if he would protest, try to talk her out of her choice, but he said, "What will you do? Stay here? Go back to Ireland?"

"I don't know," Failend said. "I don't know what I'll do. Once I get to a safe place, I'll figure that out. I'll look to God for guidance."

"He's guided your steps so far," Father Conall said. "And he will again. And now He's telling me we should go."

"Of course," Failend said. She turned to Louis. "You'll tell Thorgrim? Tell him what I've done? Tell him…you can tell him I loved him. That I love him."

Louis nodded and the two of them fell silent, looking into each other's eyes. So much to say, so much had passed between them. A week would not be enough to say it all. She stepped toward him and wrapped her arms around him as best she could, pressing herself close, feeling the smooth, cool links of mail against her cheek. She felt his arms tighten around her.

"And I love you, too, Louis de Roumois," she said. "God speed you."

"And God speed you, Failend," he said. He eased his hug and she stepped back. She looked at his face, his lovely face, one last time. And Louis looked at her as well, and gave a hint of a smile, then turned and walked off into the dark.

Chapter Thirty-Eight

Such grief he has, for rage he's like to split,
A little more, and he has lost his wit:
Says to that count: "I love you not a bit;
A false judgement you bore me when you chid."

Song of Roland

It was easier than Louis dared hope it would be. He crossed the open ground between the great hall and the stone wall that enclosed all of the king's residence, and as his eyes adjusted to the dark, after the relative brightness of the lantern light, he could see the door that Father Conall had indicated. It was just visible in the light of a quarter moon, standing out against the darker wall, and the path underfoot led in that direction.

His thoughts were not on where he was going, or how he would manage his escape. He was thinking about Failend, and the choice she had made, and all the strange adventures they had shared. He wondered if he would ever see her again. He imagined not.

With his mind thus occupied Louis didn't see the guard posted by the door until he had almost reached him, but he managed to hide his surprise. The man was standing quite still and he seemed to meld into the dark. Louis tried to keep his pace casual as he considered the best approach — bluff his way out or fight? — but he had still not decided by the time he reached the guard and the door.

As it turned out, no decision was needed. The guard did not move at all as Louis approached, save to nod in Louis's direction. Louis was, after all, armed and dressed the same as he was. What's more, Louis was not trying to get into the royal estate, he was trying to leave, so there was no real cause for alarm or suspicion.

Louis nodded back as he passed, lifted the iron hasp on the door, swung it open and stepped through, and with an overwhelming sense of relief closed it behind him.

Now what? he thought, though he kept walking as he wrestled with that question. For more than three years now he had entertained only one goal, one driving vision: return to Frankia and avenge himself on his brother. That had not changed. It had only become considerably harder.

All this time he had imagined he would return to Roumois and the men-at-arms, his old comrades, would rally to him. The people of Roumois would side with him after they learned what his brother had done in banishing him to Glendalough. Louis was well liked by the people — he and his men had been protecting them from the depredations of the Northmen for years — and he did not doubt they would assist him in taking his vengeance.

He realized now those thoughts were ridiculous, naive, the daydreams of a child. The world was far more complicated than that. It wasn't just his brother he had to contend with, and it wasn't just Roumois. Eberhard had ingratiated himself into the court of Charles the Bald, had managed to convince the king that he, Louis, was the traitor, a threat to the peace in Western Frankia. Undoing that would be considerably more difficult.

He crossed over the open area surrounding the king's residence and into one of the narrow streets that led to the main gate in the city wall, or in that general direction. He had no idea how long it would be before the gate opened at dawn, but he knew he would have to wait until then. There was no talking his way out when he did not know the language, and an English guard who did not speak English would be very suspicious indeed.

Why am I still wearing this mail and helmet? he wondered. There was no longer any advantage in walking around dressed as a man-at-arms. There was too great a chance that one of the other king's men would try to speak with him. In his regular clothing he would be taken for one of the many foreign merchants who traveled to all of the places of worth in Engla-land.

He paused in the shadows and listened but he could hear nothing beyond the scurrying of some little nocturnal creature. He pulled the helmet off and then the belt and mail shirt. He buckled the belt around his tunic and stuffed the rest down behind a couple of old barrels pushed up against the wall. He listened some more. Still nothing. He stepped out of the shadows and continued on down the deserted road.

Soon the cluster of buildings began to thin out and Louis knew he was approaching the outer wall that formed a ring around all of Winchester, and that was as far as he could go until the sun was up and the main gate opened for the day. A wheel barrow was pushed up against a wattle fence and he sat down in it and made himself as comfortable as he could and waited for the light to come.

He did not think there was much chance of his falling asleep and he was right. He stared off into the dark, his eyes wide open, his mind tumbling along like water running down a mountain stream. His return to Roumois had just become considerably more complicated, and so had his ability to get there. He had remained with Thorgrim all this time simply because Thorgrim was trying to return to Norway, which meant he had to cross over to Frankia at some point, and that would at least get Louis on the right side of the water.

Louis had even toyed with the idea of enlisting Thorgrim to help him in his fight against his brother. That, of all his plans, seemed the most dubious, and he went back and forth. Sometimes he thought it was a brilliant idea, a natural union, the reason God had put him in Thorgrim's way, and other times he was disgusted that he could even entertain the idea of making a pact with a man who was clearly Satan's minion on earth.

But none of that mattered now. Thorgrim was locked away in a prison in Winchester, thanks to his own rash ideas and his ridiculous belief in his "wolf dreams". He would not be going to Norway. After Winchester, Thorgrim's next port of call would most likely be Hell. He could be no help to Louis anymore.

Louis doubted that the other one, Bergthor, would be going to Norway either, or that he, Louis, would be welcome in that company in any case. Joining with the heathens had taken him that far, but it would take him no farther.

Lunden, maybe? Louis mused, considering his next move. He had heard of this place Lunden, on a big river, apparently just a few days' ride from Winchester. Quite a number of ships going in and out, he had heard: a good chance he might find passage to Frankia. The purses he had liberated from the guards were hanging from his belt.

It was still too dark to see what was in them, but judging by their weight they seemed to hold a respectable number of coins, or perhaps bits of silver.

I could buy a horse, he thought next. He pictured himself making his way across the countryside and the thought of walking held little appeal. He could most likely buy a horse right there in Winchester. He did not need to speak to do that, the silver would do all the talking for him. Buy a horse, ride to Lunden, sell the horse and get passage to Frankia. Figure out what to do in Roumois once he got there.

Yes, yes, that makes sense, Louis thought, and he smiled in the dark. He shuffled up onto the bed of the barrow and leaned against its side. He was not comfortable by any means, but he was close enough.

Sleep was coming on in fits and starts when the light of dawn began to spread over the narrow streets. Louis shook himself awake and slid off the barrow, glad he had not been discovered by its owner, who might not appreciate his using it as a bed. He stretched and scratched and knew there was something pressing down on his thoughts, something that had happened that was coloring his mood.

Failend... he remembered. She had gone off, to do what he had no idea. And neither did she, it appeared. For more than two years now she had been a part of his life, sometimes a friend, sometimes an enemy. Sometimes, way back, a lover. But always there. And now she was gone.

Louis shook his head, surprised at how deeply he felt Failend's absence. For years now his thoughts had been directed at his return to Roumois and nothing else. He was barely aware of any other considerations floating around in his mind.

I wonder... he thought as he started to walk. *I wonder what else is buried in there.* But such worries were for poets — skalds as the Northmen called them — or philosophers, and Louis knew he was neither, so he tried to push them aside.

He had a purpose now, a task at hand. A horse. Buy a horse. He walked slowly down one of the streets looking for some place where he might accomplish such a thing. He did not know if it was even possible in Winchester, or if he would have to go back to one of the farms he had passed on the way there.

And then, at the far end of the next street over, he saw what looked very much like a stable. He stopped and took the purses off his belt and poured the contents into his palm. There were a few bits of what looked like an armband cut up into short segments, but the rest were coins, silver coins.

Of the coins, most were stamped with the profile of a man with flowing hair and wearing some sort of robe. Louis guessed he was an English king, maybe the one who had been wounded in the recent fight. There were letters running around the edge of the coin, and though Louis could read Frankish and Latin and Greek he could not figure out what the letters spelled. He imagined that they spelled the man's name.

Not all of the coins appeared to be of English minting. One he recognized as Frankish; a few of the others seemed to have come from the Moorish countries. One was so old the markings were worn almost completely away.

Such a lot of wealth for a couple of pitiful guards, Louis thought. *I wonder where they got all this.* Then he smiled. The guards had plundered it from Thorgrim and the others after they had been taken prisoner, that was the most obvious explanation. Louis knew that his own purse had been taken.

Maybe I've stolen back that which was once mine, Louis thought. *Mine, after I stole it from someone else.*

Wherever the silver came from, it was Louis's now, and it should be more than enough to buy a horse. He poured the money back into one of the purses and continued on toward the stable. He could hear feet shuffling around, the occasional grunt and soft whinny as he drew closer. Louis looked over the wattle fence that formed the perimeter of the yard in which the stable stood. He could see a large man with a pitchfork tossing hay to a half dozen horses standing in their stalls.

Good, good, Louis thought. He walked through the break in the fence and approached, his eyes moving up and down each horse in turn. One, he could see, was far superior to the rest, a strong-looking chestnut beast, good hindquarters, a decent length of neck.

No, you idiot, you only have to ride to Lunden, Louis chastised himself. His inclination was always to go for the best possible mount, but there was no reason to pay for the best now.

He took a few more steps toward the stable and the man with the pitchfork finally noticed him. He turned, holding the pitchfork level, not a threatening gesture but one that made it clear the tool would make an effective weapon, if needed.

"I would like to buy a horse," Louis said. He spoke Frankish on the off chance that the man did as well, but he also pointed to the horse he wished to buy — not the worst in the stable but not the fine chestnut he had looked at first — and shook the purse that hung from his belt.

He saw the understanding come over the man's face. He lowered the pitchfork, nodded and spoke in what Louis assumed was English. He half turned and pointed toward the horse Louis had indicated.

Louis nodded and fished in his purse for a half dozen of the silver coins. He held them out on his palm as if he was offering the man a treat, but the stableman looked at the coins, frowned and shook his head.

You damned thief, Louis thought. The horse was not worth even that amount. But Louis did not wish to haggle, he wished to get a horse and get away from Winchester before he was missed, so he pulled out a few more coins and offered those as well.

At that the stableman's face brightened quite a bit and he nodded and snatched up the coins. He fetched the horse from the stall and led it over to Louis who ran his hand over its neck and flank and thought, *It should live long enough to get me to Lunden, at least.*

There followed more pantomime negotiations as Louis bought an old bridle and a battered and patched saddle for considerably more than they were worth. When he was done he saddled his mount and rode off, still irritated that the stableman thought he had pulled the wool over his eyes.

Bastard can't wait to tell how he made a fool of some idiot Frank, Louis thought. *Well, once they find out he helped a prisoner escape they'll probably cut his head off.*

It was a nice thought, and it made Louis happy for a moment, until he forced himself to think of other things.

By the time Louis arrived at the main gate, keeping his horse to a walking pace, there was already a fair amount of traffic going in and out. There were guards there as well, a half dozen or so. They were looking over everyone who came and went, but not with any great interest.

Louis watched a cart laden with something and covered with a tarpaulin roll past uninspected.

If the guards were told to look out for me they would certainly have searched the back of the cart, Louis figured. He took that as a good sign.

He approached the gate with a studied calm, an expression that was close to bored, looking as much as he could like a man who rode in and out of Winchester on a regular basis. He fell in behind a man pushing a wheel barrow along, full of something Louis could not identify.

As he reached the gate he looked down at the guard standing there, gave a bit of a smile and nodded in greeting. The guard nodded back and seemed not in the least interested in what Louis was up to, and not even very interested in returning the salutation. The man looked away and then Louis was through the gate, Winchester behind him, the Roman road and all of Engla-land spread out before.

He did not increase his pace at all as he continued along the road. He would figure out how to get to Lunden, somehow, once he was out of sight of the gate. But first he had to put distance between him and the city. He did not think it would be long before he was discovered missing, and when he was then the hunt would begin in earnest. Felix seemed to wield a lot of influence in the English king's court, and Felix seemed very much to want Louis in captivity.

The travelers on the road became sparser as Louis left Winchester behind, until finally he was all but alone. He continued on along the Roman road for a mile or so, then stopped at a place where the road was intersected by another that was clearly built by a civilization not quite so advanced. He turned his horse around and looked back toward Winchester. He could see nothing now but the spires and the upper edge of the wall. There was no indication of any alarm, or anything amiss.

He looked to his right, where the dirt road ran off toward the north-east, which was roughly the direction he thought Lunden to be. He suspected that there was another Roman road on the far side of Winchester, and that that road would lead to Lunden, or thereabouts. As he understood it, Lunden had always been an important place, even back to ancient times, and so the Romans would have built roads leading there.

I should just ride off on this dirt road, Louis thought. *Skirt around Winchester, pick up the Roman road on the other side.* He nodded to himself. That made sense.

He looked back at Winchester. He thought of Thorgrim and the others, probably still locked up in that lightless prison. They would be sitting on the floor, staring at the dark in silence, waiting for what would come next.

Stupid heathen bastards, Louis thought. *It was their fault. Thorgrim's fault. Riding right into Winchester like that, no real thought as to what they would do. Of course it had ended with the lot of them locked in a prison until their execution. What else could they expect?*

He did it to save Failend, Louis thought next, with an uncomfortable twinge in his mind. Stupid, yes, but they hadn't gone to Winchester for plunder or any of their heathen savagery. Thorgrim probably knew from the outset how foolish and futile it was — the man was not actually stupid, Louis could admit that much — but he had gone in anyway because he believed Failend was in danger. And he had been right.

Well, it was a good show, but he didn't do her any good, Louis thought next. *It was me who saved her. Me and that priest.*

He continued to stare blankly at Winchester's spires, his mind tumbling around.

Of course, you wouldn't have been there to save her if Thorgrim had not led us all there in the first place…

He could picture what would happen to them: Thorgrim, Harald, Godi. Hall, Gudrid. Starri Deathless. Burned at the stake, most likely. That seemed like the sort of thing that would appeal to these English.

The heathens would not go easily, that was certain. They would fight, and maybe half of them would be killed in that futile effort. Those still alive would be tied to the stakes, dry branches piled around their feet.

Just like they had almost done to him and Harald, once. He had almost died the same way, before Thorgrim stepped in.

"Oh, *merde*," Louis said out loud.

Chapter Thirty-Nine

Here shall never
men inflict harm
on one another,
evil do or kill.

The Poetic Edda

The point of land to larboard, around which Amundi was steering, had been doing far more to block the wind than he had quite realized. The boat was taking a beating from the gale and the seas it kicked up: even with the sail reduced they had been heeling hard, the canvas and rigging stretched to near breaking. Every now and again a gust would dip the leeward rail, scooping up a great mass of water and sending the men to wildly bailing once again.

At least they were free of Skorri and his band, even if they still had the seas and the wind to contend with. Skorri's boat was stove in, his rig collapsed into a heap. Amundi glanced astern as often as he could, hoping to see the entire thing slip under the surface, but he did not get that satisfaction.

Still, what he saw was satisfying enough: the crippled boat, drifting out of control toward a rocky shore hidden by the driving rain. It would be some time before Skorri was any concern of his, if ever again.

Finally Skorri's boat was lost from view, which was just as well because Amundi had all he could contend with directly ahead of him. For hours they had been trying to weather the point of land, but as they made northing around it Amundi could feel the wind gaining in strength, could hear the note it made in the rigging rising in pitch. The boat was pressed down harder, and now it scooped water with every other dip in the waves. They could not go on that way.

"Thord!" Amundi shouted. "Thord!" Thord looked up from where he was hunkered down below the rail.

"Haul up that leeward clew!" Amundi called, pointing to the corner of the sail that was pulled down to the starboard side of the boat. They had to reduce sail even further, and the only way to do that now was to haul part of it up to the yard.

Thord nodded and slapped Onund on the shoulder to get his attention. He pointed to the leeward sheet, the line holding the clew down, and Onund nodded. Then the two men made their way carefully down to the low side of the boat, careful not to get knocked off their feet in the violent rolling, careful not to get flung on top of Odd who was still lying in the bottom.

Finally they had the lines in hand, and with a nod from Thord Onund began easing out the sheet while Thord hauled on the clewline which pulled the corner of the sail up. It flogged and banged and twisted as Thord fought with it. Oleif slid down to the low side and grabbed the rope as well and soon they had the clew pulled up. That done, the motion of the boat became noticeably easier, and their speed noticeably slower.

This won't do, Amundi thought. They had sailed clean away from Skorri. There was no reason to keep risking all their lives on the open ocean. He looked off to larboard as more and more of the north shore of the point came into view.

There must be some place there to land…

Amundi's eyes were not the keenest, and they were not helped by the driving rain and the fog that half-covered the shore, but he was fairly sure he could see a beach a mile or so away.

"Oleif!" he called and the young slave made his way carefully aft. Amundi pointed. "Is that a beach over there?"

For a moment Oleif was silent, staring through the rain. "I think so," he said.

"Good enough," Amundi said. "Go tend to the sheets and tell the others to help and to tend the braces as well. We're going to come about!"

Oleif nodded and moved off in the crab-like way they were forced to move on the wildly bucking craft. He grabbed each man in turn and shouted out Amundi's orders and the men moved off to tend the various lines. Soon they were all in place, lines in hand, ready to swing the yard and sail around as the boat turned.

Amundi nodded to them and then turned his attention to the seas rolling in. If he timed this wrong, if he got the boat caught between two waves, then there was a chance that the sea would roll them right over. Amundi did not fear death in general, but he feared a watery death. He hated the thought of drowning when he had just declined the chance to go down fighting.

The bow of the boat slid into a trough between the waves, dipping down then rising on the next roller coming in. The wave moved under, lifting the stern, and at that moment Amundi put the tiller over, turning the boat on the rising sea. The yard came swinging around overhead as the stern of the boat moved through the eye of the wind.

And then they were around, the boat running west, the long point of land on their larboard side and stretching out ahead. The motion was diffcrent now, with the wind more astern. The boat lifted and twisted and settled as the seas moved under, and Amundi worked the tiller side to side to keep them running straight.

His arm ached from the effort, but he had the feel for the boat and he did not dare turn the steering over to anyone else. He had stopped shivering a while before and he did not think that was a good thing. Time to get ashore.

The waves were lifting the boat and sending it hurling along. Amundi stood as best he could and sighted down the shoreline to the spot that he took for a beach. They were already noticeably closer, close enough that he could see it was indeed a beach, a stretch of gravelly sand about a hundred yards long, an easy target even in those conditions.

He pushed the tiller a bit to one side, lining the bow up with the open place. "We're going ashore, right up there!" he shouted as loudly as he could. The boat surfed along with its crazy motion and Amundi continued to fight the tiller until the last of his strength had nearly drained from his arm. But before it was gone completely, they were there.

The beach was as good as he hoped, wet shingle that eased its way down into the sea, no surprise outcroppings of rock to snatch the bottom of the boat clean out. The surf picked them up and flung them forward and drove the bow into the gravel with a loud crunching sound.

The abrupt stop sent the men on the thwarts tumbling and nearly tossed them into the bottom of the boat, but they managed to retain their seats. Four of the men jumped over the side and hauled the boat farther up the beach, but the sea had already deposited them pretty high.

Amundi stood, every muscle protesting, his soaked clothes heavy on his shoulders. "Let's get ashore, get Odd ashore," he said, though the others were already passing those things they would need to bring with them to the men on the beach. Signy drew back the fur that covered Odd and Amundi could see Odd was blessedly dry. His head moved side to side and his eyes opened and he half sat up, looking around with bewilderment.

"We have to get off the boat, my love," Signy said, putting a hand under Odd's arm. Thord came up on the other side and together they lifted Odd to his feet.

"Some of you, come help with Odd!" Thord shouted. "Help us lift him off!"

"No, no," Odd said and his voice was surprisingly strong. "No, I can do it myself."

Thord looked back at Amundi, clearly wondering if Odd should be allowed to try. Amundi nodded his head.

Odd made his way carefully to the side of the boat and slowly, deliberately, swung a leg over the side. Thord and Signy hovered near to help, and on the beach others stood ready to catch him, but Odd swung the other leg over and dropped down to the sand on his own. He staggered a bit and made a sound like the breath had been knocked out of him, but he kept to his feet with the help of a few hands holding his arms.

Amundi climbed over the side next as the others distributed weapons and the little food they had, and drank the last of the fresh water. The rain had eased off some, which was a blessing, though they were all soaked through, save for Odd. Alfdis put a cape around Odd's shoulders and pinned the brooch.

"Odd! Odd, my boy, how are you?" Amundi said, though as the words left his lips it seemed like a foolish question. Odd was not well, clearly. But Odd gave a weak smile and nodded his head.

"Not my best, Amundi, old friend," he said. "But my strength returns."

"We'll rig up a stretcher to carry you in," Amundi said. "We have to get going, get north, quick as we can."

"No, no," Odd said. "I can walk. I won't be more of a burden." Amundi was about to protest but he could see in Odd's face that he was not just being polite, not just being considerate. He needed to do this. He needed to walk on his own legs. The old Odd was coming back.

They headed off the beach and walked west along the point of land. The country was mostly low hills, like gentle ocean rollers, with granite outcroppings and patches of brush and trees here and there, and the going was not hard. And that was good, because Amundi could tell that Odd was not nearly as strong as he was pretending to be. But he kept up, his pace did not falter.

As they walked Amundi told Odd of what had happened over the past week or so, almost none of which Odd could recall. He described Halfdan's arrival at his hall, the scene there, the rescue, Onund's decision to help Amundi. He told him about the boat and Skorri, and it was clear that Odd had been oblivious to all of it, from the moment he had attacked the guards until just then. It was astounding to Amundi, but had obviously done Odd considerable good.

"Where now?" Odd asked. They were getting closer to where the point of land they were on met the mainland. They could see the broken coastline stretching away to the north.

"I don't know," Amundi said. "We have to get north, because Halfdan is to the south. And Skorri, too, if he and his men lived to get ashore. But I don't know for certain where we are. Do you?"

Odd shook his head. "Nothing here is familiar to me," he said.

Amundi looked back at the others. "Any of you know where we are?" That was met by shaking heads, mostly. But one man named Kormak spoke up.

"I think we're some miles south of Fevik. I've sailed this way before. I think Vifil Helgason's farm is not too far from here. But I don't know for certain."

Amundi nodded. It was not much information, but it was more than he had before.

They continued on, the sky growing darker as the daylight neared its end. The rain had turned to a heavy mist, which was not as miserable, but close. It was not a terribly cold day but would get much colder as the dark came on. Amundi figured they would have to keep walking, even in the dark, if they did not find shelter. They were too cold and wet to do otherwise.

How much longer can Odd keep going? Amundi wondered. He was still keeping pace with the others, Signy on one side, Thord on the other, but Amundi could see he was growing weaker, stumbling more often, his insistence that he was fine growing less emphatic.

We'll make a stretcher soon, Amundi thought. *Hold a knife to his throat if he won't let us carry him.*

They moved inland, the shoreline behind them now, the rolling country stretching away ahead, growing less visible in the fading light.

"If we're where I think we are," Kormak said, "there should be a road ahead somewhere. Take it north and we'll come to Vifil Helgason's farm. I think."

The word *farm*, with its suggestion of a warm hall and a fire and food and drink seemed to buoy them all. Their pace increased, their steps less shuffling, even Odd's. They crossed a half mile of field through knee-high grass, the land tending gently uphill, and came at last to the road that Kormak had thought might be there. It was a muddy, beaten, rutted track, but it was one of the most beautiful things any of them had seen in some time.

Signy came up beside Amundi as they trudged along north. "Odd cannot go much longer," she said. "He'll drop in his tracks before he admits it, but I can tell."

Amundi nodded. "I'm glad to see the old, stubborn Odd is back. But you're right. We can't let him keep on."

There was a jumble of low granite ledges ahead, convenient places to sit, so Amundi said to the company, "Let's give our legs a rest, have a seat up here." That was met with a general groan of relief, and the weary band shuffled the last fifty feet and found places to sit on the wet rock.

Once they had settled and rested a few moments Amundi called Oleif and Kormak to him. "There was a stand of small trees back down the road, not far. Go cut a couple of saplings so we can make a stretcher to carry Odd. I don't think he can keep on like this much longer."

The two men nodded then hurried back down the road in the gathering gloom of evening. It was good they were doing that now:

there would soon not be enough daylight left for them to see what they were doing.

Amundi took his place on the granite ledge and felt the weariness and the ache wash over him. Alfdis was going from man to man handing out chunks of bread, pretty much all the food they had with them. Amundi took it, gratefully, though he was not sure he had the energy to eat. He held the bread in his hand for a few moments, then lifted it to his mouth. He was just chewing the last of it when Oleif and Kormak returned, carrying two stout ten-foot poles between them.

"Odd," Amundi said, standing as he did. The daylight was almost gone now, he could barely make Odd out against the rock. "We're going to make a stretcher, bear you along from here." He held up his hand as the first protests came from Odd's lips. "No argument. We didn't go to this effort just to see you die on the road like a horse run to death."

Odd began to protest again but this time Signy hushed him and made him sit still as a couple of capes were lashed together to make the sling. Thord had had the good sense to bring some small rope with him and that was lashed to the corners of the capes. They were just starting to tie the sling to the poles when Oleif stood and cocked his ear.

"Riders," he said. "Close." Amundi frowned and listened but he could not hear anything. But he could see on the faces of some of the other men that Oleif was not the only one who heard them.

"Where are they coming from?" Amundi asked. "North or south?"

No one answered at first. At last Oleif said, "I can't tell."

And then Amundi could hear them as well: horses coming closer. They seemed to be coming at a slow trot, the sound of their hoof beats muffled by the rain and the road's soft mud. Like the others, he could not tell from what direction they were coming. He stood motionless and listened and he felt suddenly overwhelmed with exhaustion, unable to move, unable even to think of what he should do.

Signy was the next to speak. "We should not be on the road," she said. "Not until we know who this is."

That made considerable sense, enough to penetrate the fog in Amundi's mind. "Right," he said. "Let's find some place to hide and..."

It was as far as he got. Before he could finish the thought the riders were there, coming down the road from the north. A few of them carried torches against the darkness, with the result that Amundi could see little of them past the bright flames. He had no idea who these men were.

Beside him he heard the scrape of Thord drawing his sword as the other men took in hand the weapons they had salvaged from the boat. A few even had shields. Amundi drew his own sword and held it with the point lowered. He felt himself tense up, ready to move, the presence of danger bringing new energy.

Maybe the gods have given me a second chance to die with a weapon in my hand, he thought. Then the lead horse stopped, ten feet away, as the rider pulled the reins back and held the torch out at arm's length.

The rider spoke. One word. "Amundi?"

The voice was familiar, but it was not the one he had expected. It was not Skorri's. The rider nudged his horse forward a few feet and now the torchlight fell on his face, enough that Amundi could see it. A narrow face, a young face, dark beard, well-tended.

"Vifil Helgason?" Amundi said.

"Ha!" Vifil said, his voice sounding of surprise and pleasure and triumph, all at once. He slid down from his horse, torch in hand, smiling wide. He was wearing a mail shirt and had a sword on his waist. There was a shield hanging from his saddle.

"Amundi Thorsteinsson!" he said. He looked around. "And by the gods, Odd Thorgrimson! I thought it was too much to hope that we might find you!"

"Why were you looking for us?" Amundi asked.

"This fellow came by, fellow named Alf. He'd run away from Halfdan's army. Not sure why, he wouldn't tell us, really. Anyway, he was tired and hungry and said he'd trade us some news we might want for food and drink. He told us how you had stolen Odd from Halfdan, how you had escaped in a boat. We guessed you would come ashore near here, that you wouldn't want to stay in a boat any longer than you had to, not in this storm. So we came to look for you. Or at least find your bodies where you washed up on the beach."

Amundi smiled. He looked past Vifil to the other riders. There were thirty men at least. He could see spears and shields. A well-equipped war band, they had come ready to fight.

"I don't know if I've been more happy to see any man in my life," Amundi said, and he embraced Vifil. "We must get Odd on a horse, he doesn't have much strength left."

"We have horses," Vifil said. "We brought more horses, in case we were lucky enough to find you."

It was then that they heard the other riders, more hoof beats, not so far off, loud enough that all conversation stopped as they listened.

"More of your people?" Amundi asked.

"No," Vifil said. "All the men I brought are here with me. Don't know who this could be."

But Amundi did, he had an ugly feeling in the pit of his stomach. It did not seem possible: indeed, Amundi told himself it was not possible. The chances of Skorri making it to shore alive were very small. But even if he had, how would he get horses? How would he know to ride north in search of them? Wouldn't he go back to Halfdan's camp?

No, Amundi thought. *He would not go back to Halfdan's camp if he could not bring us in with him. He wouldn't tell Halfdan he had failed.*

"I think I know who this is," Amundi said, and as he did the horsemen seemed to appear out of the night, coming from the south.

There were around fifteen of them. They carried no torches, but the light from Vifil's torches fell over the men and horses in the lead, and touched those farther back. It illuminated the first of them, who reined to a stop ten feet away.

"Ah, Amundi," the man said. "We thought you would be here, scurrying north."

"Skorri," Amundi said. "I'd have thought the crabs would be making a meal of you by now. I see not. But there's still time."

Skorri's eyes moved beyond Amundi. "Odd, you look well," he said. "But we'll see to that. And you would be Vifil?"

"I would," Vifil said.

"Well, Vifil, I guess your work here is over. Take your men and go, and I suspect King Halfdan will forget what you've done tonight."

"Hmm," Vifil said. He folded his arms but did not move beyond that.

"Sorry, did you not hear me?" Skorri asked. "The more you help these criminals the less forgetful King Halfdan is likely to be."

"Yes, I understand," Vifil said. "But I'm not sure you have this right."

As if on some signal Vifil's men all dismounted, moving as one, the quiet evening filled with the sound of thirty armed men getting down from their horses, drawing weapons and setting shields on arms.

"I seem to have a lot more men than you," Vifil said. "And they seem to be better armed." He took a step forward and raised his torch higher, throwing more light on Skorri, and looked him over with a puzzled expression. "You don't seem to have mail, or a sword, or a shield," he said. "Or even a seax or a knife. Neither do you or you," he added, pointing at the men on either side of Skorri. "Are you certain you came here to fight? Are you sure you want to?"

Skorri scowled. It had apparently not occurred to him that he would need to do anything more than simply issue commands. It had apparently not occurred to him he might meet a war band stronger than his.

"You don't want to do this, Vifil Helgason," he said. "None of you," he continued, speaking so all could hear. "You don't want to bring Halfdan's wrath down on you."

A voice called out from somewhere back in the crowd of Vifil's men. "Halfdan can bring his lips down on my ass!" The men laughed and banged weapons on shields and that seemed to break the tension. Vifil smiled. Even Amundi found himself smiling.

"I'll give you one last chance…" Skorri said, loud, over the noise, but Vifil cut him off.

"Here's your choice, Skorri. You and your men get down and fight, or ride off. That's it. Choose now or by the gods we'll pull you down from those horses ourselves."

It was silent after that, save for the shuffling and snorting of the many horses and the occasional thump of a weapon against something. Skorri and Vifil glared at one another. Skorri spoke next.

"Odd Thorgrimson, you'll let these others die to protect you?"

"Yes, he will," Amundi said before Odd could answer. "We've given him no choice." He braced, waiting for Odd to speak, and when he didn't Amundi wondered if Signy had her hand over his mouth.

"Go, Skorri," Vifil said. "Go now."

For a moment more Skorri just stared at Vifil, stared at Amundi and the others. It seemed to hang there, teetering, the whole thing on a cliff edge. Then Skorri jerked the reins of his horse over hard and headed back down the road, the rest of his men following behind.

Vifil, Amundi and the rest remained motionless until the sounds of their horses' hooves could be heard no more.

"That was not wise, Vifil," Amundi said.

"No," Vifil said. "No, it wasn't."

Odd stepped up beside them. In the light of the torch they could see the weariness and the pain in his gaunt, lined face. "I wish you had not done that for me," he said.

"Well, you get your wish," Vifil said. "Because I didn't do it for you. Now, let's get you on a horse and get back to my hall. We have a lot to do, I think, to prepare for a visit from our king."

Amundi smiled, just a bit of a smile. Vifil spoke the truth. There was a lot to do. And Amundi was glad to do all of it and more, and he knew the others felt the same. To do, rather than to be done unto.

There would be time enough to worry about those things. It would be their reality tomorrow, and the next day and the next, stretching off farther than they could see.

But for now there was the hall at Vifil's farm. Warmth. Dry clothes. Hot food. A comfortable bed. For the moment that was as far as Amundi's mind could travel, as far as his imagination could reach.

Chapter Forty

The same year also Æthelwulf went to Rome
with great pomp, and was resident there a twelvemonth.
Then he returned homeward; and Charles, king of the Franks,
gave him his daughter, whose name was Judith,
to be his queen.

Anglo Saxon Chronicle

The witan met in King Æthelwulf's bedchamber. The king himself was propped up in the big wood-framed bed that occupied a respectable portion of the floor space. He wore a linen shirt, bleached to a brilliant white, against which the dark-brownish splotch of blood from his wound stood out in sharp relief.

Felix frowned a bit.

He knew two things for certain. One was that Æthelwulf had a number of shirts exactly like the one he was wearing, ones that did not have blood stains on them. The king had no need to wear the that one. The other thing that Felix knew was that Æthelwulf's wound had pretty much healed up. He did not really need to be in bed. But he seemed to be enjoying it, and the drama of the bloodstained shirt as well, and it did no harm, so Felix figured the old man might as well stay as he was, a near-martyr in his battle with the Godless.

Nor was it particularly unusual to conduct business in the royal bedchamber. It was, after all, a nice room. Not cavernous like the great hall so it was possible to keep it somewhat warm in the winter months. It was one of the few rooms in the king's residence, or anywhere in Winchester, that had windows with glass in them, so the room was often filled with natural light, a wonderful thing. The walls were hung with brightly colored, intricately woven tapestries that made the room seem almost cheery when the sun was streaming in.

But what most pleased Felix just then was the bedchamber's size, which was not great and so left no room for the minor thegns and lords with small holdings to attend. They were the ones, in Felix's experience, who often talked the most, hoping to impress the king with their words since they could not with their estates or the taxes they paid. And if a man was speaking just to impress, there was a good chance he had nothing very important to say.

The men who were there were the thegns with the greatest holdings, as well as the ealdormen who ruled over the various shires in Wessex. The men whose opinions mattered.

Four of the king's five sons were there as well. The oldest, Æthelstan, had died just a few years before, though he had lived long enough to be a king himself, ruler of Kent. The remaining boys were standing dutifully near their father's bed: Æthelbald, next in line for the crown of Wessex, Æthelberht, who was after him, Æthelred, seven years old, and the youngest, Alfred, who was six and, in Felix's mind, the most clever of the lot. It seemed a shame to Felix that with four brothers ahead of him in succession Alfred would likely never be king himself.

"The heathens seem to be staying put, licking their wounds," ealdorman Byrnhorn was saying. The discussion had just commenced: what were the heathens doing, what would they do next, what should the king do about it.

"We hurt them badly, under your highness's command," Alhmund added, nodding toward King Æthelwulf, who acknowledged him with a nod as well. "Maybe worse than we thought. Maybe they're patching themselves up and making ready to leave."

"Not sure they're doing that," said Leofric, who, having stood by Æthelwulf during the battle, had earned a higher status in the king's reckoning, and thus at court. "If the heathens just meant to leave they would not have taken Nothwulf prisoner and made him lead them right into the king's residence."

An uncomfortable silence followed that. The words were humiliating to Nothwulf, who, as ealdorman of Dorsetshire, was part of the bedchamber audience.

"I led them to where they might be captured," Nothwulf protested. "It's not as if…."

"I see Leofric's point," Byrnhorn interrupted. "Don't see why the heathens would have sent a scouting party, or whatever in God's name they were doing, into the city if they just meant to leave."

"They must have been spies," ealdorman Egbert chimed in. "Must have come to get a look at the defenses, the number of men-at-arms we have. Trying to figure if it would be a smart business to attack Winchester."

Heads nodded. Egbert's was, in fact, the most logical guess. But it was wrong. Thanks to Louis de Roumois, Felix alone knew the real reason the heathens were there. They had come to rescue the Irish girl.

Still, he kept silent. He did not know why she was so important to them, and telling the witan what he knew would only confuse matters. But he meant to find out, about the girl and about many other things, once he had another go at Louis. He intended to pry quite a bit of information from the traitorous bastard before he was done.

And, happily, they would soon after be going to Frankia, to the court of Charles the Bald, where Felix would be able to deliver Louis in person.

"Well, they'll not be bringing word back to the rest of the heathen camp now," King Æthelwulf said. "Thanks to the good work of my house guard. The Godless heathens back in Hamtun still know nothing of our strength, and they're not likely to find out."

"And what do we know of the heathens' strength?" asked Hereric, a thegn who had an estate to the north.

"Eleven ships," Felix said, his first words since the witan began. "Around five or six hundred men."

That was met with silence. The numbers were not too terribly intimidating — the king's army was about the same size, maybe even bigger. But the bulk of the king's men were made up of the fyrd, the folk called up to fight when needed. Soldiering was not their profession, whereas the heathens were all fighting men. They would not have come raiding if they were not. It made them a formidable enemy.

"Well, we beat the bastards once, like I said," Alhmund observed. "No reason to think we can't do it again."

This, too, was met with silence. There was more to it than that, but none of the men there wanted to say it. They had caught the heathens unprepared the first time, and sprung a trap on them. It was a brilliant move and it had worked brilliantly, but no one thought the heathens would fall for it, or anything like it, a second time.

"I agree that we're a near match for the heathens," Felix said. "But I'm not so certain we need to fight them just now."

This he knew was the most helpful thing he could do: express doubt, suggest caution, which the others could not, or would not, do. Felix was not playing the same game as the lords. He did not have to worry about his reputation, or fear that his words would make him appear timid. It did not matter to him.

"What do you mean by that, Felix?" Æthelwulf asked.

"I mean that you have your pilgrimage to consider, sire," Felix said. "Your visit to the court of Charles, your pilgrimage to Rome and a meeting with the Holy Father. Sure, we could fight the heathens, and I have no doubt we'd kill the lot of them. But such an effort would set us back weeks at least. More, if we suffered much at their hands. No, I say better to stay behind the walls of Winchester for the time being. I don't think the heathens will try to breach our walls. They'll tire of this place and move on."

"I think Felix makes good sense," Leofric said. "We hurt the heathens once, no reason to waste our men doing it again." He looked over at Æthelwulf and added, "No reason to risk your life, sire, when you've already been nobly wounded in battle."

Byrnhorn spoke next. He was one of the most powerful of the ealdormen and that gave him leeway to ask awkward questions. "I'd like to have at 'em, of course, just like we all would, but I can see the sense in this as well. But if the heathens do come to Winchester, we're sure we can defend the place with the men we have?"

That was something to consider. Winchester was a sizable city. It was ringed with a formidable wall, but a wall was only useful if there were men to defend it, men enough to keep an enemy from scaling it. With the soldiers they had, on a wall so big around, the defenses would be spread pretty thin. It might be difficult to hold off a determined enemy.

"We have more men coming," Felix said. "Men from Kent who will be here soon."

"Very well, then," King Æthelwulf said. "We keep an eye on the heathens, and if they seem as if they plan on going away then we let them. If they plan to make trouble then we'll give them trouble, two-fold. But what of the prisoners? What's to be done with them."

"Kill them," Felix said. "Kill the lot of them. Make an example."

"Are they of no use?" Byrnhorn asked. "Ransom, or information, or some such?"

"I think not, lord," Felix said. "I've had experience with these people. They're not of much use. Even if you can understand their barbarous language, they'll never tell the truth. And they won't pay ransom because there's not the least bit of loyalty or honor among them. But here's the interesting thing. There was a Frank in their company, a traitor to King Charles. I do believe I can get information from him that will be of use."

"Good, good," the king said. "Then on the morrow we'll see those dogs burned at the stake, the whole lot of them. I know there are some in Wessex who think they can profit from cooperating with the heathens. This should give them pause."

The witan moved on to other, less pressing business. Felix struggled to pay proper attention but his mind kept going back to Louis de Roumois and the Irish girl. What could possibly have driven Louis and the heathens to do so rash a thing as to ride straight into the lions' den?

I should find out soon enough, he thought. It occurred to him that he should make Louis watch the heathens go up in flames, let him hear the bastards screaming out the last seconds of their lives. That would no doubt encourage his cooperation.

The door opened, a servant slipped in and moved silently to Felix's side. "There's a soldier here would have a word with you, lord," he whispered.

Felix nodded and stood. He followed the man to the door and stepped into the hall, closing the door to the king's bedchamber behind him. A sense of dread was already rising in his chest.

There were two men standing there. One was the captain of the guard. The other was one of the captain's men, whose worried-looking face was marked by a great bruise on one side. He wore no belt and had no weapons on him and even without knowing the specifics Felix knew he would not like whatever he was about to hear.

"The prisoners, lord," the captain said, "the Frank and the Irish girl? They escaped, lord. Some priest helped them, or someone dressed like a priest, anyway."

Felix said nothing. He felt sick with this news. But in truth he was not terribly surprised. Louis might be a traitor, but he was smart and bold.

"When?" Felix asked.

"Early, lord," the man with the great bruise said. "Before dawn." Felix guessed this man was one of the guards who had allowed them to escape, but he had no time to think about punishment just then.

Before dawn. And now it was nearly noon.

"I want them found," Felix said. "Shut the gates, search the city. Everywhere. Ask the men at the gates if they saw anyone leave who might have been the prisoners. You understand?"

"Yes, lord," the captain said. He gave a hint of a bow and the other man did as well. "We'll find them, lord," the captain said and then they turned and hurried off.

Felix watched them go. *No, you won't,* he thought. *Louis, that whore's son, is too clever to be caught by the likes of you.*

Chapter Forty-One

Now that is come to pass
which I have hoped, that thou,
dear youth, again to my halls art come.

The Poetic Edda

It was all but completely black inside the little prison. The only light, the only indication of whether it was day or night, came from the tiny space between the bottom of the door and the stone threshold. Because of that, and that alone, Thorgrim knew more than a full day had passed since they were first shoved inside there, hands bound.

He had seen the space grow bright as dawn came the day after their first night as prisoners. There had been some quiet speculation among the seven men remaining as to what would become of them, some dark humor about their fates at the hands of the English. There had been some talk of when food of some sort and water might come their way.

But none of what they discussed came to pass. They had not been removed from their cell to be paraded in front of the city folk and then killed in some manner. They had not been given food or water. It was as if they had been forgotten entirely.

The light under the door grew dim and finally went out as the last of the day lapsed into night. The men grew quiet, too hungry and thirsty even for morbid jokes. Some slept for want of anything better to do. Others, Thorgrim imagined, stared off into the dark and considered what would happen next. He did not know for certain, because he could not see anyone or anything in the unmitigated dark.

Like most of the others, Thorgrim was sitting on the floor, his back against the wall. Starri was on his right side and Hall, he thought, was on his left, but he was not certain. He heard the scuffle of feet on the stone, someone moving in the dark, the grunts of men as they were stepped on, the curses and subsequent apologies.

He guessed that the man who was moving was trying to find his way to the corner that they had designated as the toilet, a necessity that only added to the unpleasant nature of their confinement. But he heard the steps coming closer, and a voice calling in a low whisper, "Lord Thorgrim?"

"Here," Thorgrim said. He heard more steps. "Here," he said again and he had the sense of someone approaching. He heard the soft thump of a shoe accidentally kicking someone sitting on the ground.

"Careful, you dumb oaf," Starri snarled.

"Sorry," the man said and Thorgrim was pretty sure it was Brand.

"Lord Thorgrim? It's me, Brand," the voice said. "Could I have a word with you?"

"Yes," Thorgrim said, sitting a bit more upright. "What is it?"

"Well, lord," Brand continued. Thorgrim could tell Brand was kneeling now, and his voice was even lower, more conspiratorial. "Well, lord, I'm not sure this is my business…"

"Go on," Thorgrim said.

Brand took a deep breath and paused for a moment before starting in. "Like I said, this isn't my affair, but…who knows what'll become of us, and I wanted to tell you this."

He paused again before he continued, still speaking just above a whisper. "Harald and I, we've become friends, you know. I think he's asleep now, so I dared come tell you this. I admire Harald very much. And I know that you two…well, you have had some disagreements, as of late.

"But I want you to know something. Back in the battle, the fight with the English fleet, when Herjolf was in command of *Dragon*? Well, Herjolf tried to get clear of the fight. I think he thought the English ships were too big for us to tangle with. We were alone, you know, until the rest of you came up with us. But it was Harald… Harald purposely fouled the oars, got them all tangled up, so there'd be no choice but to fight. It was Harald made sure we went into the battle bold as we did. And he led the men in the fight when the English were on us."

Thorgrim was silent for a moment, considering Brand's words. Finally Brand said, "Lord…?"

"I never heard any of this," Thorgrim said at last.

"Not everyone saw what Harald did. And those of us who did see it, Harald made us promise not to tell. And Herjolf, well, he sure wasn't going to say anything. I think he's been scared ever since that Harald would tell the tale, but he hasn't."

"Thank you, Brand," Thorgrim said. "Thank you for telling me this. It…it makes a big difference."

"Of course, lord," Brand said. "I thought you should know."

Thorgrim could hear Brand stand and make his way back toward wherever he had been sitting. Near Harald, no doubt — they had indeed become good friends.

"Well, now," Starri Deathless said. "Your boy's a strange one. Makes a fool of himself fighting a whale and he won't stop bragging about it. Then he does something a man could be proud of and he doesn't say a word."

"It seems that way," Thorgrim said. "Maybe the boy learned a lesson."

"Maybe," Starri said, though he didn't sound terribly convinced.

Maybe… Thorgrim thought. Humility was not a particularly common trait among the Northmen, who entertained one another by telling tales of their exploits in battle. But Thorgrim had never been like that. He had always been of the mind that a man should keep his mouth shut and let his actions speak. Actions did not lie and they did not embellish.

It was a habit that he had hoped Harald would adopt. He hoped that Harald would learn it from his example. Listening to Harald after his fight with the whale, however, seeing him relish the admiration of the others, Thorgrim had felt certain the boy had learned nothing. But maybe he had.

It would be a good time for it. If they were all going to be marched off to their deaths on the morrow, Thorgrim hoped Harald would meet the gods with humility. He did not think the gods cared much for braggarts.

There was nothing more to say and nothing more to do, locked in the cell as they were with no way out, so Thorgrim fell into a quasi-sleep, drifting off to a world of odd, shifting dreams, waking to wonder what had become of Failend, what of Louis. And what would become of all of them, and how could they go down fighting.

He was in the middle of one of his short bouts of sleep when some sound or other stirred him. He opened his eyes and looked down at the crack along the bottom of the door and saw it was daylight, but what hour it might be he could not tell.

"Men-at-arms. Outside," Starri said.

Thorgrim listened. He could hear the chinking sound of mail, the thump of spear shafts on the ground, a single voice giving orders.

"This better be our breakfast," Godi said in the dark. "And if the bastards burned my porridge I'll kill all of them."

But it was not breakfast. Once the men-at-arms beyond the door had settled, a voice call out in words Thorgrim recognized as English. There was some shuffling around among the men in the prison, he heard someone curse, and Harald's voice say, "Shut your mouth."

It was Harald who spoke next, having worked his way over to the door. He called through the thick planks, back at the man on the other side. They went back and forth a few times, then Harald spoke in Thorgrim's general direction.

"He says they're going to open the door. At least that's what I think he said," Harald reported. "He says we're to come out, one man at a time."

Thorgrim got to his feet, his muscles protesting. There was a lot that had been left unsaid, he was sure. The Englishman had not bothered to warn Harald of what would happen if they tried rushing the guards. Thorgrim imagined there was a line of spears waiting for them, and the consequences of trying to escape would be obvious.

"You hear that, Starri?" Thorgrim said. "Just do as you're told. Nothing stupid. The time for doing stupid things will come soon enough."

Starri grunted. "As long as you promise I may be stupid later, then I'll agree."

The lock on the door clicked, the hasp opened and the door swung back with a creaking sound. The light came spilling in to reveal the seven haggard-looking, filthy, squinting Northmen inside. The captain of the English guard shouted out, just a couple of words.

"He says first man come out," Harald said.

"I go first," Thorgrim said. He would not allow any man into danger before him, and he wanted as much time as he could get to see what was going on.

The men crowding near the door stepped aside as Thorgrim passed through, and Thorgrim told them what he had told Starri: they were to do as ordered, nothing stupid. He stepped out of the door and into the early morning sun. Two dozen spearmen in two ranks faced him, weapons leveled, shields on their backs, faces set and determined. They seemed to take it as a given that the wild heathens would attack like mad dogs.

Well, at least we scared them, if nothing else, Thorgrim thought.

The captain of the guard stood in front of the ranks, two men beside him, just common men, with a great pile of chain at their feet. Thorgrim met the captain's eyes and they held one another's gaze and Thorgrim could see that that man at least was not in any way afraid. He looked angry, if anything. He pointed to Thorgrim's hands and barked a few words and Thorgrim guessed he was asking how Thorgrim's hands came to be untied.

By way of response Thorgrim shrugged, and thought, *Pointless to ask me, you dumb bastard. I have no way to answer you even if I cared to.*

But dumb bastard or not, the man had a job to do, and it did not seem to matter much to him if Thorgrim's hands were bound or not. He nodded to one of the men beside him and that man knelt down and placed a shackle around Thorgrim's ankle, an open iron band with two hinged loops of iron at either end. One loop was passed through the other and the second man passed the bitter end of the chain through that, securing the shackle and preventing it from opening. Slave shackles, meant to bind a line of men to one another.

The two men stood and one of them gave Thorgrim a shove and Thorgrim stumbled forward, barely keeping his feet as the captain barked for the next man to come out. Thorgrim looked behind him. Godi came next, looking as defiant as he could under those circumstances. Thorgrim heard the spearmen shuffle a bit, no doubt surprised and intimidated by the size of the man. Thorgrim braced for Godi to try something, to grab someone's spear or drive a fist into the captain's face, but the big man stood silently as he, too, was made fast to the chain, five feet behind Thorgrim.

Again Thorgrim was pushed forward. He heard the chain rattle as Godi was pushed as well and the captain barked for the next to come out. One by one the Northmen were linked together, then finally the captain was back at Thorgrim's side. He called out an order and the spearmen formed up in two lines with the seven chained men between them. Then the captain gave Thorgrim a shove and led the lot of them off in a grim parade.

They tramped across the open ground, following the same path they had followed going to the prison, as far as Thorgrim could tell: it had been dark then, and he had not been in a good frame of mind for careful observation. But now as they walked he could see more and more of the open ground around the corner of the great hall coming into view, and he was not encouraged by what he saw.

There were people there, a small cluster of people who seemed to be doing nothing more than standing about. And then as the guards and prisoners marched in a broad path around the corner of the hall, more and more people came into sight. A crowd to witness some spectacle, Thorgrim guessed, and he did not doubt that that spectacle would feature him and his men.

Then they were around the corner and Thorgrim could see the long side of the great hall to their left, the main gate off to the right, the whole thing enclosed by the tall gray stone wall. There were ladders leaning against the wall and men-at-arms with spears patrolling the top and others standing at the open gate. More people were coming into the courtyard to join the crowd already assembled.

At the far end stood a platform with a canopy of sorts. It was a couple hundred feet away but Thorgrim could still see bright spots of color and glints of sun off polished metal, and he guessed it was a stage set up so the king and his court could have the best view of the coming entertainment.

And it was clear now what that entertainment would be. Facing the crowd, halfway between them and the great hall, standing in a straight line with ten feet between them, stood seven posts driven into the ground and standing about eight feet high. Around each post was piled a stack of dried brush and straw, something that would ignite quickly, and under the brush more substantial pieces of wood that would really generate a scorching heat.

"Still waiting for my breakfast, sons of bitches," Godi called, and Thorgrim heard the thump of someone hitting Godi in the head. He guessed it was done with the butt of a spear. No one would dare get close enough to Godi to use a hand in striking him.

A murmur swept over the watchers, fingers pointed, heads turned, as the Northmen came shuffling into view. Thorgrim suspected that most of these people had never been so close to one of the dreaded heathens. But they had no doubt heard stories, and those stories would only add to the pleasure of what they were about to see.

The men-at-arms escorted their prisoners up to the line of stakes and stopped them there and the onlookers fell silent. The workmen who had put the shackles on began to take them off again, starting at the back end of the line which happened to be Gudrid. They knelt beside him and as they worked Gudrid looked at Thorgrim and his face seemed to ask if he should just do as he was told, just go to the post without a fight. Thorgrim gave him a little nod, and Gudrid nodded back.

Four spearmen surrounded Gudrid as two other men-at-arms grabbed him and half dragged him over to the post. They pushed him up over the pile of brush until his back was to the pole, then bound his hands behind him. Gudrid stared ahead, over the heads of the onlookers, and his face wore no expression.

Brand was next, and soon he was made fast to the next post in line, and then they came for Harald, who was after him. Starri came next. Thorgrim could see he was twitching, his arms making their odd movement, but not so dramatically as when he was right on the edge of lapsing into a frenzy. He looked over at Thorgrim as the shackle was taken off his leg. Thorgrim gave a small shake of his head, ignoring the despondency on Starri's face. But still Starri allowed himself to be led away and tied to the stake with only a bit of thrashing and jerking against the guards' grip.

They came for Godi next, took his shackle off and bound him to the stake, which looked insubstantial pressed against his massive back. When they were done they removed Thorgrim's leg iron, the last of the Northmen, and he did not struggle as they led him up to the pole.

Thorgrim's arms were pulled back around the pole. He felt the leather thong wrap around his wrists and he clenched his fists as the thong was pulled tight. He waited for the men to notice his bunched fingers, to punch him in the gut or the head to make him stop, but they didn't. If they noticed at all they seemed to think nothing of it — they just tied his wrists and stepped away.

It was only when the guards had reached the ground again, stepping off the pile that was laid down to burn Thorgrim's body to ash, that Thorgrim relaxed his fists which in turn loosened the bindings. Not much, certainly not enough for him to free himself, but a little. Enough to allow him to flex his hands, and that was good.

He began to thrash, growling, wide-eyed like he was suddenly consumed with fury. He jerked side to side as if trying to break free and felt the knife which was tied loosely to his upper arm under the sleeve of his tunic begin to shift.

He paused, breathing hard, looking side to side like some kind of trapped beast, and he could see the crowd was loving the display. It was, no doubt, confirming everything they believed a Northman to be.

Thorgrim thrashed again, made a growling sound, and he felt the knife slip down his sleeve, handle first. He flexed his fingers around and caught the knife and held it there, the blade still hidden by his tunic sleeve. He looked around. They had only one chance, and it was a small one, and the timing had to be exactly right for there to be any chance at all.

Something was happening now, the crowd parting, making way for one of the Christ priests followed by two lines of boys dressed in white, the two in front swinging golden, lidded cups from which smoke was wafting. Thorgrim had stolen dozens of similar cups from the Christ churches he had plundered, but he still did not know what they did, other than produce smoke.

Some sort of magic, he thought, and he hoped whatever magic it was was not terribly strong.

The Christ priest took a few steps toward the line of stakes. He raised his arms and spoke in a voice that carried over the grounds. He spoke with the cadence of words he had said many times before. Thorgrim looked to his right, toward Harald, to see if Harald was following this, but he could not see his son around Godi's bulk.

The priest stopped and lowered his arms to his side. He seemed to be waiting for something, but whatever it was it did not happen, apparently. He turned and walked back the way he had come, the white-clad boys following.

Now someone on the stage was speaking and Thorgrim looked in that direction. An old man, wearing a long red robe, trimmed with fur, a tunic white as snow underneath. The king, Thorgrim guessed, ruler of all this land and beyond. A powerful man.

Once again Thorgrim could not understand a word, but in this case he had a pretty good idea of what was being said: some pronouncement about how this was the inevitable fate of the enemies of the king, or something along those lines. The sort of thing they always said in such circumstances. He twisted and looked back over his left shoulder, then his right. As far as he could see there was no one behind him. He eased the knife out of his sleeve, just a few inches.

He heard a collective gasp, a rush of excitement, from the folk watching. He looked to his right. A man was pushing his way through a gap in the press of people. He carried a torch, held high, the flame bright even in the late morning sun. He stopped at the far end of the line, at Gudrid's post, and touched the torch to the pile at Gudrid's feet. A ripple of sound ran through the crowd as the first of the flames began to rise up from the dried brush, but Gudrid remained silent.

Now, now, Thorgrim thought. Now was the moment to make his move. If he had tried to free himself and the others any sooner then the spearmen would have killed them all, with little problem. But the distraction and chaos of the flames, he hoped, would help throw things into confusion. And if there was confusion, there was a chance.

He slipped the knife the rest of the way out of his sleeve. He looked over at Godi. Godi was looking down at Thorgrim's hands, watching him work the blade around. Then he looked up and gave Thorgrim a smile and a nod of the head.

Thorgrim nodded back. Beyond Godi he could see that the brush at Brand's feet had been set on fire and that at Harald's as well, and the man with the torch was just getting to Starri. There was not much time left before the flames reached the men at the posts.

He turned his eyes straight ahead, his entire concentration on the knife in his fingers. Quick as he dared he turned the knife around. He felt with his thumb to be certain the blade was facing in the right direction then tilted the knife forward, hoping the blade was pressing against the leather thong.

The man with the torch had reached Godi and was setting the brush at his feet on fire. He was lighting it at the outer edge, not near the center, closest to Godi. The flames would take longer to reach their victims that way, thus prolonging the crowd's amusement, which Thorgrim guessed was the idea.

He pressed the knife against the thong with all the force he could put into his fingertips and sawed up and down, the length of each stroke greatly limited by his bound hands. The man with the torch approached and set fire to the brush at the edge of the pile, then backed away, his part done.

Smoke rose up at first and then flames began to sputter and Thorgrim could feel the first waves of heat, even though the flames were still feet away from him.

What of the others? Has the fire reached Gudrid? he thought and pushed those thoughts aside. He had only one thing to consider now — getting though the leather thong, cutting the others free as they sheltered behind the wall of flames.

He pressed harder, sawed up and down. He heard the snapping and crackling of the dried wood at his feet, the growing shouts of the watching crowd as the flames approached their victims. He began to cough as his lungs filled with the smoke that engulfed them. He pressed harder with the knife and as he did he felt the handle, slick with sweat, slide from his grasp.

Chapter Forty-Two

The wise two,
in battle line went,
split mails
and shields,
went right through
grey-coated armies.

The Poetic Edda

Over the crackling of the flames and the shouts of the mob Thorgrim heard the crushing sound of the knife hitting the dried brush at his feet. He felt a sickening twist in his stomach. An image of the flames reaching Gudrid, reaching Harald and the others, formed like a flash of lighting in his head.

Pick it up, pick it up, he thought. If he could slide down the pole he might be able to grab the knife again. He twisted around and looked down at the base of the post behind him but he could not see the knife. He turned and looked down the other side. No knife. It had hit the brush and kept on going, sinking out of sight into the kindling.

He looked over at Godi and saw Godi was looking at him, eyes wide, face red, smoke swirling around him. Thorgrim coughed and shook his head. He did not know what else to do. They had had one chance, and it was not much of one, but now even that was gone.

His eyes remained on Godi as his mind tore through one thought after another: not genuine plans or ideas but vague possibilities, hazy visions of what he might do.

Then suddenly those thoughts were gone as he saw a look come over Godi that he had never seen before, not on Godi or on any other man, a frightening and other-worldly look, his bared teeth clenching, his eyes narrowing and his entire body seeming to draw in tight.

Then Godi let out a massive roar, like some beast from an ancient legend, a roar that tore through the royal compound, echoed off the stone walls and came back again. His body, clenched, now seemed to swell up bigger than ever. He heaved his arms aside and snapped the leather thongs binding his hands as if they were silk thread. He was still roaring his terrifying roar as he leaped off the burning pile and with two great strides was up and at Thorgrim's side.

Thorgrim twisted to see what was happening. Godi plunged his hand down into the brush at Thorgrim's feet and pulled it out gripping the knife. In his fist it looked like a toy or some delicate lady's instrument, but with one swipe Godi cut Thorgrim's bindings away.

Thorgrim felt the amazing sense of relief as the bindings came free, then Godi grabbed his wrist, lifted it and pressed the handle of the knife into Thorgrim's palm.

"Go!" he shouted, nodding toward the others to their right, the men still tied to the stakes.

"What…" Thorgrim began and stopped. He wanted to know what Godi meant to do but he knew there was no time. He gripped the knife hard and jumped off the pile of brush onto the firm, trampled ground of the yard. He was vaguely aware of the screaming and shouting of the people on the other side of the burning brush, of the crackling of the flames, of the smoke that threatened to choke him as he sprinted down the line of stakes.

He raced past Godi's stake, now empty, and came to the next one, the one to which Hall was tied. Just as he was ready to leap up onto the brush pile and cut Hall free he realized that he had to get Gudrid first, that the flames at Gudrid's feet had been burning the longest. He did not break stride as he raced past the other pyres and came to the last in the line, where Gudrid was tied fast.

Thorgrim thought at first that he might be too late. The flames were like a wall in front of Gudrid, and Gudrid in turn was thrashing and pressing himself back and kicking uselessly at the fire creeping toward him. Thorgrim took two quick steps up the pile of brush and wood and slashed down with his knife, cutting Gudrid's bonds away, probably cutting Gudrid as well, but he gave that no thought.

He grabbed Gudrid's tunic and pulled him away from the flames. Gudrid's face was red, his skin blackened by the smoke. There were dozens of small holes burned in his tunic but he seemed otherwise untouched by the fire.

Thorgrim gave him a push to get him further from the flames then leaped back to the ground and with four strides he came up behind Brand, next in line, the flames a foot or so from reaching him as he twisted away as much as he could. The heat was blistering, all but unbearable, as Thorgrim slashed the leather bindings. He pulled Brand back and pushed him off the pile and followed behind. He clambered onto the next where Harald was struggling against his bonds, and Thorgrim cut him free.

"Godi's gone, probably fighting!" Thorgrim shouted. He had expected the guards to come rushing in, spears leveled, but they had not, and he guessed that Godi was holding them off.

"Go fight with him!" Thorgrim shouted, pointing out toward the rest of the yard which was obscured by the smoke. "Get the others!"

Harald nodded and he and Thorgrim jumped down off the pile. Harald waved to the other men and raced forward between the two stacks of burning brush as Thorgrim charged up the last of the piles. Starri was there, thrashing and screaming and kicking. Not out of fear, Thorgrim knew, but out of a raging desire to get at his enemies, to kill them even as they killed him.

Once again Thorgrim slashed at the thongs and they parted under the edge of the blade. He reached for Starri's arm to pull him back as he had the others, but Starri was not there. In the instant that he was cut free, Starri launched himself forward, flung himself right through the wall of flames rising in front of him. He was screaming his berserker battle cry as he burst out of the fire and Thorgrim could hear the note of terror and panic rise from the people on the far side.

Now what? Thorgrim thought. All his men were free, and that might have bought them another few minutes of life, but probably no more. They were, after all, seven unarmed men against all of the king's soldiers and guards.

Thorgrim jumped to the ground and pushed through the wall of smoke and flames and into the clear air on the other side of the burning brush, and he could see right off what was happening. It was chaos.

Godi and Harald and the others were a dozen yards away and charging toward the crowd. They had burning branches in their hands, like great arms of flame, and they were swinging them as they ran because they understood, as Thorgrim did, that chaos was their comrade in arms.

But of course there was nothing they could do to create more panic and confusion than Starri could. He had apparently raced straight at the guards, the spearmen, who formed in a semicircle between the folk watching and the line of stakes. Thorgrim could see two guards on the ground already. Starri had grabbed up a spear and now he was jabbing and flailing at the others who tried to get at him, dancing, sidestepping, thrusting with the spearhead and the butt of the shaft.

The people who had been watching — and there were hundreds of them — were in a mindless panic now, and it was a wonderful thing to see. They were pushing and shoving and running in a hundred different directions, swarming over and around the men-at-arms who were trying to get at Thorgrim and the others. The captain of the guard who had taken them from the prison was shouting orders. His mouth was open and his arms were waving but it was impossible to hear him over the noise of the mob.

Weapons, Thorgrim thought. They needed weapons, and the most likely source were the spearmen with their long polearms and their shields. He tossed the knife aside and grabbed up one of the flaming branches at his feet and charged toward the crowd, toward where Godi and Harald and the others were fighting.

Thorgrim shouted as he came charging in, adding his part to the wild confusion, the burning branch held horizontally. A knot of guards were working their way around Godi's flank, and they did not see Thorgrim coming until he was nearly on them. They looked up suddenly, mouths open in surprise, and Thorgrim drove the burning branch right into their faces.

Two of the men took a direct hit. They screamed and spun away, clapping their hands to their cheeks, slapping at flaming beards. They dropped their spears and Thorgrim snatched them up.

"Godi! Harald!" he shouted and tossed a spear to each. Godi and Harald caught the weapons in their left hands. They flung their burning branches at the men coming at them, then took up the spear shafts with both hands and began driving them at the men-at-arms trying to encircle them.

Thorgrim had caught the guards' attention now. He could see a dozen armed men trying to get at him, but the panicked crowd were swarming around them, blocking their way, buffeting them like a fierce wind. As one of the men stumbled, just feet away, Thorgrim reached out and grabbed his spear and jerked it from his hand.

"Gudrid!" he shouted. Gudrid turned and Thorgrim tossed the weapon to him. He could see Hall and Brand had spears now as well, and they were fighting on all sides. He turned back just as another spear tip was thrust at him, chest high. He spun sideways and knocked the spear out of line with his right arm, and as the man wielding it took another step closer Thorgrim drove his left elbow into the man's jaw.

The spear wavered and nearly slipped from the guard's hands as the man went reeling back, but Thorgrim grabbed the weapon before it fell and pulled it clear. The folk in the crowd were mostly rushing for the main gate, trying to get away from the wild fight, mindless of the soldiers trying to get at the escaped prisoners.

But still the English soldiers were trying to get through the mob. Thorgrim could see swords raised, mail shirts on the men trying to push their way through, and he guessed they were the noblemen who had been standing with the king on the raised platform, eager to show they, too, were willing to jump into the battle.

Thorgrim took a step back and held the spear horizontally and waited for the men coming at him to break through the crowd. The first to push his way through was one of the guards, spear in hand, held vertically so as not to impale the people he did not wish to impale. The panicked, fleeing people parted before him and he seemed surprised to be suddenly in the open, and even more surprised to see Thorgrim five feet in front of him.

Surprised though he was, the guard brought his spear down quick, just not quick enough. Thorgrim stepped forward and held his own spear up in both hands, using the weapon as a staff. He caught the shaft of the guard's spear on his own and twisted it aside, swinging the butt of his own spear around and catching the man on the side of the head.

The shaft hit the rim of the man's helmet, striking with enough force to toss him sideways, right into the next man coming through the crowd. This one was not a guard but one of the nobles, one of the men fitted out in mail and holding a sword and shield. He stumbled as the stunned guard fell into him, but he recovered in time to get his shield up to stop the thrust from Thorgrim's spear.

Thorgrim's spear point ripped into the wood face of the shield and he felt the solid impact. His eyes moved from the shield to the man holding it and he was struck with a sense of unreality — he knew the man, recognized him, but he did not know from where.

And then he remembered. The prisoner! It was the man who had led the fight at the inn, the one they had forced to lead them into the king's compound. He had a crazed look on his face, a wild, heedless look, as if he cared nothing for his own life as long as he could take another. Thorgrim had seen that look on other men, but rarely, and those men generally did not live long.

Poor, stupid bastard, Thorgrim thought next. The man might be hungry to bring death, but he did not have the skill to do it, at least not when facing someone like Thorgrim Night Wolf.

Thorgrim pulled back hard on the shaft of the spear, pulling it free from the face of the shield as the man came at him, shield first, sword raised, screaming some incomprehensible thing.

Too close, too close, Thorgrim thought. The man had stepped up to sword distance, too close for Thorgrim to use his spear, no time for Thorgrim to take a step back. So instead he stepped forward, stepped right into the man, pressed his chest against the man's shield, felt his hot breath on his face. He was too near now for the Englishman to strike with his sword.

Thorgrim held his spear up and slid his hand down the shaft until it was right behind the spear head, until he was holding the spear as if it was a dagger with a six foot handle behind.

The Englishman saw the danger now. His eyes went up to the spear point and opened wider still. He tried to step back but Thorgrim held the edge of his shield with his left hand as he drove the spear point down with his right. It came over the top of the shield and struck the Englishman just above the collar of his mail shirt and drove on in with little resistance, down through the man's throat and further still.

Thorgrim let the spear go as the man's head rolled back and his body went limp from the shock of the fatal blow. He reached out and grabbed the man's sword before it fell and jerked the edge of the shield he still held on his left arm. The man's arm slipped out of the shield's strap as he went down and Thorgrim flipped the shield around and stuck his own arm through.

Thank you, Thorgrim thought as he watched the man's body hit the ground, the spear standing out from his chest, blood running from his open mouth. His eyes were still wide and Thorgrim guessed he was already dead, though it hardly mattered just then.

He stepped back, sword raised. He could see nothing but panicked people running, shoving. One of the men-at-arms stood in mid-stream, trying to kick his way through. Then suddenly the crowd parted and there was only space between him and Thorgrim. Thorgrim saw the determined look on the man's face as he stepped up, leveled his spear and charged.

Thorgrim let him come, let his momentum build, and just as his spear point was a couple feet from driving into Thorgrim's gut Thorgrim chopped down with his sword, splitting the spear shaft like kindling. He lifted his shield and the surprised man slammed into it as Thorgrim braced himself against the impact. The man bounced back and Thorgrim brought his sword down like an ax. But the soldier was quicker than Thorgrim would have guessed and he leaped back, colliding with the people behind him, his determined look gone as Thorgrim's sword whipped past, hitting only air.

No time for this… Thorgrim thought. This chaos, the cover that the crazed mob provided, would not last much longer. They had to get out now. Godi and the others had formed themselves up into a square, fighting off attacks from three directions. Thorgrim backed off a few feet, reached over and smacked Godi with the flat of his sword.

"We have to go!" he shouted, loud enough for Godi and the others to hear. "Out the gate, with the crowd!"

Godi nodded, thrusting with his spear as he did.

"Swine array!" Thorgrim shouted. A swine array would form them into a human wedge, an effective formation for smashing through a shieldwall, if they had men enough. Thorgrim hoped it would do the same with seven men against a frightened mob.

"Right!" Godi shouted.

Thorgrim pushed his way forward. He meant to make himself the point of the wedge, but before he could get there Godi let out a roar and charged ahead, swinging and thrusting with his spear, kicked with legs like small trees at anyone in his way. They moved forward, the others falling in behind Godi like geese flying in a V formation, and the terrified people fought to get clear.

Much as he loathed letting another man take the greater risk, Thorgrim had to admit Godi made a frightening and effective point.

"Harald, Brand, get Starri!" Thorgrim shouted and the two young men nodded and raced off to pull Starri from his personal brawl and drag him along.

The crowd was thinning some, which made movement easier, but offered less cover. Godi plunged ahead into the running mass and anyone who saw him coming stumbled out of the way and anyone who didn't was knocked aside as they made for the main gate. There were handfuls of soldiers all over the grounds, some hurrying one way or another, some not, but there was no coordinated effort to stop the Northmen. No one seemed to be in charge.

That was hardly a surprise. The entire situation had been turned on its head. Order had been turned to madness in less time than it took for a man to don a mail shirt and strap on his weapons.

And now, Thorgrim realized, the king's men were having a hard time even finding the Northmen in the crowd. He could see here and there armed men pointing, running, trying and failing to get at them through the panicked townsfolk.

Godi was no longer swinging his spear or kicking his way through. There was no need, no one was blocking their way. The seven of them found themselves carried along by the crowd, swept toward the gate like twigs in a fast moving stream.

The gate was close now, the guards trying to shut it, men shouting orders, men trying to get the running mob to stop long enough to get the big doors closed and trap the prisoners inside. But no one was willing to stop in their headlong fight. No one was interested in being trapped inside the walls with the mad heathens on the loose.

They were fifty feet away when the guards gave up trying to close the gate and formed up into a human wall instead, shields and spears ready, making one final effort to keep the heathens from getting out. Godi did not slow at all, and neither did the men behind him, Thorgrim on his left side, Harald on his right, the rest trailing astern. Twenty feet away and Thorgrim dug in, pushed harder, came up to Godi's side, and then he ran harder still until he was a step ahead and then another, leading the swine array now. Thorgrim was the only one with a shield, and tough as Godi was his flesh would not turn aside the point of a spear.

Thorgrim was ten feet from the shieldwall, running as fast as he was physically able. He saw a half dozen spear points aimed directly at him, men bracing for him to impale himself on their weapons. Five feet away and Thorgrim ducked behind the shield so the wood and canvas disk was covering him from the waist up and he had time enough before he hit to hope none of the soldiers would think to go for his legs.

Five spear heads hit the shield, five points came tearing halfway through the wood as Thorgrim slammed into the shieldwall. He felt the men in front of him buckle under the impact, felt the line of men seem to break apart.

He pulled his arm from the strap of the shield and let it go. The five spears that were stuck in the wood were useless now, leaving the men who had carried them unarmed, and Thorgrim slashed at them with his sword. He was still in the middle of his first stroke when Godi came crashing into the men to his right and Starri came screaming in to his left.

Starri had a spear in hand, the shaft broken in two, leaving a weapon three feet long, and he was using it with great dexterity. He drove the point in between two shields and Thorgrim heard a man scream as the shieldwall continued to break apart. Godi had bashed a gap in the wall and Harald and Brand and Gudrid were charging into it, spears driving out in every direction. Thorgrim brought his sword back over his left shoulder and took a powerful backhand swing at the man in front of him who was stumbling to get clear.

And then the shieldwall disappeared. It was like a magical thing. One second there were twenty soldiers standing in their way, and the next second there were not, the component parts of the wall either lying on the ground bleeding or running off.

"Go! Go!" Thorgrim shouted, and he waved his men forward and they started to run once more. They did not bother with their swine array. The way was clear now, the gates open, the streets and thatched houses and workshops of Winchester in sight past the open ground. They raced out through the gate, now nearly alone as the town folk scattered like chickens with a stray dog in the yard, and they kept on running. Where they were running to, Thorgrim did not know. His only thought was to put distance between them and the king's men.

They bolted over the open ground and toward the place where the nearest street began, Thorgrim now taking the lead. He could feel his chest burning, his legs aching, but he pressed on. And then they were in the street, where the small buildings crowded up near the dirt road offered them at least some illusion of shelter.

Thorgrim slowed his running then came to a stop, doubled over, gasping for breath. The wound in his side was radiating pain and he was sure Failend's fine stitches had been torn clean away. His knees hurt.

He could hear Godi and a couple of the others sucking in air as well. He looked up. Godi's mouth and eyes were open wide as he struggled to pull sufficient breath into his chest. Gudrid was sweating profusely, the perspiration making tracks through the soot that covered his face. Hall was still doubled over. Harald and Brand, to Thorgrim's annoyance, were pretty much breathing normally, as was Starri Deathless.

"Very well," Thorgrim said at last. He straightened and winced at the dagger-thrust pain from his half-healed laceration. He barely had breath enough to speak, but he knew there was no time to wait. The king's men would be coming soon. "We need to go."

"Where?" Starri asked.

Thorgrim gestured with his head toward the far end of the street. They had come that way only once, at night, following the Englishman, but Thorgrim thought he had an idea of how the city was laid out.

"Any of these streets will lead to the city wall," he said and he hoped he was right. "We'll go there and find a way out."

No one said anything because no one had a better idea. Thorgrim turned and headed up the street, jogging as fast as he was able. He could see faces peering out from doors and windows and from behind buildings. Word of the chaos at the king's residence, of the savages on the loose, must have spread.

They had not gone far when two things happened at once. Up ahead, through the press of houses and the jam of carts and animals on the street, they caught sight of the city wall, the great, gray stonework that encircled Winchester, the wall that was there to keep the hostile world out, but was now keeping them in. And behind them, they heard the first sounds of pursuit.

Horses, Thorgrim thought as the sound made its way through his heaving breath and his distracted thoughts. There were horses behind them, but not in sight, still a ways back. They were not running, but not walking either. Moving quickly. Horses had to mean the king's men, and if they were not at a full gallop it likely meant they were not entirely sure where the Northmen had gone.

"I hear horses," Starri said at the same moment Thorgrim heard them.

"Yes, but there's the wall," Thorgrim said, pointing. "Let's go."

He picked up the pace of his run, painful as that was to his legs and knees and lungs. They raced down the center of the road and came out in the street perpendicular to it, a street that bordered the city wall. Thorgrim stopped there, breathing hard. He looked to his right, but he could see nothing other than the ends of more streets, more carts, more animals wandering about. Across from those streets stood an unbroken stretch of wall fifteen feet high with no way to get over or through.

He looked left. A hundred yards away he saw it: the main gate. The doors were still open but no one was going in or out. The guards has shed their bored and lazy attitude. They stood poised with shields on their arms, spears held ready, looking in a dozen different directions. A general sense of alarm seemed to have spread through the city.

"There!" Thorgrim pointed with his sword and he felt a glow of hope, the first in a long time. The guards outnumbered them, to be sure, but Thorgrim did not doubt they could fight their way through. And the gates were still open.

He started to run again, the rest behind him, and covered about a dozen feet before he stopped. Riders came bursting out from the street closest to the gates, pounding into the open, and reined hard to a stop. The foremost of them had his sword drawn and was pointing to the gate and shouting something Thorgrim could not understand. But he did not need to. The meaning was clear enough as six of the guards raced off to push the main gate's two big oak doors closed.

"Oh, by all the gods!" Gudrid said in frustration.

"They're showing us no favors today," Brand said.

"Toy with us, toy with us, it's what they'll do," Starri said. "They like to play with Night Wolf this way, you know."

Even before that exchange was done, the riders had seen them. The man with the sword was now pointing their way, and the others were turning their mounts to look. For a moment no one moved, not the Englishmen or the Northmen. Both clusters of men seemed frozen in that moment, like reliefs carved in the posts of a great hall, depicting some moment before epic battle.

Then the horsemen began to move. Thorgrim saw the leader kick his heels into his horse's flanks, saw the horse leap forward into a run, the rest of the horsemen just two steps behind. The guards were running as well, but they were quickly left in the horses' wake.

Thorgrim looked around. They weren't getting out of the city, so the best they could do was find a place to make a stand. Any one of those houses might work. It would at least be a fine place to die with their weapons in their hands.

He was about to speak when he heard Harald's voice, shouting. The boy was not among them and Thorgrim had not even noticed he was gone. But now he came running out from the side of a nearby workshop and over his head he was carrying a ladder, a long ladder, twelve feet at least. Long enough to get up and over.

"Here! Here!" Harald shouted as he pounded across the street, stopping quick and letting the momentum bring the ladder down and stand it upright against the stone wall. Thorgrim looked back at the horsemen. They were fifty yards away, riding at a full gallop now. Harald was too late. There was no time left for Thorgrim and his men to turn their backs and get up the ladder.

"Sons of whores!" Starri shouted and charged toward the riders. He had covered only three steps when Godi lunged forward and grabbed him by the neck and the crotch and lifted him kicking and flailing over his head.

"Go! Go!" Godi shouted and he turned and flung Starri at the ladder, flung him so hard Starri was halfway up when he hit it and managed to grab hold of one rung and get his foot on another before he fell.

Godi grabbed Hall and shoved him toward the ladder. "Go, all of you go, I'll hold them off!"

Harald turned toward Godi, shouting and pointing at the ladder with his spear. "You're with us, Godi, you're with us!" he shouted. "Come with us!"

Thorgrim grabbed Harald's arm and pulled him back. He had seen, in that instant, what Harald and the others could not see. He saw what Godi wanted, and what the gods wanted for Godi. They called to him. They called him to their feast in the great hall.

"Let him have this," Thorgrim said to Harald. "He might make it yet."

Harald's eyes were wide, his face red with exertion. He looked as if he did not understand. The horsemen were on them now, riding up with swords drawn. Harald's eyes went from Thorgrim to Godi and back. He nodded and turned and leaped for the ladder, the last one up, save for Thorgrim and Godi.

The first of the horsemen came charging at Godi and Godi lifted his spear and jabbed. The horseman swerved away, slashing with his sword and missing, and the next came in at his heels.

"I'll see you again, soon enough, Godi Unundarson!" Thorgrim called as he reached out and found one of the ladder's rungs.

"In Odin's great hall, Thorgrim Night Wolf!" Godi called, still facing the riders coming at him. "I'll have your seat waiting!"

Thorgrim turned and ran up the ladder, moving fast up the wooden rungs. He heard the shouting and the pounding of hooves on the ground below. He pulled himself up onto the top of the wall and stood and looked down.

Godi was standing at the base of the wall like a giant rock barrier rolled in place. He was driving with his spear as the horsemen came at him, charging and retreating. He had managed to get up two rungs of the ladder, but now the riders had him fully engaged.

He took another step just as the guards on foot reached him, charging in, spears thrusting upward. Godi knocked a spear aside, lunged down at the man, drove his point into the man's guts and trapped his own weapon at the same time. Thorgrim saw Godi grab for the dead man's spear as three others drove their weapons into his huge body. Godi roared like a bear and swung his fist, leaping from the ladder as more spears came driving into him.

The first rider was back, sword lifted. Godi, incredibly, was still on his feet, lashing out, when the sword came down on his head.

Hall and Gudrid grabbed the top of the ladder and pulled it up. Thorgrim felt a hand grip his arm.

"We have to go."

He looked over. Harald was there, tears running down his face. He nodded toward the ladder now leaning against the other side of the wall. Beyond that lay open country. The rest of the men were already climbing down.

"Go. I'm behind you," Thorgrim said. Harald swung himself onto the ladder and raced down, and Thorgrim followed behind. He hit the ground and Harald grabbed the ladder and spun it off the wall and tossed it aside.

Thorgrim looked around. They had the wall to their backs and the open country before them and no obvious place to go, no sort of defense or shelter. What to do? Get as much distance as possible between themselves and the English, he guessed.

"Follow me," he said as if he had some plan in mind. He headed off directly away from the wall, not toward the Roman road but over the fields. Maybe there would be a farm near — he could see buildings in the distance — and maybe they would find some horses there.

Maybe. But he did not think they would get there. It might take the men-at-arms on their horses a moment to straighten themselves out, another moment to get the gate open, but it would not be long before they came riding out with their helmets and mail, swords and shields at the ready.

They were moving at a fast walk, six men in open country.

"Maybe we should run?" Harald suggested.

"No," Thorgrim said. There was no point. They could not possibly run far enough to do any good, and further exhausting themselves would not help.

They were still close enough to the city wall to hear the creak of the main gate as it was swung open. As one they stopped and turned. A moment later the first of the riders came charging through, then another and another. More than a dozen at least, and Thorgrim was sure these were just the men at the gate. More would be coming, as if there was any need for more.

"Let's form up into a square, back to back, all of us," Thorgrim said. It was their only means of defense now. If they tried to run they'd be cut down for certain. But Thorgrim could hear the lack of enthusiasm in his voice. The death of Godi Unundarson seemed to have taken all the strength from him.

The others gathered, back to back, spears held out. If they stood firm they could probably hold the riders off, but in truth the English were not likely to attack mounted. They would get off their horses and attack on foot and the little knot of Northmen would quickly be overwhelmed.

Thorgrim was facing the riders, watching them make their charge. They were coming on at a full gallop, with not the least reticence or uncertainty. They were a hundred yards away and Thorgrim could see the flash of the sun off the blades of their swords.

And then they stopped, the horses rearing and twisting as their riders reined them in hard. They stamped and turned in place and the warriors mounted on them looked off across the countryside and pointed with their swords.

Thorgrim frowned and turned and looked in the direction they were pointing. More riders were coming, twenty or so, riding hard over the open country. They were a half mile away. The sound of their horses' hooves came faintly to Thorgrim's ears.

"Now who by all the gods is this?" Brand said.

"They have shields," Starri said. "And helmets."

Thorgrim knew he would have to take Starri's word for it. He could not make out that sort of detail from that distance. But if he was wondering who these newcomers were, it seemed the English riders were wondering as well. They remained where they had stopped, still seated on their restless mounts, still looking in the direction of the men heading toward them across the fields.

Then the English made a decision. They decided that whoever these men were, they were not friends. As one, the riders turned their mounts and kicked them into a run and charged off toward the still open main gate of Winchester.

The horsemen, the ones coming across the fields, changed course now, swerving to their left and making not for the English riders but for Thorgrim and his band.

"Keep together, keep together," Thorgrim said. They would keep up their defensive stand, hopeless as it was, until they knew who these riders were.

As they drew nearer Thorgrim could make out more detail: he could see the shields now, and swords held up and helmets, or so he thought. But he could not make out any more than that.

But the others could, apparently. He sensed Harald and Starri and Gudrid all relaxing their posture, saw them standing their spears upright and resting them on the ground. He heard Starri Deathless shout, "Ha!"

The riders were fifty feet away when Thorgrim heard a voice call out, deep and jovial, "Thorgrim Night Wolf!"

Twenty feet away and Thorgrim could see it was Bergthor Skeggjason, his thicket of beard split by a wide grin, as usual. And beside him, Louis de Roumois.

Chapter Forty-Three

May the sword not bite
which thou drawest,
unless it sing round thy own head.

The Poetic Edda

Bergthor and Louis reined to a halt and slid down from their saddles and the men behind them did the same. Thorgrim recognized them but he did not know their names. They were Bergthor's men. Good men.

The smile did not leave Bergthor's face as he returned his sword to its scabbard and came at Thorgrim with arms spread.

"Thorgrim!" he said again and wrapped his arms around Thorgrim and hugged him, and Thorgrim was too stunned to do anything but let him. Bergthor released him and stepped back and looked over the men clustered there. "I knew the gods would not let you die like dogs at the hands of the English!" he exclaimed. "Louis here said we were too late, but that's the way these dreary Franks see things, not our people! I knew we'd make it in time."

"If you'd paused to scratch your ass once we'd be dead," Gudrid said.

"Plenty of time!" Bergthor said.

Thorgrim looked over at Louis and their eyes met. "You betrayed your friends?" he said, nodding toward the walls of Winchester.

Louis gave him a quizzical look. "Since when are the English friends to the Franks?"

"They took you out of the prison. They knew your name. They're not friends?"

"No," Louis said. "They are not friends. They wished to do to me the same as they tried to do to you. Or worse. It looks like you, Thorgrim, are my best friend in the world. God help me."

From somewhere behind the walls of Winchester they heard a trumpet sound, and then another. They turned in that direction and even Thorgrim could see the movement on top of the walls, the men-at-arms scrambling along behind the parapet. He turned back to Bergthor.

"I don't know how you happened to be here, but it was bravely done. Still, you might live to regret it. Or die regretting it."

"Ha!" Bergthor said, his big smile not diminishing in the least. "Let's mount up! See, I have brought horses for all of you!"

Thorgrim had noticed them already — seven saddled and riderless horses among the other mounts.

"Godi?" Louis asked.

Thorgrim shook his head. "He's dead. Put himself in front of the spears so that the rest of us could get over the wall."

That was met by a moment of silence, then Bergthor said, "Well, he feasts with warriors now, and when it's our turn we'll join him there. But we had best away."

A trumpet sounded again from behind the city wall, and this time it was accompanied by the drumming of hooves, a low, distant sound, like thunder far off. All of them, Thorgrim's men and Bergthor's men, turned at once and looked back toward the main gate, a half a mile away. The riders who had fled through the gate were coming out again, and with them two dozen more, led by horsemen carrying banners aloft. But this was no stately display. They were riding hard, a full gallop, and they were coming for the Northmen.

"They're very determined, aren't they?" Hall said.

"Whoa!" Bergthor shouted. "Well that's it, we'd best be on our way! Come, come! Thorgrim, you take the gray one there, she seems the best of a bad lot. Bunch of broken nags was all we could find."

Thorgrim hurried over to the gray horse that Bergthor had indicated. He slid his sword through a loop in the saddle, having no scabbard on his hip. He put his foot in the stirrup and swung himself up and the others around him did the same.

He looked over his shoulder. The English had not broken their stride at all and they were closing the distance with notable speed.

"Let's go!" Thorgrim shouted, jamming his heels into the horse's flanks. He felt the animal jump and start to dig in as it ran, and around him the other horses were likewise getting underway.

Bunch of broken nags, Thorgrim thought.

He owned horses, knew about horses, but he was not the greatest judge of them, being a sailor at heart. Still, it did seem to him that these were not the finest animals he had seen. Nor would he expect them to be. Bergthor and the others must have scoured the countryside to collect this many. They were farm animals mostly, taken from the people who worked the land thereabouts.

That would not be true of the horses coming from Winchester. A mounted warrior was in all likelihood a wealthy man, maybe one of the nobles who had been sitting with the king, or part of such a man's hird. Their horses would be the finest and the fastest. And they would not be tired from hard riding as Bergthor's horses were.

I'm about done with this… Thorgrim thought next. It was getting tiresome, having the gods toy with him that way. He no longer wished to flee. He wanted to turn his horse around, ride it straight into the middle of the English riders, take as many down as he was able. End it there.

He looked behind and felt his arms tense, ready to pull the reins to one side and spin his horse around. But he knew that if he did that the others would follow. He might be ready to throw his own life away, but he could not make that choice for his men. He turned and faced forward again and let the reins go slack.

Bergthor was in the lead now, a horse length ahead of Thorgrim, but that was fine because Bergthor had just come that way and likely knew the best way back. Thorgrim's eyes were watering from the wind, his ears were filled with the pounding of the hooves and the occasional whoop from Bergthor or Starri Deathless. They seemed to be moving very fast now, this band of wild Northmen tearing over the countryside, but when Thorgrim looked behind again he saw the English were closer yet. As fast as they might be going, the men-at-arms in pursuit were going much faster.

The horses raced down the backside of a small hill, and for a moment the fields ahead of them were lost from view, like dipping into the trough between waves. And then they were up the far side and once again Thorgrim could see farms spread out around, and cows in fields and smoke rising here and there.

It was odd. The world went on as if nothing was amiss, while he and his men, and the English behind, came charging through it, as if they were part of a different world entirely, and for that one moment the two just happened to overlap.

Thorgrim looked behind once more and caught a glimpse of the banners the English held aloft, bright colors against the sky, and the mail and helmets of the riders, the shining breastplates on the horses themselves. They were only a few hundred yards behind now, and Thorgrim could feel his horse was slowing with the effort. He wondered if the creature would just die under him. He'd had that happen before.

"Bergthor!" he shouted, and Bergthor twisted around, looking back at Thorgrim.

"We won't outrun them!" Thorgrim shouted. "We need someplace…to make our stand! Farmhouse?"

He looked up as he said it, but there was no farmhouse near that he could see. A hundred yards away a small hill rose up like an ocean roller, blocking the view of the country just beyond it, but if there had been a house there they would have seen it. Beyond that it was just fields for a mile at least. And they would not make it another mile before the English were on them.

"A little farther!" Bergthor shouted back. His face was red and covered in sweat from the effort of riding as hard as he was, but he was still smiling, as much as he could.

Thorgrim gave him a quick nod and leaned forward in the saddle. It was pointless, pressing on, but he and Bergthor could hardly discuss it just then, and besides there was nothing more to do. Ride until the horses died under them, and then stand and fight until they were dead as well.

The ground dipped at the foot of the next hill and Thorgrim could see only the green grass of the field ahead. Then they were going up the hill, Bergthor in the lead, Thorgrim half a pace behind, the rest following. They crested the hill and came down the far side and to Thorgrim's astonishment there were men there, hundreds and hundreds of men, fifty feet away. They had shields and helmets and spears and battle axes and they stood in a long line, hidden by the hill and ready to fight.

As the riders came flying over the top of the hill the men in their path scrambled out of the way. Bergthor gave a shout of triumph and hauled back on his horse's reins, skidding to a stop. Thorgrim pulled the reins of his own mount back and the horse reared a bit and tossed its head, as much as the exhausted animal could muster. Around and behind him the rest of the riders came to a stop as well.

Bergthor was already off his horse when Thorgrim swung his leg over the saddle and dropped. "How's this for a surprise, Thorgrim?" he shouted. "You didn't think I'd come alone, did you?"

Thorgrim shook his head. He did not know what to say. Bergthor turned toward the men nearest to him and spoke loud enough for his voice to carry down the line. "Our English friends will be here directly!" he shouted. "Let's be ready to welcome them!"

They could hear the pounding of the horses' hooves as the English riders, unseen, charged toward the far side of the hill. The Northmen lifted shields and leveled spears and hefted swords and braced themselves. Then the first of the Englishmen came galloping over the crest of the hill, sword held high, the rider to his left and just behind holding one of the bright-colored banners.

He did not slow as he came over the top and down the other side, but sat more upright and pulled back on the reins as he saw the army arrayed before him. He was close enough that Thorgrim could see the play of emotions on his face: determination changing to surprise, changing to confusion, changing to fear. He pulled harder on his reins and his horse reared as more and more of the riders came after him over the hill.

The first rider's horse came down again and spun in place, the man holding his sword up, looking for someone to fight. The Northmen were coming in from all sides, surrounding him and the other Englishmen as they came charging over the top of the hill. A rider hacked down at one of Bergthor's men, who turned the blade aside with his shield and swung with a battle ax and missed.

"Don't kill them! Don't kill them!" Thorgrim shouted. He had not thought this through, was still a little stunned by the turn of events, but he did know these Englishmen were of much greater value alive than dead.

There were knots of fighting now, the Northmen swarming around the English riders, going at them with shields raised, while the English hacked and slashed in manic desperation. But the Northmen seemed to heed Thorgrim's words, and rather than kill the riders in their saddles they dragged them down one after another, until soon the riderless horses were running in every direction and the well-appointed English warriors were buried under crowds of bearded heathens.

The air was filled with the shouts of the English and the shouts and laughter of the Northmen piling on. Each of the men-at-arms was at the center of his own individual scrum and Thorgrim could well imagine the eager hands liberating their purses and swords and bejeweled knives and rings and necklaces and arm bands. He could see one fellow dragging the mail shirt off of his thrashing, shouting victim.

Bergthor was standing at Thorgrim's side, arms folded, laughing at the sight. Thorgrim turned to him.

"If we let this go on they'll strip those English bastards naked, and that I don't care to see."

"We can agree on that," Bergthor said. He turned toward the fighting men. There were at least ten of the Northmen attending to each of the English riders, which meant nearly every man there was engaged.

"Hey, you thieving whores' sons, let those bastards up!" he shouted. "Come on, come on, let them up!"

Slowly the struggling came to a stop as the Northmen stood and backed away. Some were bleeding where their victims had apparently landed a blow or managed to draw a weapon, but none of the wounds seemed terribly severe. The Northmen were grinning or laughing. This was the most fun they had had since the two fleets had met on the beach, which seemed like a year ago, at least.

"Get these English to their feet, get them together here!" Thorgrim shouted. The English men-at-arms had been left on the ground but now men reached down and stood them up on unsteady legs.

They had been proud warriors, finely fitted out, when they came over the hill, but they were not so anymore. They had been stripped down mostly to their tunics, which were torn and stained with blood and grass and mud. Some did not even have their tunics left. Their hair stood in wild array, their faces streaked with blood from noses and mouths. They had the look of men too stunned to even understand what had happened to them.

Once the English were on their feet the Northmen pushed them toward the middle of the crowd until they were all in a cluster, a battered, frightened group, each beaten, stripped man trying to preserve some semblance of dignity and courage.

Thorgrim and Bergthor approached and the Northmen parted for them. Thorgrim could see the English eyes turning his way. They would recognize him, of course. The man they had tried to burn at the stake that very morning. They would guess he had reason to angry with them, and that he might not feel particularly charitable.

Thorgrim moved his eyes from one man to the next. Despite their ravaged appearance he could see they were not common soldiers. They were not even elite house guards. They were more than that. They were important men, nobles, men of means and station. They had come out for the fun of running a handful of escaped heathens to ground.

Rich men out on an afternoon's hunt.

He nodded his head. "Good, good," he said. "These men will serve us well."

Epilogue

We shall surely
drink delicious draughts,
though we have lost
life and lands.

The Poetic Edda

Felix lowered his head into his hands and closed his eyes. King Æthelwulf was ranting on about something but Felix did not think it was important, or indeed even worth listening too.

A disaster, he thought. *An absolute disaster. But what did these idiots think was going to happen?*

He opened his eyes and looked up. The man standing in front of him was a young thegn named Beadurof who owned a tolerable estate in Kent, though nothing compared to what the other members of the witan owned. He had been sent by the heathens to bring word of what had befallen the others. And what must happen next.

"That's right, sire," Beadurof said, in answer to the king's query. "The whole heathen army, or most of it, was lying in wait behind the hill. We had no notion of it. We rode right over the hill and right into their arms. That's what happened."

Felix had to marvel at the heathens' insight. Beadurof was about the least important of all the men they had taken prisoner, and he was the one they had sent to bring word. The ealdormen, whose lives were of real value, had been kept prisoner. The heathens would give up nothing or no one of real value.

How did they know? Felix wondered. *Fortunate guess?*

"Did you fight, at least?" Æthelwulf asked. "Were any of the men killed?"

"Yes, certainly, sire, we fought. Fought hard as we could," Beadurof said but Felix could hear the false note in his voice and he guessed that the nobles were so taken by surprise that they had no fight in them.

And it was clear that if there had been any fighting it was pretty one-sided. Beadurof's appearance alone told that tale. His tunic was ripped and coated in mud and he had been stripped of everything but the tunic and his leggings. There was blood on his face, partially wiped away, from a bloody nose, apparently.

"There was a great host of them, sire, as I said," Beadurof continued in his defensive tone. "But well hidden. The others, the heathen prisoners who escaped from the stakes, they led us right into their arms."

"Humph," Æthelwulf said.

"This is a bad business. A bad business," said Leofric, sitting near the king on a mostly empty bench. Leofric, ealdorman of Dorsetshire, was one of the few of that rank who had opted not to go out on the hunt.

Leofric had not been an ealdorman long. It had been no more than a day, actually, since he had been elevated to that office. Nothwulf, the former ealdorman, had fallen out of Æthelwulf's favor, thanks in part to his own blunders, but also through Leofric's subtle manipulation of the king. Felix saw what the old man was up to and could even admire it, since it did not affect him at all.

Nothwulf, already on shaky ground, would have been pretty much done for after making such a mess of his fight with the Northmen, even to the point of leading them into Winchester. But Nothwulf had managed to get himself killed trying to stop the prisoners' escape, and thus cleared the way for Leofric's advance.

Better for Nothwulf to die as an ealdorman and a hero than live as a goat, Felix thought. Nothwulf's wife, Cynewise, was sneaky and powerful in her own right, and Felix had never liked or trusted her, but he was sure Leofric would have no problem sending her packing back to Devonshire from whence she had come.

"Yes, Leofric, yes, it's a bad business," said Æthelwulf with no attempt to hide his disgust. Felix did not offer an opinion. He did not feel that he had to. Æthelwulf seemed to understand well enough the gravity of what had happened.

All the ealdormen and thegns, the men of highest rank, had been sitting on the stage near Æthelwulf, invited there by the king himself to watch the heathens die in flames. But the prisoners managed to get free of their stakes, and when they did the nobles plunged into the fight, eager to be seen risking their lives for their king. But despite those efforts, the heathens disappeared in the chaos of the panicked crowd.

At first it was assumed they were still in the city. The noblemen called for their war horses, the better to scour Winchester, and because the horses made them feel more martial, more important.

Then word came that the heathens had made it over the wall. The mounted ealdormen ordered the gates open and charged after them, joined by another twenty of their kind, horns blowing, banners waving. The heathens were barely armed and greatly outnumbered, even after more of them arrived on horseback. It seemed like the whole thing would be a grand lark, an afternoon's hunt, and a way to show off for the king, all at once.

Felix had watched them go and he had an uneasy feeling in his gut. Here the wealthiest and most important men in Wessex, Ingwald, Alhmund, Egbert, Byrnhorn, all of them, would be riding out on their own, no men-at-arms, no foot soldiers, just them against the heathens. But there would be no dissuading them, he could see that. He had no authority over those men, and Æthelwulf seemed happy to see them ride off in pursuit.

They won't be gone long… Felix thought. It was the most comforting thing he could come up with. The ealdormen would be gone and back and no harm done. Except that was not how it worked out.

"And where are they now, do you know?" Felix asked, the first words he had spoken.

"Back to Hamtun," Beadurof said. "That what they told me to tell to the king. Going back to Hamtun."

Going back to Hamtun with all the witan as hostages, Felix thought.

"And what do the bastards want?" Æthelwulf demanded.

"Ahh…" Beadurof paused, clearly not wishing to say the very thing he had been sent by the heathens to say. "They are demanding a hundred pounds of silver…"

"Ah, those dogs!" Æthelwulf interrupted. "A hundred pounds of silver? Are they mad?"

"Well, sire, that's actually a hundred pounds of silver for every hostage…" Beadurof said, and that was met with silence.

I guess the heathens know the value of their hostages, Felix thought.

"Well, Felix, what say you?" Æthelwulf asked.

Felix shrugged. "We pay, I suppose. By which I mean, each of the fools that went charging after the heathens will pay his own ransom. I don't see that we have much choice."

Æthelwulf nodded. Felix could see he was much relieved by the idea of each ealdormen paying his own ransom.

"The heathens say the silver should be brought down to them in Hamtun in a week's time," Beadurof continued. "They say if it's not they'll send one man's head to Winchester every day it's late."

"Barbarians. Damned barbarians," Æthelwulf said.

You were going to burn the heathens alive, Felix thought, but he said, "Was there anything else?"

"Yes," Beadurof said. "They want the Irish girl, the one they came for."

"Well, they can damn well have her," Æthelwulf said. "As if I had any interest in keeping her sort about."

"That may be a bit of a problem," Felix said. "We're not entirely sure where she is."

"What?" Æthelwulf said, scowling. "What's become of her?"

"We're trying to find that out now," Felix said. "But we'll find her, never fear."

He did not, however feel as optimistic as his words and tone suggested. His most trusted men had been searching her out, and thus far had come up with nothing. Felix knew that somehow Louis de Roumois was tied up in all this, which did not make him feel any better. Louis might be an enemy of Charles, his king, but he was no fool. Not at all.

"Also, the heathen that was killed, the big one? They want his body back."

"Is that a problem too, Felix?" Æthelwulf asked.

"No, sire," Felix said. He had meant to order the body thrown to the dogs but he had not gotten around to it yet.

"And one last thing…" Beadurof said.

"Yes?" Felix asked.

"Well, when the heathens were taken, lord, they were all of them wearing swords. They say they must have those swords returned."

* * *

Failend was kneeling on the stone floor. Her coarse woolen robe offered her knees some relief, but not much. That was fine. That was as it should be. Kneeling was not lying in bed. It was not sitting in a fine chair. It was an act of reverence, an act of penitence. It was just the thing for which her soul was shouting out.

The choir was singing, their lovely voices lifting to the upper reaches of the massive church, the ancient Latin words twisting and flowing around each other. Failend took that opportunity to look up, a tiny tilt of the head, no more. She was still surprised by how unencumbered her head felt, the ease of movement that came with the weight of her long hair gone.

Father Conall had cut it off right at the base of her skull. He had done it in his cell in the priests' dormitory near the church, just as soon as they had made their way out of the king's estate. With her hair mostly gone she looked passably like a boy, one too young for facial hair. She looked like an acolyte. And she was happy to pass for an acolyte. It was better than trying to pass for a tonsured priest.

As the choir sang Failend moved her eyes along the back of the church, over the altar and the tabernacle and the canopy. They lingered on the crucifix and the bloody agony of the Lord hanging there. They moved on, over the rest of the sanctuary. Nothing. Priests, altar servers, the choir, the acolytes, the nuns half hidden by the grille. That was it. No men-at-arms. None of the king's men.

They had come often, starting on the day of her escape. They came in mid-morning, after the guards had been discovered locked in the small room at the end of the hall, or so she imagined. But by then Failend was wearing short hair and boy's leggings and the heavy wool robe that Father Conall had brought her. She had been introduced to the other acolytes as Father Conall's brother, come from Ireland. But mostly the others did not care who she was, or where she was from, or why she was there.

The king's men had come several times after, searching the cells and the church and the other buildings. They showed up suddenly and in large numbers, no doubt hoping to catch the escaped prisoner by surprise. Once they even brought the guards whom Failend and Louis had overpowered and they had examined each one of the priests, who were made to stand in a long line. Failend had been there, watching, ready to step in and give herself up if she thought they might identify Father Conall. But the guards had looked at him and passed on by. It had been dark in the hall and Father Conall had been wearing the hood of his robe, and in any case the guards could not really tell one tonsured priest from another.

The king's men had examined the acolytes as well. One of the guards had been within five feet of her, had looked right at her, his eyes lingering. But then he turned away without a word, and Failend had the impression he was more interested in young boys than he was in finding the escaped prisoner.

The mass ended, the priests and the boys and the nuns all filed out, each back to their various tasks. Failend, hands held in front of her and pressed together like the other acolytes, processed slowly down the nave toward the back of the church.

They moved through the massive doors and into the narthex. Failend felt a hand on her arm and with it a stab of panic, uncertainty. Her first instinct was to lash out, her second to jerk her arm free and run, but she heard Father Conall say softly, "Come, brother."

She turned and stepped out of the line. Father Conall was already walking away, so she followed. He led her out through a side door of the church, out into the open ground surrounding the imposing building.

Once they were some distance from the church and from any of the many people hurrying by in sundry directions, Father Conall stopped and turned toward her. He opened his mouth to speak but Failend spoke first.

"There was a great commotion a few days ago. In the city. We could hear it but we were not allowed out. Or told what was going on. There were rumors…"

Father Conall nodded. "The heathens, the ones who came to find you, they were sentenced to die. At the stake. But they escaped. There was a search, and fighting." He spoke in Irish and to Failend the sound of the words was like the angelic singing of the choir.

"They escaped?" Failend asked.

"Yes. Over the city wall, or so I hear. And now there are rumors they took some of the ealdormen as hostages."

Failend nodded. A smile played on her lips. She could not help herself. She had considered the agony she would feel in her soul if

Thorgrim and the others had been burned alive trying to rescue her, after she had willfully abandoned them. But now she would be spared that torment.

"You're pleased to hear that? That the heathens escaped?" Father Conall asked. There was no rebuke in his tone. He was just asking.

"Yes," Failend said. "Yes. I won't lie. I'm happy to hear it. Is that wicked?"

Father Conall frowned. "I don't know. I'd have to think on that. But see here. I've spoken with the bishop. He's said I can go. Back to Ireland, back to my monastery."

"Oh, that's wonderful!" Failend said. "And me?"

Father Conall smiled. "The bishop doesn't worry himself about acolytes. It's no concern to him if you come or go. I did not even mention you."

"Didn't the bishop wonder why you wanted to return home? Just now? He wasn't curious?"

"God smiles on you, Failend," Father Conall said. "I didn't just today start asking his leave to return home. I've been asking for weeks. I'm quite done with Engla-land."

"But…why, after all that, did thc bishop finally give you permission to go?" Failend persisted. It seemed too easy and it made her suspicious.

"Well, here's the truth of the thing…" Father Conall said, his voice dropping to somewhere between a confession and a whispered secret. "I'm the one who defended you when you first came to the church, heard your confession. He knows I'm…part of all this. I don't think he wants to know how. But he certainly doesn't want the king to think any of this was a failure on his part, or any of his people. He's rather that I…we…just go."

Failend nodded. That made sense. "When do we go?"

"Now. This morning. I have only a few things to collect up. The abbot will give me some money for travel. It won't be an easy trip, I'll warn you. We can't go to Hamtun, because the heathens are there. We'll have to go to Lunden, or to the west, and find a ship that can take us to Ireland."

Failend nodded and smiled again. She was looking at Father Conall's face but she was not seeing him. She was seeing far beyond him, and beyond the city of Winchester and the light blue sky and the soft clouds over Engla-land.

What she saw was the wild blue ocean over which she had sailed aboard a Northman's longship. What she saw was the rugged coast of Ireland, the steep cliffs and the green fields and the rolling country that ran inland from there.

What she saw was her life made over again. Once more. What a gift from God this was. How many women had the chance to remake themselves anew, again and again?

What that new life would be she did not know. Taking her vows, perhaps, giving herself to a holy order. Or married again, to a man who was kind, who loved her. She could not return to Glendalough, but perhaps she would live in Kells, where Father Conall was bound, or to the north of that. Maybe even Dubh-linn. She could speak the Northmen's language fluently, after all, and knew all of their customs.

It did not matter at all, not just then. She would build the life she wanted to live when the proper time came. She knew how to do that now. She had the courage to do it. She was ready to begin.

"Failend?" Father Conall said. "Are you all right?"

His voice brought her back, so she was looking at his face now, his kind face. She nodded. "Yes, Father. I am all right. I am most certainly all right."

Bergthor and his men and Thorgrim's men had done a tolerable job of fortifying Hamtun, turning the place into a small but effective longphort in the short time that Thorgrim and the others had been gone. They had torn down the buildings closest to the water, the ones that could hide an enemy. They had used the beams from those buildings to build rudimentary walls around the stretch of shoreline where the ships were pulled up. They had scrounged up a few boats in the village and begun regular patrols of the bay, up and down, because they did not intend to be taken by surprise a second time.

Thorgrim ran his eyes along the wall and over the top of the wall to the roofs of the houses fifty yards beyond, the closest that Bergthor had spared. He was pleased with what had been accomplished. They could defend this place and hold it as long as they needed to. Which he hoped would not be long.

He was sitting on a barrel near where *Sea Hammer* was pulled up on the mud. His tunic was off and Harald was doing his best to sew up the spear wound in Thorgrim's side, the one he had received in the sea fight when they first arrived. The one Failend had already stitched up once.

Harald was stitching him now, happy to do the work. He liked stitching wounds for some reason, in part because he considered himself very skilled at the task, which he was not. And despite his sometimes clumsy efforts there was no one who Thorgrim trusted more.

"Hold still, hold still," Harald admonished and he took a stitch and then washed the blood away, enough so he could see to take another. "We're nearly done." It was an astoundingly painful process but Thorgrim managed to limit his reaction to a few involuntary twitches.

The storm that had raged between him and Harald had blown through, the sky clear again. Brand's hushed words about Harald's behavior in battle, Harald's failure to make any mention of it, went far in calming that tempest. The English flames that had nearly burned them alive seemed to have scorched the arrogance out of Harald, as had Godi's selfless death.

That at least was what Thorgrim suspected. The two of them, Harald and he, had never talked about it, and they never would. Things between them were once again as they had been. Thorgrim would give Harald back the command of *Dragon* and Harald would do as he was told. They both understood that. There was no need for further discussion.

Harald took another stitch and Thorgrim twitched, but only a bit.

"You miss her now, eh?" Louis de Roumois said. "Failend?" He was sitting nearby sharpening a knife which he had apparently liberated from an English guard.

"Miss her? Why?"

"She was a good surgeon. Gentle hands."

Thorgrim frowned. "Harald does well enough," he said.

But in truth Thorgrim did miss her, he missed her already, and it was for reasons well beyond her skills with a needle. There seemed to be a gap now, an empty space that Failend had once filled. Like shields mounted on a longship's side: they are all as one until one is removed, and suddenly its absence becomes sharp and obvious.

But no, that was not it. Failend was not one of many. She was something else entirely. And Thorgrim had never really understood that until she was gone.

"Yes, I miss Failend," Thorgrim added. "But we'll get her back. Or else I'll start removing our hostages' heads and sending them off to Winchester."

"Hmm," Louis said. "I would not be so sure."

Harald tied off the thread and once again wiped the blood away. He stood and stretched. "There. That should hold. If you're careful."

"Thank you," Thorgrim said. He swiveled around and looked at Louis. "Why do you say that? You think the English want to keep Failend, more than they want their noblemen alive?" Then another thought came to him, and he tried to keep his tone flat as he added, "Or do you think she's dead already?"

"I don't think she's dead," Louis said. "But I don't think she wants to come back. They didn't steal her, you know. She went to Winchester on her own."

Thorgrim looked away. He considered that. He looked back at Louis. "I know she went on her own," he said. "I don't know why." These were questions he had very much wondered about, and he knew that Louis was the only one who might have an answer.

"I think maybe she was tired of being a heathen," Louis said.

"She was never one of us…not when it came to her gods, at least."

"God. One God. And I think she missed Him. You know, Thorgrim, she didn't choose this life, the life of a raider. 'Going a'viking', as you people say. Not at first. She did come to love it, in her own way. But love rarely lasts forever."

"Hmm…" Thorgrim said. He understood what Louis was saying. He himself knew full well that one could grow tired of the raider's life. Looking back now he could see the uncertainty that had been creeping into Failend's spirit, the way her enthusiasms would wax and wane.

I should have seen it then… he thought. But actually he had seen it then. He knew that. He just had not given it much thought. And now she was gone.

He was casting around for the next question to ask, the best route to understanding what had happened, when his attention was drawn to something going on on the top of the wall, something attracting the attention of the men posted there. He stood and felt the pull of his flesh against the stitches, the sharp stab of pain, but he ignored it. He reached out and Harald handed him his tunic and he slipped it over his head. He was tugging it down into place when Hall came hurrying over.

"Lord Thorgrim? There are riders. From Winchester, I think."

"Took them long enough," Thorgrim said. "You and Louis get the hostages ashore and line them up. I'm sure these whores' sons will want to see them." The English captives had been stored aboard *Sea Hammer* under guard since their return. "Harald, come with me."

Thorgrim headed off toward the wall with Harald walking beside him. They climbed up the ladder, stepped onto the top and looked down. There were two dozen or so armed men on horseback. The two closest to the wall, their horses side by side, were dressed in shining mail and helmets, and their horses were better equipped than most of Thorgrim's men.

Behind them, a young man held a pole and banner aloft. Behind him the mounted warriors stood in two lines, and behind them was a horse-drawn cart. Thorgrim doubted it was carrying silver, but for the sake of the hostages he hoped it contained Godi's corpse.

One of the Englishmen spoke first, a string of incomprehensible words. Thorgrim turned to Harald and said, "That man on the left…don't we know him?"

Harald stopped, mouth open, and looked down. He took a moment, then turned back to Thorgrim. "Yes," he said. "He commanded the army we fought last, I think. The ones who blocked up the channel."

"But he's the one who honored his word in the end, right? The one who had the ships removed?"

"Yes, that's right."

Thorgrim nodded. That was good. Here was at least one Englishman who had already shown that his word was worth something.

"This other one," Harald said. "He says he's come to talk with us. But he says he must see the hostages first."

"Of course," Thorgrim said. He gestured to two of his men who stood nearby. "Get this ladder on the outside of the wall so these dogs can climb up."

The ladder was lifted and set down again as the two men climbed down from their horses. Behind them the one with the banner jammed the pole into the ground so it stood upright, then climbed down as well and lifted a bundle off his saddle.

The three men then climbed to the top of the ladder and stepped onto the wall. Thorgrim could see their curious eyes moving over the longphort, looking for weaknesses, counting the number of men. Then the ladder was shifted back and Thorgrim led the way down the other side and across the hard-packed dirt to where the hostages stood in a long line.

Thorgrim smiled at the sight, and almost laughed. Here were the lords of the land, but they did not look too lordly now. They had not been harmed, he knew that, but still they looked like beaten dogs. Their once fine clothing was rumpled, torn and filthy. Hair and beards and moustaches were in disarray. They looked like men trying to cling to some dignity through their fear, anger and despair.

"Here they are," Hall said. "But they don't look worth a hundred pounds of silver a piece to me."

"No," Thorgrim agreed. "We'll how much these bastards want their own back, or if they'll settle for their heads alone."

The two men who had been sent to negotiate had stopped and were looking over the line of hostages. No one spoke. Then the one man's eyes fell on Louis, standing at the far end of the line. Thorgrim saw the man pause, saw his and Louis's eyes lock. There was a moment of silence, then the man spoke. A moment more and then Louis replied.

"What are they saying?" Thorgrim asked.

"I don't know," Harald said. "They're speaking Frankish."

Frankish… Thorgrim thought. Perhaps this was part of all the strange dealings that Louis had had back in Winchester, his being pulled from the prison, his escape.

I'll find out later what this is about, Thorgrim thought. *Beat it out of Louis if need be.*

And then they were done, apparently. The one who had been talking to Louis turned to Harald and spoke, in English this time.

"He says the hostages look well enough," Harald said.

The man then turned to the boy who held the bundle and nodded toward Thorgrim. The boy stepped up and held the bundle out to Thorgrim, but Thorgrim did not take it. Instead he nodded to Hall, who stepped over and took it for him. Hall unwrapped the canvas cover to reveal the swords that Thorgrim and the others had lost.

Hall pulled Iron-tooth from the bundle and handed it to Thorgrim, and then found Oak Cleaver and gave it to Harald. He wrapped the rest in the canvas once more.

The man spoke again. "He says the king has agreed to your ransom," Harald said, "but we must wait until the silver can be collected. A week at least, he says."

Thorgrim nodded. He had never expected that so much silver could be delivered in just a few days. Even a week seemed very fast. He wondered how often they would beg for more time, and how many heads he would have to cut off to make sure they were not trifling with him.

Then the man started speaking again. He and Harald went back and forth and then Harald turned to Thorgrim.

"He says he cannot deliver the girl...Failend, I suppose. He says he does not have her, that she and Louis overpowered a guard and escaped. He says you should ask Louis where she is."

Thorgrim was silent, thinking about those words. Thorgrim had already asked Louis and Louis had told him pretty much the same thing. Thorgrim suspected this fellow was telling the truth. And he guessed that Louis was telling the truth about Failend not wanting to come back.

They didn't steal her... he had said. *I think maybe she was tired of being a heathen...*

If these English bastards did find Failend, would they have to drag her back against her wishes? She was skillful and clever. If she wanted to return to him, to this life a'viking, then she probably could, even without his help.

He had taken her prisoner once: he would not do it again.

"Very well," Thorgrim said. "Tell him he has a week to gather the silver. One week, and the silver had best be here," Thorgrim said again and waited as Harald translated the words.

One week... One week to defend this longphort and wait on the riches to flow from Winchester. One week for Failend to return, if returning was what she meant to do. One week before he could sail again, the bows of his ships pointed toward East Agder. He was closer now to his home than he had been since first reaching Ireland.

Home. It was like the horizon, it seemed. Always in sight, always impossible to reach.

Historical Note

At the time of King Æthelwulf's reign, England, or *Angel-cynn*, was by no means a single, united country. Indeed, the name Angel-cynn itself doesn't appear during Æthelwulf's time, but rather in the writings of his son, Alfred.

Ninth century England was divided into seven kingdoms: Wessex, Mercia, East Anglia, Essex, Kent, Sussex and Northumbria. Of those, Mercia had earlier been the most powerful, but by the time Æthelwulf assumed the throne of Wessex, that kingdom had come to dominate the others in the south.

The history of England had been, until then, one of constant struggle among the various kingdoms. By the end of the eighth century, however, a new threat loomed: the Norsemen, whom the *Anglo-Saxon Chronicle* records first appeared in 789. That year three longships arrived on the Isle of Portland on the southern coast of England in the kingdom of Wessex. The shire reeve was sent to investigate, and, in the course of what might have been a misunderstanding, the Norsemen killed him. It was the first of many, many bloody encounters between the Vikings and the English.

For the next sixty years the Vikings continued to plunder England, Ireland and Frankia. Prior to becoming king, Æthelwulf himself led men in battle against the Vikings on several occasions, with mixed results. But for all the terror the Northmen brought to the shores of England, their raiding was not so disruptive that it had much impact on the affairs of the kingdoms. But starting in 850, that began to change.

In 851, the twelfth year of Æthelwulf's reign, the *Anglo-Saxon Chronicle* records five Viking attacks on the shores on Æthelwulf's Wessex. That same year Northmen overwintered in England for the first time. It was a harbinger of things to come, the first step on a road that would lead to the Northmen ultimately taking as their own a huge territory in north-east England known as the Danelaw.

In that same year of 851, Æthelwulf led an army composed of men from all over Wessex against a large force of Norsemen who had sacked Canterbury and London. The victory he achieved solidified Æthelwulf's place as the preeminent ruler among the kings of the various kingdoms of England. The coin on the cover of this book is one minted by Æthelwulf, and features his likeness with his name above it.

Still, the Viking incursions did not stop, or even slow, but continued to increase in size and intensity. Ultimately the problem of defending the kingdom against massive armies of Vikings would not fall to Æthelwulf, but rather to his sons, in particular Alfred.

In 853, Æthelwulf sent Alfred and his older brother Æthelred to Rome to meet with the pope. Some historians, with the advantage of knowing that young Alfred would eventually become Alfred the Great, have suggested his being sent on that pilgrimage was a mark of how highly he was regarded by his father, but that is unlikely. It's more probable that the two youngest were sent because they were considered the most expendable.

Æthelwulf himself set out for a pilgrimage to Rome in 855, bringing Alfred and a large retinue for company. Some historians, even during the Middle Ages, considered Æthelwulf as excessively pious and irresponsible, leaving his kingdom at a time when Viking incursions were becoming larger and more prevalent. Other historians have suggested that Æthelwulf's departure signaled his confidence in the strength of Wessex, whose armies had scored a number of victories against the raiders (though, to be sure, they had also lost quite a few).

One aspect of Æthelwulf's pilgrimage was unique — he was the first Anglo-Saxon king to make that journey while still king. Prior to that, every monarch who traveled through Frankia to Rome had been in exile, either deposed and driven from England, or having given up the crown in order to die in the Holy City. Æthelwulf, however, had left his son Æthelbald as ruler of Wessex, and Æthelberht in charge of Kent, with the assumption that they would hand the kingdoms back to him on his return. That went about as well as one might expect.

On the journey home in 856, Æthelwulf spent several months in the court of Charles the Bald of West Frankia. The connection between the two kings had become closer and more involved as they both faced the increasing threat of Viking attacks. Æthelwulf's dealings with Charles were no doubt facilitated by Æthelwulf's notary, a Frank named Felix, who was responsible for the king's official letters and perhaps much more than that.

While at the court of Charles the Bald, Æthelwulf, who was by then in his forties of fifties, did yet another unprecedented thing: he married Charles's 13-year-old daughter Judith. It was not the age difference that made the marriage so surprising in the eyes of contemporary observers and historians today, but the fact that Carolingian princesses virtually never married. Instead, they were usually given over to religious life, where they would not inconvenience the dynasty with any children who might have a claim to the throne.

What's more, Æthelwulf's marriage, which introduced Charles's bloodline into the royal lineage of Wessex, was looked on as an act of subordination to the Frankish king, not what one would expect from a ruler who was secure on his throne.

Upon his return to Wessex, Æthelwulf discovered that his son Æthelbald had no intention of giving back the kingship. Rather than start a civil war, Æthelwulf agreed to divide the kingdom, with Æthelbald ruling one part and Æthelwulf and Judith ruling another. This was agreed to, and Æthelwulf reigned over his now much reduced kingdom until his death in 858.

While Æthelwulf was struggling with Viking incursions and rebellious sons, King Halfdan of Norway was apparently expanding his rule though political alliance and military conquest, though the truth of Halfdan's history is hard to pin down. Primary source material for Medieval English history is scarce enough — in the less literate world of Viking Age Scandinavia it is all but nonexistent. For the story of Halfdan and his times, historians must look to the Sagas, which are of questionable accuracy, being written many hundreds of years after the fact.

To the best of our knowledge, Halfdan the Black was born around 810 and became king of Agder when he was eighteen or nineteen years old. He spent the next thirty years increasing his kingdom and his wealth before drowning, around the year 860, after his sleigh fell through the ice. Like Æthelwulf of Wessex, Halfdan is perhaps best known for having a son who would be considered the one to unite the scattered kingdoms of his land into a single country. Just as Alfred the Great is thought of as the king who unified England, Halfdan the Black's son, Harald *Hårfagre* — Harald Fairhair — is considered, by the writers of the Sagas at least, to be the first King of Norway.

Acknowledgements

My sincerest thanks go out to the usual suspects: Steve Cromwell for the cover, Alistair Corbett for the background, and Chris Boyle for the maps. The acknowledgements might get repetitious but my appreciation for all that you folks do to make these books look as good as they do is deeply held. Thank you to Kim Reeman for her sharp eye with copy editing – you saved me from a few embarrassments.

Thanks to Nat Sobel, Judith Weber, Adia Wright, and all the folks at Sobel Weber for their hard work on behalf of these and other books.

Thank you to all the good folks at Maine's First Ship who help keep me sane by helping me forget about writing every once in a while. They include but are by no means limited to Orman Hines, Jeremy Blaiklock, Lori Benson, Rob Stevens and of course the Rigging Gang, Bob Ireland and David Bellows.

And my deepest thanks are reserved for my family: Elizabeth Lockard, Nathaniel Nelson (the IT Department of Fore Topsail Press), Jonathan Nelson (the Graphics Department of Fore Topsail Press), Abigail Nelson, Stephanie Nelson, and the COO and CFO of Fore Topsail Press, Lisa Nelson, to whom this book is dedicated. Thank you all, now and forever.

Would you like a heads-up about new titles in The Norsemen Saga, as well as preview sample chapters and other good stuff cheap (actually free)?

Visit our web site to sign up for our (occasional) e-mail newsletter:

www.jameslnelson.com

Other Fiction by

James L. Nelson:

The Brethren of the Coast:
Piracy in Colonial America
The Guardship
The Blackbirder
The Pirate Round

The Samuel Bowater Novels:
Naval action of the American Civil War
Glory in the Name
Thieves of Mercy

The Only Life that Mattered:
The Story of Ann Bonny, Mary Read and Calico Jack Rackham

Glossary

adze – a tool much like an ax but with the blade set at a right angle to the handle.
Ægir – Norse god of the sea. In Norse mythology he was also the host of great feasts for the gods.
Angel-cynn - (pronounced Angle-kin). Term used in the writing of Alfred the Great and the Old English Chronicle to denote both the English people of Teutonic descent, namely the Angles, Saxons and Jutes, and the land they occupied. This seems to be the only term used to denote the country of England until the Danish conquest, after which the island was referred to as Engla land.
Asgard - the dwelling place of the Norse gods and goddesses, essentially the Norse heaven.
athwartships – at a right angle to the centerline of a vessel.
beitass - a wooden pole, or spar, secured to the side of a ship on the after end and leading forward to which the corner, or clew, of a sail could be secured.
berserkir - a Viking warrior able to work himself up into a frenzy of blood-lust before a battle. The berserkirs, near psychopathic killers in battle, were the fiercest of the Viking soldiers. The word berserkir comes from the Norse for "bear shirt" and is the origin of the modern English "berserk".
block – nautical term for a pulley.
boss - the round, iron centerpiece of a wooden shield. The boss formed an iron cup protruding from the front of the shield, providing a hollow in the back across which ran the hand grip.
bothach – Gaelic term for poor tenant farmers, serfs.
brace - line used for hauling a **yard** side to side on a horizontal plane. Used to adjust the angle of the sail to the wind.
brat – a rectangular cloth worn in various configurations as an outer garment over a *leine.*
bride-price - money paid by the family of the groom to the family of the bride.
byrdingr - a smaller ocean-going cargo vessel used by the Norsemen for trade and transportation. Generally about 40 feet in length, the byrdingr was a smaller version of the more well-known *knarr.*
cable – a measure of approximately 600 feet.
clench nail – a type of nail that, after being driven through a board, has a type of washer called a rove placed over the end and is then bent over to secure it in place.

clew – one of the lower corners of a square sail, to which the **sheet** is attached.
ceorl – a commoner in early Medieval England, a peasant, but also a small-time landowner with rights. Members of the ceorl class served in the **fyrd**.
curach - a boat, unique to Ireland, made of a wood frame covered in hide. They ranged in size, the largest propelled by sail and capable of carrying several tons. The most common sea-going craft of mediaeval Ireland. **Curach** was the Gaelic word for boat which later became the word curragh.
dagmál – breakfast time
danegeld - tribute paid by the English to the Vikings to secure peace.
derbfine – In Irish law, a family of four generations, including a man, his sons, grandsons and great grandsons.
dragon ship - the largest of the Viking warships, upwards of 160 feet long and able to carry as many as 300 men. Dragon ships were the flagships of the fleet, the ships of kings.
dubh gall - Gaelic term for Vikings of Danish descent. It means Black Strangers, a reference to the mail armor they wore, made dark by the oil used to preserve it. *See* ***fin gall***.
ell – a unit of length, a little more than a yard.
eyrir – Scandinavian unit of measurement, approximately an ounce.
félag – a fellowship of men who owed each other a mutual obligation, such as multiple owners of a ship, or a band or warriors who had sworn allegiance to one another.
figurehead – ornamental carving on the bow of a ship.
fin gall - Gaelic term for Vikings of Norwegian descent. It means White Strangers. *See* ***dubh gall***.
forestay – a rope running from the top of a ship's mast to the bow used to support the mast.
Frisia – a region in the northern part of the modern-day Netherlands.
Freya - Norse goddess of beauty and love, she was also associated with warriors, as many of the Norse deity were. Freya often led the **Valkyries** to the battlefield.
fyrd – in Medieval England, a levy of commoners called up for military service when needed.
gallows – tall, T-shaped posts on the ship's centerline, forward of the mast, on which the oars and yard were stored when not in use.
hack silver – pieces of silver from larger units cut up for distribution.
hall – the central building on a Viking-age farm. It served as dining hall, sleeping quarters and storage. Also known as a **longhouse**.
halyard - a line by which a sail or a yard is raised.
Haustmánudur – early autumn. Literally, harvest-month.
Hel - in Norse mythology, the daughter of Loki and the ruler of the underworld where those who are not raised up to Valhalla are sent to

suffer. The same name, Hel, is given to the realm over which she rules, the Norse hell.

hersir – in medieval Norway, a magistrate who served to oversee a region under the rule of a king.

hide – a unit of land considered sufficient to support a single family.

hird - an elite corps of Viking warriors hired and maintained by a king or powerful **jarl**. Unlike most Viking warrior groups, which would assemble and disperse at will, the hird was retained as a semi-permanent force which formed the core of a Viking army.

hirdsman - a warrior who is a member of the **hird**.

hólmganga – a formal, organized duel fought in a marked off area between two men.

jarl - title given to a man of high rank. A jarl might be an independent ruler or subordinate to a king. Jarl is the origin of the English word *earl.*

Jörmungandr – in Norse mythology, a vast sea serpent that surrounds the earth, grasping its own tail.

knarr - a Norse merchant vessel. Smaller, wider and sturdier than the longship, knarrs were the workhorse of Norse trade, carrying cargo and settlers wherever the Norsemen traveled.

Laigin – Medieval name for the modern-day county of Leinster in the south-east corner of Ireland.

league – a distance of three miles.

lee shore – land that is downwind of a ship, on which a ship is in danger of being driven.

leeward – down wind.

leech – either one of the two vertical edges of a square sail.

leine – a long, loose-fitting smock worn by men and women under other clothing. Similar to the shift of a later period.

levies - conscripted soldiers of ninth century warfare.

Loki - Norse god of fire and free spirits. Loki was mischievous and his tricks caused great trouble for the gods, for which he was punished.

longphort - literally, a ship fortress. A small, fortified port to protect shipping and serve as a center of commerce and a launching off point for raiding.

luchrupán – Middle Irish word that became the modern-day Leprechaun.

luff – the shivering of a sail when its edge is pointed into the wind and the wind strikes it on both sides.

Midgard – one of nine worlds in Norse mythology, it is the earth, the world known and visible to humans.

Niflheim – the World of Fog. One of the nine worlds in Norse mythology, somewhat analogous to Hell, the afterlife for people who do not die honorable deaths.

Njord – Norse god of the sea and seafaring.

Norns – in Norse mythology, women who sit at the center of the world and hold the fate of each person by spinning the thread of each person's life.
Odin - foremost of the Norse gods. Odin was the god of wisdom and war, protector of both chieftains and poets.
oénach –a major fair, often held on a feast day in an area bordered by two territories.
perch - a unit of measure equal to 16½ feet. The same as a rod.
Ragnarok - the mythical final battle when most humans and gods would be killed by the forces of evil and the earth destroyed, only to rise again, purified.
rath – Gaelic word for a **ringfort**. Many Irish place names still contain the word Rath.
rod – a unit of measure equal to 16½ feet. The same as a perch
rove – a square washer used to fasten the planks of a longship. A nail is driven through the plank and the hole in the washer and then bent over.
ringfort - common Irish homestead, consisting of houses protected by circular earthwork and palisade walls.
rí túaithe – Gaelic term for a minor king, who would owe allegiance to nobles higher in rank.
rí tuath – a minor king who is lord over several **rí túaithe.**
rí ruirech –a supreme or provincial king, to whom the **rí tuath** owe allegiance.
sceattas – small, thick silver coins minted in England and Frisia in the early Middle Ages.
seax – any of a variety of edged weapons longer than a knife but shorter and lighter than a typical sword.
sheer strake – the uppermost plank, or strake, of a boat or ship's hull. On a Viking ship the sheer strake would form the upper edge of the ship's hull.
sheet – a rope that controls a sail. In the case of a square sail the sheets pull the **clews** down to hold the sail so the wind can fill it.
shieldwall - a defensive wall formed by soldiers standing in line with shields overlapping.
shire reeve – a magistrate who served a king or ealdorman and carried out various official functions within his district. One of the highest ranking officials, under whom other, more minor reeves served. The term shire reeve is the basis of the modern-day *sheriff.*
shroud – a heavy rope stretching from the top of the mast to the ship's side that prevents the mast from falling sideways.
skald - a Viking-era poet, generally one attached to a royal court. The skalds wrote a very stylized type of verse particular to the medieval Scandinavians. Poetry was an important part of Viking culture and the ability to write it a highly regarded skill.

sling - the center portion of the **yard**.
sœslumadr – official appointed by the king to administer royal holdings. Similar to the English **shire reeve**.
spar – generic term used for any of the masts or yards that are part of a ship's rig.
stem – the curved timber that forms the bow of the ship. On Viking ships the stem extended well above the upper edge of the ship and the figurehead was mounted there.
strake – one of the wooden planks that make up the hull of a ship. The construction technique, used by the Norsemen, in which one strake overlaps the one below it is called *lapstrake construction.*
swine array - a Viking battle formation consisting of a wedge-shaped arrangement of men used to attack a shieldwall or other defensive position.
tánaise ríg – Gaelic term for heir apparent, the man assumed to be next in line for a kingship.
thegn – a minor noble or a land-holder above the peasant class who also served the king in a military capacity.
thing - a communal assembly.
Thor - Norse god of storms and wind, but also the protector of humans and the other gods. Thor's chosen weapon was a hammer. Hammer amulets were popular with Norsemen in the same way that crosses are popular with Christians.
thrall - Norse term for a slave. Origin of the English word "enthrall".
thwart - a rower's seat in a boat. From the old Norse term meaning "across".
tuath – a minor kingdom in medieval Ireland that consisted of several **túaithe**.
túaithe – a further subdivision of a kingdom, ruled by a **rí túaithe**
Ulfberht – a particular make of sword crafted in the Germanic countries and inscribed with the name Ulfberht or some variant. Though it is not clear who Ulfberht was, the swords that bore his name were of the highest quality and much prized.
unstep – to take a mast down. To put a mast in place is to step the mast.
Valhalla - a great hall in **Asgard** where slain warriors would go to feast, drink and fight until the coming of **Ragnarok**.
Valkyries - female spirits of Norse mythology who gathered the spirits of the dead from the battle field and escorted them to **Valhalla**. They were the Choosers of the Slain, and though later romantically portrayed as Odin's warrior handmaidens, they were originally viewed more demonically, as spirits who devoured the corpses of the dead.
vantnale – a wooden lever attached to the lower end of a shroud and used to make the shroud fast and to tension it.
varonn – springtime. Literally "spring work" in Old Norse.

Vik - An area of Norway south of modern-day Oslo. The name is possibly the origin of the term *Viking.*
wattle and daub - common medieval technique for building walls. Small sticks were woven through larger uprights to form the wattle, and the structure was plastered with mud or plaster, the daub.
weather – closest to the direction from which the wind is blowing, when used to indicate the position of something relative to the wind.
wergild - the fine imposed for taking a man's life. The amount of the wergild was dependent on the victim's social standing.
witan - a council of the greater nobles and bishops of a region, generally assembled to advise the king.
yard - a long, tapered timber from which a sail was suspended. When a Viking ship was not under sail, the yard was turned lengthwise and lowered to near the deck with the sail lashed to it.

Printed in Poland
by Amazon Fulfillment
Poland Sp. z o.o., Wrocław